Virginia Andrews is a worldwide bestselling author. Her much-loved novels include RAIN, LIGHTNING STRIKES, EYE OF THE STORM and THE END OF THE RAINBOW. Virginia Andrews' novels have sold more than

VIRGINIA
ANDREWS®

TARNISHED
GOLD

POCKET
BOOKS

LONDON • SYDNEY • NEW YORK • TOKYO • SINGAPORE • TORONTO

First published in Great Britain by Simon & Schuster UK Ltd, 1996
This edition published by Pocket Books, 2003
An imprint of Simon & Schuster UK Ltd
A Viacom Company

3 5 7 9 10 8 6 4 2

Simon & Schuster UK Ltd
Africa House
64–78 Kingsway
London WC2B 6AH

www.simonsays.co.uk

Simon & Schuster Australia
Sydney

A CIP catalogue record for this book is available from the British Library

ISBN 0-7434-6829-5

Printed and bound in Great Britain by
Bookmarque Ltd, Croydon, Surrey

Prologue

"You've got to let go of innocence," Mama once told me, "or it will take you down with it when it sinks like some old rotted shrimp boat in the canal."

One spring morning I had come running up to the gallery where she sat weaving palmetto hats to sell to the tourists. In my hands I cupped a dead baby blue jay. I thought it had fallen from the nest, but Mama said its mother most likely threw it out.

I shook my head. I was only seven. It was inconceivable that a mother of any kind could cast one of its offspring out of the nest.

"No, Mama. It must have tried to fly and fell," I insisted.

She put down her palmetto leaves and looked at me with that soft, sad expression in her dark onyx eyes that brought tears to my own eyes. Her gaze went to the baby bird and then she shook her head.

"It's too small to have tried to fly, Gabriel. It was sickly and either died or would have died. The mother knew what was best."

I, too, gazed down at the diminutive creature, its eyes glued shut, its tiny beak slightly open, its tiny claws tightly closed.

"How can it be best to throw your baby out?" I asked angrily.

"She had other babies to care for, Gabriel honey, strong, healthy ones who needed her attention and the food she brought. If she spent time worrying over one that was going to die anyway, one of the healthy ones would get sick and die."

I shook my head. I wouldn't believe it.

"It's not a decision she sits around munching over, Gabriel, no. It comes from instinct. She just knows what's necessary. It's how she makes sure her good babies will survive and have a chance in that jungle you love so much."

"Is she sad about it?" I asked, hopefully.

"I suppose, but there's nothing she can do about it. Understand?"

"No," I said. "Maybe if she tried harder, this baby would live, too."

Mama sighed deeply and that's when she told me about innocence.

I didn't know what she meant then. I was too young to measure the world in terms of innocence. To me, waking up every day was still like ripping off the wrapping paper to get at the wonderful gifts that awaited as soon as I finished my breakfast and shot out the screen door, bounded down the steps to our front gallery, and turned around the corner of the house toward the swamp and the canals and all my animals. Sickness and death, violence and cruelty, were not permitted entry to this world. If something died, it was because its time had come fairly. Hope struggled to survive within me.

"Can't you bring the baby bird back to life, Mama?" I asked. "Can't you give it some herbal drink with a eye dropper or sprinkle some magic powder over it? Can't you?"

Mama was a *traiteur*, a healer whose hands did magical things. What she knew had been passed down to her from her mother and her grandmother and her grandmother's mother. She took the fire out of burns, blew smoke into the ear of a child and chased out the ache, put warm palmetto leaves on old people and helped them to stand and walk and

2

move their arms freely. Evil spirits were afraid of her. She could sprinkle holy water on the steps of a house and keep the devil out. Surely she could stir life back into a creature as small as the bird in my hands.

"No, honey, I can't bring back the dead," she told me. "Once you go through that doorway, it locks forever and ever behind you." She saw the disappointment in my face, however, and added, "But this baby bird will grow up in a better world."

How could there be a better world? I still wondered. My world was full of colors and sunshine, beautiful flowers with wonderful scents, magnificent birds that glided through the air as lightly and easily as dreams, delicious flavors in the food Mama made, fluffy white clouds that tickled my imagination so I could see them as camels or whales or even cotton candy.

"What'cha got there, Gabriel?" Daddy asked as he came out of the shack house he had built for us just before I was born. Although it was still morning, he had a bottle of beer in his hand. Sometimes that's all he had for breakfast. His dark brown hair was unbrushed, the long strands over his forehead and just parted enough for his beautiful emerald eyes to peer through. He wore only his pants, no shirt, no shoes or hip boots. A trail of curly brown hair left his belly button and shot up to his chest where it exploded into a V-shaped matting. My Daddy was tall and strong with long arms that rippled with muscles whenever he pulled on something or lifted something. Mama once told me he had wrestled an alligator for a two-dollar bet. She said that's how foolish he was, but I thought it meant he was the strongest daddy in the world.

"A dead baby blue jay," Mama answered for me.

"So?" he said. "What'cha going do with it, Gabriel? Throw it in the gumbo?"

"Jack!"

Daddy laughed.

"I wanted Mama to bring it back to life," I explained. "She said its mother threw it out of the nest."

"Most like," Daddy said. He sucked on the neck of the beer bottle, drawing its contents down his throat as his

3

Adam's apple bounced like a tiny rubber ball. "Just throw it away," Daddy said.

I looked horrified at Mama.

"Why don't you bury it in the backyard, Gabriel," she suggested softly.

"Yeah. Maybe we could have a service," Daddy said, and laughed.

"Could we, Mama?"

Daddy stopped laughing.

"Hey, child, that's just a dead bird. Ain't no person."

I didn't understand the difference. Something beautiful and precious was dead.

"I'll say some words over it for you," Mama offered.

"I got to see this," Daddy said.

"Don't tease the child, Jack."

"Why not? She's got to grow up someday. Today's as good a day as any." He pointed his long right forefinger at me. "You should be up here helping your mama make them hats to sell and not be spending your time wandering through the field anyhow," he chastised. Then he offered, "There are snakes and bugs, snapping turtles and gators."

"I know there are, Daddy," I said, smiling. "I stepped on a snake this morning."

"What? What it look like?"

I told him.

"That's a damn cottonmouth. Poisonous as hell. You didn't step on it or you'd be as dead as that bird in your hands."

"Yes, I did, Daddy. I stepped on it and then I said, excuse me, Mr. Snake."

"Oh, and I suppose it just nodded and said, it's all right, Gabriel, huh?"

"It looked at me and then it went back to sleep," I said.

"Christ, you hear what stories she's telling, Catherine?"

"I believe her, Jack. She's special to the animals out there. They know what's in her heart."

"Huh? What sort of Cajun voodoo nonsense you concocting, Catherine Landry? And now you got the child talking gibberish, too."

4

"It's not nonsense," she said, "And certainly not gibberish." She stood up. "Come on, Gabriel. I'll help you bury your bird," she said. "Maybe the creature should be pitied," she said, throwing an angry glance back at Daddy.

"Go ahead. Waste time worrying about some dead bird. See if I care," Daddy said, taking another swig of his beer. Then he dropped the empty bottle in the rain barrel. "I'm going to town," he called after us. "We're outta beer again."

"You're out of work, Jack Landry. That's why we're out of beer."

"Aaaa," he said, waving at us. He went back into the shack.

Mama got the spade and dug a small hole under a pecan tree for the baby bird because Mama thought it would always be a cool, shady spot. I put the baby bird in gently and then Mama covered her. She told me to put a stick in the ground to serve as its monument. Then she lowered her head and took my hand. I lowered my head too.

"Lord, have mercy on the innocent soul before you," she said, and crossed herself. I did, too.

We both said, "Amen."

Just as we looked up together, I saw a blue jay flit through the cypress trees and disappear in the direction of Graveyard Lake, a small brackish pond in the swamp that Daddy had named for its collection of floating, moss-strung dead cypress. Mama's gaze trailed after mine. She sighed. She still held on to my hand, but we didn't start back to the gallery and the work that had to be done.

"Being a mother, any kind of mother, is very hard, Gabriel," she said. "You don't just give birth to a baby. You give birth to worry and pain, hope and joy, tears and laughter."

"I would never throw out one of my babies," I vowed, refusing to relinquish my hold on that innocence Mama feared would pull me down with it.

"I hope you never have to even think of such a thing, honey, but if you do, remember the blue jay and make the choice that's best for your child and not for you."

I stared up at her. Mama was a wealth of wisdom, most of

5

which was years and years beyond me. But she had the eyes of a fortune-teller. She could look into the darkness of tomorrow and see some of what was to come.

I shuddered a bit even though it was a warm spring day. Mama was looking deep into the swamp, into the beyond, and what she saw made her hold more firmly to my hand.

And then, as if it had heard and had seen everything, a blue jay I imagined to be the mother started to sing its own dirge. Mama smiled at me.

"Your friend is thanking you," she said. "Come on. Help me weave a bit."

We turned away, and nervous, but secure because Mama still held on to me, I took my small steps toward tomorrow.

1

My Own Eden

The sound of the screen door being slammed sharply at my family's shack house ricocheted like a gunshot through the willow trees and cottonwood, quickening my footsteps. I was almost home from school. Part of the way I had walked with Evelyn Thibodeau and Yvette Livaudis, the only two girls in my class who cared to talk to me at all. Most of the time we had all been speaking at once. Our excitement boiled over like an unwatched pot of milk. It was our last year. Graduation loomed around the corner with all its promises and terrors hanging like so much Spanish moss.

Evelyn was going to marry Claude LeJeune, who had his own shrimp boat, and Yvette was going to Shreveport to live with her aunt and uncle on their sugar plantation. Everyone understood she would eventually marry the foreman, Philippe Jourdain, with whom she had carried on a letter correspondence all year. They had really seen each other only twice and he was nearly fifteen years older, but Yvette was quite convinced that this should be her destiny. Philippe was a Cajun, and Yvette, like most of us, would marry no one else. We were descendants of the French Arcadians who had migrated to Louisiana and we cherished our heritage.

7

It was 1944. The Second World War still raged and young, eligible Cajun men were still scarce, even though most farmers and fishermen had exemptions. Evelyn and Yvette were always chiding me for not paying attention to Nicolas Paxton, who was going to inherit his father's department store someday. He was overweight and had flat feet, so he would never be drafted.

"He's always been very fond of you," Yvette said, "and he's sure to ask you to marry him if you gave him the time of day. You won't be poor, that's for sure, *n'est-ce pas?*" she said with a wink.

"I don't know which I would hate most," I replied. "Waking up in the morning and seeing Nicolas beside me or being shut up in that department store all day saying, 'Can I help you, monsieur? Can I help you, madame?'"

"Well, you've turned away every other possible beau. What are you going to do after graduation, Gabriel, weave split-oak baskets and palmetto hats with your mother and sell gumbo to tourists forever and ever?" Evelyn asked disdainfully.

"I don't know. Maybe," I said, smiling, which only infuriated my sole two friends more.

It was a very warm late spring day. The sky was nearly cloudless, the blue the color of faded dungarees. Gray squirrels with springs in their little legs leapt from one branch to another, and during the rare moments when we were all quiet, I could hear woodpeckers drumming on the oak and pecan trees. It was too glorious a day to get upset over anything anyone said to me.

"But don't you want to get married and have children and a home of your own?" Yvette demanded as if it were an affront to them that I wasn't engaged or promised.

"Oui. I imagine I do."

"You imagine? You don't know?" Her lips moved to twist into a grotesque mockery. "She imagines."

"I suppose I do," I said, committing myself as much as I could. My friends, as well as all the other students at school who knew me, thought I was born a bit strange because my mother was a spiritual healer. It was true that things that annoyed them didn't bother me. They were always fuming and cursing over something some boy said or some girl did. Truly, most of the time I didn't even notice. I knew they had nicknamed me *La Fille au Naturel*, the Nature Girl, and many exaggerated stories about me, telling each other that I slept with alligators, rode on the backs of snapping turtles, and never was bitten by mosquitoes. I was rarely bitten, that was true, but it was because of the lotion Mama concocted and not because of some magic.

When I was a little girl, boys tried to frighten me by putting snakes in my desk. The girls around me would scream and back away, while I calmly picked up the snake and set it free outside the building. Even my teachers refused to touch them. Most snakes were curious and gentle, and even the poisonous ones weren't nasty to you if you let them be. To me, that seemed to be the simplest rule to go by: Live and let live. I didn't try to talk Yvette out of marrying a man so much older, for example. If that was what she wanted, I was happy for her. But neither she nor Evelyn could treat me the same way. Because I didn't think like they did and do the things they wanted to do, I was foolish or stubborn, even stupid.

Except for the time Nicolas Paxton invited me to a *fais do do* at the town dance hall, I had never been invited to a formal party. Other boys had asked me for dates, but I had always said no. I had no interest in being with them, not even any curiosity about it. I looked at them, listened to them, and immediately understood that I would not enjoy being with them. I was always polite in refusing. A few persisted, demanding to know why I turned them down. I told them. "I don't think I would enjoy myself. Thank you."

The truth was a shoe that almost never fit gracefully on a twisted foot. It only made them angrier and soon they were spreading stories about me, the worst being that I made love with animals in the swamp and didn't care to be around men. More than once Daddy got into a fight at one of the zydeco bars because someone passed a remark about me. He usually won the fight, but still came home angry and ranted and raved about the shack, bawling out Mama for putting "highfalutin" ideas in my head about love and romance.

"And you," he would shout, pointing his longer forefinger

9

at me, the nail black with grime, "instead of playing with birds and turtles, you should be flittin' your eyes and turnin' your shoulders at some rich buck. That pretty face and body you've been blessed with is the cheese for the trap!"

The very idea of being flirtatious and conniving with a man made my stomach bubble. Why let someone believe you wanted something you really didn't? It wasn't fair to him and it certainly wasn't fair to myself.

However, even though I never told my two girlfriends or even Mama for that matter, I did think about love and romance; and if believing something magical had to happen between me and a man was "highfalutin," then Daddy was right. I didn't want people to think I was a snob, but if that was the price I had to pay to believe in what I believed, then I would pay it.

Everything in Nature seemed perfect to me. The creatures that mated and raised and protected their offspring together were designed to be together. Something important fit. Surely it had to be the same way for human beings, too, I thought.

"I can't do that, Daddy," I wailed.

"I can't do that, Daddy," he mimicked. Liquor loosened his tongue. Whenever he returned from the zydeco bars, which were nothing more than shacks near the river, he was usually meaner than a trapped raccoon. I had never been in a zydeco bar, but I knew the word meant vegetables, all mixed up. Often I heard the African-Cajun music on the radio, but I knew that more took place in those places than just listening to music.

Of course, I burst into tears when Daddy ridiculed me, and that set Mama on him. The fury would be in her eyes. Daddy would put his arms up as if he expected lightning to come from those dazzling black pupils. It sobered him quickly and he either fled upstairs or out to his fishing shack in the swamp.

My biggest problem was understanding why Mama and Daddy married and had me. They were beautiful people. Daddy, especially when he cleaned up and dressed, was about as striking a man as I had ever seen. His complexion was always caramel because of his time in the sun, and that darkness brought out the splendor of his vibrant emerald eyes. Except for when he was swimming in beer or whiskey, he stood tall and firm as an oak tree. His shoulders looked strong enough to hold a house, and there were stories about him lifting the back end of an automobile to get it out of a rut.

Mama wasn't tall, but she had presence. Usually she wore her hair pinned up, but when she let it flow freely around her shoulders, she looked like a cherub. Her hair was the color of hay and she had a light complexion. Her eyes weren't unusually big, but when she fixed them angrily on Daddy, they seemed to grow wider and darker like two beacons drawing closer and closer. Daddy couldn't look at her directly when she interrogated him about things he had done with our money. He would put up his hand and plead, "Don't look at me that way, Catherine." It was as if her eyes burned through the armor of his lies and seared his heart. He always confessed and promised to repent. In the end she took mercy on him and let him slip away on his magic carpet of promises for better tomorrows.

As I grew older, Mama and Daddy grew further apart. Their bickering became more frequent and more bitter, their animosity sharp and needling. It hurt to see them so angry at each other. As a child, I recalled them sitting together on the gallery in the evening, Daddy holding her in his arms and Mama humming some Cajun melody. I remember how Mama's eyes clung worshipfully to him.

Our world seemed perfect then. Daddy had built us the house and was doing well with his oyster fishing and frequent small carpentry jobs. He wasn't a guide for rich Creole hunters yet, so we didn't argue about the slaughter of beautiful animals. We always appeared to have more than we needed during those earlier days. People would give us gifts in repayment for the healing Mama performed or the rituals she conducted, too.

I know Daddy believed he was blessed and protected because of Mama's powers. He once told me his luck changed after he married her. But he came to believe that

11

that same spiritual protection would carry over when he indulged in backroom gambling, and that, according to Mama, was the start of his downfall.

What I wondered now was, how could two people who had fallen so deeply in love fall so quickly out of it? I didn't want to ask Mama because I knew it would make her sad, but I couldn't keep the question locked up forever. After a particularly bad time when Daddy came home so drunk he fell off the gallery and cracked his head on a rock, I sat with Mama while she fumed and asked her.

"If you have the power to see through the darkness for others, why couldn't you have seen for yourself, Mama?"

She gazed at me a long moment before she replied.

"There's no young man you've looked at who has made something tingle inside you?"

"No, Mama," I said.

She thought for another long moment and then nodded.

"Maybe that's good." Then she sighed deeply and looked into the darkness of the oak and cypress trees across the way. "Just because I was handed down the gift of spiritual healing and became a *traiteur* doesn't mean I'm not a woman first," she said. "The first time I set eyes on Jack Landry, I thought I had seen a young god come walking out of the swamp. He looked like someone Nature herself had taken special time to mold.

"It wasn't a tingling that started within me, it was a raging flood of passion so strong, I thought my heart would burst. I sensed that when he set eyes on me he liked what he saw, and that stirred me even more. Something happens when the woman in you takes a front seat, Gabriel. You stop thinking; you just depend on your feelings to make decisions.

"You remember I told you about the shoemaker who worked so hard for everyone else, he had no shoes for himself?"

"Yes, Mama. I remember."

"Well, that was me. I couldn't see what would happen to me the next hour, much less over the next ten years. Jack Landry was all I wanted to see, and he was . . ." She smiled and sat back. "Very charming in his simple way. He was good at spinning tales and making promises. And he was always showing off for me. I remember the Daisys' shingling party. After the roof was raised, there was a picnic and games. Your father wrestled three men at the same time and whipped them all, just because I was watching. Everyone knew it. They said, 'You put the life in that man, Catherine.' Then he took to saying it, and I came to believe it.

"You're old enough for me to tell you your father was a wonderful lover. We had a few good and wonderful years together before things started to go sour." She sighed deeply again. "Beware of promises, Gabriel, even the ones you make yourself. Promises are like spiderwebs we weave to trap our own dreams, but dreams have a way of thinning out until you're left with nothing but the web."

I listened, but I didn't understand all of it, for I thought if Mama with all her wisdom could make a mistake in love, what chance did I have?

I had been thinking deeply about this after I left Evelyn and Yvette. Their questions had stirred up the same old questions about myself.

Then I heard the screen door slam a second time, this time followed by Mama's angry screams.

"You don't come back here until you return that money, Jack Landry, hear? That was Gabriel's dowry money and you know'd it, Jack. I want every penny replaced! Hear? Jack?"

I broke into a trot and came around the bend in time to see Daddy stomping through the tall grass, his hip boots glistening in the afternoon sun, his hair wild and his arms swinging. Mama was standing on the gallery, her arms folded over her bosom, glaring after him. She didn't see me coming and pivoted furiously on her moccasins to charge back into the shack.

Daddy began to pace back and forth on our small dock, raging into the wind, his arms pumping the air as he complained to his invisible audience of sympathizers. I hesitated on the walkway and decided to speak with him first. He stopped his raging when he saw me approaching.

"She send you out here? Did she?" he demanded.

"No, Daddy. I just came home from school and heard the

13

commotion. I haven't spoken to Mama yet. What's wrong now?"

"Aaaa," he said, waving at me and then turning away. He stood there with his hands on his hips, his back to me. His shoulders dipped as if he carried a cypress log on them.

"I heard her shout something about money," I said.

He spun around, his face red, but the corners of his mouth white with anger.

"I had a chance to make us a bundle," he explained. "A good chance. This city fella comes along selling this miracle tonic water, see? It comes from New York City! New York City!" he emphasized with his arms out.

"What's it supposed to do, Daddy?"

"Make you younger, take all the aches and pains out, get rid of the gray in your hair. Women especially can rub some of it into their face and hands and wrinkles disappear. If you got loose teeth, it makes 'em tight again. I seen the woman he was with. She said she was well into her sixties, but she looked no more than twenty-five. So I run back to the shack and I dig out the bundle your mother's kept hidden from me. Thinks I don't know what she's doin' with all the loose change . . . Anyway, I go back and buy up all the tonic the man has. Then I come back and tell your mother all she got to do is tell her customers what this tonic does and they'll buy it at twice the price. Everyone believes what she says, right? We make twice the money, and quickly!"

"What happened?"

"Aaaa." He waved at the shack and then bit down on his lower lip. "She goes and tastes it and says it's nothing but ginger, cinnamon, and a lot of salt. She says it ain't worth the bottle it's in and she couldn't tell anyone to buy it for any purpose. I swear . . ."

"Why didn't you bring home one bottle first and ask her to look at that before you bought all of it, Daddy?"

He glared at me.

"If you ain't birds of a feather. That's what she said, too. Then she starts that ranting and raving. I went back looking for the man, a course, but he and his lady friend are long gone. I was just trying to get us a bundle," he wailed.

14

"I know you were, Daddy. You wouldn't just give away our money."

"See? How come you understand and she don't?"

"Maybe because you've done things like this many times before, Daddy," I said calmly.

He raised his eyebrows.

"Mary and Joseph. A man can't live with two women nagging him to death. He needs breathing room so he can think and come up with good plans." He looked back at the house. "You got any money?"

"I have two dollars," I said.

"Well, give it to me and I'll try to double it at *bourre*," he said. That was a card game that was a cross between poker and bridge. Mama said she had fewer hairs on her head than the number of times Daddy had stuffed the pot, which was what the loser did.

"Mama hates when you gamble with our money, Daddy. We have bills to pay and cotton jaune to buy for the weaving and—"

"Just give it over, will ya?"

Daddy always brushed aside problems as if they were lint not worth noticing.

I dug the two dollars out of my pocketbook and handed it to him. He took it and shoved it into his pocket and then stepped into the pirogue.

"Only two more days of school for me, Daddy," I said. "Sunday's graduation. Don't forget."

"How could I forget? Your mother jabbers about it all day." He gazed at the shack again. "Don't know why she's so upset about the dowry money. You ain't got no beau lined up. You keep listening to that woman, you'll end up some spinster weaving hats and blankets to keep alive. Hear?"

I nodded and smiled.

"Aaaa," he said, pushing away from the dock. "What's the sense of talking? No one listens. That woman," he said, glaring at the house. I watched him pole the pirogue through the dusty shadows. Before I turned, I saw him reach into his back pocket and come up with a small bottle of whiskey. He emptied the bottle and then threw it over the water. It hit

15

with a splash and glittered for a moment before it disappeared, just like Daddy as he went around a bend of flowering honeysuckle.

Mama was sitting at the kitchen table, her head in her hands, when I entered the house. I put my books down quickly and went to her.

"It'll be all right, Mama. I don't need that money just yet."

She looked up, her face so full of fatigue, she looked years older. I felt like I, too, could get a glimpse of the future, but I didn't like it. It was as if a cold hand had clutched my heart.

"It's gone," she moaned. "Just like everything else that man touches." She smiled and brushed back some loose strands of my hair. "I only want you to have better," she said.

"I'm fine, Mama. Really."

She laughed and shook her head.

"I do believe you think so," she said, and sighed so deeply, I thought she had drawn up the last pail of strength from the deep well of her soul. "Well, any real good man who falls in love with you and wants you for his wife won't care about no dowry money, I suppose. He'll see the dowry's in you, in your goodness and your beauty. It's more than any man deserves."

"I'm not any more beautiful than other girls, Mama."

"Sure you are, Gabriel. The wonder is you don't notice or parade with arrogance." She looked around, resembling someone who was lost for a moment, someone who forgot who she was and where she was. "I ain't even started the roux for tonight's dinner, that man got me so mad."

"That's all right, Mama. I'll do it," I said. Every woman in the bayou had her own touch when it came to preparing the sauce we used with our fish or fowl. Mama's specialty, the one she taught me, was gumbo made with filé, a powder she said came from the Choctaw Indians, made from ground-up sassafras leaves. It was guaranteed to clear the sinuses.

"You go out to the gallery and sit awhile. Go on," I insisted.

16

"That man," she said, "stirs the thunder in me."

Finally she gave in and went out to sit on her rocker. With summer on our doorstep, the sun was still quite high in the late afternoon. Sometimes we would have a cool breeze come up from the Gulf and there was enough shade on the gallery this time of day to make it tolerable, but after I set the roux to simmering, I decided I would go for a swim.

"Smells good," Mama said when I came out. "That man don't deserve a good meal tonight and probably won't get one. Where'd he tell you he was going?" she asked, her eyes narrowing with suspicion. She was worried about what he would do next. I didn't want to tell her he had taken my two dollars and headed for a card table at some zydeco bar where he could easily get into a fight. But instead of lying, I just left out information.

"He went poling downstream, Mama."

"Humf," she said, and rocked harder. "Come home drunk as a skunk, that's what he'll do. Probably fall on his face out here and sleep on the gallery floor all night. Won't be the first time."

"Don't worry, Mama. We'll be fine," I said, and squeezed her hand.

"Just a few days until you graduate," she said. "Imagine that. Something good to celebrate for a change," she added. She leaned over to kiss my cheek and then sat back, finally noticing the towel in my hand.

"What are you going to do, Gabriel?"

"I'm just going for a dip in the pond, Mama," I said.

"Be careful, hear?"

"Yes, Mama."

I bounced down the stairs and went down to the dock where my pirogue was tied. Daddy had built it for me when I was only eight. At eight I was already a good swimmer and soon to become very good at poling through the canals. In the beginning Daddy thought it was amusing. He would brag about his nine-, ten-year-old daughter who could wind her way around the trickiest bends and through the narrowest canals better than most fishermen.

When I was younger, I kept pretty close to home, but as I grew older and stronger, I ventured farther and farther out in the swamps until I knew as much about them as Daddy did, and even found places he hadn't. My favorite was a small pond about a quarter mile east of our house. I found it by venturing through some overgrown cypress. All of a sudden it was there, quiet, peaceful, secluded, with a large rock in the middle upon which I would sun myself.

This time of the day the sun would seep through the thick moss, oak, and cypress leaves and cast a veil of soft sunshine over the tea-colored water, which this afternoon was remarkably clear. I could see small rocks and plants, turtles and bream. The frogs grew louder as the sun dipped behind the tall trees, serenading me with their croaking. Nutrias scurried in and out of their dome houses along the banks of the pond, and as usual a pair of egrets paraded on the big rock, even as I drew closer to it.

The mistress of the pond was a dark blue heron who had made her nest in a gnarled oak tree on the north side. She and I had gotten to know each other well and I had even succeeded in having her land on the rock while I was there. She kept her distance in the beginning, strutting carefully along the edges and watching me every moment. I spoke softly to her, but hardly moved, and in time she grew close enough for me to reach out and touch her if I wanted. I never did because I knew that would spook her. It was just an unwritten agreement between us. She would trust me as long as I didn't violate the trust. It was enough to see her so close and watch her swoop down from her nest, gliding gracefully over what had become our pond.

This afternoon when I poled my way to the pond, I saw her nestled comfortably in her nest. A school of bream were in a feeding frenzy among the cattails and lily pads. There was a gentle but constant breeze threading through the swamp and lifting the bed of moss on the dead cypress trees. The sun was at that point where its rays washed over the big rock. Here all my troubles and worries, my fears and dark thoughts, were chased from my heart. No one shouted, no one cried. There were no threats or complaints, except the complaints of egrets when marsh hawks came too close to their bed of eggs.

I fastened my pirogue to the branch that stuck up near the

rock and then I stripped off my dress, unfastened my bra, and stepped out of my panties. Leaving my clothing in a neat pile in the canoe, I took my towel and stepped onto the rock to spread the towel and lie down. Everything in nature was unclothed; it seemed right for me to be so, too. Nudity gave me a sense of freedom and I loved feeling the sun everywhere on my body. I put my hands behind my head and smiled at the rays that kissed my cheeks and caressed my breasts. When I got too warm, I dove into the pond and swam in circles around the rock. Then, dripping, but cool and refreshed, I returned to lie a little longer before returning home to have what I expected would be a dinner attended only by Mama and myself. For now, I didn't want to think about it.

I had almost drifted into sleep when I heard the distinct sound of a splash and opened my eyes. At first I saw nothing, and then he was there, gazing up at me from his pirogue and smiling widely. I recognized him immediately as Monsieur Tate, the owner of the biggest cannery in Houma. He was a man in his late twenties, married without children as yet. Daddy had worked for him on two occasions. He was a handsome man, slim, tall, with *chatlin* hair, which was what we Cajuns called blond mixed with brown. I had never seen him in anything but a jacket and tie.

Mr. Tate had been fishing and wore only a T-shirt and dungarees right now.

I gasped and pulled the towel out from beneath me to wrap myself in it. My heart throbbed in triple time as I held my breath. A nearly paralyzing numbness gripped me.

"You're about the prettiest creature I've ever seen in this swamp," he said. I felt my face fill with blood and my neck redden. I shrank into a tighter ball, but he simply gazed around. "Didn't think anyone else knew about this pond. I caught the biggest *sac-au-lait* here."

"I didn't know anyone knew about this pond either," I said, nearly in tears.

"That's all right. No harm done. Skinny-dipping isn't bad. I haven't done it in a long while, but it sure looks inviting here."

19

I waited, expecting he would just turn around and pole his way out, but he stood there, smiling.

"Oui, oui," he said, "it seems like a very good idea." He pulled his T-shirt over his head and began to unfasten his pants. I stared in disbelief. A few moments later, he was naked and unashamed of what I saw. He laughed and dove into the pond.

"Beautiful!" he cried. "Come on in."

"No, monsieur. I have to go home," I said.

"Oh, nonsense. Come on. I don't bite."

My blue heron, disturbed by Monsieur Tate's presence, swept down over the water and then over the trees and away, an omen I should have given more of my attention.

"No," I said, and began to inch my way toward the edge of the rock and my pirogue. He saw where I was going and what I wanted to do and swam to my canoe before I got to it. He unfastened it and started to swim back toward his own.

"Monsieur!" I cried. "What are you doing?" He laughed and tied my canoe to his.

"Now you have to swim," he said. "Come on. Dive in."

I shook my head. "Bring back my pirogue."

He behaved as if he couldn't hear me, swimming round the canoes and then to the rock. I backed away as he boosted himself up and onto it.

"It feels good to be in Nature, to be au naturel, *n'est-ce pas,* Gabriel?"

"Please, monsieur," I said.

"Don't be frightened," he said, and squatted down beside me. Then he lay back on the rock, putting his hands behind his head the way I had had my own. My heart was pounding. Here he was a married man, sprawled naked next to me. "Oh, that feels so good," he said. "How long have you been coming here?"

I was sitting with my knees pulled up, the towel wrapped tightly around my shoulders. Could he not see how embarrassed I was? He behaved as though we were having a quiet conversation at a Sunday school picnic, but my abdomen felt like a hollowed-out cave.

"A long time," I said.

"Very good. I can see why. You found a little piece of

paradise. It's a wonderful spot. I love to get away from the noise and bustle of my business, get away to a place like this where you can be with your own thoughts and commune with Nature. That's what you do, isn't it, Gabriel? Everyone calls you *La Fille au Naturel*. I see why now," he said, smiling. I continued to blush and looked away quickly.

"Please, monsieur."

"What's wrong? A beautiful girl like you must have been with a man before, no?"

"No, monsieur. Not like this."

"Really?" He turned on his side and reached out to touch my thigh. I nearly jumped off the rock. "It's all right. Nothing to be afraid of. It's just as natural as . . . as your fish and birds."

"But you are married, monsieur."

"Married," he said as if it were distasteful even to have the word in his mouth. "I married too quickly and for the wrong reasons," he added.

I glanced at him. Was no one happily wed? Was everyone fooled?

"What reasons?" I asked. He touched me again, tracing along my thigh with his finger as if he had his finger in beach sand.

"Money, wealth, power. Gladys's father owned the cannery."

"You weren't in love?"

He laughed and rolled over on his back.

"Love," he pronounced with his lips tight, as if saying it left a horrid taste on his tongue. "I said it and she said it, but neither of us believed it. We swallowed our lies like castor oil and said 'I do' in front of the priest. Even he had doubts when he pronounced us man and wife. I could see it in his eyes. *Mon Dieu.* Love. Is there really such a thing?"

"Yes," I said firmly.

"Your mother and father, are they truly in love?" he challenged with laughing eyes.

"They were," I replied. He stared at me for a moment and then he smiled.

"I could fall in love with someone like you in the blink of an eye."

"Monsieur Tate!"

"I'm not that old," he protested. "Yvette Livaudis, a girl in your class, is going to marry a man older than I am, right?" In the bayou everyone knew everyone else's business. I wasn't surprised he knew about Yvette. "You shouldn't think me too old."

"You're not old, monsieur," I granted.

"That's right. I'm not." He looked back at our canoes and then at me. "I'll swim back and get your canoe," he offered.

"Thank you, monsieur."

"For a kiss," he added, smiling.

"No, monsieur!" I cringed.

"Why not? It's harmless enough. Just one kiss and you're free again." He sat up and leaned toward me. I turned away until I felt his lips on my shoulder and then my neck. I started to protest when he reached behind my head to pull my lips closer to his. Then he kissed me. I tried to pull away, but he held me firmly. I felt his tongue between my lips and then his hand move up the side of my body until the palm found my breast. I backed away quickly and he laughed.

"There, now wasn't that nice?"

I shook my head, clutching the towel against my bosom.

"To the canoe," he shouted, and dove off the rock. He swam quickly and got into mine. "Have no fear, damsel in distress, I'm coming to rescue you."

He began to pole my canoe toward the rock, behaving as if we were two children pretending. He brought the canoe back to the rock and stood there, holding out his hand.

"Come on. I'll help you in."

"I can get in myself. I've done it hundreds of times." When I spoke, I tried not to look at him standing there stark naked.

"I'm sure you have, mademoiselle, but we're surrounded by alligators."

"We are not," I said.

"You can't see them like I can. Come," he said, beckoning. I thought there was no other way to rid myself of him, so I gave him my hand and kept my eyes down. But when I stepped into the canoe, he embraced me and pressed his body to mine. We tottered as I struggled to be free.

"Whoa," he said. "We're going to fall in."

"Please, let me go," I pleaded. And then we did fall over and into the water. He shouted as we splashed under. When I came up, I no longer had my towel and he was already climbing back into my canoe.

"Are you all right?"

"I'm fine," I said. "Get out of my canoe."

"First I have to do the gentlemanly thing and help you to safety," he insisted. "Come along now." He reached out and seized my wrist. I climbed up and over the side of the canoe, and he sat back as I got in, this time pulling me over him and throwing his arms around my waist. His mouth was on mine again and then his lips moved quickly over my neck and down to my breasts, trailing his kisses with laughter. I tried to struggle out of his grip, but he was too strong and he turned me over so that I was now beneath him. Then he leaned back and smiled.

"Quite a temptation, you lying out here like this, waiting for a man like me."

"Please, monsieur. I was waiting for no one."

"No boyfriend about to arrive?" he asked with skeptical eyes.

"No, please."

"Come on now, you don't expect me to believe that a daughter of a man like Jack Landry wasn't waiting for some excitement. Why settle for a teenage boy? You have a man at your disposal," he insisted.

Before I could offer more protest, he lowered himself toward me, squeezing himself more firmly between my legs. I felt him nudge me with the hardness that had grown between his legs and then he pushed forward, dropping the weight of his body over my arms, pinning me back as he slipped farther under until . . .

The shock of it stunned me at first, but the more I squirmed, the more he enjoyed what he was doing and the tighter he made his grip on me. I was trapped beneath him, his hot breath over my face. He was mumbling, pleading, pressing deeper and deeper into me, his thrusts faster, harder, until finally I felt him quiver. I uttered a tiny cry and stopped resisting when he filled me with his hot lust and

23

passion. All I could do was close my eyes and wait for it to end.

After it had, we were both silent. I didn't move, but I felt him lifting himself from me. I kept my eyes shut tight, hoping that I could erase what had happened from my mind and my body if I just didn't look.

"I'm sorry," he said. "I just . . . couldn't help myself. You're so beautiful and my wife and I . . . we . . . It's been a while. I'm sorry. You're okay. It's nothing. Really. You're fine."

I waited. Then I heard him dive into the water and start to swim back to his own pirogue. I opened my eyes as he pulled himself into his canoe. I sat up and took a deep breath. All the blood had drained from my face. I thought I would faint. He dressed himself as quickly as he could, looking at me periodically until he was finished. Then he seized his pole.

"It's all right. It was nothing," he said, and began to push away. "I'll never come back here. I promise. This will be your special place again. *Bonjour,*" he added as if we had just had afternoon tea. A few moments later, he was gone.

The pirogue rocked in the water. I didn't move. It was deadly quiet. Even the frogs had stopped croaking. Only the insects circled madly over the water, but the bream, frightened by the commotion above, had swum deeper and waited in the cool shadows to be sure it was safe.

I started to cry, but stopped myself. It would do no good and it would only make me look even more horrible when Mama set eyes on me. I was terrified of that. Feeling dirty and violated, I lowered myself off the side of the pirogue and scrubbed my body vigorously. Then I got back into the canoe and dressed quickly, swallowing down my sobs, choking back my tears.

It terrified me to think of what would happen if everyone found out what Mr. Tate had done. The scandal would be worse than a hurricane. Hateful gossips would find a way to blame me, I was sure. Why was I naked in the swamp? Those who had made up fantastic stories about my wild ways with animals in the bayou would see this only as a reinforcement of their terrible lies. And poor Mama, she would bear the brunt of the storm. Daddy would only get drunker and into more fights.

No, I decided, there was nothing to do but try to forget; although right now, I didn't see how that was possible. For one thing, I could never return to my beautiful pond without recalling this nightmare. The surroundings lost their pristine beauty for me. I would be afraid to return. What if he returned when I was alone again?

How horrid and guilty I felt. Maybe this was my fault. Maybe I was wrong to bathe nude. I had a woman's mature body and I would be a liar to claim I never craved to be touched, to tingle and fulfill my own longing for love; but it was a longing I had hoped to satisfy with someone who truly cherished and loved me, too.

I desperately longed to talk to Mama about it, to get her advice and wisdom, but I didn't see how I could do so without her realizing what had happened. Mama would take one deep look into my eyes and know the truth. I had to be strong and not appear to be avoiding her gaze tonight, I thought. I sat there with my eyes closed and held my breath. Then I released it and took long, deep breaths, willing my heart to stop thumping like a drum. I would be calm. I would press this memory down and smother it with other thoughts.

My legs were still trembling when I stood up to begin my poling, but as I gathered speed and momentum, they grew stronger and more sturdy. I pushed myself away from the pond, the leaves of the sprawling cypress closing like a door behind me. I didn't look back. For a while as I continued, I darted my gaze from side to side, afraid Monsieur Tate might be somewhere nearby, waiting to apologize or plead with me to say nothing. The thought of facing him ever again set my heart pounding. What would I do? What would he do?

When I reached our dock and tied up my pirogue, I checked my clothing and tried to see my reflection in the water. Mama would think my appearance was due only to my swim anyway, I assured myself. I looked up at the shack where I knew she was waiting, setting the table, lighting a butane lantern, putting a record on our windup Victrola, trying to forget her own troubles. I had to do everything I could to keep what had just happened to me buried outside the house.

I took a deep breath and started up the pathway. As soon as Mama heard my steps on the gallery, she called.

"Is that you, Gabriel?"

"Yes, Mama. I'll just go up and change into something else," I said. "I got this dress wet and dirty," I added before she could inquire. I flashed a smile at her in the kitchen and hurried up the stairway to my bedroom.

"How was your swim?" she called.

"Refreshing, Mama. You should come with me someday."

I heard her laugh.

"I don't remember when I swam last. Probably that time your father took us all to Lake Pontchartrain, before the war. Can you remember that?"

"Yes, Mama."

I studied myself in the long mirror over the oak armoire in Mama's room. My shoulders were red and there were faint patches of irritation on my neck, too. What was I to do? I put on my yellow and white dress, the one that had the buttons up to my collarbone, and then I wiped my hair vigorously with a towel, brushed it down, and wrapped the towel over my neck like a scarf. I kept my fingers crossed and descended to the kitchen. Mama looked up from the stove.

"This roux is delicious, honey. I boiled some crawfish, too."

"I'm starving," I said. I got us some napkins and some of Mama's lemonade. She brought the pot to the table and ladled out the crawfish and roux. She had thrown in some vegetables and rice. It smelled delicious.

"What'cha doin' with that towel?" she asked with a smile before she sat.

"My hair's still very wet, Mama. I'm too hungry to wait."

She laughed and we started to eat.

"Well, like I told you. Your father's not coming home for dinner. I'm locking him out tonight," she declared. "He's nothing but a thief, stealing your dowry money for that

26

stupid scheme. If he spent half the time and energy he spends on schemes doing legitimate work instead, we'd be millionaires, as least as rich as the Tates," she said, and I nearly dropped my spoon.

"What's wrong, Gabriel?" she asked quickly.

"I swallowed too fast, Mama."

"Well, take your time, honey. You got all the time in the world. Don't rush your life like I did. Think twice and then think twice more before you say yes to anything. No matter how simple or small it seems."

"Yes, Mama."

The music had stopped.

"I'm going to wind it up again," Mama said. "Tonight I just feel like hearing music. Tonight I don't want to hear silence."

I watched her get up and go to the Victrola. I hated being deceitful to her, but she was so down, so depressed and alone, I could never add even a pinch of sadness to her misery. I lowered my eyes to my food. After I ate, I helped clean up and then went upstairs to finish sewing my graduation dress. Mama had cut out the pattern. She went out on the gallery to weave some split-oak baskets, but she wasn't out there long before Mr. LaFourche came to fetch her in his Ford pickup truck. His wife was having terrible stomach cramps.

"I got to go make a visit," she called up to me. "You be all right?"

"Yes, Mama. I'm fine."

"If that no-account father of yours shows up, don't give him anything to eat," she said.

"I won't, Mama," I said, but she knew I would. After I heard the truck leave, I came out of the loom room and put on my dress. I went to Mama's mirror again and gazed at myself in the light of the butane lamp. The dress fit perfectly. I thought it made me look years older.

But I didn't smile at my image.

I didn't feel my heart burst with joy and excitement.

I began to cry. I sobbed so hard, my stomach ached. And then I ran out of tears and sat silently on my bed, staring through the window at the sliver of moon above the willow trees. I sighed deeply, took off my graduation dress, put on my nightgown, and crawled under my blanket.

When I closed my eyes, Mr. Tate's face with his lustful smile appeared. I moaned and sat up quickly, my heart pounding. How would he sleep tonight? I wondered. Was it easier for him to put the sinful act out of mind than it was for me, or would his conscience come roaring down over him and drive him to his knees to pray for forgiveness?

I was very angry. I wanted to pray to God to refuse him. I wished him centuries of pain and suffering. I hoped that when he had left my pond, he had fallen out of his canoe and been attacked by snakes and alligators. His cries would be music to my ears. I raged for a while like this and then I felt guilty for doing so and shut down my vengeful thoughts.

But Mr. Tate had stolen more than my youth and innocence when he had attacked me, he had invaded and stained my private world. My sadness was deeper because of that. I was afraid of what it meant, for before this, I never felt alone. No matter that I had no real friends; no matter that I wasn't invited to parties and did not go to dances and shows.

But if I lose my world, I thought, if I lose the swamp and the animals, the fish and the birds, the flowers and the trees, if I fear the twilight and cringe when shadows fall, where will I go? What will become of me?

Would the beautiful blue heron return to her nest above the pond?

I was afraid of the morning, afraid of the answers that would come up with the sun.

2

Paradise Lost

I was positive that Daddy's not coming home all night was the only thing that kept Mama from noticing that something serious was bothering me the next morning. Mama had been out late treating Mrs. LaFourche, who Mama believed had eaten a few bad shrimp, so Mama was pretty tired and irritable anyway. She rose, expecting to find Daddy either sprawled out on the front gallery or on the floor of our living room, but he was nowhere to be seen.

Mama didn't notice that I ate very little breakfast or that I was quiet and tired myself. I had tossed and turned, flitting in and out of nightmares most of the night. But Mama ranted and raved to herself, raking up old complaints about Daddy, criticizing not only his excessive drinking and gambling, but his laziness.

"All the Landrys were lazy," she lectured, returning to an old theme. "It's in their blood. I should have know'd what your father would be like right from the start. Oh, he charmed me in the beginning by building this house and working hard for a while, but he was only setting me up the way the Landry men always set up their women, so he could throw it back at me all the time about just how much he done for me already.

29

"Like being a husband and a father was a nine-to-five job," she complained. "But being a mother and a wife was a twenty-four-hour, seven-day-a-week job. That's the way the Landry men see it.

"Before you marry anyone, Gabriel, you ask to see his grandpere, and if his grandmere's still living, you talk to her and get the lowdown, hear?" she warned.

"Yes, Mama."

She finally took note of me, but she attributed other reasons to my appearance.

"Look at you," she remarked, "nervous as a just-hatched chicken with your graduation just a day away now."

"I'm fine, Mama."

"I can't wait to see them hand you that diploma."

She beamed, her smile washing away her scarlet face of anger.

"You're the first Landry to get a high school diploma, you know that?" she asked. Daddy hadn't told me, but she had said it a few times before in his presence when she blamed some of the things he had done on his family blood.

"Yes, Mama."

"Good. Then be proud, not nervous. Well now, we'll have to plan a little celebration for afterward, won't we?"

"No, Mama. I don't want a party."

"Sure you do. Sure," she said, nodding and talking herself into it. "I'm going to make a couple of turkeys, and I think I'll make Louisiana yam with apple stuffing. I know how you love that. Of course, we'll have some stuffed crab and some shrimp Mornay with red and green rice. I'll make some garlic grits. I'll need some biscuits, and let's see, for desserts we should have a gingerbread, one of my coffee cakes, and maybe some caramel squares."

"Mama, you'll be working all day and night until graduation."

"So? How often will I have a graduation party for my daughter?" she said.

"But we don't have the money, do we?"

"I got a small stash your daddy didn't get his hands on," she said, winking.

30

"You should save it for something important, Mama."

"This is is important," she insisted. "Now hush up and go to school. Go on," she said, pushing me toward the door, "and don't you worry about how hard I work or how much I spend. I got to do what I enjoy doing and what makes me happy and proud. Especially these days," she added, scowling with thoughts of Daddy.

I shook my head. There wasn't anything I could do or say to change her mind once Mama had made up what she wanted to do. Daddy called her Cajun stubborn and said she would stare down a hurricane if she had made up her mind to do so.

"I'll come home as soon as I can to help you then," I said.

"Never mind. You do what all the girls are doing and worry about your graduation ceremony, not me," she said.

I left the house, still feeling a cloud overhead because of what had happened to me the day before; but also feeling the excitement that came with the end of school. At school no one talked about anything else. The chatter in the classroom was so loud and furious, we sounded like a yard of hens clucking. Our teachers gave up on doing anything that even vaguely resembled education.

In the afternoon they took us out to the yard on the side of the building where a portable stage had been constructed so we could rehearse the graduation ceremony. A piano had been wheeled out for Mrs. Parlange, the school secretary, to play the processional. Our principal, Mr. Pitot, was going to accompany her on the accordion, too. Together with Mr. Ternant, who was the vocal, physical education, and math teacher, and who played the fiddle, Mr. Pitot would do a few Cajun pieces to entertain the audience of grandparents, parents, brothers and sisters, uncles and aunts, and friends before the speeches and the distribution of diplomas. Mr. Ternant was put in charge of the ceremony and lined us up according to height. He told us how to walk, hold our heads up high, and sit properly on the stage.

"I don't want to see anyone crossing his or her legs. And no gum chewing, hear? You all sit still, face forward, and look dignified. Every one of you is a representative of this

31

school," he lectured. Bobby Slater made a popping sound with his mouth. Many of us smiled, but no one dared laugh. Mr. Ternant glared fiercely for a moment. Then he explained what we had to do when we were called up.

"I want you to take the diploma in this hand"—he demonstrated—"and cross over to shake like this."

He wanted us to then turn to the audience and make a small bow before returning directly to our seats.

I tried to concentrate on everything and listen carefully to all the instructions, but my mind kept wandering and returning to the incident at the lake. Yvette and Evelyn were too occupied with themselves and with their other friends to notice my distraction. I knew anyone who did notice me just thought it was my typical disinterest in things that interested them. It wasn't so. I wanted to be just as excited; I wanted to be just as young and silly and happy as they were. But every once in a while, Mr. Tate's face, just inches from mine, would flash across my eyes and I would gulp and moan softly to myself.

I was very quiet on the way home; however, Yvette and Evelyn were far more talkative than ever. A twilight gloom had pervaded my entire being, but even if I had wanted to talk, they didn't give me an opportunity to get in a word. It wasn't until we were about to part that they noticed me.

"What's wrong with you today?" Yvette asked. "Graduation jitters?"

"A little," I said. I could never even begin to tell them the true reason for my melancholy.

"Well, if you had a future waiting, you wouldn't be so jittery," Evelyn declared pedantically. "Now what are you going to do the day after tomorrow, sit on the side of the road at your stand and wait for some handsome prince to come riding along?"

Yvette laughed.

"Yes," I said, smiling. "That's exactly what I will do."

"Well, you'll grow old waiting for a handsome prince in these parts," Yvette said.

The two of them looked at each other in a way that told me they had been talking about me at length.

"Don't you even think about being with a man?" Evelyn asked, flashing a sly glance at Yvette.

"Of course," I said, but with less enthusiasm than either of them would.

"You never talk about it when we talk about it," Yvette added. "We know you never been kissed," she said, shifting her gaze to Evelyn, who smiled. "Much less . . . touched." They giggled.

"You two don't know everything about me," I said, but in a sad, unfortunate tone of voice. It wiped the smiles off their faces for the moment. Yvette's eyes grew as small as dimes and glittered with suspicion.

"What have you been keeping secret?" Yvette said. "Someone visit you in the swamps?"

I reddened.

"Someone has!" Evelyn declared. "Look at her."

"No." Butterflies beat small wings of panic in my stomach.

"Who was it?"

"What did you do, Gabriel Landry?"

"We always tell you everything that we've done," Yvette said petulantly.

"Nothing. I've done nothing," I insisted.

They laughed.

"Liar."

"You better tell us, Gabriel Landry or . . ."

"Or we'll make something up and tell everyone tomorrow before graduation," Evelyn announced. Yvette nodded, happy for the plan. "We'll claim you told us in secret. Everyone will believe us because they know we're friends and we talk on the way home from school every day."

"That's right," Yvette said. "If we both swear to it, everyone will believe it."

"But there's nothing to tell. I . . ."

"What?" Yvette demanded. She put her hands on her hips. Evelyn stared, anticipating. I took a deep breath. If they spread rumors about me tomorrow, they could ruin graduation for Mama.

"All right, I'll tell you, but you've got to swear to keep it secret."

33

"We'll swear," Yvette said.

"On Saint Medad. Swear."

They did and crossed their hearts.

"Well?" Evelyn said.

"Sometimes in the afternoon I pole my pirogue deep into the swamp to a small pond I've found. No one else ever goes there. I take off my clothes and go swimming."

"Naked?" Yvette said, her eyes widening. I nodded. They drew closer to me.

"What happened?" Evelyn asked breathlessly.

"One afternoon about a week ago, I was sunning myself at the pond and this handsome young man came poling along. I didn't hear him."

Yvette's mouth opened.

"You were naked when he appeared?" Evelyn asked. I nodded. They held their breaths.

"I opened my eyes and found him staring down at me and smiling. I was terribly embarrassed, of course, and reached for my dress. But he . . ."

"What?"

"Sat on it."

"No!"

"What did you do?" Evelyn asked.

"I said, please, monsieur, you have me at an unfair advantage. He agreed."

"And gave you your dress?"

"No. He took off his clothes so he would be naked, too."

"You're lying," Evelyn said.

"You asked me to tell you. You swore you would keep it a secret. I'm telling you and you're calling me a liar," I said. "I kept my part of the bargain." I started to turn away.

"I believe you," Yvette declared. "Tell us the rest."

I hesitated.

"All right. I do believe you," Evelyn relented. "Go on."

"He was very polite. We spoke softly. He had the deepest blue eyes I had ever seen. I think he hypnotized me with those eyes. In fact, I'm sure he did."

"What do you mean?"

"The next thing I knew, he was kissing me."

"And he touched you?"

"Everywhere," I said. "I couldn't resist."

"And then?" Yvette said with impatience.

"I don't know. I just . . . woke up and he was gone."

"Gone?" Evelyn grimaced with disappointment. "You must have just dreamt it, fantasized," she added contemptuously.

"No, I know I didn't dream it. He had left a beautiful red rose at my side."

"A red rose? In the swamp?" Evelyn asked, smirking.

"That's how I knew I hadn't dreamt it."

The two studied me a moment in silence.

"All right. So what did you do then?" Yvette asked.

"I was so frightened I got dressed and went home as fast as I could. I told my mother."

"You did? Everything?"

"Of course."

Evelyn was impressed. "What did she say?"

"She asked me to describe the young man, and after I had, she sat down with a look on her face like I had never seen. She was quiet for the longest time. Finally I asked her what was wrong, and she then told me the story of the young fisherman who was thought to be the handsomest young man in the bayou. She said young women would swoon at the sight of him, but she said he was too handsome for a man to be and he knew it. No one was more arrogant about his looks.

"One day he went into the swamps to fish and never returned."

"Are you saying your mother said the man who kissed you was a ghost?" Yvette asked. I nodded.

"It's why I never heard him approaching. He glided on the air, I think."

Neither Yvette nor Evelyn spoke for a moment.

"Did he feel like a ghost when he kissed you?" Evelyn inquired skeptically.

"No. He felt real, very real."

"Did you ever see him again?"

"No, but sometimes I think I sense him."

"You still go out alone?" Yvette asked, incredulous.

"Yes. He didn't hurt me. Mama says he's a lonely soul.

Punished for being too much like a Greek god. The story she remembers from her grandmere is, the day he finds someone who can see the goodness in his heart and love him for that and not for his good looks, that's the day he can return to the world to live out his life, but . . ."

"But what?" Evelyn asked.

"Yes, but what?" Yvette followed.

"But whoever does love him that way dies and takes his place in the swamp. It's sort of an exchange of souls for a while."

"How horrible."

"And dangerous," Yvette said. "You had better not go into the swamp alone so much."

"I don't," I said. "As much."

"I don't know if that counts," Evelyn declared after a moment's thought. "Kissed by a ghost isn't the same thing as being kissed by a live man."

"How do you know?" Yvette said. "Only Gabriel knows for sure."

"It felt wonderful at the time," I replied. "Now, remember. You swore on Saint Medad, and if you violate this oath, you might bring bad luck to your husbands."

They were wide-eyed. The daughter of a *traiteur* had some credibility when it came to this sort of thing.

"I'll never tell," Yvette said.

"Me neither."

"I got to go home. See you tomorrow."

"*Oui*. See you tomorrow," Evelyn said.

I watched them hurry off and then continued down the road. In my heart I wished that what had happened to me yesterday was what I had described to them. It was my fantasy, and for a while at least, I would use it to cloak the ugly truth.

When I arrived home, I found Mama doing just what I feared she would be doing: slaving over the stove, chaining herself to the kitchen to prepare for my graduation celebration. She told me she had already sent word to a dozen of her friends and people she often treated.

36

"Some are offering to make food, too. It's going to be a great party, honey. We'll have music and loads of good food."

"I wish you wouldn't do this, Mama."

"Let's not start that again. It's my time in the sun and it should be your father's time, too."

"Has he been home?"

"Not that I know," she replied, and dove into her labor of love to keep from thinking and being angry. Seeing I was not going to change her mind, I offered to help, but she refused to permit it.

"It's your party. You earned it; you just enjoy yourself," she insisted. I couldn't stand by and watch her work, so I went out to our dock and sat with my feet dangling in the water, watching and hoping for the sight of Daddy poling his pirogue up the canal to home. But he never came. At dinner Mama was mumbling to herself something awful.

"That man has gone bad, gone sour like warm milk. Nothing's going to change him. He'll be the death of all of us. Truth is, I hope he never comes home," she declared, but I knew she was heartbroken about it. She sat on the gallery in her rocker after dinner and glared at the darkness, waiting for one of those shadows to take Daddy's form.

I put the finishing touches on my graduation dress and put it on to show Mama. She shook her head and smiled.

"You're so beautiful, Gabriel, it makes my heart pound."

"Oh, Mama, I'm not. And besides, you told me dozens of times that pride's a sin."

"You don't have to go overboard and fall in love with yourself, but you can be thankful and happy you've been blessed with such natural beauty. You don't understand," she added when I looked down and blushed. "You're my redemption. When I look at you, at least I can feel something good came out of my marriage to that scoundrel we call your daddy."

I looked up sharply. "He tries to be good, doesn't he, Mama? He thinks about it."

"The most I can say for him, honey, is it's beyond him. It's in his blood. The Landrys were probably first cousins to

37

Cain." She sighed. "I got no one to blame but myself for the pot I'm boiling in," she said.

"But if the Landry blood is so powerful and evil, won't I be evil, too, Mama?" I asked fearfully.

"No," she said quickly. "You got my blood in you, too, don'tcha?"

"Yes, Mama."

"Well, my blood overpowers even the wicked Landry blood." She took my hand into hers and drew me closer so her eyes could look deeply into mine. "When evil thoughts come to mind, you think of me, honey, and my blood will come rushing over those thoughts, drowning them. If it don't . . ."

"Yes, Mama?"

"Then maybe what you're thinking ain't so evil after all," she said. Then she took a deep breath as if the advice had drained her of the little energy that remained after so hard a day of cooking and baking. She also did a lot of cleaning around the shack so it would look as presentable as possible to our guests tomorrow.

"You're tired, Mama. You should go to sleep."

"*Oui.* I should," she admitted. She sighed, gazed into the darkness for a moment, her gaze sliding over the shadows in search of Daddy, and then she rose with great effort. We went into the shack together and upstairs.

"Tonight's the last night you go to bed a little girl," Mama told me after I got into bed. She sat at my feet for a few moments. "Tomorrow you graduate. You're a young woman now." She started to hum a Cajun lullaby, one she used to sing to me when I was a little girl.

"Mama?"

"Yes, honey."

"Before you met Daddy, did you have any other boy-friends?"

"I had a number of young men on my tail," she said, smiling. "My father would shoo them away like flies."

"But . . . did any of them become your boyfriend?"

"Oh, I had my little romances."

"Did you . . ."

"Did I what, honey?"

"Did you kiss and do things with the other boys?"

"What kind of a question to ask is that, Gabriel?" she said, pulling her shoulders up. She held a small smile, however.

"I just wondered if that was what was supposed to be."

"Kissing and things is supposed to be, if that's what you mean, but you got to remember what I told you my grandmere told me: 'Sex, Catherine,' she used to say, 'is just Nature's little trick to bring the two people right for each other together.'"

"What if people who aren't right for each other have sex?" I pursued, speaking softly, afraid that if I spoke too loudly or too fast, the magic moment during which Mama would tell me intimate things would burst and be gone.

"Well then, it's just sex. It might make them feel good for the moment, but afterward," she said with a scowl, "they'll feel they lost a little of something precious, something of themselves. That's what I believe. I suppose," she added, raising her right eyebrow, "your girlfriends would laugh at that, *n'est-ce pas?*"

"I don't know, Mama. I don't care what they think."

She stared at me a moment. "You want to tell me something, Gabriel, something gnawing at your insides?"

The words were on my tongue, but I swallowed them back.

"No, Mama. I just wondered, that's all."

She nodded. "Just natural. Trust your instincts," she said. "You got good ones. Well, good night, Miss Graduate," she said, and leaned over to kiss my cheek. I held on to her a bit longer than I should have, and Mama's eyebrows went up again, her eyes sharp and small.

"I'm always willing to listen and help you, honey. Don't ever forget that," she said.

"I know, Mama. Good night."

"Good night," she said, and got up even though I sensed she wanted to remain there until I told her what was behind my dark eyes.

I thought about Mama's words and wondered what part

39

of myself I had left in the swamp. My worrying caused something hard and heavy to grow in my chest, making it ache. I put my palms together under my chin, closed my eyes, and prayed.

"Please, dear God," I muttered, "forgive me if I did anything to cause this evil thing to happen to me."

I tried to throw off the dreary feelings. Fatigue closed my eyes, but sleep was driven back by my tossing and turning. Anticipating the excitement of tomorrow, worrying about what had happened, worrying about Daddy and about Mama, kept me wide-awake until the wee hours of the morning. The sun was actually turning the inky sky into a shade of red slate when I finally drifted into a deep repose. I woke to Mama's shaking the bed.

"Gabriel, you can't oversleep this morning!" she said, laughing.

"Oh. Oh, what time is it?" I looked at the clock and leaped out of bed.

We were getting our final report cards, turning in our books, saying our good-byes today, the last day of school.

"Go wash the sleep out of that face in the rain barrel," Mama ordered. "I'll have some breakfast for you."

"Did Daddy come home?" I asked.

"No. You would have smelled him if he had," she offered, and went down to make breakfast.

I washed my face in the rainwater, brushed my hair, and put on my clothes. Mama was mumbling about all the things she was still going to do in preparation for my graduation party. Every once in a while she would break to complain about Daddy.

"He better be back here today and make himself presentable for the ceremony," she warned.

"He will, Mama. I'm sure."

"You have faith in everyone and everything," Mama said. "You'd even give a snapping turtle a second chance."

I couldn't help it. Today, of all days, I wanted to think only good and happy thoughts.

There was a storm of excitement at school: torrents of laughter and giggling, smiles raining down over us, our hearts thumping like thunder. The classrooms only calmed down when Mr. Pitot visited them. Everyone sat with his or her hands folded, backs straight as we were taught, eyes forward. Some chairs squeaked.

Mr. Pitot congratulated us on a fine year, complimented the students who maintained high grades and who never misbehaved. He warned us about our behavior at the ceremonies.

"The public will be our guests. Parents, family members, friends, will all have their eyes on you, on us. It is incumbent upon us to put on our best faces."

I turned and saw Jacques Bascomb put his tongue under his upper lip so he resembled a monkey. It was hard to believe that some of the boys in my class would be out working and raising families in less than a year's time.

School ended after the morning session so we could all go home and get into our graduation clothes. When I arrived and found Mama setting up tables for our guests outside, I knew Daddy had not returned yet.

"Mama, this is too much for you to do by yourself," I complained.

"It's all right, honey. I'm fine. When you have your heart soaking in happiness, you don't feel the labor."

"But afterward you will," I chastised.

"Listen to you," she said, standing back with her hands on her small hips. "Just graduated and already bossy."

"I'm not being bossy. I'm being sensible, Mama."

"I know, honey. Okay. I'll wait for help 'fore I do anything heavy. That's a promise," she said. I hoped she would keep it. I saw the palms of her hands were red from lifting and sliding the tables and chairs. Where was Daddy? How could he be so inconsiderate?

I went inside and after eating only half of the po'boy sandwich Mama had prepared for my lunch, I got into my dress and fixed my hair again. Then I went outside and sat on the gallery, waiting for the time to pass and hoping to see my daddy come walking up to the house, full of apologies, but eager to help make this one of the happiest days of our lives.

He never showed.

Mama put on her best dress and brushed and pinned her hair. We stalled and waited as long as we could. Finally she emerged, her face burning with fury, those eyes ready to sear through Daddy's and set his soul on fire.

"Let's go, honey. We don't want you to be late," she said.

I didn't mention Daddy. We both started down the road. When we joined the Thibodeaus and Livaudises, they asked about Daddy.

"He'll meet us at the festivities," Mama said, but anyone could see that shadows had come to darken and pain Mama's happiness. No one asked why. They all looked at each other and knew the answer anyway.

There was a big crowd at the school by the time we arrived. Yvette, Evelyn, and I hurried into the building to put on our graduation gowns and caps and get into place. Mr. Ternant was as nervous as a gray squirrel, marching up and down the corridor, repeating the same orders, his head bobbing, his hands fluttering like two range chickens spooked by a fox. Finally we heard the first notes from Mrs. Parlange's piano and then Mr. Pitot's accordion. Everyone grew quiet.

"Attention," Mr. Ternant said, holding his right hand up like a general leading his troops to battle. The processional began and his arm lowered, his fingers pointing forward. "Begin!"

We got into step and trailed out to the stage. It seemed brighter than ever, the sun glistening off every shiny surface. Parents and family strained their necks like egrets to get views of their graduates. Cameras were clicking, babies were crying. I gazed at Mrs. Parlange and saw she was playing the piano as if she were in a concert hall, looking neither to the right or to the left.

Remarkably, we all wove in and out of the aisles of seats to our own and sat orderly when the processional ended. After we were all seated, Mr. Pitot stepped on the stage beside the dignitaries. He gazed at us and then nodded his satisfaction before approaching the microphone. The ceremony, my graduation, was about to begin.

I searched the audience until I spotted Mama. She had kept a seat beside her, but it was empty. My heart sunk. How could Daddy miss my graduation? Please, please, dear God, I prayed, don't let him miss it.

And then my gaze shifted to the right and I saw Monsieur Tate. He was in the first row beside his wife. His eyes were fixed on me, his lips pressed tightly together. The unexpected sight of him put my heart into triple time and took my breath away. I looked at Gladys Tate to see if she noticed how he was staring at me, but she looked like she was bored. She was very elegantly dressed, however, and had her hair cut and styled, with bubbles of pearls in her ears and around her neck. Gladys Tate was one of the more attractive women in our town. She had a regal stature and always walked and spoke with an air of superiority.

I looked away quickly, closed my eyes and caught my breath.

After Mr. Pitot and Mrs. Parlange played two numbers, Mr. Pitot returned to the stage and made a small speech about us all graduating at one of the most important times in history. He said we had a country to rebuild as soon as the war ended, and because so many young men were away and killed, we had more responsibilities. His words frightened me a bit and made me feel a little guilty about not doing something more with my life. Maybe I should have become a nurse, I thought.

After Mr. Pitot's speech, Theresa Rousseau, our salutatorian, got up and made her speech, followed by the valedictorian, Jane Crump, who had never missed a day of school or gotten a grade lower than ninety-five on a test. She was a short, plump girl with glasses so thick they looked like goggles, but her father was president of the bank and everyone expected he would find her a suitable husband after she had gone to college to become a teacher herself.

Finally it was time to distribute the diplomas. I had been sitting there, twisting my hands together as if I had a roll of yarn in them, afraid to look at Mama and terrified of looking to the right and seeing Mr. and Mrs. Tate. But when I did look at Mama this time, my heart jumped.

43

There was Daddy sitting beside her, his hair wet and brushed, his best shirt and pants on. He had even shaved. But Mama was not smiling. Daddy was, beaming, and waving at me so much, I had to wave back to stop him from embarrassing Mama. Mr. Pitot began to call out the names of the graduates. My heart began to thump against my chest. I thought for sure when I stood up, my legs would turn to butter and I would sink to the stage floor.

"Gabriel Landry," Mr. Pitot cried out.

I rose, knowing all eyes were on me, the eyes of Mama's friends and people who respected and thought highly of her, the eyes of those who thought I was *La Fille au Naturel*, and the eyes of Octavious Tate. I couldn't help but glance his way once. He had a small smile on his lips. Gladys Tate was gazing up at me with some interest.

Just as I reached for my diploma, Daddy jumped up in the audience and shouted.

"That there's my daughter, the first Landry to graduate school! Hal-le-luja!"

There was a roar of laughter. I felt my stomach sink to my knees. I turned and saw Mama tugging on Daddy's shirt to get him to sit down. Tears blinded my vision. I took my diploma quickly and ran off the stage and into the school building to escape the laughing eyes. I was supposed to go back to my seat and march away with my class, but I couldn't do it, and it wasn't only because of Daddy's outburst.

Monsieur Tate's eyes had burned through my graduation gown. I had felt naked on that stage, naked and obviously violated. I had felt as if everyone in Houma could see what had happened to me. I ran down the corridor and into the girls' bathroom where I sat on a closed toilet seat and cried, my diploma in my hands. Moments later, Mrs. Parlange came rushing in after me.

"What are you doing? Mr. Ternant is having heart failure out there. You're supposed to go back to your seat and leave the stage with your class. You knew that, Gabriel. Why are you crying?" she followed, as if she first opened her eyes and saw me.

44

"I can't go back, Mrs. Parlange. I can't. I'm sorry. I'll apologize to Mr. Ternant later."

"Oh, my dear. Dear, dear," she said, waving her right hand back and forth to fan her face. Bewilderment clouded her expression. "This has never happened before. I really don't know what to do."

"I'm sorry," I wailed.

"Yes, well, yes," she said, and walked out on tiptoes.

I choked back my sobs, feeling as if I had cried dry that bottomless well of tears. Then I took a deep breath and looked at my diploma. How proud Mama was of me and how sick to her stomach she must be right now, too, I thought. I sat there, not sure of what I should do next. My heart stopped racing, finally, and I rose. When I gazed at myself in the mirror, I saw a face flushed and streaked with dry tears. I washed and dried it, took another deep breath, and walked out just as the processional to take the students off the stage had begun. I was at the doorway when they began to enter.

"What happened to you?" Yvette demanded.

"You made a fool out of the whole class," Evelyn said. "What you do, see your ghost boyfriend?"

"What ghost boyfriend?" Patti Arnot asked, which brought a half dozen others around us quickly.

"You'll have to ask her," Evelyn said. "I'm disgusted with her behavior."

"Me too," Yvette said.

It was as if I had broken out with measles. Everyone kept away from me. I retreated to a corner and took off my graduation gown and cap, just as Mr. Ternant came looking for me.

"You graduated," he said angrily before I could apologize, "so I can't punish you, put you on detention, or have you wash blackboards until your fingers turn blue, but what you did out there embarrassed us all, young lady."

"I'm sorry, sir," I said, my eyes down.

"Why did you do such a thing?"

I didn't reply except to say, "I'm sorry."

"Well, it's not a very auspicious way to begin your adult

45

life. I'll take that," he said, seizing the box that contained my gown and cap. "Who knows what you'll do next, and these things are expensive."

He pivoted and marched off. Everyone who heard was glaring at me. Defeat seemed all around me.

I looked away and started for the exit.

"She should have graduated in the swamp with her animal friends instead of us," someone shouted, and everyone laughed. I emerged from the laughter like someone drowning in a murky pool and hurried outside where I found Mama, worried, waiting. Daddy was off to the right shouting at someone who had passed a remark about me.

"I'm sorry, Mama," I said before she could ask why I had run off the stage.

"It's all right, honey. Let's go before your father gets arrested again. Jack!" she cried. He stopped shouting, his fist dangling above him, and looked at us. Then he glared at the man with whom he was arguing.

"Lucky for you I gotta go," he spat.

When he joined us, I realized quickly why Mama had been sitting with a gray face beside him. He reeked of whiskey, despite his clean appearance.

"Why'd you run off like that, Gabriel?" he asked. "Some of these people think you're as mad as a rabid dog."

"Why do you think she run off?" Mama snapped. "The way you behaved, screaming out like that, everyone laughing at you."

"Is that why? I was just proud, is all. Can't a man be proud of his daughter anymore?"

"Proud's proud, being a fool is just being a fool," Mama replied.

"Aaa, who cares what these stuffy folks think anyway. You looked great up there, Gabriel. Let's go celebrate."

"Figures you'd get home in time for that, Jack Landry," Mama said.

"Quit whippin' me, woman. A man can take only so much before he explodes."

Mama flicked him a scathing glance. He looked away quickly and fell behind us as we trekked toward home and the party Mama had prepared all by herself.

Fewer people attended than Mama had expected, and none of my classmates appeared. I knew it was because of my behavior and I felt just terrible about it, but Mama wouldn't be discouraged, nor would she permit a single sad face. Her food and the food her friends brought was wonderful. The men and especially Daddy had plenty of homemade whiskey to drink. The Rice brothers provided the music. They played the fiddle, the accordion, and the washboard. People danced and ate until long after nightfall. Every time someone started to leave, Daddy would jump up and grab him by the elbow, urging him to stay.

"The night's young," he declared. "We got lots to drink and eat yet. *Laissez les bon temps rouler!* Let the good times roll."

I never saw him so excited and happy. He danced one jig after another, dragged Mama out to do the two-step, performed somersaults and handstands, and challenged every man to Indian wrestle.

People ate and scraped their plates clean. The women helped Mama clean up. No one bothered me about what happened at graduation, but most had some sort of advice or another when they stopped to wish me good luck.

"Don't be in a hurry to go and get married. Marry the right man."

"Think about getting a job in the cannery, maybe."

"If I were your age, I'd go to N'orleans and find work, or try to get a job on a steamboat."

"Raise a family when you're young so you're not too old to enjoy life when they finally up and leave."

I thanked everyone. Daddy drank himself into a stupor and fell asleep in the hammock, his arm dangling, his snoring so loud, we could hear him clear across the yard.

"I'm just going to leave him out there," Mama told her friends. "Won't be the first time; won't be the last."

They nodded and went their way. When everyone was gone, I sat with Mama on the gallery for a while. Daddy was still sawing trees in the hammock.

"It was a wonderful party, Mama. But now you're so exhausted."

"It's a good exhaustion. When you do a labor of love, it

don't matter how tired you get, honey. The pleasure soothes you and eases you into a restful sleep. It's just too bad your father came soaked with whiskey to your ceremony and embarrassed you that way. It near broke my heart to see you rush off that stage."

"I'm sorry I did that, Mama."

"It's all right. Most people understood."

I had the greatest urge to explain to her why it wasn't just what Daddy had done. I would begin by telling her about Monsieur Tate's eyes on me and then . . .

But I just couldn't get the words up from the bottom of the trunk I had buried them in.

Mama stood up, gazed at Daddy for a moment, shook her head, and started to go into the house.

"You coming, Gabriel?"

"In a while, Mama."

"Don't think you're not exhausted too, honey," she warned.

"Oh, I know I am, Mama."

She smiled and we hugged.

"I'm darn proud of you, sweetheart. Darn proud."

"Thank you, Mama."

She went in and I stepped off the gallery and walked around to the dock. I took off my moccasins to dip my feet in the water and sat there for a while, listening to the cicadas and the occasional hoot of an owl. From time to time I heard a splash and saw the moonlight glimmer off the back of a gator sliding along the oily surface of the water and into the shadows.

I stared into the swamp, fixing my eyes on the inky darkness, and I wished and wished until I thought I saw him . . . the handsome young Cajun ghost. He was floating over the water and beckoning to me, tempting me.

If there really was a handsome young man haunting the swamps, I thought, I could forget the terrible thing that had happened to me. I'd even be willing to fall in love with him the way I had described to Yvette and Evelyn, and exchange my soul with his. I'd rather be a ghost, floating along through eternity, than a violated young woman right now, I thought.

His smile faded in the darkness and became a group of fireflies dancing madly around each other.

All the magic of this day evaporated. The stars seemed to shrink away, and dark clouds slid from behind silvery ones and chased away the moon.

I sighed, got up, and walked back to the house, not full of hope and dreams for tomorrow, as I should be, but weighed down, soaked with terror about the days to come.

Did I have a little of Mama's clairvoyance? I hoped not. I hoped I was just tired.

3

Hiding from Mama

Summer had begun as timidly as a white-tailed deer the year I graduated high school, but a little more than a week after the ceremony, the heat became more oppressive than I had ever known it to be. Mama said it was the worst she could recall, and Daddy said she had finally gotten her wish: She had brought him hell on earth. Nights were no cooler than the days. At times the air was so heavy with humidity, my hair would become damp and my dress would cling like a second layer of skin to my body.

All of Nature appeared just as depressed. Every animal restricted its travel to bare necessity. The gators dug themselves deeper into the mud; the bream seemed reluctant to come out of the water even to feed on the clouds of bewildered insects. Part of the problem was we didn't have much of a breeze coming up from the Gulf. The air was so still, leaves looked wilted and painted against the sky, and birds looked stuffed and fastened on branches.

What little tourist business there normally was during the summer months dried up. A snake could curl around itself in the shady area of our road and feel safe. We could count on our fingers the vehicles that rumbled by between morning and night. Every day Mama complained about how hard things were getting, but Daddy continued to sweep aside problems as if they were dust on his boots. Mama made some income and bartered food from her *traiteur* missions, two of which involved bad snakebites, and another three involved insect bites. There were more skin rashes than ever, lots of heat exhaustion, and then finally there was Mrs. Toomley, who went into a strange coma that lasted nearly a month.

Even though Daddy had little or no work, when an out-of-town contractor finally came by and offered him and some of the other men work in Baton Rouge, he was reluctant to take it, complaining it meant he would be gone nearly six weeks. Mama told him he was gone nearly that long on and off, drinking and gambling anyway, so what difference did it make? At least now he could send home some money for us.

Despite the harsh line she took with him, I saw sadness in her eyes when it came time for him to get into his truck and join the others for the journey to Baton Rouge. She made him a thick po'boy sandwich filled with oysters, shrimp, sliced tomatoes, shredded lettuce, and her sauce piquant.

"You ain't made me a sandwich like this for a while, Catherine," he told her.

"You ain't gone off to do decent work for a while, Jack Landry," she replied. He shook his head and shifted his guilty eyes away a moment. They were parting on the gallery. I was just inside behind the screen door. I hated it when they argued, and I hoped if I remained inconspicuous, they might be gentle with each other.

"Sure you're going to be all right without me, woman?" he asked her.

"Should be. I've had plenty of practice," she replied. Mama could be hard as stone when she felt the need to be.

"You don't let up on me," he complained. "I'm going off, won't see you for weeks. Cut me some slack, woman. Give me a chance to gulp some air before you push my head back underwater, hear?"

"I hear," she said, a tiny smile on her lips. Her eyes twinkled. His whining amused her. I don't know why he tried to put on false faces. Mama could read the truth through a mile-high pile of dead Spanish moss, but Daddy, especially, was a windowpane.

"Well," he said, sliding his boot over the gallery floor, "well . . ." He looked at me and then he leaned forward and pecked Mama's cheek like a chicken. "You take care. And you, Gabriel, you spend more time with your mama than with them animals, hear?"

"Yes, Daddy."

"Don't worry about me, Jack. Just don't drop the potato this time," she warned him.

"Aaa, what am I standing around here for? I got to go." He hurried off and got into the truck, waving once as he turned out of our yard and onto the road. I stood at Mama's side and waved after him.

"It seems unfair he has to go so far to find work, Mama."

"He don't find it. He was just lucky it came looking for him. If he was an ambitious man, he'd make his work for himself here, like most others do. But whoever whipped up the gumbo called Jack Landry left that ingredient out," she complained. "Let's go see if we can find a cool spot in the house."

The sun looked like a ball of rust behind the thin veil of a cloud. The cloud wasn't moving. I half expected to discover that the clock had stopped as well, the hands too exhausted with the effort to tell time in this heat.

"That's a good idea, Mama," I said. She stared at me at moment, tilting her head slightly to the right the way she often did when she was a little suspicious about something someone said or did.

"It's been nearly two weeks that you graduated and just about that long that summer came down with a wrath over us, yet you haven't gone off to your swimming hole, Gabriel. How come?"

"I don't know," I said quickly, too quickly. Mama screwed those scrutinizing eyes more tightly on me. "Something scare you out there, something you're not telling me, Gabriel? One of your loving animals didn't try to feast on you, did it?"

"No, Mama." I tried to laugh, but my face wouldn't crack a smile.

"I know you, Gabriel. I know when you've laughed and when you've cried. I know when you're so happy inside, your face becomes a second sun and when you're so sad, the clouds are in your eyes. I nursed and diapered you, fed you and cleaned your bottom. Don't keep no secret locked from me, honey. I got the keys and will find it one day anyway."

"I'm fine, Mama. Please," I begged. I hated not being honest. Mama shook her head.

"It'll be only a matter of time," she predicted, but she relented and I was able to get her to talk about other things while we worked on items to sell at our roadside stand.

We had far more than we needed for our tourist booth, but we worked on hats, baskets, and wove blankets to have for sale as soon as summer ended and the tourists started flocking back to the bayou. Days passed, one day indistinguishable from the other, mostly. Every day after a week, Mama looked for the check from Daddy, but none arrived. She mumbled about it under her breath and went on to do other things, but I knew it was eating away at her like termites in a dead tree. She didn't have to say it, but we were dipping deeply into her stash.

And then one afternoon, just about ten days after Daddy had left, a late-model automobile appeared in our yard and two tall, stout men, one with a thin scar across his chin and the other with what looked like a piece of his right ear missing, came stomping over our gallery to rap hard on the front door. I was in the living room thumbing through a copy of *Life* magazine Mrs. Dancer had given Mama when Mama went to treat her stomach cramps. Mama was in the kitchen and walked quickly to the door. I got up and followed.

"Yes?" she asked.

"You Landry?"

"Yes, we are," Mama said. Instinctively she stepped back and pushed me back too. "What do you want?"

"We want to see your husband, Jack. He been here?"

"No. Jack's in Baton Rouge, working on construction."

"He ain't been here?" the man with the chipped ear demanded.

"I said no," Mama replied. "I'm not in the habit of telling lies."

They both laughed in a way that chilled my blood.

"Married to Jack Landry and you don't tell lies?" the man with the scar said. His thin lips curled into a smile of mockery.

"That's right," Mama snapped. The back of her neck stiffened and she moved forward, all retreat out of her eyes. She fixed them on both men. "Now, what is it you want with my husband?"

"We want him to pay his debts," the other man said.

"What debts?"

"Gambling debts. Tell him Spike and Longstreet been here and will be back. Make sure he gets the message. Here's our calling card," he added, and took out a switchblade knife to cut a seam in our screen door. I felt the blood drain from my face. I screamed and Mama gasped, putting her arm around me quickly. The way they stood there glaring in at us made ice water drip down my spine.

"Get off my gallery! Get off my land, hear! I'll call the police. Go on."

They laughed and took their time leaving. We watched them get into their car and drive away, both our hearts pounding.

"Now what trouble has that man brought on our heads?" Mama wailed.

"Maybe we should go to town and tell the police, Mama."

"They won't care. They know your father's reputation. I'll fetch a needle and thread and sew up that screen," she said, "before we get a flock of mosquitoes in here."

We both tried to not talk about the two men, but every time we heard a car engine, we looked up fearfully, expectantly, and then sighed and released our held breaths when the car went on past our shack. It was hard enough to fall asleep with the heat and humidity, but now with fear loitering at our door, too, we both tossed and turned and opened our eyes and listened hard whenever we heard any unusual sounds at night, and especially whenever we heard automobiles.

The two ugly men didn't return, but four days later, while

Mama and I were having a salad for lunch, we heard a horn and looked out to see Daddy's truck bouncing over the front yard. He nearly drove it into the house. He took a swig of a jug he had beside him on the front seat and then heaved the jug out the window. He practically fell out of the truck getting out. He stumbled and made his way to the gallery where we stood, both wide-eyed.

"What'cha both standin' there lookin' like ya seen a ghost?" he demanded, stopping short so quickly, he nearly toppled over. It's only me, Jack Landry, home. Ain'tcha glad to death?" he said, and laughed.

"What are you doing back here, Jack, and tanked up with rotgut whiskey, too?" Mama asked, her hands on her hips.

"Work ended faster than I expected," he replied, unable to stop his swaying. He closed his eyes, a silly smile on his lips.

"In other words, you got canned again, right?" Mama asked, wagging her head with anger.

"Let's just say me and the foreman had a disagreement to a point beyond compromise."

"You came to work drunk as a skunk," Mama concluded.

"That," Daddy said, waving his long finger in the air like the conductor of an orchestra, "is a dirty, low-down lie."

"I bet you ain't got a penny in your pocket, neither," Mama continued.

"Well . . ."

"And you never sent home a dollar, Jack."

"You didn't get nothin' in the mail?" he said, his eyes wide.

Mama shook her head. "When you get to hell, the devil's gonna learn a trick or two."

"Catherine, I swear on a stack of—"

"Don't say it. It's blasphemy," she warned. He gulped and nodded.

"Well, I did put some money in an envelope. Them postal workers stole it, for sure. They open the envelopes with a candle, Gabriel, and then they reseal them with the wax," he said.

"Oh, Daddy," I said, shaking my head.

"Don't you two look like a pair of owls." He started to

55

laugh, but Mama stepped to the side and pointed to the screen door where she had sewn up the slash.

"See that, Jack? Your friends came a-calling and cut up our screen door when they didn't find you here."

"Friends?"

"Mr. Spike and Mr. Longstreet."

"Here?" His face turned paper white and he spun around as if they were waiting for him behind a tree. "What'dja tell them?"

"That you were working in Baton Rouge. Of course, I didn't know I was telling a lie."

"When were they here?"

"A few days ago, Jack. What do you owe them?"

"Just a little money. I'll straighten it out," he said.

"How much is a little, Jack?" she pursued.

"I got no time to talk to you, woman," he said. "I gotta go upstairs and rest from the journey."

He climbed the stairs, pulling himself up and nearly pulling out a rafter at the same time. Then he went into the house and stumbled up the stairs, leaving a cloud of sour whiskey stench behind him.

"I bet his will be the first corpse the worms reject," Mama said, and plopped into her rocking chair. It made me sick to see her so defeated and depressed. I thought it was that and the heat and my own gloom that upset my stomach something awful that night. Mama thought I might be coming down with some sort of summer dysentery. She gave me one of her herbal drinks and told me to go to bed early.

But the next morning I woke up just as nauseous and had to vomit again. Mama was worried, but once I finished throwing up, I suddenly felt better. My headache was gone and my nausea passed.

"I guess your medicine worked, Mama," I told her. She nodded, but she looked thoughtful and unconvinced. I wasn't sick again for nearly a week, but I was continually tired and sluggish, once falling asleep in Mama's rocker.

"This heat," Mama said, thinking that was the cause. I tried to keep cool, wrapped a wet towel around my neck, drank lots of water, but I was still tired all the time.

One afternoon Mama noticed me returning from the outhouse.

"How many times you been to the bathroom today, Gabriel?" she asked.

"A few. Just to piddle, Mama. My stomach's okay."

She still stared at me suspiciously.

And then the next morning I woke and had the same nausea. I had to vomit again.

Mama came to me and put a wet towel on my forehead and then she sat on my bed and stared at me. Without speaking, she pulled the blanket back and looked at my breasts.

"Is it sore there?" she asked. I didn't reply. "It is, isn't it?"

"A little."

"You tell me the truth and mighty quickly, Gabriel Landry. Did you miss your time?"

"It's come late before, Mama."

"How late is it, Gabriel?" she probed.

"A few weeks," I admitted.

She was quiet. She looked away and took a deep breath and then she turned to me slowly, her eyes sad but firm. Her lips were pressed together so hard, the color drained from them, but there was a redness in her cheeks and in her neck. She sucked in some air slowly and looked up before she looked at me again. I couldn't remember Mama ever looking at me this sadly.

"How did this happen, Gabriel?" she asked softly. "Who made you pregnant?"

I shook my head, the tears burning beneath my eyelids. "I'm not pregnant, Mama. I'm not."

"Yes, you are, honey. You're as pregnant as pregnant is. They're ain't no half-pregnant. When did this happen? I ain't seen you with no boy here and don't remember you going off except to go . . ." Her eyes widened. "Into the swamp. You been meeting someone, Gabriel?"

"No, Mama."

"It's time for the whole truth, Gabriel. No half sentences."

"Oh, Mama!" I cried and covered my face with my hands. "Mama!"

"What in tarnation's going on here?" Daddy complained. He came to my doorway in his tattered underpants. "A man's trying to get some rest."

"Oh, hush up, Jack. Can't you see something's happened to Gabriel?"

"Huh? Whaaa . . ." He scrubbed his cheeks with his rough palms and ran his long fingers through his hair. "What happened?"

"Gabriel's pregnant," she said.

"What? When . . . Who . . . How did this happen?" he demanded.

"I'm trying to find that out. If you'll just clamp down on that tongue . . ."

My shoulders shook with my sobs. Mama put her hand on my head and petted me.

"There, there, honey. I'll help you, don't worry. What happened?"

"He . . ."

"Go on, honey. Just spit it out," Mama said. "Best way to get something bitter and distasteful from your mouth is quick," she assured me.

I took a deep breath and sucked back my sobs. Then I raised my head and took my hands from my face.

"He had his way with me in the canoe, Mama. I couldn't stop him. I tried, but I couldn't."

"That's all right, Gabriel. That's all right."

"What?" Daddy said, stepping closer. "Who did this? Who had his way? I'll—"

"Hush, Jack. You'll frighten her."

"Well . . . no one's gonna . . ."

"Gabriel, did this happen at your swimming hole?"

"Yes, Mama."

"Who was it, honey, did this to you? Someone we know?"

I nodded. Mama took my hand into hers.

"These young bucks, these worthless, good-for-nothing . . ." Daddy rattled.

"It was Monsieur Tate," I blurted, and Daddy stopped ranting, his jaw falling open.

"Octavious Tate!"

"Mon Dieu," Mama said.

"Octavious Tate done this?" Daddy fumed. He stood there, his eyes widening, his face a magenta color from his rage. Then he frightened both Mama and me by slamming his fist into the wall so hard he bashed in a hole.

"Jack!"

"Gabriel, you get up out of that bed, hear? You get yourself dressed and out of that bed right now," Daddy directed, jabbing his right forefinger at me.

"Jack," Mama cried. "What are you going to do?"

"Just get her dressed. I'm the man of this house. Get her dressed!"

"She's not—"

"It's all right, Mama," I said. "I can get up." I never saw Daddy so full of fury. There was no telling what he would do if he didn't have his way.

"Well, what's he planning to do?" Mama cried. She looked at me. "My poor baby. Why didn't you tell me this all before?"

"It happened right before graduation, Mama. I didn't want to start anything then and . . . I wasn't sure whether or not it was partly my fault."

"Your fault? Why?"

"Because I . . . swim without my clothes," I said.

"That still don't give no man the right to do what he done," Mama said.

"Get her up and dressed!" Daddy screamed from the other room.

"I will not," Mama replied.

"No, Mama. I'll do what Daddy wants. I made this trouble worse by not telling you about it." I rose and began to dress, my hands trembling, my legs shaking, feeling as if I were sinking, drowning, going under in a pool of hopeless despair, and not even thinking for the moment that there was a baby growing inside me.

"Where you taking her, Jack?" Mama demanded. After I was dressed, Daddy took my hand and led me out and to his truck, practically dragging me along. Mama followed to the gallery steps.

"Get in the truck," he ordered, and then turned to her.

"You hush up now, woman," he said to Mama. "This here's a man's job to do."

"Jack Landry . . ."

"No. If you didn't let her wander about freely, this probably wouldn't have happened, hear?" he accused.

I felt terrible for Mama and buried my face in my hands. What had I done? It was all my fault. First, I shouldn't have been so unaware and trusting in the swamp, and afterward, I should never had kept it such a deep, dark secret from Mama. She looked so small and defeated on the gallery and so disappointed. I knew she blamed herself for bringing me up to believe I led a charmed life. It was true I always felt nothing in Nature would harm me, but I never counted on another human being invading the sanctity of my precious perfect world.

Daddy started the truck and slammed it into gear. He pressed down hard on the accelerator, tearing up some grass and gravel as we shot off. The truck bounced so hard my head nearly hit the roof. Daddy mumbled angrily to himself and slammed the steering wheel with the ball of his palm. I kept my eyes low. Suddenly he turned sharply to me.

"You didn't offer yourself to this man, didja, Gabriel?"

"Oh no, Daddy."

"You was just swimming in your pond and he come on you?"

"Yes, Daddy."

"And you tried to get away, but he wouldn't let you?"

"He took my clothes," I said.

"That low-down . . . rich . . ." Daddy's eyes got so small, I didn't think he could see the road. The tires squealed as we went around a turn.

"Where are we going, Daddy?"

"You just keep your head low and your mouth closed until I tell you to speak, understand, Gabriel?"

"Yes, Daddy."

A short while later, we drove over the gravel in front of the Tate Cannery. Daddy brought the truck to a sharp stop, the wheels sliding and jerking.

"Come on," he said, opening the door.

60

I got out slowly. Daddy came around the truck and seized my left hand. He marched us up to the office door and pulled so hard on the knob, the door nearly came off the jamb. Mr. Tate's secretary, Margot Purcel, looked up from her desk sharply. She was typing an invoice, but when her eyes fell on Daddy, they widened and she looked terrified.

"Where is he?" Daddy demanded.

"Sir?"

"Don't you 'sir' me. Where's Tate?"

"Mr. Tate's on the telephone in his office," she said. "Can I tell him why you want to see him?"

She started to rise.

Daddy glared at her and just tugged me once toward the inner office door.

"Sir!"

Daddy opened the door and pushed me in ahead of him. Then he slammed the door behind us.

Octavious Tate sat behind a large, dark hickory desk. He wore a cream shirt and tie and had his suit jacket over the back of the chair. The fan in the corner hummed and created a nice breeze that circulated around the office. The shades on the east side were drawn to block out the late morning sunlight, but the shades were up on the west side, so we could see the trucks loading up and men working.

Mr. Tate was on the phone, but he told whomever he was speaking to that he would call him back and quietly returned the black receiver to its cradle. Then he sat back.

"What is this?" he asked so calmly, I wondered for the moment if I had indeed dreamed everything.

"You know what this is," Daddy said.

Mr. Tate shifted his eyes to me, but I did what Daddy had told me to do and looked down.

"I don't know what you're talking about, Landry. I'm a busy man. You've got no right to come busting in my office. If you don't turn around and just march out that door, I'll—"

Daddy walked up to his desk and slapped his hand down. Then he leaned over until his face wasn't a foot from Mr. Tate's.

"That's my daughter standing there and she's pregnant with your baby. You done raped her in the swamp, Tate."

"What? Now . . . see . . . see here," Mr. Tate stammered. "I did no such thing."

Daddy straightened up and gave him a crooked smile.

"Everyone knows my daughter ain't no liar." He stepped to the side. "This the man who jumped you, Gabriel?" he asked.

I lifted my head slowly and looked at Mr. Tate. He curled his lips in and stared at me.

"Yes," I said softly.

"Well?" Daddy said.

"I don't care what she claims. It's ridiculous."

"You're going to pay, Tate. It's either going to be easy or hard, but you're going to pay."

Mr. Tate swallowed hard and then gathered his strength. He lifted the receiver again. "I'm going to call the police and have you arrested if you're not out of this office in ten seconds," he threatened.

"Okay then," Daddy said. "It will be hard."

He spun around, scooped my hand into his, and jerked the office door open. Without closing it behind us, he marched us out. Margot Purcel stood up and looked toward the inner office as we went past her and out the door.

"Get in the truck," Daddy said.

"Where we going now, Daddy?"

"Just get in. I know how to deal with the likes of him," he said.

Ten minutes later we turned up the long driveway to the Tate mansion, which was known as The Shadows because of the grand moss-draped oaks, willows, cypress, and magnolia trees that surrounded it and kept it in long, cool silhouettes most of the day. I had seen it only from the road before this. Our family was never invited to the famous parties that the Tates held there, nor was Mama ever called upon to treat Monsieur or Madame Tate.

As we continued up the long driveway, my heart throbbed in triple time and I shrank into a tighter ball, fearful of what Daddy had in mind to do next. Daddy's battered truck rattled over the gravel, kicking up dust clouds behind us. The grounds were so immaculate and neatly trimmed, I felt as if we were tracking mud over a new carpet.

All the oak trees had beds of azaleas and camellias under them. Queen Anne's lace bordered both sides of the driveway. To the right toward the canal, I saw the seemingly endless vegetable gardens and fruit trees. A short, stout black man with stark white hair and a tall, lean black woman with her ebony hair pinned up were harvesting crops. They looked our way for a moment and then went back to their labor.

I turned toward the house.

Before us the two-and-a-half-story structure rose with a majestic confidence that bespoke its grandeur and richness. It had classic columns rising from the ground to the entablature that supported the roof. There were upper and lower galleries and shutter-enclosed stairs. When we turned toward the front, I saw that the bayou side had a recessed gallery with brick arches below and turned Doric columns above. Ferns and palm leaves worked their way up and around the brick. There were three gabled dormers on the roof over the upper front gallery, each with four rows of paneled windows. The chimney rose from the rear of the building.

"What are we going to do here, Daddy?" I asked. Daddy turned off the truck engine and glared at the house for a moment.

"I know about the Tates," he said. "Octavious had nothing until he married Gladys White. She wears the britches in this family. Get out," he said.

I stepped down gingerly. This close, the house looked even more intimidating. Late morning shadows curved and then soaked the front in shade so thick, I felt as if we were stepping across one world and into another when we approached the tall, paneled door flush with fixed glass panes. Clumps of purple wisteria dangled from the scrolled iron railing above us. A half dozen silver bells on leather strings were hung over the door.

Daddy rattled them hard and then he let them fall against

63

the door. A few moments later, a tall, spindly-looking, almond-complected, balding man with a long, thin nose and very thin lips opened the door. He wore a butler's uniform, but he had his tie loosened and apparently was just finishing chewing something. He swallowed quickly and raised his light brown eyebrows. They lifted at the middle as if there were an invisible hook hoisting them into his crinkled forehead.

"Yes?" he said, unable to hide his disapproval of the way Daddy was dressed, his hair wild, his shirt half in and half out, and his dungarees worn nearly clear through at the knees.

"I want to see Madame Tate," Daddy said.

"Really? And who wishes to see Madame?" the butler asked. He spoke with his head pulled back a bit so that the underside of his nose was clearly visible. There was a small but distinct dimple at the tip. He had a nasal tone and tucked his lips in at the corners after he spoke.

"Jack Landry and his daughter, Gabriel," Daddy said. "And I don't mean to be turned away," he added.

"Really? What is the nature of your visit, monsieur?"

"That's private."

"Really?"

"Yeah, really, really. You going to get her or am I going to get her?" Daddy asked.

The butler's eyes widened and those eyebrows were jerked even higher.

"One moment, please," he said, and closed the door.

"Snobby, rich . . . dirty . . ." Daddy mumbled. He looked around and nodded. "They think they own everything and everybody and can do whatever they please. Well, they ain't met Jack Landry head-on yet," he said.

"I think we should go home, Daddy," I said softly.

"Home? We ain't going nowhere till I get some satisfaction," he remarked. He shook the bells again. A moment later the butler opened the door, but this time standing beside him was Gladys Tate.

She looked formidable, towering, her shoulders back, her spine a steel rod. Her eyes were burning with indignation.

She looked like she had been interrupted doing something very important or was about to leave the house for an important appointment. She wore a polka-dot dark blue dress with a thin scarf. There was a matching polka-dot belt with a large bow at her waist.

This close up, confronting her, I realized how stunningly beautiful she was, but also how hard those slate-cold brown eyes could be. Steely faced, she stepped forward.

"How dare you have me summoned like this? What is it you want?" She threw me a glance, her mean look so sharp, I thought it could cut glass.

"I have business with you," Daddy said, undaunted.

"My husband handles the business."

"Not this business. This business is private," Daddy insisted.

"Really, monsieur, I don't think—"

"You're gonna hafta talk to me, madame, sooner or later. It be better sooner," Daddy said.

She shifted her eyes to me again. I could feel the curiosity twirling around in her brain, and her face softened.

"All right, Summers," she said to the butler. "I'll speak with these people." She said "people" as if we were lower than grasshoppers. "First room on the right," she ordered, and we entered the mansion.

I had never been inside a house this large and couldn't help but gape at everything: the mauve marble entryway, the great tapestries depicting grand plantation houses and grounds and Civil War scenes. Before us to the left was a square, polished mahogany stairway, and above us, from the high ceilings, dangled teardrop chandeliers with glittering brass necks. Beyond the entryway, the house seemed to go on forever. I saw pedestals with sculptures, and beside the tapestries, there was artwork covering every available space. It didn't look like a home so much as it looked like a government building or a museum.

We entered the room on the right. The first thing that caught my eye was the parasol roof. We stepped onto a rich beige carpet. The room had honey beige straw-cloth walls, blond beige woods, rosy beige leather on the French chairs.

Everything looked so clean and neat and new, I was afraid to touch anything. Gladys Tate stopped in the middle of the room and turned to Daddy. She ran her eyes from his head to his feet. He wore his old boots stained with mud. She looked like she was trying to decide where he could do the least damage. Finally she nodded at a small chair to the right.

"I'll give you five minutes," she said.

Daddy grunted and sat. He looked like he would bust the chair into pieces merely by leaning back. Gladys Tate sat on the settee, her back squarely against the cushion. She looked at me and then at Daddy.

"Well?"

"Your husband raped my daughter and made her pregnant," he said without hesitation.

I held my breath and didn't swallow. Gladys Tate did not change expression, but it was as if the shadows that carpeted the front of the great house had somehow penetrated the walls and darkened her face.

"I assume," she said after the heavy pause, "you have some proof to support this astounding accusation."

"My daughter's the proof. She'll tell you how it was exactly. She don't lie."

"I see." She fixed her stone eyes on me. "Where did this alleged incident occur?"

"In the swamp, madame," I said softly.

"The swamp?"

"In the canals. He was fishing when he come upon her in her pond, a place she goes swimming," Daddy said.

Gladys Tate stared at him as if it took a few moments for Daddy's words to be translated, and then she turned back to me.

"You know who my husband is?"

"Yes, madame."

"You say he came upon you while you were swimming?"

"I was actually sunning myself on the rock at the time. When I opened my eyes, he was there. I was . . ."

"Nude?"

"Yes, madame."

She nodded. Then she smiled at Daddy.

"Do you know what it means to make false accusations, especially accusations of such a serious nature?"

"It ain't false," Daddy said.

"I see. And you have brought your daughter here for what purpose?"

"What purpose? He made her pregnant. That's gonna be a costly thing."

"Oh, so it's not justice you seek so much as it is money, is that it?" she asked with a wry smile painted across her lips.

"That's justice, ain't it?" Daddy retorted.

"Have you spoken with my husband?"

"Yeah, and he don't want to own up to it. But he will," Daddy threatened. "Look at her," Daddy said, pumping his hand toward me. "Look at what he done to my little girl. How's she supposed to find a decent husband when her stomach's two feet ahead of her, huh? And all because your husband had his way with her!"

Gladys Tate stared at me again. "You're the girl who ran off the stage at graduation, aren't you?" she asked.

"Yes, madame."

"And you," she said, turning to Daddy, "are the man who made that ridiculous scene."

"That ain't got nothing to do with this."

She stared again. These silent pauses sent chills up my spine, but Daddy didn't seem to notice or care. Finally she sighed, shook her head.

"I wish to speak with your daughter alone," she said.

"What? Why?"

"If you want me to give you any more of my attention or time, you will do as I ask," she said firmly. Daddy thought a moment. It was easy to see she was determined and he would do best if he listened to her.

"I'll be right outside," he said, standing. "And only for a few minutes. Don't you try nothing sneaky on her neither," he added. He gazed at me, his face full of fury. "Call me if she does," he said, and walked out.

"Close the door," Gladys Tate ordered. I did so. "Sit where your father sat," she said. Then she sat forward. "Have you ever seen my husband before this incident in the swamp?"

"Just here and there, madame, but we never spoke."

"I see. Now, in your own words, tell me what you say happened."

I began slowly, explaining how I went swimming often in the pond and how this particular afternoon I had fallen asleep sunning myself. I described how he had taken off his clothing and climbed onto the rock. She didn't change expression until I told her what he had said about his marriage. Her eyes became smaller and a white lined etched about her tightened lips.

"Go on," she said. I described the way he teased me, how we fell out of the pirogue and then what followed. I felt the tears streaming down my face, but I did not wipe them off. They dripped from my chin.

She sat back when I was finished. Then she stood up abruptly and went to the door. Daddy was obviously eavesdropping and nearly fell into the room when she opened it.

"Well?" he said.

"I want you to wait right here," she told him.

"Why?"

"Do what I tell you to do," she ordered without hesitation. Even Daddy, fired up the way he was, was taken aback with her strength and firmness. He entered the room and sat on the settee. "I'll see that Summers brings you something cool to drink," she said, and left.

"What's that woman doing?" Daddy asked me. "You tell her something I didn't hear?"

"I told her exactly what happened, Daddy."

"I don't trust these rich people," he said, eyeing the door. A few moments later, the butler appeared.

"Would you like some lemonade?" he asked.

"Ain't ya got nothing stronger?"

"We have whatever you want, monsieur," he said, grimacing.

"Get me a cold beer. No glass."

"Very good, monsieur. Mademoiselle?"

"I'll have the lemonade."

He nodded and left.

"Maybe they'll poison us," Daddy said. "That's why I

68

ordered it in the bottle." He winked. "Don't drink the lemonade."

"Oh, Daddy, she wouldn't do that."

He sat back and drummed the arm of the chair with his long fingers.

"Look at this place. I could live a year off what this room costs. Maybe longer."

The butler brought us the drinks. Daddy sipped his beer cautiously. He shook his head when I drank my lemonade, but it tasted good and refreshing.

A short while later, we heard the front door open, and after that, Octavious Tate appeared.

"I'm calling the police," he said, but when he turned, Gladys Tate was right behind him, standing as solidly as a statue.

"Just go inside and sit, Octavious," she commanded.

"Gladys, you're not going to give these thieves a moment of our time. You're—"

"Go inside, Octavious."

He shook his head and came into the room, sitting across from Daddy. He glanced at me once and then looked at his wife. She closed the door and remained standing.

"Well?" he said.

"Look at this girl, Octavious. Go on."

"I'm looking at her."

"Are you going to deny her story to her face?" she challenged.

He swallowed hard. "Gladys . . ."

"I want to know the truth and I want you to admit to it. She told me things you said about us, Octavious, intimate things she would not know otherwise."

"I . . ."

"You were in that swamp fishing, weren't you, Octavious?" she said, beginning her relentless interrogation.

"Yes, but . . ."

"And you poled to that pond, didn't you? You saw her there?"

"That doesn't mean I did what she claims I did."

"But you did do it, didn't you?" she pursued.

"I . . ."

69

"Took off your clothes and climbed up on the rock to sit beside her? Well?"

"Look, she invited me to . . ."

"Octavious, you made love to this girl, didn't you?" she demanded, stepping toward him, her eyes wide and furious. He looked down. "Answer me and tell the truth! You're only prolonging this horrible moment and driving the knife deeper into my heart."

He nodded slowly, biting down on his lower lip. Then he looked up sharply.

"Ha!" Daddy said, slapping his hands on his knees.

"There's no way she can prove that her baby is my baby," Octavious said quickly. "This sort of girl—"

"Doesn't lie," Gladys said, nodding. She looked at me and then at him before she took a deep breath and looked away for a moment. When she turned back to us, I saw the glitter of tears in her eyes, but she sucked in her breath and blinked away those tears.

"How much does he want?" Octavious asked, glaring at Daddy.

"It's not only what he wants," Gladys replied. We all looked at her, Daddy the most surprised. "It's what I want," she said, and regained her composure to make the most astounding demands of all.

4

Bought and Sold

"What is it you want?" Daddy asked Gladys Tate before Octavious could. Octavious sat there seemingly hypnotized by his wife's movements. Mama once told me there's no hate such as that born out of a love betrayed. Like Octavious, I wondered what sort of revenge Gladys was concocting.

She walked to the window, hesitated a moment, and then jerked the curtains closed as if she thought someone might be spying on us. It darkened the room and her face when she turned slowly back to us. Octavious squirmed in his seat. The dark cherry grandfather clock in the corner bonged the noon hour. While it did, Gladys fixed her eyes on me like a marsh hawk sighting in its prey.

"Who else knows what's happened to you?" she asked sharply.

"Just my mother," I replied. A small smile trembled over her lips as she nodded slightly. Then she swung her gaze at Daddy, her face tightening, her shoulders rising.

"And who else have you told, monsieur?"

"Me?" He looked at Octavious and then back at her. "I just found out about this today, so I ain't had time to tell anyone, but you can be damn sure that I'll talk and talk plenty if—"

"You'll get your money, monsieur," Gladys spit. "Far more than you expected, too."

Daddy's eyes lit up with glee. He sat back and smiled, nodding his head.

"Well, that's more like it. You can't treat folks miserably just because they ain't as rich as you," he said. "You can't just go about abusing and—"

"Spare me the lecture, monsieur," Gladys commanded, her hand up like a traffic policeman. "What my husband has done is terrible, but I'm sure it pales beside some of the things you have done in your life," she declared.

"What? Why, I ain't never been arrested or—"

"Never?" Gladys smiled coolly. Daddy glanced at me and then at her. "It's not important. Nothing you've done or even said matters here. That's not what interests me in all this."

"Well . . . what does?" Daddy cried, his face red with frustration.

"Her," Gladys said, pointing her thin finger at me. She had rings on every finger, but on the forefinger she had a large ruby in a silver setting. Her long, rose red fingernails looked like tiny daggers aimed at my heart. I shuddered, ice sliding down my spine.

"Me?"

"Since no one but your mother and the people in this room know you're pregnant with my husband's baby," she began, "I propose, no, I insist, that you remain here until you give birth to the child."

"What?" Daddy said. "What for she should do that?"

I could only stare at her, dumbfounded. Why would she want to set her eyes on me, much less have me in her presence now?

Gladys turned to Daddy and flashed that oily smile at him again.

"You're so ignorant, you don't even understand what a wonderful thing I am offering your daughter and your family," she said. "Do you think a mere sum of money extorted from us will cure all the problems your daughter, your wife, and even you will endure once she begins to show her unwed pregnancy?"

"Well, no, but . . ."

"What are you proposing to do, Gladys?" Octavious asked in a dry, tried voice. She glared at him in silence for a moment.

"I'm proposing to become pregnant," she said.

"What? I don't understand," Octavious said. He shook his head. "How can you . . ." Then he paused and looked at me, his face lighting with comprehension. "But, Gladys, why do you wish to do this?"

"It's not only these swamp people who will be the talk of the bayou once this is out, Octavious. And do you for a moment think that we can buy this man's silence?" she followed, nodding toward Daddy.

"If I give my word," Daddy began, "you can be—"

"Your word." She threw her head back and laughed and then fired a look of fury at him. "What happens when you go to one of your zydeco haunts and guzzle too much whiskey, monsieur? Will you still keep your word? Do you take me for a fool because my husband . . . my husband has done this dreadful thing?"

"Well," Daddy said. He chewed on his thoughts for a moment, not knowing how to react and not sure yet what it was Gladys Tate was proposing. "I don't think I understand all this."

She croaked a short laugh. "And you think I do?" She raised her eyes toward the ceiling. "Some women drop children like calves in a field all day and all night." She glared at me and then, looking sad, she said, "And some . . . are denied the blessing of their own child because of some quirk in nature." She turned to Octavious. He looked away, his chin resting on the palm of his hand.

"What I am proposing," she continued, glancing at me first, "is that Gabriel remain here at the house during the entire period of pregnancy. She will live upstairs and no one will know she is here, not even my servants. I will see to it that she is well taken care of until the baby is born and everyone thinks it is mine. In order for that to happen, I will pretend to be pregnant myself and go through all the stages of pregnancy."

"Well, how you gonna do that?" Daddy asked, smiling. "Swallow a watermelon?" He laughed and looked at me. I was too shocked and frightened by her suggestion to move an inch, much less smile or laugh.

Gladys Tate's face went paper white for a moment and then she shot Daddy a stabbing glance.

"Let that be my concern, monsieur, and not yours," she said, her voice resembling a snake's hiss. She straightened her back again and looked at me. "After it's over, Gabriel can return home and no one will know any of the dreary details. She can go on with her life and be the candidate for marriage to a decent man you hoped she would be."

"What about the baby?" Daddy asked, undaunted.

"The baby," she said after a deep breath. "I told you. Everyone will think the baby is mine. The baby will remain here and be brought up a Tate. He or she is a Tate anyway," she added.

"I don't know," Daddy said, shaking his head. "My wife, she may not put up with this, no. . . ."

"What's the alternative?" she fired. "Your wife will live in utter shame forever, I'm sure. Surely," she said, turning to me, "you don't want your mother to go through the indignity, to be the subject of gossip forever, to have to avoid the looks of others, to know people are whispering about you. Blaming my husband won't be enough to exonerate you, Gabriel," she charged, nodding at me. "Men will still think you were somewhat responsible, especially when everyone learns you were swimming nude."

I tried to swallow, but my throat lump was like a rock. She kept her eyes fixed on me so intently, I was unable to look away. I couldn't help but think about Mama. Gladys Tate was right. Mama would never show it, but I knew she would feel terrible. Some people would stop using her as a *traiteur*, and others would treat us like lepers.

"Daddy?" I said after a moment. "I think she might be right."

74

"What? You saying you want to do this, give up the baby and all?"

I nodded slowly and lowered my head like a flag of defeat. It did seem like a sensible solution to all the problems.

"I don't know. Keeping my daughter like a prisoner, keeping the baby . . ."

"Octavious," Gladys said sharply, and then smiled like a Cheshire cat, "why don't you take Monsieur Landry into the office and discuss the financial considerations, while Gabriel and I have our own little chat."

Octavious looked at her a moment and then stood up as if he had to lift three times his weight. She pulled him aside at the door and whispered something in his ear that made him crimson.

"Are you crazy?" he said. "He'll just drink it up, waste it."

"That's not our concern," she said. "Monsieur," she added, turning to Daddy. He glanced at me and then rose slowly.

"This ain't a done deal," he said. "Not till I hear what they have to offer, hear, Gabriel?"

"Yes, Daddy."

"Good." He exchanged a look with Gladys Tate, but she couldn't be intimidated. He knew it and followed Octavious out of the room and to the office. Gladys Tate closed the door behind them and took a seat in the high-back chair. She rested her arms over the chair arms and kept her back straight. To me she looked regal. Even though we were on the same level, I felt as if I were gazing up at her or she were looking down at me.

"I assume," she began, "that this will be your first baby."

"Oh, of course, madame."

She sneered. "You want to sit there and tell me you were a virgin when my husband made love to you?"

"But it's true, madame."

She stared a moment, her eyes blinking quickly. "Perhaps it is," she said in what I thought was a much sadder, deeper voice. She sighed and looked toward the shaded windows. "It is my fault, me," she said, and brought her lace silk handkerchief to her eyes. "He can obviously make a baby. I'm having trouble."

"I'm sorry, madame."

She spun on me as if she just realized I had heard her words, and her eyes turned crystal-hard.

"I don't want your pity, thank you. What were you doing out there in the pond? Setting a trap for him?"

"What?"

She nodded, her smile slight and twisted. "Bathing in the nude, knowing he was poling nearby, a good-looking, rich man . . ."

"No, madame. I swear."

She grunted and tightened her face again, her skin resembling the surface of an alabaster statue. Then she took a deep breath. "I meant what I told your father: Despite what Octavious has done, this is more of a favor for you and your family than it is for me."

"I know, madame."

"In order for this to work, you will have to obey my every command and be very, very cooperative. It will not be pleasant for me, but it will especially not be pleasant for you for the next six or seven months. You will have to endure loneliness and be quieter than a church mouse. Can you do that?"

"I hope so. I think so, madame."

"I hope so, too. If you disobey me just once," she said, "I'll throw you out and leave you to explain your big stomach, understand? It will be messy, but I think I can convince people around here that you made it all up, despite your mother's good reputation. I have money, friends in high places. People depend on my factory for a living. Whose side do you think they will all take? A poor Cajun girl's or mine?"

I didn't reply. She knew the answer.

"So will you obey my rules?" she pursued.

"Yes, madame. But surely I will be able to see my mother."

"Infrequently and very secretly. What I will do," Gladys Tate thought aloud, "is let it be known I am using a *traiteur* for my own pregnancy. People will believe she is coming here to see me, but you can see no friends, no other visitors, is that clear?"

76

"Yes, madame. But where will I stay?"

"I will show you your quarters when you return. I want you to return at night, tonight, in fact. Come at midnight. The house will be quiet. I'll have my butler away, and the maids will, of course, be asleep. Just come to the door. Bring very little. You understand?"

"Oui, madame."

"Good," she said, and rose.

I stood. "I am sorry for all this," I said. "Despite what you might think, I did not want it."

"What I think doesn't matter. What has happened and what we can do to repair the damage to my family and yours is all that matters," she lectured.

I nodded. Was she really so generous, so big of heart, to be able to forgive her husband and plan such a solution? I was hopeful, even grateful, but I didn't like the way her eyes skipped away when I tried to catch them. Was it because she didn't want me to see how deep the pain in her was? Or how deep the thirst for vengeance was?

She opened the door and called to Octavious and Daddy. Daddy came in first, and by the look of delight on his face, I saw he was satisfied with the offer he had gotten.

"Is everything settled?" Gladys asked Octavious. He nodded unhappily.

"I got to get back to work," he said.

"Yes, sir, you go back to work," Daddy told him, and patted him on the back. "I don't want you going bankrupt. Not now." He winked at me. "Come on, Gabriel. We got to tell your mother what we decided here."

"I told her I want her back here at midnight tonight," Gladys said. "She's to come to the front door herself, understand, monsieur?"

"Sure. What's there to understand?" Daddy said. Then he scowled. "If I hear you don't treat her right, the deal's off," he countered.

She simply smirked. It was as if a fly had threatened an alligator.

"Remember," she told me. "No one is to know and you are to bring very little."

"Yes, madame."

Octavious left first. Daddy stood in the entryway a moment and gazed around, nodding.

"Not a bad place to be living in for a few months, eh, Gabriel? I'm sure you'll have good things to eat and all."

"Yes, Daddy. Let's go," I urged. He sauntered to the door and then turned on Gladys.

"Don't think any of this makes it all right. It's still a crime, what he done."

Gladys didn't change expression, but her eyes full of accusations shifted to me. I opened the door and stepped out quickly, Daddy following with a wide grin. But when we got into the truck and started away, he stopped smiling.

"You got to help me convince your mama about this, Gabriel. She's gonna think it's some plan I hatched to make more money. You be sure to tell her it was Gladys Tate's idea, not mine, hear?"

"I will, Daddy."

"Good," he said. And then, thinking about the money, he did break into a wide smile again.

"Is it a lot of money?" I asked.

"What? Oh. Well, not as much as I would have liked, but it will do fine. I'll make sure your mother has a bundle to stash and then I'll buy us some things for the house and maybe even a new truck and tools for me so I can get more work."

"That's good, Daddy," I said. I gazed back at the mansion and thought at least something good has come out of this terrible thing.

Mama said nothing for a few long, heavy moments. She listened to what Daddy told her, spewing it all in nearly one breath, and then she looked at me and got up from the table to go stand by a window. The plank shutters were open and the breeze blew the cheesecloth we had hung over it so that it flapped about her.

"I don't like it," she finally said. "It don't sound natural, her pretending to be having a baby and all."

"What?" Daddy's eyes bulged as he floundered. "Here we are getting all this money, Gabriel don't have to walk in broad daylight with her stomach out a mile and take the stares and gossip, and there's a good place for the baby, and you don't like it?"

"Most women I know wouldn't be so gracious about it and want to keep the child as their own, Jack."

"Well, look at the women you know. They ain't got her class. Am I right, Gabriel?" he asked, and nodded. "Go on, tell her."

"I think it's for the best, Mama. She told me so far she hasn't been able to get pregnant. She blames herself, and I think that's why she's not so hard on Octavious and why she wants to keep the baby."

Mama stared at me a moment. "You understand quite a lot for a young woman, Gabriel. You're growing up so fast," she said, shaking her head. "But it ain't right this way."

"What you complaining about now, woman? That the child got good sense? Well, she inherited it from you," Daddy offered.

"That, I believe, Jack Landry," she said, fixing her eyes on him. "How much money did they offer you? Come on, tell me quick and no lies."

"Five thousand dollars!" he said. "How's that?"

Mama was impressed, but she still shook her head sadly. "Blood money," she said. "I don't feel right taking it, Jack."

"Well, you're not taking it. I'm taking it," he said. "And it's just your luck I see fit to give some of it to you and do things around here you wanted me to do," he added.

"It's still the same as if I took it."

"Gabriel," he cried, throwing up his hands. "Will you talk sense into this mother of yours? I'm about outta steam."

"Mama, it's the best solution and at least something good will come from it. Gladys Tate is going to let you visit me, pretending you're treating her."

"What will I tell people about your not being here?" she asked, relenting somewhat.

"You'll tell them she went to visit my brother's family in Beaumont," Daddy suggested. "That'll do just fine, no?"

"No. My friends know I would never let her go visit a Landry," Mama replied. "I'm not a good liar anyway. Don't have your experience, Jack."

"Then don't say nothing. It ain't none of their business anyhow."

"You can tell them I went to visit with your aunt Haddy, Mama. I've always wanted to visit her anyway. It's almost not a lie."

Mama laughed. "You're getting to sound like him," she said, but kept her smile. She walked over to me and stroked my hair and then kissed my forehead. "Poor child. You don't deserve this. It wasn't your fault, but it isn't the first time and it won't be the last something unfair happens in this world. You sure you want to do this?"

"Yes, Mama."

She took a deep breath with her hand on her heart. "You just promise me if you're not happy, you'll come home no matter what, Gabriel."

"I promise, Mama."

She sat again. "When you supposed to go?"

"Tonight at midnight," I said. She looked frightened, her eyes growing glassy. "It will be fine, Mama."

She bit down on her lower lip and nodded, swallowing back her tears. It made my chest ache.

I went upstairs to choose the few things I would bring with me. I decided to take the pictures of Mama and Daddy when they were first married. I packed some underthings, two nightgowns, three dresses, another pair of moccasins, some ribbons for my hair, my combs and brushes. While I was choosing things, Mama prepared a package that contained her homemade soap, some herbs she wanted me to take with my meals, and a small statue of Saint Medad. I put some books and magazines in my bag and a pad and pen for writing my journals and doodling. I was sure Gladys Tate would give me other things to do when I asked. I could embroider and weave to pass the time.

That evening Mama prepared one of my favorite meals: her crawfish étouffée. She kept busy to keep from worrying and made some lace cookies. Daddy had gone to town to shop for some of the things he was planning to buy with the money. He returned with a box of chocolates and a bottle of French toilet water for Mama. It had been a while since I had seen him so buoyant and happy. He cleaned himself up for dinner and wore his best shirt and pants. As we ate, he rattled on and on about things we should do in the house.

"What'cha say we buy a new stove, Catherine?"

"The one I have is fine, Jack."

"Well, that ain't the point. I was thinking we would get one of them new radios and maybe I'll get you one of them Mixmasters so you don't have to stand over the bowl and churn and churn all day, how's that? And what about one of them whatchamacallits that suck dirt up?"

"You need electricity for all those things, Jack," Mama reminded him dryly.

"Well, we'll get the electricity now. I got the money coming, don't I?"

"Don't spend it all in one day, Jack," Mama warned.

"Oh, I know that. I'm giving you a stash, but I'll need some money to invest. Can't live off five thousand forever, you know," he said as if he were already a big businessman. "Maybe instead of a truck and tools, I'll see about getting me my own shrimp boat with a down payment or—"

"Stop it," Mama said. Tears were streaming down her cheeks.

"What? What I do?"

She got up from the table and ran out the front door.

"What I do?" Daddy asked me, his arms out.

"It's all right, Daddy. Let me talk to her."

I followed her. She was sitting in her rocker, staring at the darkness.

"Mama."

"I can't abide him sitting there gloating over all the things he's going to do with that money, Gabriel. I'm sorry. It's tainted money, no matter what," she insisted.

"I know, Mama. But it's not the money that matters so much. It's having a good place for the baby and keeping the shame from our door. Gladys Tate is right: Even though it's not my fault, people will think bad things about me, and what good man will want to know me?"

"She said that?"

"Yes, Mama."

"She really wants this baby, don't she?"

"It certainly seemed that way, Mama."

81

Mama sighed deeply and then held out her arms. I knelt beside her and buried my face against her bosom the way I used to when I was just a little girl and she held me close and rocked a bit. Then she kissed the top of my head.

"All right," she said. "I'll be all right. Just tell him to stuff his mouth with a pound of hemp."

I laughed and hugged her again. Mama was my best friend. There would be no one like her in the world for me, ever. It was knowledge that made me happy, but sad too, for I knew I would lose her someday and have to face mornings and days, nights and the stars, without her wisdom and comfort, her love and her smiles. It would be like a cloud forever and ever blocking the sun.

We returned and finished our meal. Daddy had sense enough to be quiet and went out back to smoke his corncob pipe and muse about his newfound wealth. After we cleaned the kitchen and dishes, Mama and I went back to the gallery and talked. She told me what it had been like when she was pregnant and how my birth went. She told me about the two babies her mother had lost, one in a miscarriage and one in a silent birth. I had never known it.

Just about eleven-thirty, Daddy appeared to tell me it was near the time.

"How's this going to work?" Mama asked.

"I just drive her up there and she goes into the house herself, right, Gabriel?"

"That's right, Mama."

"You see that she goes in safely, Jack."

"Of course I will," he snapped. "I don't care how rich them folks are. They ain't going to do nothing to make Jack Landry upset," he threatened.

"It's not Jack Landry I'm worrying over," Mama retorted.

"I'll go get my things, Daddy," I said, and hurried upstairs. I stood in my room for a while and gazed around. It wasn't a big room, but it was cozy and warm and the place where I had suffered through my childhood illness, cried my tears of frustration, dreamed my fantasies, and had some wonderful conversations with Mama at night. It was where

she had sung her lullabies to me and where she had tucked
me in and made me feel safe. Tonight would be the first
night of my life that I would sleep someplace else. I choked
back my tears, for fear I would upset Mama more than she
already was upset. Then I said a silent prayer for her and for
Daddy and for me and left my room quickly, not looking
back.

Daddy turned off the truck's headlights when we reached
the entrance to The Shadows's driveway. Then he drove very
slowly over the gravel. A heavy layer of dark clouds had
come pouring in from the Gulf, drawing a sheet of thick
raven darkness to shut out the twinkling stars I often looked
to for comfort. Now the sky looked like a giant inkwell,
purple-black, deep and endless. It stirred me with a strange
sense of foreboding as we drew closer and closer to this
magnificent Cajun mansion. I knew that under any other
circumstances, I would love simply visiting such a home,
much less actually living in one for a while.

With only a light on here and there, the house appeared
dismal, ominous. Its roof loomed in a silhouette against the
ebony sea of clouds. Off to the right, I could hear the
plaintive howl of a chained hound dog, and in the distance I
could see lightning around the thunderheads. Bats swooped
over the driveway, clicking their wings with a mechanical
precision as they dipped to scoop up an insect invisible to
my eyes. When Daddy turned off the engine, we could hear
the monotone symphony of the cicadas.

Daddy was a bit more agitated than usual. After he had
brought the truck to a stop, he kept his gaze locked on the
front door of the mansion while he spoke.

"Well," he said, "I guess this here's good-bye for a while,
Gabriel. I know you'll be in good hands. Don't take no guff
from no one, hear?"

"Yes, Daddy."

"Your mother will be visiting you shortly and bring back a
report."

"Okay, Daddy," I said in a voice that seemed smaller and
younger even to me.

"Okay," he said. "Best you hop out and go up there by yourself like she said." He leaned over and gave me a quick peck on the cheek.

"'Bye, Daddy," I said, and opened the truck door. It groaned with a metallic complaint that seemed to echo over the whole property. Even the bullfrogs paused to listen.

"Soon I'll have me a new truck without dents and squeaks," Daddy bragged.

I closed the truck door and carried my bag and myself up the gallery steps to the front door of the house, but before I could shake the bells, the door was thrust open with such force, I thought it had created a draft of air that would suck me inside the dimly lit entryway. Gladys Tate stood there dressed in a dark blue robe over her ivory lace nightgown. She held a small kerosene lantern in her hand. Her hair was down around her shoulders, and her face, now without a drop of makeup, looked as if candle wax had been melted and smeared over her forehead and cheeks, giving her a ghostly white complexion. The tiny flame in the lantern flickered.

"Get in, quick," she croaked. As soon as I stepped through the doorway, she closed the door and turned toward the stairs. "Follow me."

Without another word, she led me up, hustling me along so I wouldn't have a second to pause and gaze around. I half expected to see Octavious, too, but he was nowhere in sight. When we reached the upstairs landing, she turned left and took me down a short corridor to a narrow door. She dipped into a bathrobe pocket to produce a set of keys and unlocked the door. She stood for a moment listening. Satisfied, she reached in and threw a switch to illuminate a short stairway that led to an attic landing where there was a second door.

"What's up there?" I asked.

"What do you mean, what's up there? Your room's up there. Where did you think I would put you, in my bedroom or with Octavious?" she retorted. Even in the dim light, I could see the grotesque smile.

"No, madame, but . . ."

"But what?"

"Nothing," I said.

84

"Just watch your step and step very lightly. Tiptoe," she advised, and started up the short, steep stairway, practically floating on air herself. When she reached the second door, she inserted a second key and unlocked it. I entered behind her. She set the lantern down on a bare, rectangular cypress plank table carefully and turned it up to reveal the claustrophobic small room that had one window facing the rear of the house. Now it had a shade drawn and a curtain closed over that.

The walls had once been papered in a flowery print, but that had long since faded so that the flowers were barely visible in the eggshell background, a background I was sure had once been bright white. On my right were a set of shelves now full of dolls of all sizes and apparently some from different countries. There were cobwebs between many of the dolls, and their faces and doll clothing were faded almost as badly as the wallpaper.

Directly in front of me was the short box spring mattress in a low, dark oak bed frame with no headboard. There was a tiny night table to its right, and adjacent to that, a dresser no more than three and a half feet tall, if that.

"Once," Gladys Tate said, "this was my playroom. Some of my cutouts, puzzles, toy dishes, pots and pans, as well as some other children's games are in that closet." She nodded toward the narrow cabinet just to the right of the small dresser. "It's not the Waldorf, but it will serve our purpose," she added, and turned to me. Her words were cold and uncaring. The purpose could easily be to punish someone for misbehaving.

Without replying, I set my bag down on the table and went to the bed. I sat on it and heard the mattress squeak like a family of rats. Although it was too dark to see it, I expected there was enough dust in here to fill a pillow.

"I changed that linen myself today," Gladys bragged. "It's the same linen, blanket, and pillow I used when I used to sleep in here. I always took good care of my things and they lasted. I expect you will take good care of everything, too," she said, and I gazed around, wondering what it was she expected me to take good care of: a small lantern, tiny furniture, faded wallpaper, old toys. . . .

"Of course, I couldn't have my maids clean this room without drawing some suspicion. You'll have to do most of that, but you'll have plenty of time for it, won't you?" she said.

"Where's the bathroom facilities?" I asked without replying to her comment.

"Bathroom facilities? You're used to an outhouse, aren't you?"

"Yes, but how can I go to an outhouse if you don't want anyone to know I'm up here?"

"Exactly," she said, and crossed to the small closet. She took out a chamber pot. "You'll use this. Once a night, after everyone's asleep, I'll come by and tell you and you can carry it down to the bathroom at the bottom of the attic stairway and to the right. You can wash and bathe then, too. I don't want you coming down with any diseases and endangering my child," she added.

My child? I thought. She was getting into that frame of mind very quickly. I was impressed with her determination.

"It's stuffy in here," I said. "Is that window open?"

"Yes."

"We need to open the curtain and pull up the shade then," I said, "to get some breeze." I started toward it.

"You can do that now, but you must remember to draw the shade in the morning. We don't want anyone spotting you up here. Don't ever, ever look out that window during daylight hours, understand? You'll ruin everything if you are seen."

"Never look out the window?"

"Don't even peek. Someone might see the shade moving and I would have to explain it. If that happens, I won't bother. I'll just have you tossed out on your ear," she threatened. Then she smiled coldly, the right corner of her mouth cutting into her cheek. "I could simply tell people we were keeping you here as a favor to your parents, but you misbehaved. Anything I say will be believed faster than anything your father says," she added confidently.

Despite what Octavious had done to me, I couldn't imagine why he would have married such a coldhearted woman. Her eyes had the glint of polished stone and her mouth looked thin and drawn with a pencil. I half expected to discover that her alabaster face and body had no veins carrying blood around, and instead of a heart in that bosom, there was a jar filled with angry honey bees.

"Besides, you should be grateful I have provided you with these safe, comfortable quarters during your period of disgrace," she said.

Safe, comfortable quarters? I was going to sleep, eat, and go to the bathroom in a room not much bigger than some people's closets, and in this mammoth house that had a dozen grand rooms. I would be shut away, forbidden to see the sun or feel the breeze on my face, and permitted to look out only when the sun went down, permitted to emerge like a bat.

"Now," she continued, folding her arms across her chest, "as to the rules."

"Rules?"

"Of course, rules. Everything must be spelled out and followed to the T.

"First and foremost, you are never to leave this room without my permission. As I said, I will come by and let you know when it is clear for you to go down to empty the chamber pot and wash yourself.

"Second, don't even wear those moccasins up here. Walk barefoot and walk as little as you can so that you create as little noise as you can. If anyone hears any scuffling about, I will tell them it's field mice, but we obviously can't have any clanging or banging. No singing, no music, and when you talk to yourself, as I imagine you will, keep your voice down to a whisper. All this must be true especially in the morning when my maids are cleaning the upstairs area. Is that clear?"

"Oui, madame," I said.

"Good. Third, food. I will try to be up here twice a day, but it might just be once a day occasionally. You will notice a gallon jug of water on the other side of the bed. Don't waste it. When you go down to the bathroom, you can refill the jug, but remember, you won't be doing that but once a day. I'll see to it that you have the proper things to eat so my baby is kept healthy. You'll have one fork, one spoon, one knife, one plate, one cup, and one glass because I will have to wash everything myself. Obviously we can't have the maids doing it.

"Fourth, there is no electricity up here. You'll use this kerosene lantern only when the sun goes down and keep it as low as possible and as far from the window as possible. In fact," she said, stepping forward, "I have made a mark on the floor here. Look," she commanded, and pointed. I gazed down and saw a black streak over the plank floor. "Don't bring the lantern across this line at any time, understand?"

"Oui, madame," I said, shaking my head, amazed at how well she had thought out every detail.

"You can laugh to yourself all you want," she snapped, "but I took great pains to plan this out today, and it's for your benefit as much as it is for anyone else's. I don't know if you truly appreciate that."

"Of course I do, madame."

"Umm," she said, nodding skeptically. "We'll see.

"Fifth, amusements. There are some books in the closet. You're welcome to play with the games, of course. I understand you weave and embroider, so I will bring some of that up to you. There can be no radio, no Victrola, for obvious reasons.

"Last, every Thursday night, my maids and my butler have the night off and leave The Shadows. I will come up to fetch you and you can come down to stretch your legs and eat dinner in the dining room. You can, if you wish, walk about in the rear of the house. I do have some field workers living nearby, but I'm not worried if they see you occasionally during the first few months when you won't show as much. Toward the second half of the pregnancy, however, you will not be permitted to go outside, even at night. Understood?"

I nodded.

"Good. Do you have any questions?"

I gazed around. "What if I need something during the day?"

"You'll have to wait until I can safely come up here," she said.

"I don't like this any more than you do," she continued. When I didn't reply, her eyes became glazed with fury.

"How do you think I feel housing the woman my husband made love to in the swamps, the woman who hosts his child, the child that should have been my child, in my body? What do you think it will be like for me sleeping beneath you and gazing up at the ceiling every night knowing you're here?"

"I'm sorry, madame, but this was your idea and—"

"I know it was my idea, you little fool, but that doesn't mean I have to like it because it was mine, does it? I was just smart enough to think of a way out for everyone." She pulled her head back. "Does your mother appreciate what I'm doing, too?"

"She understands," I offered.

"Umm. She understands? Well, I don't, but I'm not a *traiteur*. I'm just a . . . an abused wife." She sighed. "I'm tired," she said. "This has been a terribly emotional and draining day for me. I will bring you something to eat late in the morning after the maids have served us and cleaned up the kitchen and moved on to other parts of the house. If something prevents that, you'll just have to be patient, and don't, whatever you do, try to find out why I'm not here when I said I would be. Be smart enough to figure out that something serious is preventing it at the moment.

"This all requires great cooperation on your part to work," she explained. "I assure you, if it fails, it won't be because of something I've done."

"I'll do my best, madame."

"Your best might not be enough. Do what I want," she corrected.

"I will try."

"Yes, try," she said, twisting her mouth. "It's so much easier to conceive a child, isn't it? You just lie back and the man puts his hardness in you and grunts his pleasure."

"I didn't just lie back, madame," I retorted.

She stared at me with that wry smile.

"I'm telling the truth. I was raped!"

"It's not a big secret around here that Octavious is not a man of great strength. My father chose him, trained and schooled him in our business, prepared him to be my husband. He was afraid I wouldn't find a decent enough, proper man, so he found one for me.

89

"He arranged for our courting and practically dragged us both to the altar. Octavious is a meek individual. I find it hard to believe that he could force himself on anyone, even a supposedly helpless young girl.

"But whatever happened, the damage has been done, and once again, I had to come up with a solution to a problem."

"You should never have married a man if you weren't in love with him, madame," I criticized, my anger and indignation fueling my courage.

Her smile became crooked and mean as she shook her head.

"You young girls today amuse me. You go to picture shows and see all these movie stars in their dream romances and think that can be you, too. You think you'll meet a man and suddenly there will be music and you'll skip off into the sunset together. Well, life isn't like a movie. It's real and in the real world, people are brought together for more practical reasons, and even if there is love in the beginning, it doesn't last long.

"Are your parents still in love?" she asked disdainfully. "Do they still cherish and adore each other until death do them part? Well? You're not answering me," she said before I could take a breath.

I sucked in air and straightened my back the way Mama often did. "Not everyone has a perfect life, madame, but you began yours believing it wasn't perfect to start. You knew and yet you did it. That," I said firmly, undaunted, "was your mistake."

The smile left her face. "You're pretty insolent for a girl your age, but I'm not surprised, considering where you live and how you've been brought up. We'll tolerate each other and do what we have to do, but the day this baby is born, that's the day you leave this house and my life," she declared.

"Madame," I said. "That's the first real thing we agree about."

It seemed all the blood in her body rushed to her face. She jerked up her shoulders and straightened her back. For a moment she simply glared at me. Then she turned and went to the door.

"Remember all I have said," she ordered, and left, closing the door softly behind her. I heard her tiptoe down the stairs and go out the second door. But then I heard her insert the key and turn the lock.

Now I was alone.

I gazed about my new world. I felt like Alice but in a stranger wonderland. The diminutive furniture, the faded walls, the dusty dolls, made it all seem unreal, dreamlike. I had been deposited in Gladys Tate's past, a past obviously rarely visited, a past draped in cobwebs and filled with discarded memories. It was as if I had fallen into someone else's nightmare.

The dolls glared down at me with distrust. The thick shadows cast by the lantern danced with the flicker of the flame. Below me and even above me, the great house creaked. I was afraid to move, afraid that if I made the slightest sound, Gladys would come rushing back upstairs to order me out of the house. But I took off my moccasins and rose slowly to go to the window and raise the shade a few inches. A slight breeze flowed through and I caught the lovely scent of blooming jasmine. When I peeked out, I saw the darkness and the cypress and oak trees silhouetted like sentinels against the still purple-black night sky.

I unpacked my bag, setting Mama and Daddy's picture on the tiny dresser along with my combs and brushes, and the small statue of Saint Medad. Then I took off my dress and underthings and put on my nightgown.

There was nothing to do but put out the light and crawl into bed. I said my prayers and lay there with my eyes open, staring into the darkness. I envisioned Mama miles away getting ready for bed herself, hiding her tears from Daddy, maybe gazing into my empty room and feeling the emptiness in her heart.

I felt that same emptiness now.

And then, for the first time since all this had begun, I thought about the baby forming inside me. Was it a girl or a boy and how would he or she like living under this roof? How would Gladys Tate really treat the child? Would she be cruel to him or her or would she really accept the baby as her own and find a place in her heart for the infant? It would be horrid to learn she mistreated the baby. Right now she seemed capable of taking her vengeance out on anyone or anything, and yet . . .

And yet, I had this abiding faith, this deep-set belief that she somehow saw me as a necessary evil, a temporary place of incubation for her own long-sought-after child. She was hard and filled her sentences with threats, but surely she wanted it all to go well. I would not be neglected or abused, I thought.

My hope, no, my prayer, was that time would pass quickly and I would go home to the only world I had known and cherished. Just as I closed my eyes, I heard the cry of a night heron. I went to the window and peeked out to see it had landed on the railing outside my window. It turned and looked at me and then lifted its wings as if in greeting and as if to tell me all the animals of the swamp I loved and I believed loved and trusted me were here, watching over me.

The heron lifted off the railing and swooped toward the shadows and trees, its neck bent in that S shape. A moment later it was gone and all was quiet. I returned to the tiny bed, crawling in as quietly as I could, and then I closed my eyes and pretended I was falling asleep in my own room. In the morning Mama would call to me and all this . . .

All this would have just been a nasty dream.

5

Denied the Sun

Sometime during the night someone must have come into my tiny room and pulled down the shade so that when dawn came it provided only a dim light through the sole window. Of course, it had to be Gladys. It shocked and amazed me that I hadn't heard and awoken when she had entered the room. But the emotional strain associated with coming here and my own pregnant condition had put me into a deep sleep.

The moment my eyes snapped open and I had scrubbed the drowsiness from them, my instinct was to rise and pull up the shade, but Gladys Tate's warnings buzzed around in my head like a bee trapped in a jelly jar. How dismal it was to open my eyes and not see the bright sunshine or be able to look out the window and see the birds flitting and flowers spreading their blossoms to catch the invigorating rays. Mama always said I was like a wildflower and needed the sunshine to make me happy and help me grow and be healthy.

I sat up, but I couldn't peel back the blanket of depression. Would I be able to endure this for the number of months I had left before the birth of the baby? Had I made promises I couldn't keep? All I could do to counter the dreariness and despair was remind myself of how this would keep the shame from our doorstep and provide a good home for the baby who bore no blame for its existence. Why should a child suffer for a father's sin?

The aroma of freshly brewed, dark Cajun coffee, just-baked bread, fried eggs, and sausages permeated my room, slipping in under the floorboards. It made my stomach churn in anticipation. I rose and, because of the dimness, turned on the lantern. Then I dressed and, using the back of one of Gladys Tate's toy cooking pans as a mirror, brushed and pinnned my hair. I used the chamber pot and some of the water to wash my face and feel as refreshed as possible under these conditions. After that, I sat on the bed and listened hopefully for the sound of footsteps that would signal Gladys's arrival with my breakfast. I could hear the muffled voices of people below, the slam of a door, the barking of dogs, some grounds workers shouting to each other outside, but I heard no footsteps heralding her arrival.

Bored with the wait, I rose and began to explore the room. First I took the lantern to the small closet and, after blowing the dust away, brought out the books, which were all children's stories. What had Gladys Tate been thinking when she had said I could read these books to pass the time? They were designed for a child who had just learned to read and consisted mostly of pictures with occasional simple words.

The most impressive thing in the closet was the hand-made dollhouse with everything inside it constructed to scale. I quickly realized that it was a model of The Shadows, and by studying it, I could learn where every room was and what was in each room. However, absent from the model was the room in which I was presently living.

There was tiny furniture, even tiny books in the bookcases and tiny kitchen implements in the kitchen. My fingers were too thick to fit in some of the small openings, so I imagined it had been built for Gladys when she was very little. Aside from the dust that had made it a home, the dollhouse was in perfect condition. Exploring it further, I discovered that the roof could be detached and I could have a godlike view of the interiors. I saw what I was sure was meant to be Gladys's mother and father lying beside each other in the king-size bed in the master bedroom. What looked like Gladys's room had a bed with a canopy, but the miniature doll meant to represent her was gone. There were wee dolls to represent the maids, cooks, and the butler, even minuscule replicas of some hound dogs sleeping in the den by the fireplace.

There were no other children in the dollhouse, and the only other bedrooms were for the maids or empty guest rooms. The kitchen, as in most Cajun homes, was in the rear, and just behind it was a pantry filled with things so small, my fingernail was twice the size. I decided whoever had built this toy world had been a master craftsman, an artist in his or her own right.

I put the house aside and rummaged through the old magazines. I found coloring books and a pad of dry watercolor paints with stiff brushes. There were moldy crayons, pencils, and a toy sewing kit with some material meant for doll's clothing. I found a toy nurse's set with a stethoscope, a nurse's cap, a fake thermometer, and some real bandages and gauze. That, too, looked barely used.

At the bottom of the pile, I discovered a notebook that had been used as a drawing pad. The first few pages had crude line drawings, but as I turned the pages, I felt I was turning through the years of Gladys Tate's development until I reached the point at which her drawings were more sophisticated. One page in particular caught my interest.

I thought it looked like Gladys Tate's self-portrait: the face of a little girl who had similar features. Behind the little girl was the looming face of a bearded man. She had drawn nothing more of his body, but hovering just above her shoulder was what was obviously meant to be his hand, the fingers thick, one with a marriage band.

When I lifted the notepad a little higher to bring it closer, I saw something slipping from between some pages. It was a card with a small bird on the outside. Inside were scribbled the words: *To my little Princess. Love, Daddy.* There was a second card, also with a bird on the outside. This time the scribbled words read: *Never be afraid. Love, Daddy.*

I turned a few more pages, observing crude drawings of a

man without a shirt, his chest covered with what I was sure was meant to look like curled hairs. In the middle of the torso was a light drawing of a face with the mouth stretched in what looked like a scream.

Curious and now intrigued, I flipped past the drawings of birds, trees, and a horse to find the picture that made me gasp. It had been drawn with a shaky hand. The lines wobbled, but it was clearly meant to be the body of a man, waist down, naked, his manliness drawn quite vividly. I closed the notebook quickly, put it back in the closet, and stood up, slapping my hands together to shake off the dust. What strange things for a little girl to draw, I thought. I was afraid to permit myself to wonder what it all meant.

I went to my door and opened it slowly, listening keenly for the sound of footsteps. Surely she would be bringing me something to eat soon, I thought. I was very hungry and my stomach was growling with anger. Frustrated, but aware that if I didn't occupy myself, my hunger would only bellow louder, I turned to the shelf of dolls.

I found some cloth to use for dusting and took the first doll down to carefully wipe its arms, legs, and face. All these dolls looked like they had been expensive ones. Some had features so perfect, I was positive they were handmade. Observing the line of them on the shelf, I realized that there were only two male dolls, and they had been placed a little behind the others.

As I put the first doll down on the table, I noticed something odd when the doll's dress was raised. I peeled back the skirt and gazed with horror at what had been done. A blotch of black ink had been painted between the doll's legs where its female genitals would be. I inspected the other dolls and found either that or a chipping away of the area that had been done with some crude implement. The worst damage, however, was inflicted on the two boy dolls. They had been smashed so that their torsos ended just under their belly buttons.

I hated to think what this all possibly meant. Suddenly I heard the distinct sound of footsteps on the short stairway. I hurriedly returned the dolls to the shelf and sat on the bed just as Gladys Tate opened my door, my tray of food in her hands.

"Well," she snapped. "Don't just sit there waiting to be served. Come take it."

I hopped off the bed, took the tray, and placed it on the table.

"Thank you," I said. I pulled the chair close and sat.

"Why is that lantern on?" she asked.

"It's so dark in here with the shade drawn."

"You're just wasting the kerosene. I can't be bringing up kerosene every day too. Use it sparingly," she ordered, and turned it out, draping us in shadows. Nevertheless, I began to eat and drink the coffee while it was still warm.

"I see you've been looking at things already," she said, noticing the things on the floor by the closet.

"Yes, madame. That's a very nice dollhouse, a replica of this house, isn't it?"

"My father made that for me. He was artistic," she said, "but he did those things only as a hobby."

"It is a work of art. You should have it on display, downstairs."

"I don't think I need you to tell me how to decorate my house," she snapped. "It belongs up here and here is where it will remain."

"I'm sorry. I just thought you would be proud to have other people see it."

"If you must know, it's personal. He gave it to me for my fifth birthday." She closed her eyes as if it had been painful to explain.

"You must have loved it. I looked at the books. They're all for very small children."

"Umm. I'll see about bringing up something more equal to your maturity. My father used to make me read Charles Dickens. He had me stand before him and read passages aloud."

"I have read some of Charles Dickens's novels in school, yes."

"Well, any one of them will keep you busy awhile," she said. "You were sufficiently quiet this morning," she offered

97

in a tone as close to a compliment as she could manage. "No one noticed anything or mentioned anything to me. That's good. Keep it that way," she commanded.

"One thing you must do, however. Rise before dawn and close the shade. It has never been up during the day, and someone will surely notice."

"Why has it never been up?" I asked.

"It just hasn't," she shot back. "This room has been abandoned up until now."

"Why?" I persisted. "I would think your old playroom would have some nice memories for you, and you would want to keep it nice."

"You would, would you? Who do you think you are continually offering your opinion as to what I should and shouldn't do in my house?" She flicked her stony eyes over me.

"I'm sorry," I said. "I didn't mean to . . ."

"Just worry about yourself. There's plenty to do there," she said. "I'll be right back," she added, and left the room.

While she was gone, I finished eating. When she returned, she had a pail of water and a handful of rags in her hand.

"I brought you this so you could start cleaning this room. Do it as quietly as possible."

"I'll need more than one pail of water, madame," I said. She snapped her head back and lifted her shoulders as if I had slapped her.

"I know that, you fool. You'll start with this. You don't expect me to cart pail after pail of water up here, do you? Tonight you can dump this out with your chamber pot and bring up another pail of water along with your drinking water. I was just being nice giving you the first pail."

"I'm sorry. I don't mean to sound ungrateful," I said, which took the steel out of her spine. She didn't smile, but her eyes warmed.

"If you're finished eating, we have some very important matters to go over," she said.

"Certainly, madame." I turned, waiting.

She folded her arms over her chest and took a few steps toward the window. "I, as you know, have never been pregnant. I know as much about it as any woman my age should," she added quickly, "but there is nothing like the actual experience. That's true about everything, I suppose, but especially true when it comes to pregnancy."

I nodded, not sure what it was she was trying to say.

"If we are to make this work, have people believe me when I say I am pregnant, I had better behave as if I am. I know you're just about two months pregnant, right?"

"That's right, madame."

"Well," she said, and waited. When I didn't say anything, she snapped, "Tell me about it."

"Tell you? Where should I begin, madame?"

"At the beginning, where else? How did you find out you were pregnant?"

"Mama told me. I woke up nauseous and had to vomit. After it happened again, she asked me if I had missed my period."

"Yes?"

"I had and then she asked me if I was sensitive here," I said, indicating my breasts.

"Sensitive?" She stepped closer. "Exactly what does that feel like?"

"It feels like my breasts are fuller. Sometimes they are tender and sore."

"Really?" she said, raising her eyebrows.

I felt odd describing these things to her. For the moment it seemed as though I were the adult and she were the younger woman. How could she appear so sophisticated in other ways but be so ignorant of womanly things? I wondered.

"Yes," I said. "Sometimes they actually hurt." Her eyes widened. "I'm also tired more often and find myself dozing off."

"Yes?"

"And I have to go to the bathroom more . . . urinate," I said.

"Did you throw up this morning?" she asked.

"No. Mama gave me some herbs that help me."

"Good. For her first visit, I'll have her bring me the herb, too," she said. "If it works, why not?" she added, which I thought was a strange thing to say. Why would she actually want it? "Now, what about your stomach? I can't tell

99

because of that skirt, but you don't seem to be showing much."

"No. Mama told me she didn't show until she was nearly five months, but I do see a small difference," I said.

She stared at me a moment and then nodded. "I want to see for myself," she said.

"Pardon, madame?"

"I want to see. I have to know exactly what you look like now and as time goes by to do this right, don't I? Take off your clothing."

I hesitated.

"What's wrong? You go parading about in the swamp nude, don't you?"

"I don't go parading about," I said, tears coming to my eyes.

"It's the same thing, whatever you want to call it. Now, just get undressed. I told you, warned you, you would have to be cooperative," she said in a threatening tone. "Either you do what I ask or march right out of here now. Make up your mind."

I swallowed back a throat lump and sucked in my breath. Then, first turning away from those glaring eyes of stone, I lifted my dress over my head. I unfastened my bra and slipped out of my panties. Before I could turn around, her arms came over my head, a tape measure in her hands. She had brought it up with her, planning all along to do this. She wrapped it roughly around my stomach and pulled to take a measurement.

"Turn around," she ordered. I did so and she gazed at my breasts. "You're not normally this big?"

"No, madame," I said. "And the color has changed here," I said, pointing to my nipples. "Darkened."

"Oh?" She studied me with interest. "I'll have to stuff my bra a bit," she mused, and nodded. "Once a week I'll take the measurement of your stomach and adjust my own dimensions accordingly. You can get dressed now," she said.

She waited as I dressed myself and then in a kinder tone of voice she said, "I'll bring you some Charles Dickens with some dinner tonight. The maids are about to begin upstairs and will be working right beneath you, so keep as quiet as possible when you clean. I hope," she added, "that if you do vomit, you do it as silently as possible." She took my tray. At the doorway she turned back to me. "I'll be sending for your mother very soon, perhaps later today."

"Thank you, madame," I said. I couldn't wait to see Mama. Even though I had been here only one night, I missed her terribly.

Gladys Tate closed the door softly behind her and tiptoed down the stairway. I stood there for a moment, realizing that I was trembling, and then I set about cleaning the room and keeping my mind occupied so I wouldn't dwell on this strange, hard woman who would someday soon be the mother of the child I carried.

Gladys Tate brought Mama up to see me after dinner. One look at Mama's face when she came up the stairway and stepped into the room told me she was infuriated.

"You're keeping her up here, in this . . . closet?" she said, turning sharply on Gladys.

"It's the only secluded place in the house," Gladys said, unflinching. "I'm trying to make her as comfortable as possible."

Mama gazed about the room and then fixed her eyes on my empty dishes. Of course, I wasn't sure if it had been done for Mama's benefit more than my own, but Gladys had brought me a gourmet feast: a bowl of turtle soup, Cornish hen in a grape cognac sauce, sweet potatoes in oranges, and tangy green beans. For dessert, there was a slice of pecan pie. Gladys proudly ticked off the menu, explaining I would always eat what they ate.

Mama's eyebrows rose with skepticism.

"I wish to speak with my daughter alone," she said. Gladys tightened, her mouth becoming a tiny slice in her taut cheeks. She then gave Mama a small smile, tight and cold.

"Of course," she said, and pivoted sharply. She closed the door behind her and descended, her feet barely tapping down the stairway.

101

"You can't stay here," Mama began immediately. "This is horrible. I had to sneak up here with her, like some kind of swamp rat."

"It's not so bad, Mama. I'll keep busy and the time will pass quickly."

"I don't like it," she insisted. "You're too much a creature of Nature, Gabriel. You can't be shut up like this."

"I'll manage, Mama. Please. What will be the alternative? These are rich and important people here. They will make me look like the bad one, and the baby, the baby will grow up an outcast. Besides," I said with a smile, "I bet Daddy's already spent some of the money."

"Some? I'll wager he's spent most of it or gambled it away by now." She sighed deeply and sat on the bed. "Look how tiny everything is. What was this room?"

"Her playroom."

"Playroom? What does she think, this is another childish game, you're another toy, a distraction? That woman irks me, Gabriel. Something's very wrong with her. She wants me to bring her herbs."

"I know. She's determined everyone will believe the baby is hers. She's really getting into the pretending."

"Too much. I was alone with her and she was telling me she's had nausea in the morning and lately she's had to go to the bathroom more often. Why tell me those things without anyone around?" Mama pointed out.

I shrugged. "Maybe she was just practicing."

"I don't know. I'm not getting good vibrations here," Mama said, gazing around with that special vision. "This was not a happy room. It wasn't a playroom so much as it was . . . a hideaway," she concluded. "And that's what she's made it into now," she added, turning to me.

"If it gets unbearable, Mama, I'll come home," I promised.

Mama squinted and curled the corner of her mouth. "You have a lot more tolerance for abuse than most people, Gabriel, and you're too forgiving. I'm afraid you won't do what's in your own best interests. You'll think of everyone else first."

"No, Mama, I promise. . . ."

She shook her head and then her face reddened a bit with anger.

"Has he come around? Do you see him?"

"No, Mama. I haven't seen Octavious Tate once since I arrived. I think he's afraid of her," I offered.

Mama nodded. "That's what your father says. He's not much of a man to live under his wife's shadow and to have done what he did to you. I want you to know I was tempted to turn your father loose on him. When he drove off with that in mind, I wasn't eager to stop him. I was just as angry, but . . ." She sighed. "Maybe having a good home for the baby and keeping you from the disgrace that some would lay on you no matter what, like you say, is for the best. I just don't like the thought of you being caged up."

"I'll get out as much as possible, Mama. And you'll be by to see me now and then."

"You can bet on that," she said. She dug into her split-oak basket and took out some more herbal medicines, a jar of homemade blackberry jam, a loaf of cinnamon bread, and a package of pralines. "Don't eat all this at one time," she warned. "You gotta watch you don't get too fat, Gabriel."

"I won't, Mama," I said, and laughed.

She sighed again and stood up. We heard Gladys coming up the stairway. She knocked on the door, which was something I was sure she would never have done if Mama weren't there.

"Yes," Mama said.

Gladys entered. "I'm sorry, but if you remain up here much longer, my maids will notice."

"You should get maids you can trust," Mama shot back. Gladys didn't respond, but she made her eyes small and sucked in her breath. "I'll be by in a couple of days," Mama said. Then she turned to Gladys. "You see she gets time out of this room. She needs exercise or the birthing will be difficult, even dangerous."

"Of course, Madame Landry. I will permit whatever is possible."

"Make it possible," Mama insisted. "See that she has plenty of water to drink, too. There's two to take care of here. Keep that in mind."

"Anything else?" Gladys asked with visible annoyance.

"Yes. You should have a fan up here."

"Why? You don't have fans in your shack, do you?"

"No, but she's not locked up in a room in our shack," Mama retorted.

"There's no electricity up here, and even if there were, the noise would attract attention," Gladys explained.

"It's all right, Mama. Really," I said.

"Humph," Mama said, and then turned back to Gladys. "You make sure your husband doesn't come within ten feet of her."

Gladys turned so red, I thought the blood would shoot up and out the top of her head.

"Don't bother to make promises," Mama followed before Gladys could open her tight mouth. "Just make sure it don't happen." Mama turned to me. "I'll see you soon, honey," she said, and kissed me on the cheek. Then she glared at Gladys once more before she started out. Gladys took my tray of empty dishes and shot me an annoyed look before leaving. When they got to the bottom of the stairway and went out the corridor door, Gladys did not lock it. I was glad of that.

After Mama left, I relaxed on my bed and read some of the Charles Dickens novel Gladys Tate had brought me. Since the sun had gone down behind the trees, I was able to pull up the shade and permit more air to come into the room. The sound of a flapping bird's wings interrupted my reading and I went to the window to look out on the night heron. She did a little dance on the railing and turned to peer back at me.

"Hello," I said. "Shopping for dinner or just out for a stroll?"

She lifted her wings as if to reply and then the muscles in her neck undulated as she dipped her beak before rising to swoop down and toward the forest and ponds where she would hunt for her dinner. Never did I wish I had the power of flight so much as I did at the moment. If I had it, I would fly alongside the heron and glide over the swamp before lifting myself higher and higher toward the glittering promise of stars.

The sound of the door being opened below and footsteps on the stairs startled me. I turned from the window to greet Gladys Tate.

"You can bring your chamber pot down now and take a bath, if you like. My maids have gone to bed. Empty that pail of dirty water and get some more to do some more cleaning tomorrow," she instructed. "Don't forget to fetch water for yourself and our baby," she added. "When you get to the bottom of the stairs, it's the first door on the right. Towels and soap and everything else you need is there."

"*Tres bien*, madame," I said. "Thank you."

"I hope," she said, "you told your mother I'm doing all I can to make the best of a horrible situation. It's not easy for me either. She should understand that when she comes here," she whined.

"I don't have to tell Mama anything, madame. She has the power to see the truth. She always knows what's truly in a person's heart. That's her gift."

"Ridiculous folklore. No one has that power, but I asked around and people say your mother is the best midwife in the bayou," she admitted. "I was told she's never lost a baby in birthing, except for those already dead." She smiled. "Everyone thinks it's a good idea to have her look after me."

She stared at me a moment and then she brought her hands to her breasts as if she had just experienced the sort of tenderness I had described I experienced.

"It bothers you when you sleep on your stomach sometimes, doesn't it?" she asked.

"*Oui*, madame."

"Then it will bother me, too," she vowed. "Don't go anywhere else in the house. My butler is still wandering about," she warned, and descended.

A moment later, I took the chamber pot and followed. The bathroom was almost as big as the room I now lived in upstairs. It had pink and white wallpaper with a fluffy blue throw rug beside the bathtub. All of the fixtures were brass. The vanity table had bath powders, soaps, and colognes. I emptied the chamber pot and then closed the door and began to fill the tub with warm water. I found some bubble bath and put some in as the water filled the tub. Then I undressed and soaked for nearly twenty minutes. It was really rather delightful and something I couldn't do at home. I made a mental note to tell Mama so she would be less anxious about my staying here.

The towels were big, soft ones. After I washed my hair, I scrubbed it dry with one and then wrapped a towel around myself as I sat at the vanity and brushed out my long strands. Staring at myself in the mirror, I thought I detected more chubbiness in my cheeks and remembered Mama's warning about getting too fat. I indulged myself by spraying on some of the cologne and then I put on my dress and, after cleaning up the bathroom, carried my chamber pot back upstairs. I returned to fill my water jug and get a clean pail of water for the cleaning I would do.

As I was leaving the bathroom again, I heard a horrible sound. It resembled someone retching. I stood completely still and listened. It was definitely someone retching and it was coming from the first doorway down left. My curiosity was more powerful than Gladys Tate's warning not to wander. I tiptoed along, keeping close to the wall. When I reached the doorway, I inched my head around to peer into what I remembered from the model house was the master bedroom. I could see clearly through the room and into the bathroom because the bathroom door was open. Octavious was nowhere, but Gladys Tate was on her hands and knees, hovering over the toilet, vomiting.

I snapped my head back, an electric chill shooting up my spine.

Was she vomiting because of something she had eaten that was too rich or not good or . . .

No, I told myself. That's too far-fetched. She couldn't imagine it and then actually have it happen, could she?

My jug of water tapped the wall.

"Octavious?" I heard her call. "Is that you?"

I didn't move.

"Octavious? Damn you, I'm sick."

I waited, my heart pounding. Then I heard her retch again and I quickly retreated to the doorway and ascended the stairs, taking care not to spill any of the water out of the pail.

I closed the door behind me and stood there, catching my breath and wondering if I had made the right decision after all. These people were rich, Gladys Tate's family was one of the most famous and respected families in the bayou. Their factory gave many people employment, and everyone, from the priest to the politicians, showed them respect. But there were shadows and memories looming in the corners and the closets of this house. I wondered if I could stay here and not be touched by the sadness and evil that I suspected had once strolled freely through the corridors and rooms. Perhaps, I thought with a shudder, it was all still very much here.

Sleep did not come easy the second night. I flitted in and out of nightmares and tossed and turned, waking often and listening to the creaks in the wood. Sometimes I thought I heard the sound of someone sobbing. I listened hard and it would drift away and I would fall back asleep. Shortly before daybreak, I was awake again and this time heard the soft sound of someone tiptoeing up the stairway. The door opened slowly, and for a moment, no one was there. My heart stopped. Was it a ghost? The spirit of one of Gladys Tate's angry ancestors, enraged by my presence in the house?

Then a dark figure appeared and made its way across the room to the window shade. I pretended to be asleep, but kept my right eye slightly open. It was Gladys Tate. She pulled down the shade, waited a moment, and then tiptoed out of the room, closing the door softly. I could barely hear her descend the stairs. She had moved like a sleepwalker, floating. It filled me with amazement. It did no good to close my eyes. I remained awake and saw the first weak rays of sunlight penetrate the shade and vaguely light the room to tell me morning, the beautiful bayou daybreak, had come. Only I would not be outside to greet it as I had all my life.

The next few days passed uneventfully. I cleaned and scrubbed the room until I believed it looked as immaculate as a room in a hospital, the old wood shining, the window so clear it looked open when it was closed. I took everything off the shelves and out of the closet, dusted and organized it, and then I dusted and polished all the small furniture.

Despite herself, Gladys Tate was impressed and commented that she was happy I was taking good care of my quarters.

I was lonely, of course, and missed Mama terribly, as well as the world outside; but every night, without fail, my night heron paid me a visit and strutted up and down the railing a little longer each time as I spoke to him through the window. I told him to tell all my animal friends in the swamp that I had not deserted them and I would be back before long. I imagined the heron visiting with nutrias and deer, snakes and turtles, and especially blue jays, who were the biggest gossips I knew, giving them all the news. At night the cicadas were louder than ever, letting me know that all of Nature was happy I was all right and would return. It was all silly pretending, I know; but it kept me content.

On my first Thursday morning after my arrival at The Shadows, Gladys Tate announced that I would enjoy my first meal downstairs in the dining room and then be able to wander about freely. I decided to wear the nicest of my three dresses, not to impress and please her but to please myself. I brushed down my hair and pinned it and then waited as the time drew near for her to call up to me. I heard the downstairs door open, followed by her declaration.

"It's all right for you to come down, Gabriel."

I appeared instantly. "Thank you, madame," I said, and descended.

She gazed at me and then smiled coldly. "Octavious will not be joining us," she said. "There was no need to make any extra preparations. I made a promise to your mother that you would not see Octavious, and I mean to keep that promise."

"I made very little preparation. I have no desire to see him, Madame Tate. In fact, I'm rather relieved he won't be there," I added. She raised her eyebrows, but looked at me skeptically before we went down the stairs to the dining room where our dinner of whole poached red snapper had been laid out. Although I thought the table was rather fancy, Gladys Tate made it perfectly clear at the start that it was dressed nothing like it was when she had significant guests.

However, the fish itself was covered thickly with sauce and decorated with parsley to cover the separation marks at the head and tail. Radishes had been placed in the eyes and a row of overlapping slices of lemon and hard-boiled egg was down the center. The platter was garnished with lettuce, cucumbers, tomatoes, olives, pimentos, and stuffed eggs. If this was an ordinary meal, I wondered what an elaborate one looked like.

She told me to sit at the opposite end of the table so we faced each other. The chandelier had been turned down and two candles were burning. Shadows danced on the walls and had a strange and eerie effect on the faces of the people painted in the scenes of sugar plantations and soybean fields that hung on the adjacent walls. The sad or troubled faces of the laborers looked like smiles, and the smiles on the rich landowners looked sinister. The far wall was all mirror so that I was looking at Gladys Tate's back and myself, only in the mirror, I seemed miles away.

"You may pour us each some iced tea," she said, and I rose to do so. The crystal goblets sparkled and the silverware felt heavy. The dishware had a flower print.

"This is a beautiful table setting," I remarked.

"It's our everyday tableware. But it has been in the family a very long time," she admitted. "I suppose you're used to eating off a plank table with tin forks and spoons."

"No, madame. We have plates, too. Not as elegant as these, of course, but we do have dishes."

She made a small grunting noise and took some of the red snapper. "Help yourself," she said.

I did so and found it delicious. "You have a very good cook."

"She was trained in New Orleans and never ceases to surprise us with her Creole creations. As you can see," she said, throwing a gesture in no specific direction, "our baby will enjoy only the finest things available. You have made a very wise decision."

"I think the events made the decision for me, madame," I said. No matter what she claimed to be doing for me, I wanted to be sure she understood I was the real victim, not her.

"Whatever," she said. "How's your appetite in general?" she inquired.

"Unpredictable. Sometimes I'm very hungry in the morning, and sometimes I don't feel like eating anything. Even the thought of food upsets my stomach."

"Pregnant women have these weird cravings, don't they?" she asked, once again making me feel as if I were the adult and she the young woman.

"They can. Mama told me about a pregnant woman who used to eat bark."

"Bark? You mean from a tree?"

"*Oui,* madame."

"Ugh," she said, grimacing. "I was just referring to strange combinations. Do you have any such cravings?"

I thought a moment. "I had a passing craving for pepper jelly smeared over a piece of pecan pie."

She nodded. "Yes, that's more like it," she remarked. I started to smile, but she suddenly looked very angry.

"I want you to tell me these things as they occur. Hold nothing back," she ordered. "I must know exactly what to say to people. We'll be showing soon and they will have questions about my pregnancy. Understand?"

"*Oui,* madame."

"Is there anything else you want to tell me right now?"

I thought and then shook my head.

"Very well, eat your dinner," she said, and ate silently for a while, her eyes vacantly focused on some thought rather than on me. All the food was delicious. I enjoyed every morsel.

"There's French chocolate silk pie," she announced, and lifted a cover off the dish.

"I'll have just a small piece, madame. Mama told me to watch my weight."

"Oh? There!" she pounced. "You see, there was something else for you to tell me. Watch my weight. Must I discover these things by accident?"

"I didn't think . . ."

"You've got to think." She leaned forward, her eyes beady. "We have an elaborate and complicated scheme to conduct. We must trust each other with the most intimate details about our bodies," she said, and I wondered what

110

detail about her body she imagined I would have the vaguest interest in. I decided to risk a question.

"Have you ever seen a doctor or another *traiteur* about your difficulty getting pregnant, madame?"

She pulled herself back in the seat. Her face turned crimson and her eyes widened. "Don't assume because you are living here under these circumstances that you may take liberties with my privacy," she declared.

"I meant no disrespect, madame. You yourself just said we must trust each other."

She stared a moment and then, just as suddenly as she had become indignant, she erased that indignation and smiled.

"Yes, that's true. No. I haven't gone to any physicians or *traiteurs*. I trust in God to eventually bless my fertility. I am, as you can see, in every other way a healthy, vigorous person."

"Mama's helped some women get pregnant," I offered.

She raised her eyebrows.

"I'm sure she would help you, too."

"If I ever get that desperate, I will call on her," Gladys said. The grandfather clock bonged and she shifted her gaze to the door.

"Did you want me to return to my room before Octavious comes home?" I asked, assuming that was what concerned her.

"Octavious won't be home until much later," she said. "Your mother said you must exercise to make the birthing easier. You can go for a walk around the house, but don't go down the driveway, and whatever you do, don't speak to any of my field workers if one of them should be nearby. My maids, however, will return around eleven, so you must be upstairs before that."

"Oui, madame."

She stared at me again, her face softening. "Do you want coffee?" she asked, nodding at the silver pot on a warmer.

"Please," I said. She rose and actually served me. Then she sat down and sighed deeply.

"I am not happy with what Octavious has done, of course." she began, gazing around the large dining hall, "but

111

the prospect of little feet pitter-pattering over these floors, and hearing another voice in this house, is a wonderful thing. I will spend all my time with my baby. Finally I will have a family."

"You have no brothers or sisters, Madame Tate?"

"No," she said. "My mother . . . my mother did not do well when she was pregnant with me, and the delivery, I was told, was very difficult. She almost died."

"I'm sorry."

"My father wanted a son, of course, and was very unhappy. Then he finally settled on finding a proper son-in-law, proper in his eyes," she added, almost spitting the words. She glared at the table a moment and then raised her eyes quickly. "But that's all in the past now. I don't want to think about it." She smirked. "I would appreciate it if you would not ask me so many personal questions," she continued, her voice taking on the steely edge of a razor. "For me to answer them is like tearing a scab off a wound."

"I'm sorry, madame. I didn't intend . . ."

"Everyone has such good intentions. No one means any harm," she said with a sneer. Then her face crumpled and she looked like a little girl for a moment. "Daddy, my daddy, he never meant any harm either. All the men in my life meant no harm." She laughed a thin, hollow laugh. "Even Octavious meant you no harm, he says. He meant to give you the gift of the love experience. Can you imagine him telling me such a ridiculous thing? I think he really believes that."

I shook my head, my heart pounding, not sure what to expect next. She didn't fail to surprise and shock me. Her face turned into granite again.

"Where do you think he has gone tonight?" she asked with venom. "To give some other poor, deprived young woman the benefit of his love experience. So," she said, her eyes steaming as she leaned over her plate toward me. "Don't feel sorry for yourself. Feel sorry for me and do whatever I ask to make things right."

I could barely nod. My throat wouldn't swallow and my fingers felt numb.

She sat back. The granite softened again and she sighed

deeply. "Go enjoy your walk," she said with a wave of her hand. "Your inquiries have given me indigestion."

I rose slowly. "Can I help you with anything?" I asked, nodding at the table.

"What? No, you fool. Do you think I do anything with the dishes and food? My maids will take care of it all when they return. Just go, go."

"Thank you, madame. It was a delicious dinner," I said, but she seemed lost in her own thoughts. I left her sitting there, her head tilted slightly to the right, her eyes watery and her chin quivering.

I did feel sorrier for her than I did for myself at the moment. Despite her big house, filled with the most expensive and wonderful artifacts, furniture, paintings; despite the money her and Octavious's factory made, she appeared to be one of the saddest and most unhappy women I had ever met.

What was happiness? I wondered. From what well was it drawn? Money and wealth in and of itself didn't guarantee it. I knew far poorer families in the bayou who had ten, no, twenty smiles for every one on Gladys Tate's face. If she doubled her life span, she wouldn't laugh and sing as much as they had already laughed and sung.

No one was truly happy unless he or she had someone who loved him or her and someone she or he could love, I realized, and with that realization came the understanding of why Gladys Tate had so eagerly, willingly, and now cleverly worked on taking the baby into her home and into her life.

She would finally draw up a pail of pleasure from the well of happiness, but the path to get there was still cluttered with obstacles and even dangers. How I wished this journey would soon be ended.

6

Madame's Secret Pain

Days passed into weeks, and weeks into months, with me following the same routine. I had no clock, so I told time by the rays of light that filtered through the shade and by the sounds and noises in the house to which I had grown accustomed. The maids followed a strict schedule and always cleaned the rooms right below me about the same time of day. I could hear their muffled voices and envied them for their occasional laughter. I couldn't recall the last time I had laughed so freely. Most of the time my thoughts were tangled with knots of worry and weighted down with rocks of sorrow, for I knew how troubled Mama was about my state of affairs and could easily imagine her tossing and turning at night, dwelling on me trapped in this small room.

The silvery sounds of water swishing through pipes in the morning told me when the Tates were rising, and the aromas of foods being cooked suggested how soon my meals would be served. Despite her veiled threats to the contrary, Gladys Tate didn't miss delivering a meal, nor did she make me wait as long as she had first threatened. I think that was Mama's doing. Mama frightened her by telling her the baby's health could be in jeopardy if I was in any way denied my basic needs.

114

The only time I was denied anything was once when my lamp ran out of kerosene. I told her and she chided me for leaving it on too long or too high. To emphasize her point, she didn't bring me a new supply of kerosene for two days, claiming she didn't have it. I had to sit in the darkness once the sun went down and I couldn't read or sew. I asked her to bring me some candles at least, but she said she was afraid of my causing a fire.

"I often sit in the darkness," she told me. "It's soothing."

It wasn't soothing to me, but I knew she would have the kerosene miraculously for me on the third day, for that was the day Mama was scheduled to visit. Everything was always made perfect when Mama came. I began to feel like a prisoner of war visited occasionally by the Red Cross. To pass the time and amuse myself, I pretended that I was a spy the Germans had caught and Gladys Tate was the prison camp warden. I plotted an escape, which I discussed with my night heron while he paraded on the railing.

"I'll tie my bedsheet to my blanket and my clothes and make a rope down which I will slide," I said. "But I better wait until midnight. The guards are careless then."

My heron lifted his wings and bobbed his neck as if to say, "Good plan."

It finally brought me some laughter. The evenings had become my favorite time. When I was permitted to raise the window shade, I could measure the passing of the hours with the movement of the moon or with the movement of stars and planets like Venus. Mama had taught me about the heavens, the constellations, and I knew how to read the night sky. I loved to sit by my small window on the world and watch the evening thunderstorms, the sizzling lightning that slashed the darkness and sent a strong breeze my way.

I would sit for hours at the window and listen to the sounds of the evening, bedazzled by the flickering fireflies that looked like sparks of someone's campfire shooting through the darkness. Even the drone of insects was pleasing to someone like me, someone shut up for almost all the day and night. I took such pleasure in the hoot of an owl or the caw of a hawk. Aside from Mama and Gladys Tate, I hadn't spoken with another human being for so long.

Gladys Tate brought out her tape measure more frequently, and after the fifth month, Gladys decided I was showing enough for any casual observer to notice and accurately guess about my being pregnant. Gladys said it meant that I could no longer take a walk outside on Thursday night for fear some worker would see a pregnant young woman and wonder who she was and why she was always here. Although those walks weren't much because I was confined to the area around the house and couldn't go into the woods or approach the swamp, they had been something to look forward to, a change and a chance to visit with Nature.

Just as she promised she would do, Gladys Tate took to wearing something under her own clothes that, to my amazement, continued to accurately match my own development. She even padded her bra. She would have me stand beside her and confirm that we were about the same size. I couldn't understand why it was so important to her that she be that precise, but I didn't ask because questions like that only infuriated her.

On the other hand, her interrogation of me concerning my symptoms and my health was incessant. She went so far as to ask me if I was having any strange dreams, especially about the baby, and if so, would I describe them? When she told Mama I was eating nothing less than what she was eating, she wasn't lying. Before Mama arrived, Gladys reviewed every meal and told me what I had finished, she had finished; what I had left over, she had left over, not that I left over much. She was constantly changing the menu, cataloging foods to see what I fancied and what I didn't.

"The cook understands my finickiness," she told me. "It's just part of being pregnant. In some ways it's nice being pregnant. Everyone excuses your eccentricities," she concluded. I told her I'd rather not be pregnant and not be excused, but she didn't appreciate my reply.

One day I didn't hear her come up the stairway, and when she opened the door, she found me crying. She demanded to know what was wrong, grimacing as if I were doing her a terrible injustice.

"I'm feeding you well. You're getting whatever you need. You're not going to suffer any embarrassment after this

116

ordeal is over. What more do you want from me?" she wailed, her hands on her padded hips.

"I don't want anything from you, Madame Tate. I'm not crying right now because of this," I said, indicating the room and my confinement.

"Then why are you crying?"

"I don't know. Sometimes . . . I just cry. Sometimes I just feel so sad, I can't help myself. I'm on emotional pins and needles."

The anger left her face and was quickly replaced by curiosity and concern.

"Does it happen often?"

"Often enough," I said.

"Did you ask your mother about it?" she pursued.

"Yes. She said it's not uncommon for pregnant women to be this way."

"What way?"

"Shifting abruptly from happiness to sadness and without any apparent reason," I explained. "I'm sorry," I said. She stared at me a moment and nodded.

That night, when I went to the bathroom to empty my chamber pot and bathe, I heard sobbing coming from her room, and when I peered in the doorway, I saw her sitting on her bed, wiping real tears from her cheeks. Suddenly she stopped and then laughed. Then she started again. I left before she discovered me watching her, and for the first time, I began to consider that this situation might be just as emotionally draining for her as if was for me.

Of course, I realized that even though pregnancy made me emotionally fragile, some of my gloom had to have to do with my being caged up in Gladys Tate's old playroom. I didn't want to complain and make everyone feel bad and suffer any of Gladys Tate's lectures about how much she was doing to solve this terrible problem and how much I should be grateful.

But despite my books, my embroidery, my sketching and keeping of the journal, I had so much time on my hands and nothing left to discover about my tiny, new world. Where could I put my eyes where they hadn't been dozens of times? I spent hours daydreaming, imagining myself free and outside, walking through the tall grass, dipping my hand into the canal water, smelling the honeysuckle and magnolia blossoms or the damp odor of the hydrangeas and pecan and oak trees after a good rain. I imagined the cool breeze coming in from the Gulf caressing my face or making strands of my hair dance over my forehead. I heard the quacking ducks flying north for the summer and saw the nutrias working feverishly on their dome houses.

When Mama found out I was no longer permitted to take my walks on Thursdays, she complained to Gladys and told her it was unhealthy for a pregnant woman to remain sedentary.

"You have to keep her legs and stomach strong," Mama chastised. "She needs exercise."

Gladys's solution was to permit me to wander through the house after dinner.

"Just keep away from the windows. I don't want anyone knowing you're here, especially now," she emphasized. To make the point, she drew every curtain and kept the rooms as dimly lit as possible.

The Tate mansion was filled with expensive furnishings, many of them antiques, some of which predated the Civil War. The living room looked like a room in a museum. It seemed to me that no one ever used it. The maids kept it polished and clean, not a cushion out of place, not a speck of dust on a table. The Persian rug looked like it had never been trod upon. There were artifacts everywhere, some Oriental vases, ivory figurines, crystal and glass pieces on tables and shelves and in a cherry-wood glass case. Rich satin drapes framed the windows.

Gladys Tate let me peruse the library to choose new books to read, but I always had to restrict myself to no more than two at a time and always replace the two I had finished before taking any additional volumes. This way, she explained, no one would notice any were missing. Of course, I was forbidden to touch anything else. I could look at everything, go practically anywhere, but never disturb a thing. It made me feel like I was walking through a house made of thin china, terrified that I would bump into a table and send some very valuable piece shattering or leave footprints on the immaculate floors.

One Thursday night I ventured farther into the upstairs corridor. Usually the doors were kept closed and Gladys Tate made it very clear that I was never to open a closed door during my walk. This particular night, however, one of the always-closed doors was almost half open. I paused and gazed in, as timidly as a turtle at first, and then more like a curious kitten when I saw a pair of man's trousers draped over a chair. The closet door was open, so I could see the contents: all men's clothing. I realized that Octavious used this room. What did that mean? He and Gladys weren't sleeping together? Was it because of her fabricated pregnancy or was it always this way? I wondered.

I said nothing about it until Gladys and I sat down to our usual cold Thursday night dinner the following week.

"Your mother says that walking up and down the stairs is actually good for a pregnant woman, as long as she doesn't overdo it," Gladys remarked. "She says too many women baby themselves and are babied when they become pregnant. I'm sorry you can only do the big staircase on Thursday nights. However, you can walk up and down your own little stairway quietly when you come down to use the bathroom, I suppose.

"I'm not babying myself," she continued. "I used to have breakfast in bed occasionally. And everyone expects me to now, of course, but I am not going to appear to be one of those spoiled women your mother talks about," she said. She thought a moment and then said, "I never realized exercise was so important for a pregnant woman. I always thought they had to lie in bed and be waited upon hand and foot, but your mother thinks it should be exactly the opposite. She says unless the woman has some problem, she never tells her to stop working. Some have worked right up to the day she's delivered them."

"Mama's delivered enough babies to know," I assured her. "One time she delivered four in one day: a baby boy in the morning, a pair of twin girls in the afternoon, and a baby girl in the evening."

She nodded and then, after a pause, screwed those inquisitive eyes on me and asked, "You don't sleep well these nights, do you?"

"No."

"You wake up a lot and moan and groan. I can hear you through the ceiling sometimes. You've got to control that," she warned. "Remember, the window is open at night."

"I don't realize I'm doing it," I said. "Did I wake you and Octavious?"

"Not Octavious. His bedroom is across the corridor," she said quickly.

"You don't sleep in the same room?" I asked before I could stop my tongue.

She fixed her eyes on me with a stone glint this time. "No. We have different sleeping habits. It's not uncommon. My mother and father slept in separate bedrooms from the first day they were married."

I said nothing.

"You knew Octavious was sleeping in his own room anyway, didn't you?" she said with a tone of accusation. "You're snooping around the house now. You're into every nook and cranny, I suppose."

"No, madame. I . . ."

"It doesn't make any difference," she said, and then gave me one of her crooked smiles. "You can't tell anyone anything about this place and our lives or it will be known you were here and then questions will be asked and you'll have ruined everything. Then, instead of your baby having a good home and all that he or she needs, he or she will be labeled an illegitimate child and it will all be your fault. You understand that, don't you?" she asked, sounding more concerned than threatening.

"Of course, madame. I don't mean to be snoopy. I just meant . . ."

"You'll learn for yourself one day," she said, and then sighed. "You'll learn just how hard it is to live with a man. Men are more than just physically different; they're more selfish. They want to be satisfied all the time, no matter how we feel. All they care about is their own raging lusts," she said, practically spitting the words.

She leaned forward and then in a loud, raspy whisper, she said, "It's because of their hormones. They overflow and it makes them throb all over until they get satisfied. That's what my father told me."

"Your father discussed such things with you?" I asked, unable to hide my surprise.

She shrugged. "My mother was too prudish to do so. She wouldn't even tell me about the birds and the bees. Do you know we had skirts on our piano legs because my mother thought naked piano legs were too suggestive?" She laughed a thin laugh and then screwed her face into a serious expression and added, "Of course, young people in my time weren't as concerned about sexual matters as they seem to be today.

"It was different then," she continued, looking around as if she could see the room twenty years ago. She smiled softly. "Things were less complicated. Everything was in its proper place. Courting was more civilized, proper. I so wanted it to be that way forever, but . . ."

I just stared at her, but she looked like she was gazing through me. It gave me the shudders because she appeared to be talking to herself more than to me. Something she saw in her own memory made her eyes hateful and small. She shuddered and twisted her lips into a crooked smile before continuing.

"Octavious has never forgiven me for our honeymoon," she said angrily. "He accused me of planning it that way. He said I should have known, have kept track with the calendar."

"Calendar?" I wondered aloud. "I don't understand."

She blinked her eyes and then looked at me and smirked. Then she sat back, wagging her head.

"Girls like you drive me mad," she began. "You have your fun, but you don't know what's what with your own bodily functions."

I shook my head, still confused.

"Octavious accused me of having a period for three weeks instead of one," she snapped with impatience. "I know you know what a period is."

"Oui, madame," I said. "Of course."

"Well, sometimes mine's irregular and it just worked out that way after we got married and Octavious couldn't gratify his lust on our wedding night, nor the night after or the one after that. Is that spelled out simply enough for you to understand, or do I have to draw pictures?"

She looked away and then, when she turned back, there were tears in her eyes. "It's very difficult when your husband is not sensitive to your needs. It's just better for a man and a woman to have separate bedrooms. It was better for my mother and it's better for me. Does that satisfy your need to know? Does it?" she demanded.

"I'm sorry, madame. I don't have a need to know the private details of your life. I didn't mean to pry."

"Of course not. You didn't mean to come barging into my life either."

"No, Madame Tate. I did not," I said firmly. "It was the other way around. Octavious came barging into my life."

She glared a moment and then her face softened. "You're right. Of course. Anyway, we shouldn't be having this kind of nasty talk. We have to cooperate and help each other get through this ordeal," she said in a sweetened voice. "Have you had enough to eat?"

"Oui, madame."

"Good. Take your exercise then. Wait," she said when I started to rise. "I'll walk with you. I want to study how you walk."

"How I walk?"

"Yes. Pregnant women do walk differently. I've seen you rubbing your lower back when you walk sometimes. You have a sort of pregnant waddle."

"Oh," I said. I nodded and she followed along, keeping a step or two back so she could analyze and imitate me. I tried not to be self-conscious of my every move, but when someone is studying you under a magnifying glass, you can't help but think about every gesture, ever movement in your face, every twinge in your legs and back. I found I was even holding my breath at times.

But after a while, the walk through the house became more pleasant because she began to explain things, point to this work of art or this vase and tell me its history, who bought it and why. She explained why she held affection for certain of her household possessions. I noted that anything her mother bought, she spoke about with joy, but things her father bought seemed to resurrect painful memories. As she went on about them, I realized that most of the things her father had bought, he had bought to compensate for some sad moment or something he had done that had displeased her mother. She called them "Gifts of Repentance," and then added, almost casually, "That goes for my wonderful dollhouse, too." She looked mean, wrathful, when she said it.

"Didn't you love your father, Madame Tate?" I asked softly.

She replied with a short, thin laugh, and then said, "Love him? Of course. He demanded it."

"How can you demand love?" I asked.

"My father could demand the sun to rise or fall."

"I don't understand," I said.

"Be happy you don't," she replied, and then, with her hand on her lower back as if she really did suffer from the same aches I experienced, she groaned and added, "I've walked enough. Watch the time," she warned, "and be sure to get upstairs before anyone can discover you."

She left me standing in the corridor.

On my way back upstairs, I paused in the doorway of the den and gazed up at the portrait of Gladys Tate's father. What sort of a man thought that love demanded was any sort of love at all? I wondered. His painted eyes seemed to be shooting needles my way and his firm lips appeared caught in a sneer. I didn't linger and went up to my tiny world even though I had more time to wander about this dark and foreboding house.

Gladys Tate had lived up to her promise to Mama: She had kept Octavious from me from the day I had arrived. Only once or twice did I hear what I was sure was the sound of his muffled voice below, and once, when I was gazing out the window at night, I thought I saw him standing in the

123

shadows looking up at me, but either I imagined it or he stepped back into deeper darkness and was gone in an instant.

Almost a week after Gladys Tate had told me about her disastrous honeymoon, I went downstairs after hours to take my bath and empty my chamber pot as usual. After I undressed, I studied the changes in my body, noting the stretch marks on my breasts and abdomen. It was harder to get in and out of the bathtub, too. Every muscle seemed to be aching these days. I had a good soak, brushed my hair, and put on my nightgown, but the moment I returned to my quarters, I sensed something different. When you have spent as much time every day in a room as small as mine was for as long as I had, you get so you can smell the slightest change, much less see it. The lamp was very low, so I turned it up, and when I spun around, I found him standing there in the corner, his back to the wall.

"Monsieur Tate!" I exclaimed.

He stepped forward quickly, his finger on his lips. "Please. Don't scream."

"What is it you want?" I demanded. "You frightened me," I said angrily.

"I had to sneak up here, of course. I'm sorry," he said. "Please, relax. I'm not here to hurt you or bother you."

"What do you want?" I demanded, my heart thumping like a tin drum.

He wore a white cotton shirt and a pair of dark slacks. His hair was combed neatly, and the aroma of his cologne reached my nostrils in waves. He smiled.

"I just want to talk to you for a few moments," he said, his hands up to keep me from screaming.

"We have nothing to say to each other. I must ask you to leave immediately," I said, jabbing my finger toward the door and then pressing my nightgown against my bosom to give me some more cover from his searching eyes.

"I don't blame you for hating me," he said. "Nothing I can say will change what I have done to you or make things better, but I thought since you have been here awhile, you might at least understand a little more about my situation,

124

and perhaps, I was hoping . . . you would be somewhat more sympathetic."

"I don't understand anything except you are a horrible person, mean and selfish."

"Perhaps I am," he admitted. "I don't want to be." He lowered his head. I retreated to my bed and sat with my arms folded over my bosom. With his eyes staring, I couldn't help but feel naked even though I wore my nightgown. He raised his head and smiled again. "How is everything?" he asked. "Is there anything you need?"

"My freedom," I replied.

He nodded, the thin smile evaporating. "I understand everything's going along as it should and it won't be much longer."

"To me each day seems like a week, each week a month, and each month a year. Not to be able to go outside when the sun is up, to have to walk through the house on tiptoe and stay within the shadows until I feel like a shadow myself, is torture," I pointed out with tears in my eyes.

"I'm sorry," he said, his voice cracking. Then he added, "I pray for your forgiveness every night. I know you probably don't believe that, but it's true. Despite what I have done, I am a religious man. Why, Gladys and I haven't missed a Sunday service since we got married. We even attended church during our honeymoon."

"It's not only my forgiveness you must pray for, monsieur," I replied, my voice as cold as ice. If indeed there was any forgiveness to sprout in my heart, it was far too early for the seeds to open. I was still in the winter of my suffering, and my heart was far from a fertile place for a pardon to blossom.

His smile returned, and even in the dim light I could see it was a small, tight smile.

"If you are referring to my asking for the forgiveness of my illustrious wife, I don't think the weight on my conscience is as heavy as you would imagine. By now, even confined to these quarters and restricted in your movements around our home and property, you must have reached a realization about our relationship," he said.

"That's not my business."

"I know. Unfortunately, it's no one's business but my own. Remember the things I told you at the pond? They weren't lies, only now you probably see it's even worse than I described. We haven't been as husband and wife for some time. I'm hoping that when the baby is born and she becomes a mother, things will change."

"Monsieur, none of this—"

"Oh, Gabriel," he said, falling to his knees and reaching out for my hand. His gesture took me by surprise. I held my breath, but my heart continued to pound like rain in a storm drain. "I want you to understand everything. Only then will you perhaps find some small place in your heart for an infinitesimal amount of forgiveness."

He swallowed hard and then continued. "Gladys and I don't sleep together because making love for her is too painful. She just lies there and whimpers. Can you imagine what that is like for me? I'd like to be a real husband and sire children with her as I should, but she makes it so difficult."

"Why tell me, a stranger? Why not bring her to a doctor, monsieur?" I asked in my same hard, sharp voice. I had used all my power of pity for Mama and myself. I certainly had nothing left for him, the man whose lust had shut me up in this tiny room.

"Because a doctor can't help her unless he can wipe away years of horrid childhood memories," he blurted.

I felt a wave of blood flow up my neck and pulled my hand back from his.

"I do not understand, monsieur," I said, even though the dark thoughts had been lingering in the corners of my mind from the day I had discovered the strange drawings in the closet and the damaged dolls. These thoughts were so horrid and frightening to me, I kept them smothered.

"Gladys's father used her . . . sexually, when she was just a little girl," he said, and I gasped. "I realized something was wrong from the first day after we had been married. In order to postpone our consummation of the marriage, she secretly had one of her laborers butcher a pig and put some of the blood into a small bottle, which she brought along on our honeymoon and then used to pretend she had gotten her

126

period. One afternoon, toward the end of our week, I found the bottle buried in a drawer. When I confronted her with it, she broke down and cried and babbled some of the past.

"Naturally, I was horrified. Her father was a well-respected and important man, a man I personally admired. He had brought me into the business and treated me like a son from the first day forward. It was he who arranged for my courting of Gladys, and although she was somewhat aloof from my advances, I thought it was only because of her shyness. She had never had a boyfriend before me, really.

"So I was willing to give it time, and when our marriage was arranged, I thought we would surely learn to love each other and things would be fine. When I discovered her past, I confronted her father, who, as you might know, had been suffering from emphysema for some time. It had grown very serious. He could barely get around and spent most of his time confined in bed, hooked to an oxygen tank. It looked like an umbilical cord and he shriveled until he appeared no more than a baby. I was running the business already."

"What happened after you confronted him?" I asked, unable to prevent myself from being interested in his story even though a part of me abhorred the details.

"He denied everything, of course, and told me Gladys had always been a fanciful child who actually believed her own imaginings. He begged me not to give up on her, however, claiming I was the only hope she had for a normal life."

"You believed him?"

"I didn't know what to believe. It didn't seem to make any difference whether or not it was true. The result was the same. Gladys was, as one psychiatrist I conferred with told me, impotent. He said he had seen other similar cases in which a woman's psychological condition actually affected her ability to get pregnant. He called it mind over matter.

"Oh, I forced myself on her a number of times, hoping to break through this wall of frigidity, but it has, until now, proven impenetrable. Can you understand what it has been like for me to live under such conditions?

"I had made promises to her father and accepted her and the holy sacrament of marriage, but . . . I am only a man with a man's needs and weaknesses.

"I know," he said quickly, "that is no excuse for what I have done to you, and it's laughable for me to even suggest you forgive me because of it, but I wanted you to understand that I am not an evil person and I do suffer remorse." He lowered his head.

"You denied it when my father first came to you," I reminded him.

"Who would have admitted such a thing to Jack Landry? He looked like he would tear my arms out and rip off my head. I was terrified. I know his reputation. Don't think my legs weren't quaking under that desk when you and your father burst into my office and I tried to frighten him with my own threats.

"I know you have no reason to believe this now, but I was preparing to send you money to help you with your pregnancy and with the child. I was going to do it anonymously. I never expected your father would go to Gladys, and as you remember, I was quite surprised by her reaction and decision.

"Well," he said, sitting back, "that's the whole truth. Now you know it and perhaps you won't hate me as much as you did."

"How much I hate you isn't what matters," I said, and then I added in a softer voice, "I don't hate you. Mama always says hate is like a small fire kindled in your soul; it eventually burns away all the goodness and consumes you in its rage."

"She's right and you're very sweet to tell me that. That's what's made this so terrible, your goodness." He smiled. "Really, is there anything I can do for you? Something I could bring you?"

"No, monsieur."

He stared at me and smiled. "I wish I had been born years later and met a girl like you first," he said.

"But my father doesn't own a big cannery," I reminded him.

His smile widened. "You're a very clever girl besides being a very beautiful one, for someone who claims she hasn't been with men very much," he said. "Tell me the truth now. There were others, weren't there?"

"I have told you the truth and I don't care what you believe about me, monsieur."

He smiled as if to humor me and then he looked around, remaining on the floor at my feet. "It has to have been very lonely for you here, *n'est-ce pas?*"

"*Oui*, monsieur."

"You miss your friends, I'm sure."

"I miss my mother and my freedom to go where I want when I want."

"I'm sorry. Really, there must be something else I can do for you," he insisted. Then he rose and sat beside me. "I know. I could visit you more often," he suggested. "Amuse you, comfort you. You're a lovely girl. You shouldn't be so alone. It's not fair."

"I'll endure it. As you said, it's not for much longer." I shifted on the bed so I wouldn't be sitting so close to him.

"Yes, but as you said, every day is like a week, every week a month, a month a year, when you're so locked up and without company. We can play checkers or just talk, and I can comfort you with my shower of affection whenever you need it. Pregnant women need affection, even more than women who aren't pregnant, no?"

He reached across my lap and took my hand into his. I started to pull back, but he held on to me.

"You needn't worry now. The damage, as they say, has already been done. You can't get any more pregnant. You won't have twins," he added with a laugh.

"Please, monsieur." I pulled my hand from his, but he took it again, pressing firmer, more desperately.

"Gabriel, I'm lonely, too. It's not just for you that I make the suggestion."

"Monsieur Tate . . ."

"Pregnancy does make a woman even more beautiful," he said. "Here you are locked away in this closet, shut away from the sunlight you love so, and yet you still bloom with a freshness and a radiance that makes my heart skip beats."

"I don't feel fresh and radiant."

"But you are," he insisted. "These past months I've lain in my bed and stared up at the ceiling thinking about you closed up in this room. I go into Gladys's bedroom to hear every movement, every squeak, and a few times," he confessed, "I've watched you from a distance or from the shadows and admired you for what you are doing for your parents and for the baby."

"I do what must be done," I said, my voice weak because of the way my heart thumped with fear and anxiety, imagining him hovering below listening for a squeak in the ceiling.

"Your courage takes away my breath and in my eyes makes you more beautiful. If you will only let me give you real comfort," he said, and leaned toward me to kiss my cheek, his hands moving up the sides of my body toward my breasts.

Surprised and terrified, I put my hand on his chest and held him away. "Get out, monsieur. Now!" He hesitated. "I will scream. I warn you." My throat tightened, but he saw the determination in my eyes.

"All right," he said, standing and pumping his palms against the air between us. "Stay calm. Relax. I'll go. I just thought you needed some comfort and . . ."

"I don't want you here," I said, tears burning beneath my eyelids. "I don't want this kind of comfort."

"Okay. Fine. But what I'll do is look in on you from time to time to see if you are all right."

"No, don't bother."

"It's not a bother."

"Monsieur," I said firmly, swallowing back my tears to make my words sharp and firm, "if you set foot in this room again, I will complain to Madam Tate and I will leave this house. I swear I will."

He shook his head. "Where do you get your strength?"

"From my sense of what is right," I replied pointedly.

He was silent and then he retreated to the doorway where he paused once more to look back at me. He sighed deeply and shook his head. "I'm sorry," he said, and descended the stairs quietly.

I waited until I heard the downstairs door close. Then I let out a breath and felt my tears pour hotly over my lids and down my cheeks. Now that he was gone, I was filled with amazement. How could he come up here and, pretending to be remorseful, try to seduce me again? Madame Tate was right, I thought, men must have raging hormones that turn them into monsters. Had he no shame?

I went to the window to take deep breaths. My heart was still pounding.

If Mama knew what had happened, she would rip me from the place in an instant, I thought. Maybe what I was doing was not so wise. Maybe I shouldn't leave my baby in this house, rich people or no.

Oh, I didn't know what was right and what was wrong anymore. I couldn't throw myself on Mama for the answers. I knew she was so selfless she would choose what would make life easier for me, no matter what the consequences to her. If only there were someone else to speak to, someone else I trusted and loved and someone who loved me.

I gazed up at the stars, hot tears still streaking down my cheeks; and then my heron appeared out of nowhere, it seemed, and landed on the railing. He lifted his wings and did a small jump as if to amuse me. I laughed.

"What are you up to tonight, Mr. Heron?" I asked. He bobbed his head.

Then he turned and soared off into the night.

My animals had no false faces. They were exactly who they appeared to be. They broke no promises. They lived in a world without any false hope. Maybe I should have been born a heron. Right now it seemed a better thing to be.

I sighed and sat back, and then I felt the strange twinge in my stomach. I felt it again and my eyes brightened, my tears fell back.

It's the baby, I thought. It was the first time I had felt it move within me.

And suddenly all the dark clouds lifted and a ray of sunshine brightened the dark corridors in my heart, causing it to beat with a joy I never felt before. The pain I felt now was the pain that came from having no one with whom I could share this new excitement.

Loneliness was just as difficult to withstand when you had happiness as it was when you had sadness, I thought, for you needed to share it. I began to understand what loving someone really meant. It meant sharing every discovery, every realization, every tear, every laugh, every dream, and even every nightmare.

It meant having someone to trust with your fears and your hopes.

It meant so much more than the people in this house thought it did. Maybe the birth of the baby would bring them the understanding they lacked. The Tates might stop doting on themselves and their problems and dote on the child. It could bring them together in a good way. They would share the baby's development, laugh at its smile, be in awe of its growth, its first steps, first words. And then maybe Octavious would prove to be right: Gladys would want more children, children truly of her own.

When something bad happened, Mama, quoting Scripture, often said, "To everything there is a season and a time to every purpose under heaven . . . a time to rend and a time to sew."

The baby kicked again.

I had passed through the season of rending.

Now I was about to begin the season of sewing.

7

A Friend Appears

Now that I had felt the life stirring within me, what remained of my pregnancy seemed less terrible to endure. Starting my eighth month, I felt as if I had rounded a long, windy bend in the road and could see my destination looming just ahead. Despite her unhappiness over my being kept secretly in the Tates' house for months and months, Mama seemed pleased with the progress of my pregnancy and the baby's development. Now, during most of the time Mama visited with me, I would ramble on about how the baby had kicked and jumped, how it felt to have a living thing turning and twisting, anticipating its own birth, forgetting for the moment that Mama knew all this better than I did. After all, she had been pregnant with me!

"The baby kicked so hard last night, I nearly fell out of the bed, Mama! I had to sit up and then I spent most of the night rubbing my stomach and talking soothingly to him or her. I wish I knew whether it was a boy or a girl."

"It sounds like a boy to me," she said.

"That's what I thought," I whispered. "I just feel it's a boy and I've been talking to the baby assuming it's a boy. It doesn't feel like I'm being kicked with a dainty foot," I said, and laughed.

Mama listened with her face frozen in a wise smile that gradually turned into a look of concern and worry. I was so wrapped up in my excitement and fancy that I didn't notice for a while, and then I felt my heart skip a beat when I saw how her eyes had darkened.

"What's wrong, Mama?" I asked. "Has Daddy done something?"

"Your daddy always does something to curl the hairs at the back of my head, but no, it's not him I'm thinking of right now."

"Then who? What?"

"It's time we talked about what it's going to be like afterward, honey."

"Afterward?"

"Something magical happens when a woman gives birth, Gabriel," she explained. "There's all those months of discomfort, labor pain and the birthing pain, of course; but once the baby emerges and the mother sets eyes on this wonderful creation that took shape inside her, all the agony slips from her memory and she is filled with a joy beyond description. I seen it hundreds of times, honey. Especially with first births, the mother can't believe her eyes. I couldn't believe mine when you were born." She sighed so deeply when she paused, I had to hold my breath until she continued.

"That's going to happen to you, Gabriel, and then, in the same instant, the baby's going to be ripped away from you. You got to prepare yourself for it, although, to be honest, I don't know what to tell you, what to do for you to make that ordeal any easier."

Mama held my hand while she told me these things, and I could see from the grimness in her face that she had already seen my future misery and was feeling sad for me.

"First you were raped and then you had to go through all this with what follows. I'm not going to sugarcoat it, honey. It's a wrenching the likes of which you'll never know again," she said. "I've seen the horror when a baby's born dead. For you, it will be just like that, I'm afraid," she concluded.

I tried to swallow, but my throat wouldn't work. Tears

clouded my eyes as my heart drummed the fear Mama had stirred in my chest. Suddenly she smiled with a new thought.

"You remember once when you were a little girl you came to me with a dead baby bird and I told you the mother bird had probably thrown it out of the nest?"

"Yes, Mama. I remember. We buried the bird under the pecan tree."

She laughed. "Yes, we did. Anyway, honey, that mama bird did what she thought was best for the other babies. You couldn't accept that then. What I was trying to explain was the mama bird had to think more of her babies than she thought of herself, of her own sadness.

"That's something you're going to have to do, too. I'm just telling you this now because I want to prepare you for it, prepare you for what you have already decided to do."

I nodded, deep sadness continuing to cloud over the sunshine that had been in my heart. "You told me I had to give up my innocence, Mama." I nodded. "Now I understand."

"I'm sorry, honey. I should have talked to you more about this before you made your decision, but you were so determined it was the right decision."

"I still believe it's the right decision, Mama," I said softly.

She closed her eyes and sighed again. "Okay," she said, patting my hand. "If you really still believe that, you'll be fine then. And I'll be with you every moment."

She left me some of her herbal medicines and told me she would be coming around more often now that I was in what she called the downhill slide. She remarked that the baby had dropped more than she anticipated it would during the past few days. I did feel like a duck waddling around my small room and pulling myself up the short stairway. Lately I had to stop in the middle and catch my breath. I thought I looked pretty comical and burst out laughing at myself a few times.

But our conversation did leave me in gloom, and despite the prohibitions against it, after Mama left I decided I had to look out on sunlight and nature. I lifted the shade on the window to permit the sunshine to warm my face.

Suddenly, out of nowhere, it seemed, I saw a boy about fifteen come walking on his hands over the lawn on my right. He paused and did a flip, landing on his bare feet; and when he did, he set eyes on my window. I backed away quickly, but when I sat forward to peer out again, he was still there, standing fixed in the same spot, gazing up at my window. I feared he had spotted me. My heart pounded, anticipating trouble. If Gladys Tate found out, there was no telling what she would do in the state of mind she was in these days. The closer I was getting to delivery, the more nervous and irritable she became.

I moved to the side and stared down at the boy, while he studied the window, trying to decide if he really had seen anything, I imagine.

Then he smiled and did a back flip. He went down on all fours and kicked his feet up to start walking over the grass on his hands again. He turned, folded into a somersault, and then jumped to his feet, spinning like a ballet dancer. He had such grace and smoothness to his gymnastics, I couldn't help but watch. He smiled, stopped, and magically turned into a puppet right before my eyes.

His shoulders rose as if strings were attached and his arms lifted, his hands limp. His hands snapped up and he jerked his head to the right and then to the left. Before I could shake my head with amazement, he folded his body, imitating a puppet when the strings were released. As soon as his knees touched the grass, however, he snapped back up, his arms floating higher, his hands flapping. I couldn't help but laugh. It came out of my mouth before I could subdue it, but if he heard me, he didn't acknowledge. Instead, like the puppet he was pretending to be, he started to walk to his right, his legs lifting and falling with that jerky movement reminiscent of a doll on a string. He went around in a circle and then, once more, as if the strings broke, he folded to the ground and just lay there, frozen, his eyes like glass.

Finally he widened his eyes, smiled, and stood up. He gazed at me, but he didn't speak; at least, not with his tongue. Instead, he began a series of hand movements I recognized as sign language. I watched him for a while and saw the frustration when I didn't respond. Even if I could, I didn't know how to respond, what to say. Was he asking questions?

I had seen only one deaf-mute before, Tyler Joans, who was eight when I met him. I had accompanied Mama on a *traiteur* mission to help Tyler's mother cure some warts on the back of her hands. The Joans family had moved away years ago and I never really got to know Tyler.

The boy below stopped and put his hands on his hips. He was a tall, slim boy with dark brown hair that fell over his forehead and covered his eyes. He wore a pair of khaki pants and a faded white T-shirt torn at the collar.

I pulled back when a tall, stout man appeared carrying a rake. I heard him call, "Henry!" and then I saw him gesture angrily for the boy to follow. "Finish your chores, boy, before I tan that hide of yours." He signed quickly with his big hands and shook the rake in the air.

The boy put his right forefinger on the top of his head, spun like a top, and shot off to the left, leaving me laughing quietly and wondering who he was.

That night I was drawn back to my window when I thought I heard my heron strutting about on the balcony railing. But instead of the nocturnal bird, I found a bouquet of hyacinth tied with a string. Their lavender blossoms were pale with a dab of yellow on the center petals, surrounded by some green leaves. Surely my heron hadn't brought them, I thought, and gazed into the darkness, looking for my benefactor. How could he have known how much I missed the sight of hyacinths stretching from bank to bank on the bayou surface? I was always fascinated by the way their color changed with the changing skies, shimmering from lavender to dark purple with a passing cloud. To me it was as if a divine artist were continually repainting the world in which I lived. It was never boring, never without surprise. And that was something I craved dearly these past, dark months, shut away from the world I loved.

"Thank you," I called into the night, and waited for a response. All I heard was a mournful owl and the monotonous symphony of cicadas.

I hid the flowers under my bed before I went to sleep. I would have to cast them out the window when they faded and dried so Gladys Tate wouldn't find them. She lingered in my room the next morning after she had brought my breakfast, and I was afraid she knew that the strange but fascinating boy had seen me.

She sniffed and gazed about suspiciously as I ate. "Smells like spring in here suddenly," she said.

"The breeze is bringing in the scent of flowers," I replied, but she stood there, still looking suspicious.

"Octavious hasn't been here, has he?" she suddenly demanded. Terrified of what would happen if I said yes, I shook my head quickly. "That cologne he wears turns my stomach now."

"No, madame."

"Stand up," she commanded. I put down my fork and did so. She stood beside me, her hands on her stomach, and gazed at mine. "You're lower down than me." She molded her padding a bit. "Any other pains?"

"No, madame."

She sniffed the air again and then, just before leaving the room, paused, her eyes focusing on something on my floor. She knelt down and picked up a tiny piece of the hyacinth stem.

"What's this? How did it get here?" she demanded.

"What? Oh. There's a heron that lands here every night," I said, pointing to the window. "She dropped some leaves and sticks."

Gladys screwed her eyes on me for a moment and then smirked. "I'll have my gardener check on that. We don't want a bird attracting attention to the window. Just stay away during daylight."

"Yes, madame," I replied, and went back to eating my breakfast. She paused for a moment, but I didn't look at her and she finally left.

Later that morning, I heard a tapping sound on the small balcony and against the window. I approached it slowly and observed that someone was throwing tiny pebbles. Peering between the curtain and the window frame, I saw my young gymnast again. This time he was juggling apples and got up to five. He stopped and offered me one.

I smiled and nodded. "I'd love one," I said, expecting he would throw one up, but in a flash he disappeared beneath the balcony. Moments later, I heard him scaling the wall and saw his hand on the railing. He pulled himself up and over as quickly as a cat. It surprised and frightened me.

"You mustn't come up here," I said, shaking my head emphatically. I gestured for him to go back down. "Please."

He tilted his head and wore a grimace of confusion. Then he smiled and pointed to himself. "Hen ree," he said, and pointed to me. When I didn't respond, he repeated the action. "Hen ree."

"I'm Gabriel," I told him.

He shook his head and held up his hands, pointing his right forefinger at his left palm.

"I don't know how to say anything with my hands. Please, you must climb back down. No one is supposed to know I'm here." I shook my head and pointed to myself.

He shook his head as if I had said something in a language foreign to him and then boosted himself up on the railing. When he stood on his hands and turned to me, I cried out in fear, but he just laughed and bounced back onto the balcony. He squatted and started to speak in sign language again. He was explaining that he was mute and could speak only with his hands. He continued these rapid hand movements, carrying on what I was sure was a long conversation.

"I'm sorry," I said. "I don't know how to read your hand movements." I held up my hands and shook my head.

He paused and stared at me a moment, thinking. He had eyes the color of pecan shells and moved nervously from side to side as he struggled to think of another way to communicate his thoughts.

"You've got to go back down," I said, waving toward the railing. "Madame Tate will be angry. She doesn't want anyone to know I'm here, understand?"

He raised his eyebrows and grimaced, holding out his arms, questioning. It was so frustrating. I started to act out what I was telling him, first trying to look like Madame Tate, scowling, walking about with exaggerated authority, shooing him away. All I did was make him laugh.

Finally I pointed to myself and then put my finger on my lips and shook my head. He seemed to understand what I was telling him now.

"It's just something that has to be kept secret. Please don't tell anyone I'm here." I wagged my head and kept my finger on my lips.

He smiled. Keeping a secret was obviously fun to him. He nodded emphatically and then his gaze fell to my stomach.

His eyes widened and then he put his right palm under his left hand and rocked his arms as if he had a baby in them.

"Yes," I said, nodding. "I'm pregnant and I'm going to have a baby soon."

I saw that he wasn't going to get off the balcony quickly, and I did enjoy the company, even if he was a mute.

"Do you work here for the Tates?" I asked, and pointed to the house and the grounds. To indicate work, I raised and lowered my arms as if I were chopping wood and then carrying something. He nodded and began to make gestures to indicate his work as a grounds person raking up leaves, trimming hedges and trees, planting. "Shouldn't you be in school right now?" I asked him. I pointed to him and then seized a book and held it up, pretending to read. Then I pretended to write. His face brightened.

"Skooo."

"Yes, school," I said, and pointed to him.

He nodded, and from the expression on his face when he did so, I understood that he wished he were in school rather than working. He shook his head and went through the gestures to indicate grounds work again. Then he leaned in to look at my room. It filled his face with more curiosity. This close to him, I could see the tiny freckles under his eyes and a small scar under the right corner of his lower lip. He had a complexion almost as dark as Daddy's, and I could see that although he was slim, his arms were lean with muscle and his stomach rippled like a washboard. His eyes raked over the dolls and then settled on my embroidery. I could read the question in his face and gestures.

"Yes, I do that," I said. He nodded, smiling and gesturing with appreciation. "Thank you. Of course, if I didn't keep busy, I would go nuts," I mumbled. He looked confused, so to indicate going nuts, I rolled my eyes and shook my head. His right eyebrow lifted. I was sure I looked absolutely ridiculous going through these silly gestures.

He began to sign another question.

"I don't understand. I'm sorry." He worked harder and I caught on.

"Oh. I can't go down." I shook my head. "I told you," I said, pointing to myself and then holding my finger on my lips. "I'm here secretly." He grimaced with confusion, but he didn't let it linger. He indicated he wanted to crawl through the window. "No," I began, but he was already moving into the room. When he stepped down, I brought my finger to my lips and pointed to the floor to indicate he must keep very silent. He understood and walked with exaggerated care. It brought a smile to my lips, which made him smile.

Then he reached up as if he were plucking a fly out of the air and opened his hand in front of my face to reveal a single costume-jewelry pearl in his palm.

I laughed. "How did you do that?"

He held up his forefinger and closed his eyes, pretending great concentration. After a moment he opened them and reached behind my ear to produce another pearl.

I laughed again. "You're very good."

He nodded, smiling emphatically.

"Who taught you all this?" I pointed to the pearl and then to him. Either he was very bright or he could read lips, too.

"Graaaaa pppaaa," he said.

"Your grandpere?"

He nodded.

"Why can't you speak well?" I asked, pointing to my tongue and making movements with my fingers. He pointed to his ears, to his stomach, and then to himself.

"You were born deaf," I concluded.

And for the first time, I wondered how my baby would be at birth. Would he or she have some defect? Mama thought it was all going well, but even Mama couldn't know everything. If a baby was born out of unwanted sex, would that affect the baby's health? I had been treating my pregnancy like an illness, not wanting this baby inside me until the

141

moment I felt it move. I'd hate to be responsible for it being born deaf or blind. I should have asked Mama, but then I thought she might not tell me the truth for fear I would sit here and worry all day.

Henry walked about the room, gazing at the dolls and then at the dollhouse, which intrigued him. He knelt beside it, and after a moment, he, too, realized it was the Tate house. He pointed to it and to the walls.

"Yes." I nodded.

Just then the baby kicked especially hard and I moaned and seized my stomach. I had to sit on the bed. Henry gazed at me with curiosity and concern, and I pointed to my stomach and then kicked my foot in the air. His eyes widened. The baby kicked again and again. I gestured for Henry to put his hand on my stomach. He stood up slowly and approached timidly. The baby was still very active. When Henry hesitated, I reached out, took his hand, and brought it to my stomach. I held his palm there as the baby continued to kick.

Henry's face beamed with excitement. Then he laughed. He started to sign question after question. I shook my head. He pointed to my stomach and then made his arms into a cradle.

"Oh, you want to know how long?" I thought and counted out six fingers to indicate six weeks, but I could see that he didn't know whether I met six days or six months.

He folded his legs and sat on the floor in front of me, gazing up with wonder. When I looked into those dark brown eyes, I could just sense the myriad questions that swirled around in his pool of curiosity. Who was I? Why was I being kept secretly here? Perhaps he even wondered about the father of the baby. What did it all have to do with the Tates?

He pointed to himself again and again said, "Hen ree," and pointed to me. He wanted to know my name very badly and was frustrated with my inability to tell him. I thought for a moment, wondering how far he had gone in school. I rose, got a pen and paper, and wrote out my name. He sat beside me on the bed and looked at the notepad. Then I pointed to my lips and sounded out my name slowly.

"Ga-bri-el."

He shook his head. I realized he was illiterate. Perhaps he had never been to school or had only been there a very short time, I thought. How sad. I considered the problem and then I took his right hand and put it on my throat. His eyes were filled with surprise and even a bit of fear. I repeated my name, hoping he would feel the vibrations. Then I put his hand on his own throat. I did it a few times until I saw a brightness in his eyes.

"Ga."

"Go ahead, that's it," I said excitedly.

"Ga brrr."

We repeated the action until he pronounced the second syllable and then finally the third. I gestured for him to say it faster.

"Gabri . . . el."

"Yes, that's my name."

Henry beamed, enjoying the success. Then, timidly, he put his hand on my stomach again. The baby was much quieter. Henry looked disappointed.

"He's sleeping," I said, and laid my head on my shoulder and closed my eyes. Henry lifted his hand away, but stared at me sweetly. I smiled at him and he smiled back. Then he stood up slowly as if he saw something in the air. He walked with exaggerated steps, like a hunter sneaking up on prey. He snatched the invisible air and brought his hand to his nose, taking in a delightful whiff. I laughed and he bowed, put his hands behind his back, stepped before me, and then voilà . . . he held out a tiny magnolia blossom.

The astonishment on my face filled him with delight. I assumed, of course, that he had been keeping it under his shirt, but it was such a wonderful surprise, I couldn't keep the tears from filling my eyes.

"Thank you," I said. "And thank you for the hyacinth you left last night."

He bowed and looked toward the window.

"You have to go back to work?" I mimed the raking of leaves, pruning of hedges, and he nodded. I held out my hand for him to shake. "Good-bye," I said. "Thank you."

He held my hand for a moment and then went to the window. "Be careful," I said. He smiled and then slipped out the window and over the railing, scampering down the gutter pipe like a squirrel. I glanced out the window and saw him hurrying around the corner of the house. Like a dream, he was gone, but my magnolia blossom smelled delicious and wonderful. It filled me with pleasing memories and allowed me to close my eyes and put myself back in the bayou, free to enjoy the world I loved, at least for a few moments.

That night, right after I had my dinner, I had my first bad fright. I hadn't been sleeping well these last weeks as it was. The baby was so active. When I woke each morning now, I felt as if I had been dragged through the swamp by my swollen feet. Just sitting up took great effort, and my lower back ached so badly at times, I had to lie down again. When Gladys saw these symptoms, she began to imitate them to the point that she looked worse than I felt when I saw her in the mornings. She complained about coming up the stairs as if she were really carrying a child, groaning and rubbing her lower back.

One morning when she had gone on and on about how poorly she was sleeping and how hard things were for her, I exploded.

"What are you talking about? Why are you complaining so loudly? I'm the one who is actually suffering," I cried.

She stared at me with ice in her eyes. "How can you say you're the one who is actually suffering? Do you think just pretending to be pregnant is enough? I have developed the ability to feel what you feel, know what you know, and yes, suffer what you suffer so that no one, no one, do you understand, will doubt this child is my child, this birthing is my birthing. And I'm doing all this for you, as much as for the baby. I don't expect any gratitude. That's too much, but at least I expect understanding. So stop your whining. You're not the only one who's been put through turmoil," she snapped, and pivoted to leave me in the wake of her outburst.

I was too uncomfortable to care. Mama told me much of it was normal, but I could see some concern in her face during the last visit, so after dinner, when I felt a little nauseous, I lay down. As soon as I did so, I was stricken with contractions and I became very frightened. I kept waiting for them to end, but they remained intense.

"Mama!" I moaned. What was I to do? The cramps were so severe, I could barely sit up. The pain continued, seizing me in a vise that reached around my stomach to my back, shortening my breath. I gasped, unable to even call out for help, not that there was anyone who would hear me.

Then I heard a sound behind me and turned to see Henry crawling in the window. He saw the grimace of pain on my face and immediately became concerned. He rushed to my side, signing questions, but I didn't have the patience. I groaned and gasped when my stomach tightened again. I had my skirt raised and Henry put his cool palm on my stomach. The tightness amazed and frightened him, too. He pulled his hand away as if my stomach were on fire. I took deep breaths and waited. It eased and I let out a sigh of relief.

Drips of sweat trickled down the side of my face. Henry found a handkerchief and returned to my side to dab my face. I looked up at him and smiled. My bosom rose and fell with my heavy breaths. I've got to send for Mama, I thought. She didn't tell me this would be happening now. It's too soon.

With his hands and gestures, Henry asked if my baby was coming now.

"I hope not," I said. "It's not supposed to." I shook my head, but another contraction began. And then I felt the warmth leaking down the inside of my thighs. The sensation sent an electric shock up my spine and into my heart. Henry saw the look of terror on my face. Slowly I raised my head and ran my fingers along my leg. When I looked at my fingers, I screamed. They were covered with blood. The expression of fear on Henry's face reinforced my own.

"Mama!" I cried. I struggled to sit up, and Henry rushed to help me. "Madame Tate!" I screamed her name. The blood continued to flow. I tried to walk, but the cramps were so severe, I had to double up. Henry helped me back to the bed. With all the strength I could muster, I screamed again.

"Madame Tate!"

Silence followed. Where was she? She always claimed that every little sound made in this room could be heard below. She said she heard me moaning in my sleep. Why couldn't she hear my scream?

Henry pointed to himself and then to the door, asking me if I wanted him to go for help. I did, but that also meant Gladys would know he had been here and my secret presence and pregnancy had been discovered. Gladys would be furious. I really didn't know what would be worse: my waiting for her to eventually hear my cries or having her know about Henry. With the contractions coming faster and lasting longer each time, and the blood still streaming down my leg, I felt I had no choice. I took a deep breath and nodded, gesturing for him to go fetch Gladys Tate. He opened the door and bounded down the stairs.

I took deep breaths and waited, but instead of hearing Gladys coming, I heard Henry rattling the door below. He came running back up to tell me the door below was locked.

"What? Why?" I moaned.

Henry gestured that he would go out the window, down and around to the front of the house for help.

"No, wait," I cried, holding out my hand. He stood, confused as I tried to think sensibly in the midst of suffering another contraction. It nearly took my breath away. I gasped and gasped, but I kept my hand up so Henry wouldn't leave the room.

I realized that if Henry went busting into the house exclaiming my predicament, everyone would know about my existence up here and the secret would be exposed. Gladys wouldn't go through with her part of our bargain. I couldn't let Henry do that.

When the contraction eased, I gestured for Henry to hand me the pen and paper on the dresser. He did so and I wrote, *Mama, come quickly.* Then I folded the paper and on the outside wrote, *For Catherine Landry. Urgent.* I pointed to it.

Henry looked at it, but shook his head. He didn't know who Mama was. But then he smiled at me and gestured that he would find out and get the note to her. He patted my hand and headed for the window. In moments he was over the railing and gone. All I could do was hope that the deaf-mute boy would find a way to Mama.

Another contraction came, but it was of shorter duration. It was followed by a longer respite and then the next contraction was bearable. I took my washcloth and cleaned off the blood. It seemed to be easing, too. As my pain and fear lessened, my thoughts went back to the door below and my anger intensified. Why had Gladys Tate decided to lock that door tonight of all nights?

Stronger, breathing easier, I rose and went to the top of the short stairway.

"Madame Tate!" I called. "Madame Tate!"

It seemed quite a while before I got any response, but finally I heard the key being turned in the lock below and saw the door open. She poked her head in and cried in a raspy loud whisper, "Quiet! You hear me? Quiet."

"Madame Tate, I need you right now," I said.

She stepped into the hallway and gazed up at me. I was still clutching my stomach and bent over. She was in a formal black dress, wearing a diamond necklace with matching teardrop diamond earrings. Her hair was done up and she wore makeup.

"Lower your voice," she said.

"Why did you lock that door?"

"We have guests, business associates and their wives. I had to show them the house and be sure you didn't just pop out of here. What's wrong?"

"I'm bleeding," I said.

"What? Bleeding?" She paused. "We're bleeding!" she exclaimed, her face in a twisted grimace.

"No, we're not bleeding. I'm bleeding and I've been having contractions. Something's not right. Something's happening," I said.

"Oh, dear me. I have these guests. What will I do?"

"I've sent for Mama," I blurted without thinking. I was so

147

angry about her worrying about her guests and not me, I didn't think.

"Sent for? How?"

"Never mind right now. Something's seriously wrong, I told you. I think I'm having a premature delivery. The contractions are starting again."

"Oh!" she cried, and suddenly clutched her own false stomach. "Contractions! Bleeding! The baby's coming. . . . Octavious," she yelled. *"Octavious."* She turned from the door, her hand on the jamb and bent over.

"Madame Tate!" I called. "Wait!"

"Octavious!"

She slammed the door shut and then I heard the key turn in the lock.

"Madame Tate!"

Another contraction came rushing through me, tightening so quickly this time, it felt more like a punch in the stomach. My lungs hurt. I tried to take a deep breath. The room began to spin and I lost my balance, stumbling to the right. I fell sideways, landing on the dollhouse, splintering and smashing it with the weight of my body, just managing to break my fall a little with my extended right hand. But the contraction was so severe, I couldn't get up. I lay there, sucking in air.

This close to the floor, I could hear the commotion below: footsteps followed by shouts and exclamations, Octavious's voice, the voices of servants, guests, and then Gladys Tate's moans. With her bedroom right below, I was able to hear her screams. I heard her scream, "Blood! Contractions!"

My own contraction subsided again. I struggled to sit up and then I crawled and pulled myself back to the bed. During my moments of relief, I prayed for Mama's imminent arrival and I asked God to forgive me for any sin I might have committed.

"Don't punish the baby," I pleaded.

When my next contraction came, I muffled my cries by putting my closed fist in my mouth and biting down on my own knuckles and fingers. I couldn't let the people below hear me, not that they would have with all the noise Gladys Tate was making. It was strangely like an echo of my own inner screams and shouts of agony. It was as if my pain did travel through the floor and ceiling below until it settled in her so she could sense when to cry out and when to be silent.

I never found out how Henry located Mama, but he did so. To me it seemed like hours and hours before she came, but later I realized it had been less than an hour. I heard her voice below first and then I heard doors slam and the landing grow very quiet. Soon after, the door below was opened and Mama came bounding up the stairs. I was never so happy to see her face.

I told her what had been happening. She examined me and looked at the bloodstained sheets.

"What's it all mean, Mama?"

"The baby's been stirring a lot. He wants to be born sooner, honey."

"Is it going to happen right now?"

"It's hard to say exactly when, but maybe very soon," she replied. "Maybe very soon."

She sat back and held my hand.

"I think I passed out from one of the contractions, Mama. I can't remember how long ago the last one occurred."

She nodded and looked around, seeing the crushed dollhouse. "You fell on that?"

"Yes, Mama."

"You can't be alone anymore, honey, and I don't want you up here any longer. That woman wants you in her bedroom now anyway," she added with a smirk. "I don't know what she did to herself, but she had blood on her thigh when I was brought up to see her.

"Who was that boy you sent?"

"His name's Henry. He works here. I didn't want Gladys Tate to find out that he knows I'm here, but I was desperate, Mama."

"Let's not worry about what she thinks anymore, honey. I want to bring you downstairs where you'll be more comfortable and things will be easier."

I saw in her eyes that she was more worried than she wanted me to believe.

"Will the baby die, Mama?"

149

"Babies can be born early and be strong, honey."

"But it's usually the other way, isn't it? It's my fault," I moaned. "I wanted to be out of here so much, I forced the baby to hurry."

"Nonsense," she said.

"It doesn't deserve this. It's not the baby's fault. It didn't ask to be born this way," I wailed.

"Gabriel, stop this right now," Mama commanded. Her face was firm, her eyes blazing with authority. "If you're going to lie there and worry about everything, you'll make it harder and more dangerous for both you and the baby, honey. Trust in God now. It will be what He wants, and we will do what we can. This is not the time to be weak."

I swallowed back my tears and nodded.

"I'm sorry, Mama."

"Okay, honey."

"Where's Daddy?"

"Your father is downstairs with Octavious Tate. He jumped for joy when he heard you might be giving birth."

"Why?"

"Another opportunity to ask for more money. He's been sitting on this like a fat hen on a fat egg, just waiting for the chance to put the squeeze on the man. I don't know who to dislike more for it, your father for his greed or Octavious Tate for what he's done to you. The man deserves to have your father on his back, but your father ain't doing this to get justice for you. I'm sure he's gambled away most of what he took from the Tates and got himself into new debt."

"It just gets worse and worse, Mama. Maybe it was all my fault."

"Nonsense, and don't you even think it," she snapped. *"Oui,* it's hard, but like any storm, it will come to an end and the sun will shine again for you, Gabriel." She wiped away the strands of hair dampened with my sweat. "Can you stand or should I go get those scoundrels to help carry you down?"

"Let me try first," I said.

"Good girl."

She helped me to my feet.

"Suddenly my stomach feels ten pounds heavier, Mama, and my legs feel like two sticks of lard."

Mama laughed. I breathed easier. With her at my side now, I wasn't afraid.

Of course, I was still like someone poling in the canal for the first time. I was excited and anxious to do well, but I didn't know what was around the next bend.

8

Mine for a Moment

In anticipation of my arrival, Gladys Tate had Octavious move a second bed into her room and place it beside her bed. Mama said she heard Gladys tell Octavious to tell the servants it was for Mama because she would have to be at Gladys Tate's side continually now. Neither Mama nor I understood why Gladys didn't just move to another room for the time being or put me into one of the guest rooms, but the bed had been prepared and was waiting. After I entered the room, the door was kept locked and only Octavious and Mama were to be permitted into the room. Gladys insisted the curtains be kept closed, and of course, she ordered us to keep our voices down.

Gladys was impressed with how difficult it was for me to come down the stairs to her room and the effort it took to get me comfortably situated in the bed.

"How soon could it be?" she asked Mama, and Mama told her it could be hours or could be days.

"There's a strong possibility it's false labor and it'll take the remaining weeks it was meant to take. We'll have to wait and see," Mama said.

Nevertheless, Gladys told Octavious to go out and forbid the servants to come up the stairs.

"In fact," she decided after a moment's thought, "discharge them, all of them, immediately."

"Discharge them?"

"Give them all a week's holiday," she insisted.

"But what am I to say is the reason?"

"You don't have to give them a reason, Octavious," she replied haughtily. "They work for us. We give the orders. Just do it," she snapped, and waved her hand at him as if he were one of her servants, too. If there were any doubts as to which of them ran the house and their lives, those doubts died.

"But . . ." Octavious looked to Mama.

"I told you the bleeding doesn't always mean the birthing's coming shortly," Mama explained. "A week, two weeks, who knows?"

"I don't care," she told Mama, and turned back to Octavious. "Just have everyone out of the house. I don't want anyone to suspect anything. I've come all this way convincing people it is I who is giving birth. I don't want to risk any mistakes, any accidental discoveries," Gladys insisted.

"Which reminds me," she said, turning her steely eyes to me. "How did your mother know to come? How did you send for her?" she demanded. "And don't tell me you told some bird to go fetch her."

Fearful, I looked at Mama. Would Gladys Tate cast us out now, and with us all the effort, the suffering and loneliness, I endured for the sake of the baby and my family?

"Better tell her everything, honey," Mama said.

"There was this boy," I began.

"Boy? What boy?" she pounced, her eyes widening.

"I saw him doing handstands on the lawn behind the house, and he saw me in the window. But he won't tell anyone I'm here. He promised," I added quickly.

"What boy is this?" she asked Octavious. "Whom is she babbling about?" He shrugged.

"What's his name?" she asked me.

"Henry," I said.

"The deaf-mute," Octavious said, realizing. "Porter's son."

153

"Get rid of them," Gladys snapped. "Today. I want the whole family off the property."

"But, Madame Tate," I cried. "He's harmless. He won't tell anyone anything, and he did help by getting Mama. Don't punish his family because of me."

"I want them off my property before the sun goes down, Octavious. Do you understand?" she said, ignoring my pleas. He nodded.

"Don't worry. I'll take care of them," he assured her, but she didn't look calmed.

"You were not supposed to let anyone know you were here," she flared at me, looking red and very angry. "That was our bargain. Why do you think I've been going through all this discomfort and pain?"

"Pain? What pain?" Mama asked.

"Pain! Pain! I'm supposed to be the one giving birth. I can't be without aches and pains, can I? When you pretend as well and as accurately as I have pretended, you actually feel it. No one knows how much I've endured," she cried, her face in an ugly grimace. "I'm the one who's making all the sacrifices here just to make everything look right." She put her hands through her hair, looking as though she might tug out strands of it, and turned on Octavious, who stood by, watching with fear and amazement on his face, too. *"Why are you still here? Get rid of them! Now! All of this is your fault. All of it!"*

"All right, all right," he said, holding up his hands. "Calm down. I'll do it."

He ran from the room. I turned away so no one would see my tear-filled eyes. I shouldn't have looked out that window and I shouldn't have laughed and shown myself to Henry. Because of me, Henry and his family would be thrown out and have to go searching for a new place to live and work.

It seemed like anything and everything I did now would hurt someone. Was it because I had been touched by evil, deeply stained in my very soul? Perhaps no act, no matter how unselfish, could cleanse me of the pollution. Maybe I was better off staying away from the people I loved, I thought sadly. Look at what I had done to this innocent, handicapped boy. If I hadn't panicked, if I had waited for Gladys Tate instead of sending Henry for Mama, Henry's family wouldn't be destitute. I deserve to be miserable, I thought. Somehow, I make everyone else more miserable.

Mama saw the regret and guilt in my face and knew I was suffering remorse. "If she said the boy wouldn't tell anyone, he won't," she told Gladys. "Becoming hysterical over everything isn't going to help the situation right now."

"I am not hysterical," Gladys insisted in a raspy whisper, but her eyes still looked like two hot coals.

Mama shook her head. "I don't want Gabriel upset at this juncture. I want her to have a clear mind and concentrate. If indeed the baby's coming, we ain't out of the woods. Not by a long shot," she said, and for the first time, Gladys considered the baby's well-being rather than her own.

"Something can happen to my baby?" she asked anxiously.

"A baby crosses from one world into another. Nature pushes him out of the safe, happy one and into this turmoil. The road's always fraught with some danger. We don't need to add any of our own to it."

Suddenly Gladys Tate's eyes became two slits. The blood rushed to the surface of her cheeks and her shoulders lifted. She looked from Mama to me and then to Mama again, shaking her head very slowly as she took a step back. Then her smile came crooked and mean, her cold brown eyes shooting devilish electric sparks.

"You want the baby to die, don't you?" she said, nodding to validate her own suspicions. "Sure. You made this happen too soon with one of your secret herbal concoctions. You backward Cajun faith healers believe in all sorts of superstitions. You probably think the baby will curse you or something. Isn't that true? The baby's death would solve the problem for you, wouldn't it?"

"What? Of course not," Mama said. "What a terrible and ridiculous thing to say. If anyone is thinking like a backwards Cajun, it's you!" Mama retorted.

But Gladys continued to nod, convinced of her own suspicions. "I heard stories about *traiteur* ladies killing babies because they thought the babies were born with evil souls. When they wash them off, they deliberately drown them or they suffocate them when no one's looking."

"Those are stupid lies. No *traiteur* would take a life. We are here to ease pain and suffering and drive away bad things."

"You said it. There. You said it," she accused, pointing her right forefinger at Mama. "Drive away bad things. If you think a baby's bad . . ."

"A baby can't be bad," Mama insisted. "The baby can't be blamed for its own birth," she explained, "especially if the mother was raped," she added pointedly, but Gladys didn't look convinced.

"I'll be right here, every minute," she said, "watching your every move."

"Fine," Mama said. "You do that."

Gladys folded her arms across her chest and dropped herself into the pink cushion chair across from me.

"You can make yourself useful if you're going to stay here all the time," Mama told her. "Get me a basin of warm water and some clean washcloths. I want to bathe Gabriel."

Gladys Tate stared at us as if she hadn't heard a word. In fact, it was more like she was looking through us. Her eyes had turned glassy and she didn't move a muscle. There was just a slight twitch under her right eye. Mama studied her for a moment and then looked at me and lifted her eyebrows. She patted my hand and went to the bathroom herself to get what she wanted. I threw a glance at Gladys and saw she hadn't moved, hadn't shifted her eyes. They looked like they had turned to glass. It added chills to my already tense and shuddering body.

Mama washed me down and made me as comfortable as she could. All the while Gladys glared silently at us. She didn't change expression or move until Octavious returned. When he did, she spun on him as he approached.

"Well?" she said.

"They're all packed and gone. I gave them an extra week's wages so they wouldn't complain." He turned to Mama. "Your husband said to tell you he had to go," Octavious said.

"To play *bourre* for sure," she whispered to me. "The new money's burning a hole in his pocket. Couldn't even wait to see how you were," she added, choking back her anger. "Probably better he's not here anyway. He'd only drive us all mad," she added, more to calm herself than me.

I nodded, smiling. A small pain had begun in my groin and traveled into my stomach and around to my back, but I didn't say anything about it because it wasn't as bad as the early ones were yet.

"Well," Octavious said, looking from Gladys to Mama, "maybe I should bring something up for you to eat and drink. This may take a while, eh?"

"Bring some ice tea," Gladys ordered, "and make sure the front door is locked. Draw all the curtains closed, too. And don't answer any phone calls or make any."

Octavious closed his eyes as if he had a terrible headache and then opened them and turned to Mama.

"What can I get you?" he asked.

"Just cold water," Mama told him. She had brought along what she wanted for herself and for me.

He nodded and left, and soon after, the pain began to build.

"Mama," I said, "it's starting again."

"Okay, honey. Just squeeze my hand when you hurt. I want to know how bad it really is."

She pulled Grandmere Landry's silver pocket watch out of her bag and put it beside me on the bed.

"What's that?" Gladys demanded, looking over Mama's shoulder.

"Just a watch to tell me how long her contractions last and how much time between them. That's how I know how close we are to the birth."

"Oh," Gladys said, and placed her palms over her fake stomach. "It tightens, doesn't it? It gets as tight and as hard as a rock."

Mama just looked at her, nonplussed, which caused something in Gladys Tate's eyes to snap. A crimson tint came into the crests of her cheeks.

"I've got to know every detail, don't I? People ask

157

questions. I want to be able to describe the birth as if I really did have the baby."

"Yes, it gets hard," Mama said. "In the beginning for a very short time and then longer and longer as you get closer to delivering the baby."

"Yes," Gladys said, and grimaced as if she really did suffer a contraction.

Mama sighed and turned back to me with a small smile on her lips. She rolled her eyes. I wanted to smile back, but the pain grew longer and more severe.

"Take deep breaths," Mama advised.

"Is it coming? Is it coming?" Gladys asked, excitedly.

"Not yet, no," Mama said. "I told you. I'm not sure this is real labor yet, and besides, babies don't come busting into this world that fast, especially when a woman's giving birth for the first time."

"Yes," Gladys said, more to herself than to us. "My first time."

She waddled over to her own bed and sat down, her hands on her padded stomach. She closed her eyes and bit down on her lower lip. Mama wiped my face with a cold washcloth. I forced a smile and gazed at Gladys, who looked like she was breaking into a sweat herself. Watching her actions, her silent moans, her deep breaths, distracted me from my own pain for the moment. Mama just shrugged and shook her head.

Mama said the contractions were a good five minutes apart and didn't last long enough to be that significant yet, but it went on for hours. All the while Gladys Tate lay in her bed beside mine. She ate nothing, drank a little ice tea, but for the most part, just watched me and mimicked my every action, my every groan.

As the sun began to go down and the room darkened, my labor pains grew longer and with shorter and shorter intervals. I saw from Mama's face that she thought something significant was happening now.

"I'm going to give birth soon, aren't I, Mama?"

She nodded. "I believe so, honey."

"But it's too soon, isn't it, Mama? I'm barely eight months."

She nodded, but made no comment. Worry and concern were etched in the ripples along her forehead and the darkness that entered her eyes. My heart pounded. In fact, it had been beating so hard and so fast for so long, I was worried it would just give out. These thoughts brought more cold sweats. I squeezed Mama's hand harder and she tried to keep me calm. She gave me tablespoons of one of her herbal medicines that kept me from getting nauseous. Gladys Tate insisted on knowing what it was, and when Mama explained it, Gladys insisted she be given some.

"I want to be sure it's not some Cajun poison that works on babies," she said.

Mama checked her anger and let her have a tablespoon. Gladys swallowed it quickly and chased it down with some ice tea. Then she waited to see what sort of reaction she would have. When she said nothing, Mama smirked.

"I guess it ain't poison," Mama said, but Gladys looked unconvinced.

Suddenly it began to rain, the drops drumming on the window, the wind coming up to blow sheet after sheet of the downpour against the house. There was a flash of lightning and then a crash of thunder that seemed to shake the very foundation of the great house and rock my bed as well. We could hear the rain pounding the roof. It seemed to pound right through and into my heart.

Mama asked Gladys to turn on the lamps. As if it took all her effort to rise from the bed and cross the room, she groaned and stood up with an exaggerated slowness. As soon as she had the lights on, she returned to her bed and watched me enduring my labor, closing her eyes, mumbling to herself and sighing.

"How long can this last?" she finally inquired with impatience.

"Ten, fifteen, twenty hours," Mama told her. "If you have something else to do . . ."

"What else would I have to do? Are you mad or are you trying to get rid of me?"

"Forget I said anything," Mama muttered, and turned her attention back to me.

Suddenly, at the end of one contraction, I felt a gush of warm liquid down my legs.

"Mama!"

"It's your bag of waters," Mama exclaimed. "The baby's going to come tonight," she declared with certainty. Gladys Tate uttered a cry of excitement, and when we looked over at her, we saw she had wet her own bed.

Neither Mama nor I said anything. Our attention was mainly focused now on my efforts to bring a newborn child into the world.

Hours passed, the contractions continuing to grow in intensity and the intervals continuing to shorten, but Mama didn't look pleased with my progress. She examined me periodically and shook her head with concern. The pain grew more and more intense. I was breathing faster and heavier, gasping at times. When I looked at Gladys, I saw her face was crimson, her eyes glassy. She had run her fingers through her hair so much, the strands were like broken piano wires, curling up in every direction. She writhed on her bed, groaning. Mama was concentrating firmly on me now and barely paid her notice.

Mama referred to the watch, felt my contractions, checked me and bit down on her lip. I saw the alarm building in her eyes, the muscles in her face tense.

"What's wrong, Mama?" I gasped between deep breaths.

"It's breech," she said sorrowfully. "I was afraid of this. It's not uncommon with premature births."

"Breech?" Gladys Tate cried, pausing in her imitation of my agony. "What does that mean?"

"It means the baby is in the wrong position. Its buttocks is pointing out instead of its head," she explained.

"It's more painful, isn't it? Oh no. Oh no," she cried, wringing her hands. "What will I do?"

"I have no time for this sort of stupidity," Mama said. She hurried to the door. Octavious was nearby, pacing. "Bring me some whiskey," she shouted at him.

"Whiskey?"

"Hurry."

"What are you going to do, Mama?" I asked.

"I've got to try to turn the baby, honey. Just relax. Put your mind on something else. Think about your swamp, your animals, flowers, anything," she said.

A few moments later, Octavious appeared with a bottle of bourbon. He stood there in shock. Gladys was writhing on her bed, her eyes closed, moaning and occasionally screaming.

"What's wrong with her?" he asked Mama.

"I wouldn't even try to answer that," she told him, and took the whiskey. She poured it over her hands and scrubbed them with the alcohol, while Octavious went to Gladys's side and tried to rouse her out of her strange state, but she didn't acknowledge him. Whenever he touched her, she screamed louder. He stood back, shuddering, confused, pleading with her to get control of herself.

Mama returned to my bedside and began her effort to turn the baby. I thought I must have gone in and out of consciousness because I couldn't remember what happened or how long I was crying and moaning. Once, I looked over and saw the expression of utter horror on Octavious's face. I knew Mama was happy he was in the room, witnessing all the pain and turmoil, hoping he would see it for years in nightmares.

Fortunately for me and the baby, Mama had miraculous hands. Later she would tell me if she had failed, the only alternative was a cesarean section. But Mama was truly the Cajun healer. I saw from the happy expression on her face that she had managed to turn the baby. Then, guiding me, coaxing and coaching me along, she continued the birthing process.

"Push when you have the contractions, honey. This way two forces, the contraction and your pushing, combine to move the baby and saves you some energy," she advised. I did as she said and soon I began to feel the baby's movement.

My own grunts and cries filled my ears, so I didn't hear the grunts and cries coming from Gladys Tate, but I caught a glimpse of Octavious holding her hand and continually trying to calm her. She had her legs up and was actually pushing down on her padding so that it slipped off her stomach and toward her legs.

"He's coming!" Mama announced, and we all knew it was a boy. The room was a cacophony of bedlam: Gladys's mad cries (louder than mine), Octavious trying to get her to stop, my own screams, Mama mumbling prayers and orders, and then that great sense of completion, that sweet feeling of emptiness followed by my baby's first cry.

His tiny voice stopped my screams and Gladys's as well. Mama held him up, the placenta still attached and dangling.

"He's big," Mama exclaimed. "Big enough to do well even though he's early."

I tried to catch my breath, my eyes fixed on the wonder that had emerged from my body, the living thing that had dwelled inside my stomach.

Mama cut and tied the cord and then began to wash the baby, doing everything quickly and with an expertise born of years and years of experience, while I lay back trying to get my heart to slow, my breathing regular. When I gazed at Gladys Tate, I saw she was mesmerized by the sight of the baby. She didn't move. Octavious watched with interest and awe. Mama wrapped the baby in a blanket and held him for a moment.

"Perfect features," she said.

"Give me my baby," Gladys demanded. "Give him to me now!" she screamed.

Mama gazed at her for a moment and then at me. I closed my eyes and put my hand over my face. I had wanted to hold him, at least for a few moments, but I was afraid to say anything. Mama brought the baby to Gladys, who cradled him quickly.

"Look at him, Octavious," she said. "He is perfect. Little Mr. Perfect. We're naming him Paul," she added quickly, "after my mother's younger brother who died a tragic death in the canals when he was only twelve. Right, Octavious?"

He looked at us. "Yes," he said.

Mama didn't respond. She returned her attention to me. "How are you doing, honey?"

"I'm all right, Mama." I turned to Gladys. "Can I look at him? Please," I asked.

She glared fire at me and turned the baby so I couldn't view his face. "Of course not. I want you out of here immediately," she said. She looked at Mama. "Get her up and out of that bed and out of this house before anyone comes around."

"I can't rush her like that," Mama said. "She needs to recuperate. She's still bleeding some."

"Octavious, take them into another room, your room for all I care," she said.

Mama turned on her, her back up, her eyes blazing back. *"No!* You go into another room. My daughter will rest here until I say she's fit to leave, and that's my final word on it, hear?"

Gladys saw Mama was adamant. "Very well," she said. "I'll go to Octavious's room to recuperate and put the baby in his nursery."

"Exactly how to you plan to feed the infant?" Mama asked.

Gladys smiled coolly. "We've thought of that. I've hired a wet nurse. Octavious will fetch her now. Won't you, Octavious?"

"Yes, dear," he said obediently. He was unable to look at me and just gave me a passing glance.

"The child needs a lot of attention," Mama said. "Remember, he's premature."

"We'll have a real doctor here in less than an hour. He's someone we can trust, but I still want you out of the house as soon as possible," she said. She handed the baby to Octavious as she rose from her bed. Then she took the baby back quickly and started out of the bedroom, taking care, it seemed to me, to prevent me from getting a good view of him. She paused at the doorway.

"Once you're gone, I don't want to ever see you on this property again," she told me.

"She'd rather step in quicksand," Mama retorted.

Gladys smiled, satisfied. "Good," she said, and walked out with my baby. I hadn't even seen him for a full minute and he was already gone from my life forever. My lips trembled and my heart ached.

Octavious remained behind a moment, stuttering some apology and some thanks. "Take as long as you need," he concluded, his eyes down. Then he hurried to follow his wife and new child.

I couldn't help but burst into tears. Mama put her arm around me and kissed my hair and forehead, trying to comfort and soothe me.

"Is he really perfect, Mama?"

"Yes, honey, he is. He's one of the prettiest babies I've seen, and you know I've seen a few in my time."

"Will he be all right?"

"I think so. He was breathing strong on his own. It's good that they're having a doctor come around, though. Let me tend to your bleeding, Gabriel, and then let you rest. Damn your father for hurrying away. I could use him now," she muttered.

I lay back, exhausted, not only from the delivery, but from the emotional pain of having only a glimpse of baby Paul and then seeing him swept away from me instantly. Mama was right: This was a terrible feeling. I felt like I was trapped in a nightmare that would haunt me forever.

It was very late by the time I felt strong enough to get out of the bed and stand on my own. Mama held me cautiously and had me walk around the room first. Then she sat me down and went to find Octavious. Since Daddy hadn't returned, she had to ask Octavious to drive us home.

The house was dim and quiet with all the servants gone. I paused outside the bedroom door on the upstairs landing because I heard my baby crying. I looked at Octavious.

"I want to see him," I said.

He looked at Mama and then me.

"I won't leave before I do," I threatened.

He nodded. "Gladys is sleeping. She claims she's exhausted. If you're very quiet about it . . ."

"I will be. I promise," I said.

"Gabriel. Maybe it's better you just leave, honey. You're just prolonging the pain and . . ." Mama's voice trailed off.

"No, Mama. I've got to look at him. Please," I begged.

She shook her head and then turned to Octavious and nodded.

"Very, very quiet," he said, and practically tiptoed down the hallway to the nursery he and Gladys had prepared. The wet nurse was already there. She was a young girl not much older than me. Octavious whispered something to her and she left without glancing at me.

I stepped up to the cradle and peered in at baby Paul, wrapped in his blue cotton blanket, his pink face no bigger than a fist. His eyes were closed, but he was breathing nicely. His skin was so soft. It was a little crimson at the cheeks. All of his features were perfect. Mama was right. His fingers, clutched at the blanket, looked smaller than the fingers of any doll I had ever had. My heart ached with my desire to touch him, to kiss him, to hold him against my throbbing breasts filled with milk that was meant to be his and would never touch his lips.

"We better go," Octavious whispered.

"Come on, honey," Mama urged. She put her hand through my arm and held me at the elbow.

"Good-bye, Paul," I whispered. "You'll never know who I am. I'll never hear your cry again; I'll never comfort you or hear your laugh, but somehow, somehow, I hope you'll sense that I'm out there, waiting anxiously for the day I can set eyes on you again."

I kissed my finger and then touched his tiny forehead. My throat felt like I had a stone caught in it. I turned and walked away like one in a trance, not feeling, not seeing, not hearing anything but the cries of sadness inside me.

Somehow, we got down the stairway and out the front door to Octavious's car. Mama and I sat in the back, me lying against her, my eyes closed, my hand clutching hers. We slipped through the night like shadows indistinguishable from the blanket of darkness that had fallen heavily over the world. No one spoke until we arrived at our shack. Octavious opened the door and helped Mama get me out.

"I'll take her from here," Mama told him sternly.

"Will she be all right?" he asked. Mama hesitated. I felt her turn to him and I opened my eyes.

"She will be fine; she will grow strong again, whereas you

165

will grow weaker and smaller under the burden of your sin," she predicted. He seemed to shrink. "You be sure that that madwoman you call your wife treats that child with love and kindness, hear?"

"I will," he promised. "He'll have everything he needs and more."

"He needs love."

Octavious nodded. "I'm sorry," he muttered one final time, and went back to his car.

Mama turned me to the shack and we made our way to the door as Octavious drove away, the sound of his car drifting back into the darkness. I was still in pain. My legs felt so heavy and my head even heavier, but I didn't complain. I didn't want to make things any harder than they were for Mama. She managed to get me in the house and up the stairs to my little room. It was actually a bit smaller than the room I had been living in at the Tate house, but it was my room and full of my memories. It was like seeing an old friend again.

"It's so good to be home, Mama," I said.

She helped me into bed. "Just get some rest, honey. I'll be right here if you need me," she added. She said something else, but I didn't hear it. Before she had completed the sentence, I was asleep.

Daddy returned sometime before morning, bitter and angry about the money he had lost gambling, raging that he had been cheated and that he would get revenge. He was quite drunk and smashed a chair in anger, splintering it to bits. It woke me and sent Mama flying down to bawl him out. I heard the shouting, his pounding the walls and stomping the floor. I heard the door slam so hard, the whole shack shook, and then it was deadly quiet. My eyes shut themselves and didn't open again until the sunlight brushed my face. They fluttered open, and for a moment I didn't know where I was. After a moment, it all came rushing back over me, including the racket I had heard in the middle of the night. Mama, anticipating my awakening, stepped into the room with a cup of rich Cajun coffee, the steam rising from the mug.

"Got to get you up and about, honey. Women who lay around like sick people after they give birth usually develop some problem or another," she said.

I sat up and took the mug of coffee. "Was I dreaming or was Daddy screaming and yelling last night?" I asked her.

She shook her head. "I wish you had been dreaming. No, he came home in one of his drunken states again, claiming he had been cheated out of the money he lost at cards. Instead of finding a good job and working hard, he keeps trying to make a killing somewhere. He works harder at not working than he would if he worked," she added.

"Does he know I'm home?"

"I tried to tell him, but he wasn't hearing anything but his own stupid voice last night."

"Where is he?"

"He fell asleep in his truck last I saw, but when I looked out before, the truck was gone. No telling what he's up to now. I'll fix you some good breakfast, honey. You rise and stretch those legs, hear?"

"Yes, Mama. Mama?" I said before she left the room. She turned.

"Yes, honey?"

"What about . . ." I held my hands under my ample breasts.

Mama's face turned sad again. "I was going to tell you about that today," she said sadly. "You'll have to just pump it out or you'll develop milk fever."

"But the milk . . ."

"We can't offer it to anyone's baby, and that woman won't let Paul have your milk," she added bitterly. Mama hated waste in any shape or form.

"How long will I have to do this, Mama?"

"From the looks of you, a few weeks at least, honey. I'm sorry."

My tears burned under my eyelids. Every time I did this, I would think of my baby forced to drink the milk of a stranger while his mother's milk was poured into the ground. From the way I ached, I couldn't postpone it much longer either. After breakfast Mama showed me what to do. All the hot tears I had held back streaked down my cheeks.

They seemed to singe my heart as well as my face. I think Mama turned away and left me because she, too, was close to crying.

Afterward, when I lay back and closed my eyes, I thought I could hear my baby's cry. I recalled his tiny face and imagined what it would have been like to have his lips on my nipple drawing the milk from me. Perhaps, if I did this every time, it would make it a little easier, I thought.

Late in the afternoon, Daddy returned. He had a swollen left cheek and a black eye. There was a thin gash along the top of his forehead, and his clothes were wrinkled and marred with mud and grime as if he had been dragged through the swamp. He limped when he entered the house. Mama and I both looked up and gasped.

"What did you do now, Jack," Mama asked after a moment, "to get such a beating?"

"They ganged up on me is what happened," he wailed. "Those thieves down at Bloody Mary's." He fixed his eyes on me. "You shouldn't have left that house so fast, Gabriel. We coulda made them pay to have you leave."

"What for, Jack? So you can go and throw it away at some bar or over some game of chance?" Mama snapped. "Just like you did every other nickel?"

"It was what was coming to us," he declared, his arms spread.

"Us, Jack? How's it us? She's the one's suffered and she don't get one penny because you've gone and lost or spent it all, right? Or did you put away a little for her?" Mama asked, knowing the answer.

"I . . . I just been trying to build something for this family, is all. But I got cheated, so I went back to get back what's mine and they jumped me." He stared at me a moment. "They give you anything before you left?" he asked.

"No, Daddy," I said.

"And if they had, we wouldn't tell you, Jack Landry," Mama said.

"Ahh. Women never appreciate what a man tries to do for them," he complained, and sank in his worn easy chair. "I got to think up a new plan here. Those Tates can't get off this easy," he muttered.

"Instead of spending all this time sitting there trying to think up a new plan to rob people, why don't you go look for honest work, Jack?" Mama said, her hands on her hips. He gazed up, his nearly closed right eye twitching.

"What'cha talking about, robbing people? It's them who's robbed us, robbed our daughter of her pure innocence. Just like you not to see the point."

"I see the point," Mama said. "I been seeing it grow sharper and sharper, too. It's cutting right through here," she said, holding her hand over her heart.

"Ahh, stop your wailing. I need quiet and something to eat. I got to think hard," he said.

Mama shook her head and went back to her roux.

"I said I need something to eat!" Daddy cried. Mama continued to stir her gravy with her back to him as if he weren't in the shack. I rose and put together a plate of food for him.

"Thank you, Gabriel," he said, taking it and wolfing it down. "At least you care."

"Mama cares, Daddy. She's just tired. We're all tired," I said.

Daddy paused in his chewing, his eyes growing darker. "Damn if I'm going to sit here and watch my women suffer while that rich family enjoys the fruits of my daughter," he declared. "I'm going back, and this time I'm going to demand twice as much."

"Jack, don't you dare," Mama snapped.

"Don't tell me what not to do, woman. Cajun women," he spit. "Stubborn . . ." He put the plate down and rose.

"Jack Landry," Mama called, but he was already heading for the door.

"Just sit tight and let me be the man of the house," he yelled back, and shot through the door.

"Man of the house don't mean blackmailing people forever, Jack Landry," she called after him, but he didn't stop. He got into his truck and pulled away, leaving Mama and me standing by the door. "It's going to come to no good," she predicted, and shook her head. "No good."

169

Sure enough, late in the afternoon, the police arrived to tell us Daddy was in the lockup.

"He caused a terrible commotion over at the Tate Cannery," the policeman explained. "We're holding him until Mr. Tate decides whether or not to press charges."

Mama thanked the policeman for coming by to tell us.

"What are you going to do, Mama?" I asked after they left. "Are you going to go over to speak to Octavious?"

She shook her head. "I'm tired of bailing your father out of trouble, Gabriel. Let him sit in the clink for a while. Maybe it will drum some sense in his head."

That evening after Mama and I had a quiet dinner, we sat on the gallery and watched the road, both wondering if Daddy would come driving up. Mama was very troubled, and those worries made her look so much older to me.

"Things have a way of going so sour sometimes," she suddenly muttered. "I guess I'm not doing so well as a *traiteur*. I can't do much for my own family," she moaned.

"That's not so, Mama. You've done a lot for us. Where would I be without your help and comfort?" I reminded her.

"I should have looked after you better, Gabriel. I should have warned you about the evil that lurks deep within some people, and I shouldn't have left you alone so much. It's my fault," she said.

"No it isn't, Mama. I was stupid and blind. I shouldn't have been wandering around in my own dreamworld so much."

"It's been hard," she said. "It's like you never had a father. Be so careful about who you fall in love with, Gabriel," she warned. "It's so important. That first decision decides the road you'll follow, all the turns and hills, the twists and gullies."

"But, Mama, if you couldn't see the future, how can I expect to do so?"

"You don't have to see the future. Just don't be as trusting anymore and don't let your heart tell your mind to shut up." She rocked and shook her head.

"Will Daddy ever change, Mama?"

"'Fraid not, sweetheart. What's rotted in his heart has

taken hold of him. Now he's just a man to endure. Looks like you and I will have to tend to ourselves."

"We'll do fine, Mama. We always have."

"Maybe," she said. She smiled. "Of course we will," she said, and patted my hand. We hugged and then talked about other things until we both grew tired and decided to go to sleep.

I had to pump my breasts again and again; I conjured the image of baby Paul as I did so. I fell asleep dreaming of his tiny fingers and his sweet face.

Late in the morning Daddy returned. He was sullen and quiet, so Mama had to drag the story out of him. He did go back to Octavious to demand an additional payment, only this time, Octavious had his men throw Daddy off the grounds. Daddy sat in his truck, beeping his horn and creating a disturbance until Octavious called the police.

This morning the police told him Octavious wasn't making a formal complaint, but Daddy was warned to stay away from the Tate property. If he came within a hundred yards of it, they would lock him up again. He ranted and raved about how the rich controlled the law. He vowed to find a way to get back at them. Mama, refusing to talk to him, nevertheless made him something to eat. Finally he calmed down and talked about taking up Fletcher Tyler's offer to hire him as a guide for hunters in the swamp.

"Nobody could do it better than me. It pays all right and they give you tips," he told Mama. "Well?" he said when she didn't comment. "What'cha so quiet for? It's what you want me to do, honest work, ain't it?"

"I'll believe it when I see you actually doing it," she told him.

That set him on a tirade about how Cajun women don't give their men the support the men need. He raged about it for a while and then went off to trap some muskrats.

The day passed slowly into another hot and muggy night. Fireflies danced over the swamp water and the owls complained to each other. After I went up to my room, I sat by my window and listened to the cicadas. I wondered if Paul was asleep or being nursed. I imagined his little arms swinging, his excitement coming with every new discovery about his own body, and I turned to find a pen and some paper to write the letter I would never send.

Dear Paul,

You will probably grow up never hearing my name. If we do see each other, you will not look at me any differently from the way you look at anyone else. Perhaps, when you are old enough to realize, you might see me looking at you with a soft smile on my face and you might wonder who I am and why I am gazing at you this way. If you ask your parents about me, they won't tell you anything. We will remain strangers.

But maybe, just maybe, on a night as warm and as lonely as this one is for me, you will feel a strange longing and you will realize something is missing. You may never tell anyone about this feeling, but it will be there and it will come often.

And then, one day, when you're old enough to put the feeling into a thought, you will remember the young girl who looked at you with such love and you will realize there was something more in her eyes.

Maybe you will confront your father or your mother and maybe, just maybe, they will be forced to tell you the truth.

I wonder then if you will hate me for deserting you. I wonder if you will want to know me. I wonder if we will ever have a conversation.

If we did, I would tell you that when you were born, I thought it was glorious and I was filled with such love for you, I feared my heart would burst. I would tell you I spent night after night crying when I thought about you. I would tell you I was sorry.

Of course, you might hate your father and resent your stepmother, so I have to think hard before I tell you these things. It might be that for your sake I never do, because your happiness is far more important to me than my own.

I just want you to know I love you, and even though I didn't want it to happen, you became a part of me and always will be.

Love,
Your mother Gabriel

I kissed the paper and folded it tightly. Then I stuck it in my top drawer with my most precious momentos. It felt good to write it even though I knew Paul would never read it.

The moon poked its face between two clouds and sent a shaft of yellow light over the swamp. It looked magical for a moment, and I could swear I heard the cry of a baby. It echoed over the water and drifted into the darkness. I curled up in my bed and pretended I had baby Paul in my arms, his tiny face pressed up against my breast, my heartbeat giving him comfort.

And I fell asleep, dreaming of a better tomorrow.

9

A Tormented Spy

On warm nights when the moon peered through clouds no thicker than dreams, I would sit on Daddy's dock with my bare feet just above the water that lapped gently against the dark wooden posts, and I would listen for the cry of a raccoon. To me, a raccoon sounded like a human baby crying. I would think about Paul and how much and how quickly he had grown these past three years. Occasionally I would catch sight of him either in town with the Tates or at church whenever they would bring him along. I hoped God would forgive me, for I went to church more to catch a glimpse of my baby than I went for the service. However, most of the time the Tates would leave Paul at home with the nanny on Sundays. I learned Gladys didn't like being bothered with a baby when she was in public. I'd never complain, I thought.

The small patch of blond hair with which Paul had been born had become a full head of *chatlin* hair, the blond strands just a little thicker and brighter than the brown. His eyes were the soft blue shade of the sky in the morning when the sun was just climbing from the east and the sable darkness was sliding down the horizon on the west.

Whenever Gladys Tate saw that I had caught Paul's eye,

whether it be in town or at church, she would immediately toss him from one side to the other so her body would block me from Paul's sight. It was difficult for me to get close to him. Once, only once, when they were leaving the church and I had deliberately lingered behind at the doorway, I was no more than a few inches from him. I saw how graceful his hands were and how creamy pink was his complexion. I heard his sweet peal of laughter and when he turned his head my way, I saw him smile, his eyes brightening as if there were tiny blue bulbs behind them. I could see he was a happy baby, plump and content. I was glad about that, but I was also saddened by the thought that he might really be better off with the rich Tates, who could give him so much, and not with me, who could give him so little.

For this particular day at church, he was dressed in a little sailor's outfit and his shoes were spotless, bone white. There was no question he had everything he needed and would ever want. He looked healthy, alert, and loved. I was no more than a passing shadow in his presence, nothing more than just another strange face; yet his bright round eyes lingered long enough for Gladys to realize it. When she turned and saw it was I standing there, her cheeks turned crimson with anger. She hoisted her shoulders and quickened her step, practically flying past Octavious, who was surprised for the moment. She muttered something to him and he spun around to look at me, too. He grimaced as if he had just experienced a gas spasm in his stomach and then hurried to catch up to Gladys, who had already dropped Paul into the arms of their nanny as if he were nothing more than a rattlesnake watermelon. The baby was quickly shoved into the car, and a few moments later, they were off, the dust clouds rising behind their luxurious automobile.

I couldn't help wanting to see Paul as often as possible, to see the changes and the development in him. I cherished a newspaper photo of the Tates that had appeared in the local paper's society pages because Paul was just visible between Gladys and Octavious. I kept the clipping close to my bedside so I could look at it under the light of a butane lantern every night. I had opened and folded the clipping so many times, the words were practically illegible.

175

Mama knew the pain I was in, the way I tossed and turned at night regretting the agreement I had made. She could see the agony in my eyes every time someone appeared with a baby in her arms, whether it be one of our neighbors or a tourist stopping to buy something from our roadside stand. I volunteered to watch anyone's baby. I needed to be around the diapers, the pablum, the rattles. I needed to hear the giggles and the cooing and even needed to hear the cry for food or attention.

"I know why you upped and volunteered to watch Clara Sam's baby this afternoon, Gabriel," she would say whenever I offered. "You're just tormenting yourself, child."

"I can't help it, Mama. I'd rather have a few moments of pleasure, even though I know when Clara Sam comes to take her baby home, I will feel my own emptiness that much more."

"That you will," Mama predicted, and threw an angry glance in Daddy's direction.

Most of the time Daddy pretended none of it had happened. Whenever Mama made reference to the money he had gotten from the Tates and then squandered, Daddy would either act deaf or say she didn't know what she was jabbering about. We knew that even though he had been thrown off Octavious Tate's property and threatened with being arrested and put in jail, he had tried on at least two subsequent occasions to get more money out of him; but always to no avail.

"The man has no conscience," Daddy would wail. "Rich men like him who make their fortunes on the backs of honest laboring men never have a conscience."

"What honest laboring man might that be, Jack?" Mama snapped. "Surely you're not referring to yourself."

"And surely I am! Just 'cause I've been through some hard times, it don't mean I don't put in a hard day's work, woman. Look at me now. I put food on the table, don't I?" he protested.

Mama just shook her head and returned to weaving her palmetto basket. She couldn't argue. Daddy had been employed at his present job longer than he had at anything else I could remember. He was working as a guide for Jed

Atkins, who ran a swamp touring company and who provided boats, tackle, and guns for tourists and for rich city men who came to the bayou to hunt ducks or white-tail deer.

Jed was Daddy's favorite sort of boss. He drank a great deal of homemade whiskey himself, smoked, and cursed every fourth word. He lived alone in the rear of his gun, tackle, and boat shop, which was a wooden building so rotted, it looked like it would collapse the moment the vermin and insects that had made it their home decided to leave.

Despite his drinking, gambling, and fighting, Daddy had developed a good reputation as a swamp guide. It seemed he fit the bill because he looked and talked the way rich Creoles from New Orleans expected a Cajun swamp guide would look and talk. For an extra dollar, he would pose for their pictures: his hair wild, his beard straggly, his skin tan and leathery.

The truth was, Daddy always found them ducks or got them to get off some good shots at deer. Daddy knew his swamp; he was as much a part of it as a nutria or gator, but I hated the work he was doing because the men he guided were men who killed for sport and not for food or clothing. Some of them left the animal carcasses where they shot them because they weren't big enough or impressive enough trophies.

But between what Daddy made, or what he would bring to Mama before he gambled or drank away, and what Mama and I would make weaving baskets and blankets and selling jams and gumbo, we were doing better than ever. Daddy got himself a later-model truck, and Mama bought a new set of dishes from the Tin Man who came by in his van. On my nineteenth birthday, Mama had Daddy buy me a watch. It was silver with Roman numerals. It had a thin, black band. Daddy thought it was a waste of money.

"She can tell the time better than any watch just by looking at the sun," he explained. "No one reads the signs in Nature better than Gabriel."

"A young woman nowadays should have a nice watch," Mama insisted.

"I wouldn't mind it if she went places where some young man could consider her for to be his wife," Daddy said. "Actually," he added after mulling it over a moment and chewing on his lip, "I'm glad she has a watch. She can hear time tickin'. 'Fore you know it, she'll be twenty and unmarried. Then who'll come for her? Huh, Catherine? Not one of your well-to-do respectable town boys, no. And if one comes along and learns she ain't a virgin . . . she'll be lucky she gets one of my swamp rats."

"You stop that talk, hear, Jack Landry?" Mama said, snapping her forefinger at him, the way someone would snap a whip. "I'll put a curse on any man who talks poorly about Gabriel, hear? Any man," she emphasized, her eyes blazing.

"Well, she don't go to no dances; she don't talk to anyone at church, she don't go anywhere 'less you go, and all she does is follow you around on your *traiteur* missions. Most men round here think she's strange because of all the time she spends in the swamp. I know," he said, poking his own long right forefinger into his own chest so hard, I had to wince with the imagined pain. "I hear 'bout it all the time at the boathouse.

"'Can ya daughter really talk to gators, Jack? Does she really sleep on a bed of water snakes?'" he mimicked, wagging his head. "And what you doin' to get her lookin' presentable for a suitor, Catherine? Huh? Lettin' her walk around here barefoot with vines and wildflowers in her hair? Keepin' baby turtles, nutria, frogs, every varmint in the swamp, as a pet."

"She's a fine-looking young lady, Jack Landry. I don't have to do anything to get her suitable. Any man who doesn't see that doesn't deserve her," Mama told him.

"Ah, you're just as highfalutin as she is. Any man who doesn't see that . . . Ya got to know the garden's ready for some plantin' before you come around to put your seeds in," he said, pumping the air with his long arms. "That's what my daddy used to say."

"Swamp wisdom," Mama threw back at him. "And don't you go bringing any of those swamp rats around here to court her, neither, Jack. I want her to have a good husband, one who'll take good care of her, hear?"

"I hear. I hear. Trouble is, you don't hear. You don't hear the clock tickin'. Put your ear to her watch, too."

Lately, maybe because I was closing in on twenty, Daddy was complaining more and more about my failure to find a suitable husband. He threatened to write BRIDE AVAILABLE, ASK INSIDE on a sign and post it on our front lawn if I didn't find my own man soon. Of course, Mama told him she would rip it right out and smash it over his head if he tried to put such a sign on our lawn.

But the truth was, my mind wasn't on young men and marriage. Daddy was right. All I could think about was baby Paul and how I would get to see him again. Romance and love, marriage and husbands, seemed the stuff of movies and books, far-off like a thunderhead in the distance, bursting over someone else and not over me.

One afternoon because, my heart was so empty it had put a twilight gloom in my very soul, I poled my pirogue east on the canal and docked near the Tates' mansion. I found a deserted path to the road under a canopy of cypress trees and then crossed the highway and slipped through the forest to come around behind the house where I knew they had put up swings and a sliding pond. The Tates' nanny would bring little Paul out to play. I found a shaded spot under a large willow tree nearby and crouched down behind some branches and leaves of the vines that were woven through the fence to watch him laugh and giggle, stumble about and make discoveries, or just sit in his sandbox and push his toy cars.

Paul's nanny was a girl the Tates had imported from New Orleans. She had honey-colored hair, but a plump face and a pear-shaped figure. She waddled lazily behind the baby, her face revealing her annoyance with any extra effort Paul demanded of her. She didn't look all that much older than I was, and every time I saw her with the baby, she always looked bored. Whenever he played in the sandbox, she would sit with an emery board and work on her fingernails for hours, as if she were carving out some great marble statue, or she would be reading one of her movie magazines and chewing gum like a milk cow chewing on a blade of grass. Sometimes she would let him cry for nearly ten

179

minutes before she looked to see what was bothering him or what he wanted. It took all my strength to keep my lips sealed or keep myself from jumping up and running over to him. It was probably more painful to do what I was doing than not to be there at all.

But sitting undetected in the woods by the house, I could imagine myself there, beside him, maybe reading him a story or caring for his needs. Usually he played so well and so quietly by himself. I could see he was going to be a bright young man; everything attracted his curiosity. I was disappointed when his nanny realized the time and scooped him up to bring him into the house.

However, I returned the next day and the day after that, sometimes waiting for hours before she would bring him out. And when it rained, I was terribly frustrated, for I knew he wouldn't be out at all. Then one day while I was sitting in my spot watching him play, crawl, and toss the sand in his box while his nanny sat reading a magazine with her back to him, I spotted what I was positive was a cottonmouth snake slither over the grass and curl just beside the sandbox. It raised its triangular head ominously. Paul caught the movement out of the corner of his eye. He studied it a moment and then laughed and started toward the snake. The nanny continued to be absorbed in her magazine.

"No!" I screamed from the woods. She spun around. "He's going right for a cottonmouth snake. Quickly!" I screamed, and pointed. For a moment it looked like she wouldn't get over the shock of seeing me pop out of the woods, but she got herself together quickly enough to reach down and scoop him up just as the snake recoiled.

She screamed, too, and the cook came charging out the back door, followed by Gladys Tate.

I was too amazed to retreat quickly enough, so when the nanny started to explain and point, Gladys focused in my direction, her face filled more with disgust about me than the snake. The cook went around the sandbox and killed the snake with a metal rake. Gladys ordered the nanny to take Paul into the house. I turned and ran through the woods, my heart pounding all the way to my pirogue. I never poled up the canal as quickly to get home.

I was afraid to tell Mama what I had done and what I had been doing. Lucky for me, she was busy with a customer for her linens, so I was able to sneak by and go into the house and up to my room. When twilight fell, Mama called.

"You all right?" she asked after I appeared on the stairway.

"Yes, Mama. Just resting."

"Well, I'm not preparing anything new for dinner. We'll eat the crawfish étouffée. Your daddy sent word he won't be home for dinner. Claims he has work to do, but I know he'll be playing cards in some garage or barn and losing a week's wages."

She was so distracted about Daddy, she didn't notice anything in my face, but we no sooner had sat down to eat when we heard an automobile pull up to the front of the house. Whoever it was started to honk his horn and wouldn't stop until we appeared in the doorway. My heart sunk. I recognized the expensive, big Cadillac.

"Who is that?" Mama wondered, and then her squint changed to wide eyes and her face filled with annoyance. "What does that woman want?"

Gladys Tate got out of her automobile and strutted toward our shack with her familiar arrogant gait. I stood a few inches behind Mama, my heart thumping so hard, I was sure Mama could feel the pounding, too. Gladys looked taller in her black cape. She had her hair down. As she drew closer, she glared up at me with her cold brown eyes shooting hateful sparks. A white line was etched above her tightened lips.

"How can I help you?" Mama asked.

"I'll tell you how you can help me. You can keep your daughter off my property and away from my baby. That's how you can help me," she replied.

"Property?" Mama turned to look at me.

"That's right. She was there today, spying on my family, hiding herself in the bushes."

"Is this true, Gabriel?" Mama asked. "You were at the Tates'?"

"Yes, Mama, but I wasn't spying on her family. I was just . . ."

"Just what then?" Gladys demanded, her hands on her hips. She looked like a giant hawk about to pounce.

"Just watching baby Paul. I wanted to see how he plays. That's all."

"Oh, Gabriel," Mama said, shaking her head and fixing her eyes of pity on me.

"Everywhere I go, in town, to church, stores, every time I turn, I see her gaping at us. I won't have it, I tell you," Gladys said, her voice coming almost like the hiss of a venomous snake. It reminded me of what happened.

"If I wasn't there today, Paul might have been bitten by a cottonmouth. Go on, tell it all," I said with defiance. "Tell Mama how your nanny doesn't pay attention to the baby."

"That's none of your affair," Gladys replied, but a lot less firmly.

"The baby was almost bitten by a cottonmouth?" Mama asked.

"She exaggerates. There was a snake in the yard. My girl had plenty of time to protect the baby. Besides, it's none of her business," Gladys insisted. "We paid to keep you away and I intend to see that the deal is kept. The next time your wild daughter is seen on my property, I'll have her arrested, do you understand? And if she continues to follow us around wherever we go, I'll go see a judge and get a court order that will slap the lot of you into jail."

"I don't follow you around," I moaned.

"You've got nothing else to do with your meaningless life than seduce grown men and then follow their wives around," Gladys continued. "You should be in a convent, away from good and decent people."

"That's quite enough," Mama said. "You've made your point. Gabriel will never again set foot on your property, and if she sees you people in town or in church, she will look the other way."

"That's more like it. If you kept a tighter grip on her in the first place, we all might not be in this situation," Gladys added, her face flushed with satisfaction.

"I think you have it all a bit muddled," Mama said softly. "If you had given your husband the loving home a wife should provide her man, he might not have wandered into the swamp to rape my daughter."

"What?" She raised her shoulders. "If that's not the pot calling the kettle black . . . Why, your husband is probably the worst degenerate in the bayou."

"At least he doesn't pretend to be a saint and put on false faces in church," Mama retorted.

Gladys Tate's face reddened. She pressed her lips together and then lifted her right arm slowly to point her long, thin forefinger at me, the fingernail a silver shade.

"Keep her away or else," she warned, pivoted, and marched back to her car.

I couldn't swallow. I felt numb and incapable of movement. It was as if my feet had been nailed to the gallery floorboards. We watched her churn the lawn with her tires and then spin out and away.

"A horrid woman," Mama said. "It's like she has a snake eating away her heart." She turned and looked at me. "Gabriel, you have got to let go, honey. It's over; he's gone."

"Yes, Mama. I'm sorry."

"It's all right, honey," she said, embracing me and petting my hair. "It's all right. Let's have a good dinner and think about tomorrow."

I nodded. In the distance we could hear Gladys Tate's car squeal around a turn and accelerate. With it went my hopes of ever really knowing my own baby.

We never told Daddy about Gladys Tate's visit. He would have just ranted and raved and threatened reprisals. He might even have seen it as a new opportunity to extort some money from them.

He surprised us the next day anyway when he brought home a new dress for Mama and a new dress for me. Now it was her turn to think he was extravagant, for she could make a dress as good or better than any store-bought one.

"And what did you do, Jack Landry," Mama asked with suspicious eyes, "win a big pot at *bourre?*"

"No. This comes from all honest work, woman." He poured himself some lemonade and sat at the dinner table, smiling widely.

Mama gazed at me, looked at the new dresses, and then shook her head. "Something's up."

"Nothin's up. I was just thinkin' it was about time I took you and Gabriel out for a night. We should go to the *fais dodo* at the Crab House this Saturday night."

"Fais dodo? A dance? You want to take me to a dance?" Mama asked with amazement.

"And Gabriel. It's a good place for her to meet someone. I been thinking I ain't done enough to provide the opportunities for her."

Mama stared at him, still not believing what she heard.

"That's all, woman. It's no big thing here," he said, looking down quickly.

"You ain't asked me to a dance for a long time, Jack Landry," she told him. "Something smells rotten."

"What? Howja like them apples, Gabriel? A man asks his wife to a dance and she says it smells rotten."

"Well, I can't help it, it does," Mama said.

"Well nothing. I realized we ain't been out together for a long time and thought it was time I asked, is all."

"You ain't going to take us there and then get stupid drunk, are you, Jack?" she asked, her head tilted, her eyes scrutinizing him.

"On my honor," he said, holding up his right hand. "I have changed. You see that, don'tcha?" He nodded emphatically to drive home his own claim.

"You going to get cleaned up?"

"Absolutely. You'll see."

Although she was still suspicious, Mama agreed. She said she was doing so mostly for me. She tried on the dress. It was pretty and she was very pleased at how she looked in it. She made me try my dress on, too. She decided to take in the waist and let out the hem a bit, but otherwise, she thought Daddy had made amazingly fine choices.

"It's been so long since we did something like this," she told me. "It's against my better judgment, but I think I'll let myself go a bit and trust him."

On Saturday Mama washed and ironed Daddy's pants and shirt and then sat him on a rain barrel behind the house and trimmed his hair, beard, and mustache. He didn't put up his usual opposition. Scrubbed and pruned so even his fingernails turned from green-brown to clean, Daddy looked his handsome self again. It was as if a human being had peeled off this smelly, grimy swamp creature and stepped forward.

I watched Mama brush out her own hair and put her fancy combs in it, and when she put on the new dress and a little lipstick, she was about the prettiest woman in the bayou.

Daddy rained compliments over her. He said it made him proud, proud to be escorting the two prettiest women in the bayou. Mama blushed like a young girl. She helped me with my hair, and after I put on my new dress, she stepped back and said, "You might just catch yourself a handsome young man tonight. I hate to say your daddy could be right, but he could be."

I hadn't been to a *fais dodo* since I was in school. I hadn't made any new girlfriends, and most of the girls in my class had gotten married or were off living with relatives because there was someone nearby who would soon be marrying them. Evelyn Thibodeau had married Claude LeJeune, just as she had planned. He was doing well shrimping and owned two boats. Evelyn had a two-year-old boy and was pregnant with her second. Yvette Livaudis married her uncle's foreman, Philippe Jourdain, just as she had said she would, and then, a year later, gave birth to twin girls. I had just gotten a letter from her a month ago with a photo of her daughters inside. It took me a week to write back. I really had nothing new to tell her about myself, and it looked like her and Evelyn's predictions for me would come true: I would remain a spinster working beside Mama at our roadside stand forever.

The night of the dance was warm, although a bit overcast with sprinkles threatening. I remember as the three of us, all fancied up, stepped out of the house, I felt hopeful. Maybe we could be a family yet. Maybe Daddy was telling the truth about himself, about the changes in him. Maybe there was a new future for me, waiting out there, waiting like some beautiful pink rose, waiting to be plucked.

It wasn't until we were halfway to town that Daddy let out what his real motives were. Mama almost made him turn back. The truck took a big bounce. Daddy laughed and told us to hold on.

"Don't want to see my beauties messed up 'fore we get there," he said. "By the way," he added, "I went ahead and promised out Gabriel's first dance."

"What? What are you talking about, Daddy? Promised me to who?"

"Jed Atkins's brother's boy Virgil is visiting from Lafayette."

"An Atkins?" Mama wailed.

"Nothin's wrong with him. He's got a good job working for Jed's brother."

"And what sort of work is that?"

"They have a busy service station in Lafayette. Jed says the boy's a master mechanic, a natural with engines."

"Uh-huh," Mama said. "And what else about him, Jack?"

"Nothin' else." He paused. "'Cept one minor physical thing."

"Physical thing? What might that be, Jack? Spit out the whole truth," she added quickly. "I know how truth always tastes bitter in your mouth anyway."

"Zat so?" He hesitated. "Well, he has this birthmark on his cheek. Just a minor thing . . . a big blob of red, but I told Jed my Gabriel especially ain't one to look down on a man because he got a little birthmark on his cheek. Ain't that right, Gabriel?"

"Yes, Daddy," I said cautiously.

"That's what I thought."

"There's more to this story, Jack Landry," Mama said, focusing her eyes on him so intently, he couldn't look at her. "What is it, Jack?"

"Nothin' else. He's a strapping young man, tall, about my height, rich dark hair. . . ."

"How come he hasn't asked anyone to marry him, and how come he's not in the army, Jack? Mechanics ain't being excused."

"Well . . . he was in the army," he replied quickly.

"Was? What happened?"

"He got accused of something, but he swears he was innocent."

"Accused of what, Jack?" Mama said. Daddy hesitated. "This is worse than pulling ticks out of a child's hair."

"Attacking a nurse. Now, don't that sound stupid?"

"Attacking? You don't mean sexually, do you, Jack? You do," Mama said, answering her own question. "And you want Gabriel to meet this man after what's happened to her?"

"He was innocent. The woman was one of them, you know, one of them who likes men, all men, and he refused her, so she accused him and—"

"And they threw him out of the army?"

"After he served his time in the brig unfairly, yes. He's better off anyway. Probably would have been killed. He's a good boy, Catherine. I'll vouch for that."

"It's like the devil swearing for Judas."

"What's that?"

"Nothing. And how much did Jed say his brother would give you if you arranged this marraige, Jack?"

"How much . . . ! How could you accuse me of that?"

"Easy," Mama said. "Now I know why you were so eager to get us to this *fais dodo*," she added, her voice thick with disappointment.

"Why, that's a downright lie."

"Just tell us how much money you were promised and get it all out, Jack, so we don't discover nothing under a rock later."

"It ain't that he's paying me anything. He just said he would be sure we had something for our own nest egg. He's just a generous man when it comes to those who are members of his family," Daddy explained. "Now, ain't that a nice family to marry yourself into?" he asked.

"Jed Atkins's family can't be much to holler about," Mama replied.

"There you go, putting my friends down again. You don't let a man breathe, Catherine."

"Breathing is not what worries me about them; it's what they do with their breath and how it stinks," Mama said with a knowing, small smile.

"Nevertheless, Gabriel," Daddy said, leaning over to speak to me, "we ain't folks who look down on other folks because they've had some bad luck, are we?"

"No, Daddy."

"Tell your mother. It ain't like we don't have our own skeletons to keep in the closet, right?"

"Yes, Daddy."

"All I ask is you give the boy a chance. He's a shy one, which goes to prove he couldn't do what they accused him of doing in the army."

Mama smirked. "Why did I let myself get talked into this?" she muttered. "I should have known."

"Just relax, Catherine. Relax and let's have a good old time of it, no?"

Mama closed her eyes as the truck bounced and swayed, but I had grown very nervous.

The Crab House was a restaurant with a big ballroom in the rear. In it there was a small stage for the musicians who played the accordion, the fiddle, the triangle, and guitars. This *fais dodo* was one of the most popular of the year. People were streaming in and out the front door, and we could hear the zydeco music as we pulled into a parking space. Cajuns brought their whole family to dances like this. A room was set aside in the Crab House for the small children, many of whom would fall asleep while their parents danced or played *bourre*.

When we entered, there were those who knew Mama and were surprised and happy to see her attend. Many of them used the opportunity to complain about one physical ailment or another and get her advice. A number of Daddy's friends were gathered around the beer barrel, drinking and sucking on crawfish. I saw Jed Atkins wave to him and then saw Jed coax a tall, slim young man forward.

"Come on, Gabriel," Daddy said. "I'd like you to meet Virgil."

Reluctantly, with Mama flashing warnings and disapproval my way, I walked alongside Daddy. He and Jed shook hands vigorously, and Jed handed him a cup of home brew.

"Hello there, Gabriel," Jed Atkins said, turning to me.

"You sure grow'd into a fine young lady since I seen you last."

"I saw you just a few weeks ago, monsieur."

"Oh, yeah? Must've been a little under the weather. Don't recall." He laughed. "This here's my brother's boy, Virgil," he said, pulling him forward.

Half of Virgil Atkins's left cheek was covered with a patch of cardinal red skin, the ridges in it lifted slightly. He had dark eyes, a thin nose, and dark brown hair, the strands unevenly cut just below his earlobes. His lips were thin, too, resembling a stretched-out rubber band.

"Hello," he said. He sipped some beer.

"Well, ain'tcha going to ask her to dance, Virgil? If I were your age, I would," Jed said. "I used to do a mean two-step when I was younger," he added.

"Sure. You wanna dance?" He had a silly, soft smile, impish like a boy who liked to tease.

I gazed back at Mama, who was watching us while two elderly ladies jabbered in both her ears.

"I think I'll have something to eat and drink first," I said diplomatically.

"Fine. Go fetch her a plate, Virgil. Show her you got manners," Jed said. "These dances are more for you young people than for us old coots," he added, looking at me.

"Right," Virgil said. "Everything's better on a full stomach." Daddy and Jed laughed. Virgil and I walked toward the food.

"I'll getcha a bowl of gumbo," he said, elbowing in between two young boys. After he got us the food, he nodded toward an empty table. "I could getcha a beer."

"No. I'll just have a lemonade," I said.

"Don'tcha drink? All the young girls I know drink these days," he said with a wry expression.

"No," I said.

"You go to a lot of dances?"

I shook my head. He scooped the gumbo into his mouth quickly, his eyes fixed on me.

"You're a pretty girl," he said. "My uncle told me your daddy been keepin' you hidden away." He flashed that small smile again.

"No one's keeping me hidden away," I said sharply. He laughed.

"Why ain'tcha got a steady boyfriend then?"

"I did have," I lied, "but he had to go into the army."

"Oh?" His smile evaporated. "Uncle Jed didn't say anything about that."

"Not everyone knows. He writes me a letter every day."

"Where's he at?"

"I don't know. It's a secret."

He gazed at me suspiciously and drank some more of his beer. Then he smiled with confidence again, as if he had concluded I was making it all up.

"If I get up and get me another beer, will you still be here when I get back?" he asked.

"I haven't finished eating yet," I replied, which satisfied him.

I was nearly finished by the time he returned. He had brought me a glass of beer, too.

"Just in case you change your mind," he said.

"I don't like beer."

"Oh? Whatcha like, wine?"

"Sometimes."

He nodded. "You look like a girl who has rich tastes. Betcha that's why you're still not married, huh? You're waiting for a rich catch?"

"No. Money has nothing to do with it."

He laughed, skeptically. I felt sparks of anger catch in my chest and send a heat through my body.

"I'd like to return to the dance hall," I said, rising.

"Okay. I ain't the best dancer in the world, but I'm as good as most."

I froze for a moment. I hadn't meant I wanted to dance with him, but he obviously had taken it that way.

"You wanna dance, don'tcha?"

"Okay," I said. My tongue was so reluctant to form the word, I almost choked, but I got up and went on the dance floor with him. When I looked over toward Daddy and Jed Atkins, I saw them grinning from ear to ear. Mama, who was standing with some of her friends nearby, glared in their direction, the sparks flying out of her eyes. Daddy ignored her.

The truth was, Virgil wasn't a bad dancer, and I did enjoy the music. He took it as a sign I was comfortable with him and liked him.

"I play a mean washboard," he shouted into my ear, and laughed. "Me and some friends get together at the garage and fool around. We played for a *fais dodo* once."

"That's nice," I said. The music got louder and faster. Virgil started to sweat profusely. He unbuttoned his shirt and gulped some more beer.

"Let's get some air," he cried finally. I was going to excuse myself and join Mama, but she was into a heavy conversation with two of her friends and had her back to me, and I couldn't think of a good excuse. "Come on, let's have a smoke."

"I don't smoke," I said.

"So you'll watch me." He took my hand and I went out with him, looking back once to see Jed Atkins pat Daddy on the back and the two of them toast each other.

We went out the rear door into the parking lot. Virgil dug a pack of cigarettes out of his top pocket and pounded one out. He lit it quickly and threw the match into the air, laughing.

"Bombs away. So you like living here?"

"Yes," I said.

"I got my car right here. Wanna see it? I souped up the engine myself." He pointed to a customized automobile with a lightning streak painted in yellow across the driver's side. "It's a drag car, you know."

"I don't know much about cars."

"Whatcha think of it?"

"It's nice," I said with thick indifference.

"Nice? It's more than nice. It's a prizewinning vehicle. You know, I won five hundred dollars in races already this year?"

"I'm very happy for you," I said. "I think we better go back inside." I started to turn toward the door when he reached out to seize my wrist.

"You're very happy for me? Boy, you're sure stuck on yourself, ain'tcha?"

"I am not."

"You sound like you are." He flipped his cigarette into the air and it bounced over the parking lot, sparks flying every which way. He still held my wrist. "Whatcha want to hurry back inside for? Just a lot of old people and kids. Come on, I'll take you for a spin in my car."

"No, thank you."

"No, thank you," he mimicked, laughed, and then he put his left arm around my waist and drew me to him before I could resist. He pasted his lips to mine with a wet kiss as his hand fell to my buttocks and squeezed. I struggled to free myself, but he held on tighter, pressing his tongue into my mouth with such force, I couldn't even block it with my teeth. I gagged and finally broke free, wiping my lips with the back of my hand.

"How dare you do that?"

"What's the big deal? You've been kissed before, ain'tcha?"

"Not like that and not without my wanting to be kissed."

He laughed. "Don't put on airs. I know all about you, how you was pregnant with someone else's baby," he added. I felt the breath leave my body and my blood drain down to my feet. "It's all right. I don't care about it. I still like you. The truth is, I learned it's better to have a woman already broke in. Learned that in the army. We'll go for a ride and get to know each other and maybe we'll get hitched. Come on," he urged, stepping toward his car.

"I wouldn't go with you if you were the last man on earth," I said.

He laughed. "For you, I might just be. Once everyone knows about you, no one's going to come around asking you to marry him. You wanna be livin' with your ma and pa till they got no teeth? I can make you happy. Better than that other man did," he added with a leering smile.

"You're disgusting," I said, and pivoted.

"Last chance," he called, "to have a real man."

I didn't reply. I couldn't get away from him fast enough. When I stepped back into the dance hall, I looked desperate-

192

ly for Mama and spotted her talking to Evelyn Thibodeau's mother. She took one look at me and excused herself quickly to walk across the hall.

"Gabriel?" she said. "What's wrong, honey?"

Tears were streaming down my cheeks. "Oh, Mama," I said, "he told. Daddy told about me so that boy thought he was doing me a favor to ask me to become his wife."

She straightened as if her spine had turned to steel. When she looked for Daddy, she found he was already well on his way to a good drunk, all his buddies around him, laughing and guzzling beer and whiskey as fast as they could. She and I stood behind him. He stopped laughing and looked around fearfully for a moment.

"We're going home, Jack," she said. "Now!"

"Now? But . . . I'm jus . . . havin' some fun."

"Now," she said again.

He grew angry. "I ain't running home," he replied, "to hear you roll out complaints."

"Suit yourself," Mama said. She took my hand and we marched to the front door. "We'll walk home," she told me. "It won't be the first time I left him behind and I know it won't be the last."

10

Falling

Mama wouldn't speak to Daddy for days after the *fais dodo*. He didn't come home that night anyway, and when he appeared the next afternoon, looking as if he had slept in a ditch, she refused to give him anything to eat. She even avoided looking at him. He moaned and complained and acted as if he were the one who had been violated and betrayed. He fell asleep on the floor in the living room and snored so loud the shack rumbled. He woke with a jerk, his long body shuddering as if electricity had been sent through him. His eyes snapped open to see Mama hovering over him like a turkey buzzard, her small fists pressed against her ribs.

"How could you go and do that, Jack? How could you run down your own daughter for an Atkins, huh?"

He sat up and combed his fingers through his hair, gazing around as if he didn't know where he was and couldn't hear Mama screaming at him.

"We put Gabriel through all that horror living in that dreadful woman's house secretly just so no one would know what a terrible thing had happened to her, and you go and spill your guts out to the likes of Jed Atkins? Why? Tell me that, huh?"

Daddy licked his dry lips, closed his eyes, and swayed. He

lay back against the settee for a moment, making no attempt to respond or defend himself.

"And then you go and promise your daughter to a no-account slob, no better than the vermin living in the rotted shrimp boats. Where's your conscience, Jack Landry?"

"Aaaa," he finally cried, putting his hands over his ears. Mama paused, put she continued to stand over him, her little frame intimidating as she glared down at him. He took his hands from his ears slowly.

"I just done what I thought would be good for everyone, woman. I ain't no *traiteur* with spiritual powers like you. I don't read the future like you, no."

"Oh? You don't read the future like me? Well, it ain't hard to read your future, Jack Landry. Just go follow a snake. How it lives and how it ends up is about the same as you will," she said.

Daddy waved his hand in the air between them the way he would swat at flies. "Never mind all this. Where's that stuff you made for headaches and bad stomach trouble?"

"I'm all out of it. You get drunk so much and so often, I can't keep up with the demand anyway," she scolded. "Besides, there's no *traiteur* alive who can concoct a remedy for what ails you, Jack Landry."

Whatever blood was left drained from Daddy's face. His bloodshot eyes shifted my way and then back to glance at Mama.

"I ain't staying here and be abused," he threatened.

"That's 'cause you're the one who's been doing the abusing, not us."

"That did it," he said, struggling to stand. "I'm going to go move in with Jed until you apologize."

"When it snows in July," Mama retorted, her eyes turned crystal-hard.

Daddy kicked a chair and then marched out of the house, slamming the screen door behind him. He wobbled down the steps and tripped on his own feet before making it to the pickup. Mama watched him struggle to get into his truck, gun the engine, grind the gears, and then spit up dirt as he spun the vehicle around and shot off.

"Every time I get to feeling too good for my shoes, I'm reminded how stupid I've been," she muttered. Despair washed the color from her face as she sighed deeply.

"Oh, Mama, this is all my fault," I moaned.

"Your fault? How can any of this be your fault, honey? You didn't go and pick who'd be your daddy, did you?"

"If I cared more about being married, Daddy wouldn't do these things," I wailed. I flopped into a chair, my stomach feeling like a hollowed-out cave.

"Believe me, child. He would do these things anyway, your being married or no. Ain't no rock around that Jack Landry can't crawl out from under," she said. "Pay him no mind. He'll come to his senses and come crawling back, just like he always does." She gazed after him one more time and then went back to work.

But days passed and Daddy didn't return. Mama and I worked and sold our linens, our towels and baskets. In the evenings after dinner, we sat on the gallery and Mama talked about her youth and her mama and papa, whom I had never seen. Sad times always made her nostalgic. We listened to the owls' mournful cries and spotted an occasional night heron. Sometimes there was an automobile going by, and that would make us both anticipate Daddy's return, but it was always someone else, the car's engine drifting into the night, leaving the melancholy thick as corn syrup around us.

I had a lot of time to pole in my canoe in the late afternoons, to sit alone and drift through a canal and think. Through my mind flitted all kinds of dreary thoughts. Virgil Atkins was probably right with his predictions, I concluded. I would die a spinster for sure now, working beside Mama, watching the rest of the world pass by. All the eligible young men would find out about me and no one decent would ever want me. I would never fall in love. Any man who showed any interest in me would show it for only one reason, and once he had his way with me, he would cast me aside as nonchalantly as he cast aside banana peels. Real affection, romance, and love were things to dream about, to read about, but never to know.

Every one of Mama's friends and even people who just

stopped by to get Mama's help or buy something we made usually commented about my good looks. It became more and more painful to face them and hear the compliments. Most were surprised I wasn't married or pledged, yet whenever I went to town or to church, it seemed to me that all the respected, decent young men looked through me. I felt invisible and alone. The only place I experienced any contentment was here in the swamp with the wildflowers, with the animals and the birds; but how could I ever share this pleasure with anyone? He would have to have been brought up in the swamps, too, and love it with as much passion as I did. Such a person surely did not exist. I was as lost as a cypress branch, broken, floating, drifting toward nowhere.

Sometimes I lay in the bottom of my canoe and just let the current take me wherever it wanted. I always knew where I ended up and how to get back, but it felt good just floating without purpose or direction, gazing up at the powdery blue sky and the egrets and marsh hawks that glided through the air between me and the clouds. I'd hear the bullfrogs or the bream breaking the surface of the water to feed on insects. Sometimes a curious gator would swim alongside and nudge the canoe; and often I would fall asleep and awaken with the sun down below the tree line, the shadows long and deep over the brackish lake.

This is how I thought my life would be now: a life of drifting, going along with the breeze, uncaring, like a leaf tossing and turning in the wind, indifferent, resigned. I did not understand my destiny or my purpose, but I was tired of the questions and the struggle to find the answers. I didn't take any real interest in how I looked and I avoided talking to people, saying as little as possible to the tourists who came by to make purchases.

My behavior upset Mama. She said the look of age in my eyes pained her heart. Unfairly, my youth had been stolen from me. She blamed herself, telling me that somehow, she, a woman with great spiritual powers, had left her own home and family unprotected. She said she had been too arrogant, thinking the evil eye could never focus on her and her own. Of course, I told her she was wrong, but in my secret, put-away heart, I wondered about these dark mysteries that had a way of weaving themselves into our lives.

Late one day Daddy finally came home, acting as if he had been gone only a few hours. He drove up, hopped out of his truck, and came through the front door whistling. Mama didn't say much to him, but she didn't turn him out, and without any fanfare, she put a plate of food on the table for him. He sat and ate and spoke with animation about some of the tours he had guided, describing the long alligators or the rich flock of geese they hunted. Before he finished eating, he sat back and dug into his pocket to produce a roll of dollars and some change.

"All tips from my rich customers," he boasted. "Get whatever you need," he told Mama, and went on eating. She eyed the money, but didn't touch it until he had left the table. After dinner he sat on the gallery and smoked his pipe. I sat outside, too, and listened as he described some of the wealthy Creoles he had been guiding through the swamp. He talked about them as if they were gods because of the way they threw around their money, and because of the fine clothing, boots, and guns they had.

"One of these days and soon, I mean to take me a trip into New Orleans myself," he told me. "How'dja like to go along, Gabriel?"

I widened my eyes. I had never actually been to New Orleans proper, never to the Vieux Carré, but I had heard so much about it, I couldn't help but be curious.

"That would be nice, Daddy. We would all go, I suppose."

"Of course we would all go, and in style, too. That's why I don't want to go until I have enough money to do it right, get nice clothes for you and your mama to wear and enough to stay in a fine hotel and eat in the finest, expensive restaurants. And we'll go shopping and buy you and your ma clothes and—"

"And just how do you expect to do that, Jack Landry?" Mama said from behind the screen door. She had been listening to us talk for a few minutes without revealing herself.

Daddy spun around and smiled. "You don't think I can do that, do you, Catherine? It ain't in your crystal ball, no?"

"I just like to be sure you're not filling the girl up with more hot air, Jack. We got enough in the swamp as it is."

Daddy laughed. "Step out and hear, woman," he said. "Feast your ears on the delicious meal of words I'm gonna deliver."

Mama raised her eyebrows, hesitated, and then came out, her arms folded under her bosom.

"I'm out. Deliver."

"I ain't working for Jed Atkins no more," he said, nodding, his face full of excitement.

Mama gazed at me and then back at him. "Oh, is that so? So who are you working for now?"

"Jack Landry," he replied. "I'm working for myself. And why shouldn't I?" he followed quickly. "Why should I be gettin' only a quarter of what Jed gets, huh? I'm the one who does all the work. He just sits on his fat rump and schedules the trips. I got my own pirogue and there's Gabriel's, and soon we'll get a third. I got my own dock and I got it all up here," he said, pointing to his temple.

"I see," Mama said. "So what are you going to do, put up a sign and hope they come riding by and stop to buy your services?"

"That I'll do, but I've already done more," he said, smiling from ear to ear.

"What more? What do you mean?"

"I been telling some of Jed's customers about myself this past week or so and I give them directions how to get here and I got two trips already scheduled, the first tomorrow morning. There's a party of wealthy Creoles from New Orleans going to be here early. So," he said, putting his thumbs in his vest and pumping out his chest, "meet Jack Landry, businessman."

"What's Jed Atkins say about this?"

"He don't know it all yet. I just told him I ain't coming to work no more." He leaned toward Mama. "I'm givin' them a better deal than he gives them, but I'm making it all. Smart, huh?"

"If you make appointments with people and promise them service, you're going to have to provide it, Jack," Mama warned.

"I will."

"You'll have to stay off the rotgut whiskey, stay away from the zydeco bars and gambling and be home at a decent hour."

"I will. I swear," he said, raising up his right hand. "I'm tired of bein' everyone else's po'boy."

Mama looked hopeful. "Well, if this is true . . . Gabriel and I could cook up some food for the customers. Maybe we could make this into something."

"I was hoping you'd say that," Daddy said, slapping his knee. I couldn't recall seeing him so excited. "With what you can do in that kitchen and with what I can do in the swamp, we could have us a pretty successful little business, no?"

"Maybe," Mama said. "But if I go in there and cook and no one shows tomorrow morning, Jack . . ."

"They'll show, all right." He pulled a slip of paper from his pocket. "Father and son and two of their friends. Name's Dumas. These rich people tell other rich people and then they come here, too. We're going to be well off," Daddy concluded, "or my name ain't Jack Landry."

"I don't have to go out in the canoe, too, do I, Daddy?" I asked.

"Not if you don't want to, but it would sure be nice to have you along, Gabriel. You know these swamps better than me."

"I can't stomach seeing men go out there and shoot the animals, Daddy."

He grimaced. "Then don't come along, but don't you go preaching or sayin' anything stupid to them, hear? I don't want them feelin' bad about comin' here, no."

"Can't you just run swamp tours and show people the plants and animals, Daddy? Maybe you can get one of those glass-bottom boats and—"

"No, there ain't as much money in it, and besides, if we don't kill off some of them animals, they'll overrun us. Tell her I'm right, Catherine."

"You let her believe and think what she wants, Jack. Besides, Gabriel doesn't need me telling her what's right and what's wrong. She knows more in her heart than you think."

"Oh, don't start that mumbo-jumbo on me," Daddy wailed. "I'm trying to make something for this family. No preachin'!" he warned. "I mean it."

He stumped off to check on his canoe and the dock.

"Come on, honey," Mama said, looking after him. "I don't have the power to turn a frog into a prince, but if he's doing honest labor and it keeps him from drinking, we got something better than we had. Sometimes that's all you can hope for," she concluded, and went into the house to start a fresh roux.

Mama was up early the next morning, but Daddy surprised both of us by rising before her and putting up a pot of rich Cajun coffee. The aroma drew both of us downstairs where we found Daddy dressed and ready, wearing his best hunting clothes and clean boots.

"They'll be here in an hour," he predicted. "I patched up the dock and cleaned up my canoe and Gabriel's. I see you made some beignets. That's good. They're used to that, only yours will be better than anything they get in the city."

"Don't go saying that, Jack. New Orleans is just full of great cooks."

"Yeah, but you're the best in the bayou. Ain't she, Gabriel?"

"Yes, Daddy."

"I don't need your flattery, Jack."

"Ain't flattery. It's just the truth," Daddy said, winking at me. His excitement was contagious, and despite what work he was doing, I couldn't help but be flooded with delight.

"I'll go get us some wildflowers for the tables outside, Mama," I said, and went off right after having a beignet and coffee myself.

I knew where there was some lush flowering honeysuckle and wild violets as well as hibiscus and blue and pink hydrangeas. This early in the morning billows of fog rolled in over the swamp. As I drew closer to the water, I could hear a bass flapping and a bullfrog falling off a log into the water. Ahead of me a white-tailed doe sprinted through the bushes. It saddened me to think that rich grown men could possibly get pleasure from killing such beautiful creatures. It seemed such a great betrayal, but I knew there was little I could do to stop it, and if I did speak up, Daddy would be enraged. Things would return to being dreadful in our home.

I spent longer than I had intended to spend in the swamp gathering flowers. By the time I started back, Daddy's party of hunters had arrived and were unloading their vehicle near the dock. I paused to watch for a moment. A slim young man, only about an inch or two shorter than Daddy, with thick chestnut hair stepped out from behind the car. Just as he did so, a rice bird landed on my shoulder. It was something they often did. Most birds had no fear of me because I often fed them and spoke softly to them. The young man stared at me with a gentle smile on his lips. I shifted some flowers to my left arm and extended my right for the rice bird to trot down to my wrist before flying away. As usual, his tiny feet tickled and I laughed.

And so did the young man. I could see him asking Daddy about me, and then he looked at me more intently, shaking his head. I glanced shyly at him and continued toward the house. He gazed back at the work going on at the dock before crossing over the grass to meet me halfway.

"Hello," he said. As he drew closer, I saw he had soft green eyes and a slim but firm torso. "When you came walking out of the fog like that, I thought you were some sort of swamp goddess."

"I'm far from being a goddess," I said.

"Not really too far," he replied, his smile spreading from his eyes to his lips. "I've never seen a wild bird land on someone and strut around as if it were on a tree. Does that happen often?"

"Oui, monsieur."

"Why aren't they afraid of you?"

"They know I mean them no harm, monsieur."

"Astounding." He shook his head and then he smiled. "My name's Pierre Dumas. Your father told me your name's Gabriel."

"*Oui*. I'm just bringing some flowers to our tables," I said, continuing on my way.

"Let me help," he said, following.

"Oh no, I . . ."

"Please," he insisted, taking a bunch of the violets from my arms.

The sun had already begun to burn through the morning mist, and the grass around the shack glistened with the dew. There was a gentle breeze up from the Gulf and soft puffs of milk white clouds moved lazily across the brightening blue sky. Pierre accompanied me to the tables.

"People stop by for lunch?" he asked. "Is that what these tables are for?"

"*Oui*, monsieur. We sell bowls of gumbo and we sell cakes and coffee."

"I had some of your beignets already. Delicious."

"*Merci*, monsieur," I said, moving from one table to the other. He trailed along and I wondered when he would return to the loading of the canoes. Suddenly he just sat himself on a bench to watch me, that small smile on his lips, those green eyes radiant.

"Pardon, monsieur," I said, feeling very self-conscious, "but surely you should get back to the dock."

"I'll tell you a big secret," he said, gazing toward the dock and then at me. "I'm not really much of a hunter. I come along only to please my father."

"Oh?"

"I'm a terrible shot. I always close my eyes before pulling the trigger. I just hate the thought that I might hit something and kill it," he admitted. I smiled.

Mama came out the front door and paused on the gallery when she saw me speaking with Pierre. She was carrying some of our woven blankets in her arms to bring to the stand.

"I must help my mother," I said. "I hope you have a very poor day of hunting," I added, and he laughed.

"Those are very pretty flowers, Gabriel," Mama said, keeping her gaze fixed on Pierre Dumas. He rose, nodded to her, and walked toward the dock.

"I'll bring out the towels, Mama," I said, and hurried inside, my heart feeling light. It fluttered when I thought about Pierre Dumas's soft green eyes, and it felt as if the tiny rice bird had gotten into my chest.

"So," Mama said when I brought a pile of our goods to the stand, "you were speaking to that nice young man, I see."

"Yes, Mama. He says he doesn't really like to hunt but goes along for his father's sake."

Mama nodded. "I think we have a lot to learn from your animals and birds, Gabriel. After the babies are nurtured, their parents let them go off and be their own selves."

"*Oui,* Mama," I said. When I looked up at her, her eyes were wider and bright with curiosity, but she wasn't looking at me. She was gazing over my shoulder toward the dock. I turned and saw Pierre strolling back while Papa and the other men were casting off in the canoes.

"I'll go check on my roux," Mama said, and headed for the house.

"Monsieur," I said, "aren't you going on your swamp hunt?"

"Don't know why," he said, "but I have a little headache and decided to rest instead. I hope you don't mind."

"Oh no, monsieur. I'll speak to my mother about your headache. She's a *traiteur,* you know."

"*Traiteur?*"

I explained what she was and what she did.

"Remarkable," he said. "Perhaps I should bring her back to New Orleans with me and set her up in business. I know a great many wealthy people who would seek her assistance."

"My mother would never leave the bayou, monsieur," I said with a deadly serious expression. He laughed. "Nor would I," I added, and his smile faded.

"I don't mean to make fun of you. I'm just amused by your self-assurance. Most young women I know are quite insecure about their beliefs. First they want to check to see what's in style or what their husbands believe before they offer an opinion, if they ever do. So," he said, "you've been to New Orleans?"

"No, monsieur."

"Then how do you know you wouldn't want to live there?"

"I know I could never leave the swamp, monsieur. I could never trade cypress and Spanish moss, the willow trees and my canals, for streets of concrete and buildings of brick and stone."

"You think the swamp is beautiful?" he asked with a smile of incredulity.

"*Oui*, monsieur. You do not?"

"Well, I must confess I haven't seen much of it, nor have I enjoyed the hunting trips. Perhaps," he added, "if you have the time, you would give me a little tour. Show me why you think it's so nice here."

"But your headache, monsieur," I reminded him.

"It seems to have eased quite a bit. I think I was just nervous about going hunting. I would pay you for your tour, of course," he added.

"I wouldn't charge you, monsieur. What is it you would like me to show you?"

"Show me what you think is beautiful, what gives you this rich look of happiness and fills your face with a glow I know most of the fancy women in New Orleans would die to have."

I felt my cheeks turn crimson. "Please, monsieur, don't tease me."

"I assure you," he said, standing firm, his shoulders back, "I mean every word I say. How about the tour?"

I hesitated.

"It doesn't have to be long. I don't mean to take you away from your work."

"Let me tell my mother," I said, "and then we'll go for a walk along the bank of the canal."

"*Merci.*"

I hurried to the shack to tell Mama what the young man wanted. She thought for a moment.

"Young men from the city often have low opinions of the girls from the bayou, Gabriel. You understand?"

"*Oui*, Mama, but I don't think this is true about this young man."

205

"Be careful and don't be long," she warned. "I haven't looked at him long enough to get a reading."

"I'll be safe, Mama," I assured her.

Pierre was standing with his hands behind his back, gazing over the water.

"I just saw a rather large bird disappear just behind those treetops," he said, pointing.

"It's a marsh hawk, monsieur. If you look more closely, you will see she has a nest there."

"Oh?" He stared. *"Oui.* I do see it now," he added excitedly.

"The swamp is like a book of philosophy, monsieur. You have to read it, think about it, stare at it, and let it sink in before you realize all that's there."

His eyebrows rose. "You read philosophy?"

"A little, but not as much as I did when I was in school."

"How long ago was that?"

"Three years."

"You're an intriguing woman, Gabriel Landry," he said.

Once again I felt the heat rise up my neck and into my face. "This way, monsieur," I said, pointing to the path through the tall grass. He followed beside me. "What do you do, monsieur?"

"I work for my father in our real estate development business. Nothing terribly exciting. We buy and sell property, lease buildings, develop projects. Soon there will be a need for low-income housing, and we want to be ready for it," he added.

"There's some very low-income housing," I said, pointing to the grass dome at the edge of the shore. A nutria poked out its head, spotted us, and recoiled. Pierre laughed. I reached out and touched his hand to indicate we should stop.

"What?"

"Be very still a moment, monsieur," I said, "and keep your eyes focused on that log floating against the rock there. Do you see?"

"Yes, but what's so extraordinary about a log that . . . *Mon Dieu,"* he remarked when the log became the baby alligator, its head rising out of the water. It gazed at us and then pushed off to follow the current. "I would have stepped on it."

I laughed just as a flock of geese came around the bend and swooped over the water before turning gracefully to glide over the tops of the cypress trees.

"My father would have blasted them," Pierre commented. We walked a bit farther.

"The swamp has something for every mood," I explained. "Here in the open with the sun reflecting off the water, the lily pads and cattails are thick and rich, but there, just behind the bend, you see the Spanish moss and the dark shadows. I like to pretend they are mysterious places. The crooked and gnarled trees become my fantasy creatures."

"I can see why you enjoyed growing up here," Pierre said. "But these canals are like a maze."

"They are a maze. There are places deep inside where the moss hangs so low, you would miss the entrance to a lake or to another canal. In there you rarely find anything to remind you of the world out here."

"But the mosquitoes and the bugs and the snakes . . ."

"Mama has a lotion that keeps the bugs away, and yes, there are dangers, but, monsieur, surely there are dangers in your world, too."

"And how."

He laughed.

"I have a small pirogue down here, monsieur, just big enough for two people. Do you want to see a little more?"

"Very much, *merci.*"

I pulled my canoe out from the bushes and Pierre got in.

"You want me to do the poling?"

"No, monsieur," I said. "You are the tourist."

He laughed and watched me push off and then pole into the current.

"I can see you know what you're doing."

"I've done it so long, monsieur, I don't think about it. But surely you go sailing, *n'est-ce pas?* You have Lake Pontchartrain. I saw it when I was just a little girl and it looked as big as the ocean."

He turned away and gazed into the water without replying for a moment. I saw his happy, contented expression evaporate and quickly be replaced with a look of deep melancholy.

"I did do some sailing," he finally said, "but my brother was recently in a terrible sailing accident."

"Oh, I'm sorry, monsieur."

"The mast struck him in the temple during a storm and he went into a coma for a long time. He was quite an athletic man and now he's . . . like a vegetable."

"How sad, monsieur."

"Yes. I haven't gone sailing since. My father was devastated by it all, of course. That's why I do whatever I can to please him. But my brother was more of the hunter and the fisherman. Now that my brother is incapacitated, my father is trying to get me to become more like him, but I'm failing miserably, I'm afraid." He smiled. "Sorry to lay the heavy weight of my personal troubles on your graceful, small shoulders."

"It's all right, monsieur. Quick," I said, pointing to the right to help break him from his deeply melancholy mood, "look at the giant turtle."

"Where?" He stared and stared and then finally smiled. "How do you see these animals like that?"

"You learn to spot the changes in the water, the shades of color, every movement."

"I admire you. Despite this backwoods world in which you live, you do appear to be very content."

I poled alongside a sandbar with its sun-dried top and turned toward a canopy of cypress that was so thick over the water, it blocked out the sun. I showed Pierre a bed of honeysuckle and pointed out two white-tailed deer grazing near the water. We saw flocks of rice birds, and a pair of herons, more alligators and turtles. In my secret places, ducks floated alongside geese, the moss was thicker, the flowers plush.

"Does your father take hunters here?" Pierre asked.

"No, monsieur." I smiled. "My father does not know these places, and I won't be telling him about them either."

Pierre's laughter rolled over the water and a pair of scarlet cardinals shot out of the bushes and over our heads. On the far shore, a grosbeaked heron strutted proudly, taking only a second to look our way.

"It is very beautiful here, mademoiselle. I can understand your reluctance to live anywhere else. Actually, I envy you for the peace and contentment. I am a rich man; I live in a big house filled with beautiful, expensive things, but somehow, I think you are happier living in your swamp, in what you call your toothpick-legged shack."

"Mama often says it's not what you have, it's what has you," I told him, and he smiled, those green eyes brightening.

"She does sound like a woman who can draw from a pool of great wisdom."

"And what of your mother, monsieur?"

"She passed away a little over a year ago."

"Oh. I'm sorry."

"She developed heart trouble soon after my brother Jean's accident, and eventually . . ." He leaned over the pirogue, his hand trailing in the water. Suddenly he pulled it up and sat back. A green snake slithered past. "A moment ago that was a stick. This place is full of all sorts of magic."

I laughed.

"Just Nature's magic. Swamp creatures blend in with their surroundings to survive. Mama says that's true for people, too. If we don't like where we live, if we hate where we are, we will fade away there."

He nodded. "I'm afraid that might be happening to me," he said sadly, and sighed.

I was gazing at him so intently, I didn't pay attention to the direction in which my pirogue was going. We struck a large rock protruding out of the water and the impact caught me off balance. I fell over the side of the canoe and into the water, more surprised than frightened. When I bobbed to the surface, I was again surprised, this time to find Pierre Dumas in the water beside me. He put his arm around my waist to keep me afloat.

"Are you all right?"

I spit out the water, coughed, and nodded. He and I took hold of the side of the pirogue. He got up first and then helped me into the canoe. I caught my breath quickly, but I was still a bit dazed. Of course, we were both soaked to the skin.

"Oh, I'm so sorry, monsieur," I wailed. "Your fine clothes are ruined."

"Hardly, and it wouldn't matter if they were. Are you all right?"

"I'm fine, but quite embarrassed. This has never before happened to me."

He smiled. "How lucky I am to be here for a first."

I looked down at myself. My blouse was stuck to my bosom, the thin material nearly transparent. His eyes drank me in, too, but for some reason, even though I folded my arms across my exposed bosom, I didn't mind as much as I thought I would.

"I'm soaked to the bone," I moaned, and he laughed. "Mama will be furious, especially when she sees what I have done to you, and my daddy . . ."

"Stop worrying. It's nothing. I'll tell you what," he said, gazing to our right and nodding, "let's land over there by that clearing and sprawl out in the sun to dry for a while. We won't look so bad when we go back," he suggested.

I nodded and started to get up to pole, but he stopped me and took over. When we struck shore, he hopped out and pulled the canoe up before helping me get out. For a moment we stood so close to each other, we could feel each other's breath on our faces. His eyes held mine magnetically.

"My hair's a mess," I said softly.

"You look even more beautiful."

I started to disagree, but he put his finger on my lips and held it there a moment. Then he lifted it away and slowly, but surely, replaced his finger with his lips. It was so gentle a kiss, I could have imagined it, but when I opened my eyes, I saw his eyes were still closed. He looked like he was devouring the sensation with great intensity so as to get every bit of pleasure from it. His eyes opened and he smiled.

"I feel unreal, like I've entered your magical kingdom."

"It's not magical, monsieur, it's . . ."

"Oh yes, it is, and your kiss is the key," he said before

kissing me again, this time harder, longer. I let myself sink into his arms, our wet clothing rubbing, the heat of his body caressing my skin, my breasts.

We sank to our knees and he sat back, bracing himself with his hands, his face to the sun.

"I'm not sure which kiss is warmer, the sun's or yours," he muttered with his eyes still closed.

"I don't know how this could have happened. I can pole a canoe better than my daddy can," I said, still ashamed.

"I'm glad it happened," Pierre replied. "Here," he said, lying back and extending his arm. "Just lie back on me and it will be comfortable."

I did as he suggested, my head against his chest, his arm around my shoulder. We lay there silently, our wet clothing steaming in the hot Louisiana midday sun.

"I feel like a Cajun peanut," I muttered after a few moments.

"What's that?"

"Shrimp dried in the hot sun."

He laughed. "You're so full of surprises, every expression, every word, is something unexpected. What a delight. Tell me how it can be that you have not been stolen away and married. Are all the young men blind here?"

I said nothing. The silence was heavy.

"No boyfriend?" Pierre pursued.

"No, monsieur." I sat up.

"I'm sorry. I don't mean to pry," he said quickly.

"I should take you back," I said. "Mama will be angry no matter what."

I started to stand, but he reached out and seized my left wrist.

"I haven't known you long, but somehow, I feel I can be honest with you, and I hope you feel you can be honest with me. There's a pain in your heart. I wish I could remove that pain. I wish I had some of the magic that's in this place."

I sat again. He released my wrist, but took hold of my hand.

"Gabriel. Your name is like music to me." He took my other hand and gently, but firmly, pulled me closer to him. "You're too beautiful to be unhappy. I won't permit it," he

211

said, and kissed me again. When we parted, he wiped away the fugitive tear that had escaped from under my burning eyelid. "Someone hurt you? Some young man?"

"Not some young man," I said.

"An older man?" I nodded. "He took advantage of you? This happened recently?" he asked, firing one question after another.

"Yes. Often I go into the swamp alone. He came upon me one day and . . ."

"I hope he was made to suffer for it."

"No, monsieur. He is a wealthy man, and wealthy people often escape pain and suffering," I said bitterly.

"That's not true everywhere," Pierre said, and looked down. "At least, it's not true for me."

"Your brother," I said, recalling what he had told me. He nodded.

"There's more. I don't wear the ring all the time," he said, "but . . ."

My heart stopped and then started. "You're married, monsieur?"

With great reluctance, he nodded.

"Oh," I said, as if my heart had turned to lead. For a moment I couldn't breathe. The air seemed even more humid, more tepid.

"But it's not a happy marriage," he said quickly. "We are childless and the doctors say that is the way it will always be. My wife has some difficulties."

Despite the weakness in my legs, I stood up quickly.

"We must return to the shack, monsieur. I must help my mother prepare for the day's selling."

"Of course."

"I am sorry I caused this to happen to you. Mama will get your clothing dried quickly. It will be better if we just walk along the bank," I added.

He stood. "Gabriel. My wife is even more bitter about our marriage than I am. She thinks I think less of her. It's as if a wall has fallen between us these days. A house, a home, a marriage, should be filled with love. Two people should do everything they can to make each other's lives more meaningful, happier; but we are like two strangers sharing coffee these days.

"My heart hasn't felt as light and happy for some time as it did when I first saw you emerge from the fog in the swamp. You are truly like a breath of fresh air. I assure you, I mean it when I say I would do anything in my power to keep sadness from your door."

"*Merci*, monsieur," I said, but I started to walk away. He followed.

"Gabriel." He took my hand into his again and I turned. "You felt something special when we kissed, too, didn't you?"

"I do not trust my own feelings anymore, monsieur. Besides," I added, gazing down, "you are married, monsieur. I don't want to go looking for any more trouble; it has a way of finding me itself."

"I understand." He nodded and then smiled. "Can we be friends?"

I shook my head.

"Why not? I'm really a nice guy," he said, smiling. "I'll bring you references."

"I'm sure you are nice, monsieur."

"Then?"

I lifted my gaze to look into his mesmerizing green eyes. "Being friends with you . . . it's like being a starving person in Mama's kitchen and promising only to take a small taste of the shrimp étouffée, monsieur. Why fool yourself into believing the impossible? Once you taste it, you can't help yourself."

He laughed. "Not only beautiful and magical, but wise, too. I'm tormented by the possibility we will never see each other again. You won't turn me away, will you?"

"I'm sure you have fine, well-to-do friends in New Orleans, monsieur. You don't need a poor Cajun girl in the bayou."

"That's exactly what I need," he said as we continued to walk along. He still held on to my hand. "Someone who will tell me the truth and listen with sincerity to what I say. I'll pay you for your time. I know. I'll hire you as my personal swamp guide," he added. "I'm sure there is a great deal more you can show me."

"But, monsieur . . ."

"As long as you don't dunk me in the water every time we go poling," he added.

I couldn't help but laugh.

"That's better. Look at me, soaked but happy. I'm like a little boy again," he said.

His exuberance swept me along. I thought of dozens of reasons to protest and refuse him, but he was too cheerful and too determined.

And something inside me kept me from shutting the door.

11

The Hidden Ring

"What happened?" Mama asked the moment she set eyes on us.

"A little accident, Madame Landry," Pierre replied quickly, before I had a chance to explain. "It's no one's fault, or if it is anyone's fault, it's mine. I was talking so much and asking so many questions, Gabriel was distracted while we were in her canoe."

"You turned your canoe over in the canal?" Mama asked me with surprise. She knew how expert I was at poling a pirogue.

"No, Mama. I hit a rock while we were in the small pirogue and I fell out."

She was nonplussed for a moment, her eyes shifting from Pierre to me.

"Go change," she ordered me. She turned back to Pierre. "I have some clean, dry clothes for you to put on, monsieur. One moment."

"Please, don't go to any trouble," Pierre said, but Mama was already off to fetch the clothing. Pierre gazed at me and shrugged.

"Gabriel!" Mama called from the stairway.

"Coming, Mama." I hurried up behind her.

"How did such a thing happen, Gabriel?" she demanded in a loud whisper.

"Just the way he described, Mama. I wasn't paying attention and I poled us right into a rock. I lost balance and fell overboard."

"How did he get soaked, too?"

"He jumped in to help me."

"He jumped in?"

"*Oui*, Mama."

She stared at me a moment and then shook her head. "Change your clothes," she said.

By the time I came downstairs, Mama had Pierre dressed in Daddy's best pair of slacks and one of his best shirts. He was barefoot while Mama dried his shoes and socks, pants and shirt, on the stove. His underpants were hanging on the line in the sun. He looked up at me from the plank table in the kitchen. He had an impish grin and appeared to be positively enjoying every moment of my disaster. Before him on the table was a mug of steaming Cajun coffee and a bowl of gumbo.

"Our unexpected swim has made me ravenously hungry," he explained. "And I am glad of that because this is absolutely the most delicious shrimp gumbo I've ever eaten. So you see . . . at the end of every storm, there is some sort of rainbow."

I started to smile, but Mama raised her eyebrows.

"Sit down," she directed, "and I'll get some nourishment in your stomach, too. Honestly, Gabriel, how could you take Monsieur Dumas into the swamp to show him a pond filled with alligators and snapping turtles and snakes and then be so careless as to fall out of your canoe?"

"I didn't take him to any pond filled with alligators, Mama."

Pierre's smile widened. Just as I sat, we heard a car horn.

"Customers," Mama said.

"I'll get my own gumbo, Mama. Thank you."

She gave us a once-over, her eyes filled with suspicion and reprimand, before hurrying out to the stand.

"Your mother's wonderful," Pierre said. "The sort of

woman who takes command. I was afraid to say no to anything."

"When you leave, she will bawl me out for endangering a rich gentleman from New Orleans," I told him, and dipped into the black cast-iron pot to ladle out some gumbo for myself. I, too, was suddenly starving.

"I eat in the finest restaurants in New Orleans, but I don't think I ever enjoyed a meal more," he said, gazing around the small kitchen. "My cook has a kitchen to rival the best restaurants, and your mother does so much with so little."

"Where do you live in New Orleans, monsieur?"

"Please, call me Pierre, Gabriel. I live in what's known as the Garden District."

"What is it?"

"The Garden District? Well, it began as the area for the rich Americans when New Orleans became part of the U.S.A. These people were not accepted by the French Quarter Creoles, so they developed their own lavish neighborhood. My grandfather got our property in a foreclosure and decided we weren't above living there. Elegant gardens visible from the street give this section of the city its name. Tourists visit, but there are no buses permitted. There are some famous houses in the Garden District, such as the Payne-Strachan House. Jefferson Davis, president of the Confederacy, died there in 1889.

"I'm sorry. I don't mean to sound like a tour guide," he said, laughing at his own enthusiasm.

"Is your house very big?"

He nodded.

"Is it bigger than any house you've seen in the bayou?"

He nodded again.

"How big is your house?" I demanded, and he laughed.

"It's a two-story Grecian with two galleries in front. I think there are fourteen or fifteen rooms."

"You think? You live in a house so big you're not sure of how many rooms?"

"It's fifteen," he said. Then he paused. "Maybe sixteen. I don't know if I should count the cook's quarters as one room or two. And of course, there's the ballroom."

"Ballroom? In a house?"

"We have some rooms that haven't been used for anything yet. If I count them, too . . ."

"*Mon Dieu!* Is there much land around it?"

"We have some outbuildings, a stable, a pool, and a tennis court. I never measured it, but I bet it's over an acre of land."

"You have a stable in the city?" He nodded. "Are you the richest family in New Orleans?" I wondered, wide-eyed.

He laughed. "Hardly. In this section there are a number of large estates like ours."

"How tiny and poor our shack must seem to you," I said, gazing down as ashamedly as someone caught with holes in the soles of her shoes.

"But how large and rich it is because you live in it," he replied. I blushed and continued eating, feeling his eyes constantly on me.

"Perhaps one day you will visit New Orleans," he said.

"Daddy says he will take us as soon as he earns enough money to take us in style."

"Of course. New Orleans is a city to which you should go in style," Pierre said. "As for earning enough money . . . I expect he will have my father for a steady customer. He is impressed with your father's knowledge of the swamp."

"My daddy is the best Cajun guide in the bayou. When I was little, he taught me about the animals and he showed me how to pole a pirogue."

"Did you fall out then?" Pierre asked with a wide grin.

"No, monsieur. I'm sorry. Really, I don't know how that happened. I . . ."

"I'm only teasing you, Gabriel." He reached across the table to put his hand over mine. "I can't think of when my heart felt more filled with happiness than it is at this moment," he added. His words were so sincere and yet so overwhelming, they took my breath away.

"I must help Mama," I said, my voice cracking.

"Fine. I'll help too."

"You, monsieur? Selling our wares to the tourists?" I started to laugh at the prospect.

"I happen to be a crackerjack salesman," he said, feigning

indignation. "Why, just last week I sold a building worth nearly two million."

"Dollars?"

"*Oui*," he said, smiling at my look of amazement. "I wish Daphne was as impressed and as appreciative," he added, and then regretted it quickly.

"Daphne is your wife?"

"*Oui*," he said.

I rose to put my bowl in the sink. He did the same and for a moment, stood right behind me, so close I could feel his breath on my hair. My heart thumped. His hands went to my waist.

"Gabriel, I feel something truly magical with you. I can't deny or ignore it."

"You must, monsieur. Please," I said, afraid to turn.

"I must see you again, that's what I must do, even if it's only to chat. Surely you will turn my grayest days to blue sky. And," he said, forcing me to turn so I faced him, "I will fill your heart with happiness. I promise."

I started to shake my head, but he brought his lips to mine to kiss me gently.

I broke away. "I must help Mama," I muttered, and charged out the front door.

Mama had two couples at the stand, the women going through our linens and towels, the men off to the side smoking and talking.

"Gabriel, fetch those pillowcases we wove day before yesterday, please," she said the moment she heard me approaching.

"*Oui*, Mama."

Pierre stepped out on the gallery as I hurried back and into the house, passing him without a word. When I returned to the stand, Pierre was conversing with the men, getting them interested in buying jars of swamp insects.

"They'll make great conversation pieces on your desks in your offices. Not something easily acquired in the city, *n'est-ce pas?*" he told them.

They agreed and bought two jars apiece to add to the items their wives had taken. When they left, Mama thanked Pierre for making the sale.

"It's nothing, madame, but it was more fun than being in the canoe hunting," he added. Mama smiled. He asked her about some of her herbs and listened as she described how to use them and what they would cure. I could see he was very impressed with her. He decided to buy a variety of herbs himself.

"We have a cook who's very much into this sort of thing herself," he explained. He flashed a smile at me. Mama returned to the house to bring out some other items, happy at how well the day's sales were going.

Pierre sat in the rickety old cypress chair Daddy had made years ago and, at my request, described his mansion in New Orleans in greater detail. I sat on the grass at his feet. Nearby, curious gray squirrels squinted and waited to see what we were about and if there would be any crumbs.

"You have beautiful wildflowers here, but on our estate, our garden walls enclose huge banana trees and drip with purple bugle vine. In the morning I wake to the scent of blooming camellias and magnolia, and the streets of the district are under a canopy of oak."

"It does sound like you live in a beautiful place, too."

"It's beautiful and quiet, but minutes away by streetcar is the bustling city," he said with visible excitement in his eyes. I listened, enchanted as he described the art galleries, the museums, the grand restaurants, and the famous French Quarter where the jazz musicians played and people sat in coffee stalls drinking café au lait.

"The French Quarter is really more Spanish than French, you know. All of the buildings that date from colonial times are Spanish in design and architecture. And the so-called French market is Spanish from foundation to chimney pots."

He knew a great deal about the history of New Orleans and enjoyed having so attentive an audience as me and, later, Mama. In fact, he ended up talking more with her about Louisiana's history than he did with me.

Late in the afternoon, the hunting party returned. Pierre's father had more than two dozen ducks, as did their friends. Before they reached the dock to disembark the pirogues, Pierre went into the shack and retrieved his clothing. Mama had ironed everything, as well as dried it, and it looked at least as good as it had been.

"No reason to tell your father about our spill into the canal," Pierre whispered to me as the men shouted from the dock. I nodded. I knew Mama wouldn't say anything.

Even in his hunting clothing, Pierre's father looked the distinguished gentleman with his full head of stark white hair and his matching goatee. His cheeks and forehead were pink from the sun, deepening the wrinkles around his bright, emerald green eyes. I guessed from the expression on Daddy's face that he was giving Daddy a sizable tip. He then gazed at me for a long moment before approaching Pierre.

"How's your headache, son? Did you try some of Madame Landry's secret potions or," he added, smiling in my direction, "find another way to cure yourself?"

"I'm fine, Father," Pierre replied curtly. "I see you did well."

"Excellent. We've already booked another trip with Jack. Think you might be up to it next time, Pierre?" he asked, still with that demonic grin on his handsome face. Pierre blushed and turned away. Before they left, Pierre thanked Mama for her hospitality, and she thanked him for the purchases he had made. Daddy was busy with his gear at the dock, so he didn't see Pierre approach me to say good-bye.

"I had a wonderful day. I mean it," he said, pressing my hand in his. "I will be back sooner than my father thinks," he added, "or you, for that matter."

"Please, Monsieur Dumas. You should not. . . ."

"Watch for me," he said with a twinkle in his eyes, "where and when you would least expect to see me."

He hurried to join his father and their friends in their big limousine and rolled down the window to wave as they pulled away. Mama, who had just sold something to another traveler, stepped up beside me.

"He's a very nice young man," she said. "But he's married, Gabriel," she added in a dark voice.

"I know," I said sadly. "He told you?"

"No."

"Then how did you know, Mama?"

"When I put his pants on the stove to dry, I felt the

221

wedding ring in his pocket and gave it to him to hold with his other things. A man who takes off his wedding ring so easily does not wear it so well," she commented.

"Beware of him, Gabriel," she said softly. "He has an unhappy heart, and unhappiness is too often contagious," she said. She went to speak to Daddy and left me trembling a little as I gazed after Pierre's limousine, his beautiful words falling away like teardrops in the wind.

Weeks passed and Pierre Dumas began to fade, his face pressed to my memory like some embossed cameo to cherish deep in my heart, but never to see or feel again. At night I would fantasize about him, think of him as I would my dream lover, the ghost who emerged from the swamp to win my heart even though I knew the price I would pay for loving him. I couldn't help but replay his words, relive his kiss, hear again his laughter, and feel my heart warmed by his soft, green eyes, smiling.

Mama in her wisdom saw me moping about the grounds, drifting rather than walking along the banks of the canals, and knew what was making me pale and wan. Often she had to say something to me twice because I didn't hear her the first time; I was too lost in my own thoughts. I played with my food and stared blankly while she and Daddy talked and argued at the dinner table. Mama said I was losing weight, too.

She tried to keep me busy, giving me more to do, filling my every quiet moment with another chore, but it took me double the time to do anything, which only exasperated her more.

"You're like a lovesick duck, Gabriel," she told me one afternoon. "Get hold of yourself before you fade away or get blown off in of our famous twisters, hear?"

"Yes, Mama."

She sighed, troubled for me.

But I couldn't just forget Pierre. Whenever Daddy talked about a new booking for a hunting tour, I would listen keenly to see if it was the Dumas family; but it never was. Finally one day I went down to the dock where he was preparing for another trip and asked him.

"I thought that rich man from New Orleans was returning, Daddy. His son told me his father thought you were a wonderful swamp guide."

"Rich family? Oh, you mean Dumas? *Oui*, he was supposed to be back, but he canceled on me two days ago. You can't depend on them people. They lie to your face, smiling. My motto is, take whatever I can from them when I can and don't put no stock in any of their promises.

"Why you asking?" he said quickly. "You ain't gonna start on me again, are you, Gabriel? You ain't gonna start complaining about the little animals they shoot. Because if you do . . ."

"No, Daddy," I said abruptly. "I was just wondering. That's all," I replied, and hurried away before he went into one of his tirades against the animal lovers and the oil industry that was destroying the bayou. He could ramble for hours, working himself into such a frenzy, it would take as many hours for him to wind down. Mama could get just as upset at whoever started him on a rampage as she could get at him.

The days passed and I began to try to do what Mama wanted—fill my mind with other thoughts. I did work harder, but I always had time to go into my swamp, and whenever I poled in my small canoe, I couldn't help but think of Pierre. After another week went by, I concluded Daddy was right—rich people tell grander lies. Their wealth gives them more credibility and makes us more vulnerable to their fabrications. Maybe Daddy was right about all of it; maybe we were victims and should take advantage of them every chance we could get.

I hated thinking like Daddy, but it was my way of overcoming the deep feeling of sadness that filled my stomach like sand. I began to wonder if this wasn't why Daddy was so negative and down on everything. Perhaps it was his way of battling his own sadness, his own defeat, his own disappointments. Ironically, I became more tolerant of him than Mama. I stopped complaining about his hunting trips and was even there at the end of the day to bring him a steaming cup of Cajun coffee or help him put away his gear.

Between the money he was making and the good season Mama and I were having selling our wares at the roadside, we were doing better than ever. Daddy repeated his promise to take us all on a holiday to New Orleans real soon. The prospect excited me, especially when I thought about the possibility of walking through the Garden District and perhaps seeing the Dumas estate. I even imagined seeing Pierre without permitting him to see me.

Mama said I shouldn't count on any of Daddy's promises. "One day he'll dig into his pocket, see how much money he's got buried under his cigarette paper, and go off on a bender to gamble and drink away his hard-earned profits. I try to take as much from him as I can, claiming we need more for this and more for that, and I hide it because I know that rainy day is coming, Gabriel. Storm clouds are looming just on the other side of those trees," she predicted.

Maybe she was right, I thought, and tried not to dwell on New Orleans. And then, one afternoon, I took my usual walk along the bank of the canal. It was a beautiful day with the clouds small and puffy instead of long and wispy. The breeze from the Gulf gently lifted the palmetto leaves and made little ripples in the water, now the color of dark tea. There seemed to be more egrets than ever. I saw two great snapping turtles sunning themselves on a rock, not far from a coiled-up water moccasin. White-tailed deer grazed without fear in the brush, and my heron glided from tree to tree, following me as I ambled along, really not thinking of anything in particular, but just pleased by how well everything in Nature seemed to coexist and enjoying this relatively untouched world of mine.

Suddenly I heard my name. At first I thought I had imagined it; I thought it was just the low whistle of the breeze through the cypress and Spanish moss, but then it came again, louder, clearer, and I turned. At first I thought I was really looking at an apparition. When he had left, Pierre told me to watch for him where I would least expect to see him. Well, there he was poling a pirogue my way, something I would never have anticipated.

Shocked, I stood with my mouth agape. He wore dark pants and a dark shirt with a palmetto hat. He poled very well in my direction and then let the canoe glide to the bank.

"Bonjour, mademoiselle," he said, scooping off his hat to

make a sweeping bow with laughter around his eyes. "Isn't it a fine day we're having in the swamp?"

"Pierre! Where did you come from? How did you . . . Where did you get this pirogue?"

"I bought it and put it in just a little ways up the canal," he said. "As you can see, I've been practicing, too."

"But what are you doing here?"

"What am I doing here? Poling a canoe in the canal," he said as casually as he would if he had been doing it all his life. "I just happened to see you strolling along the bank."

I could only laugh. His face turned serious, those green eyes locking tightly on mine.

"Gabriel," he said. "I've been saying your name repeatedly to myself since the day I left. It's like music, a chant. I heard it everywhere I went in the city; in the traffic, the tires of cars were singing it; from the streetcar, in the rattle of its wheels; in the clatter of voices in our fine restaurants; and of course, at night in my dreams.

"I've seen your face a hundred times on every pretty girl who's crossed my path. You haunt me," he said.

His words took me on wings. I saw myself gliding alongside my heron, and when he stepped up to me and took me in his arms, I could offer no resistance. Our kiss was long, our bodies turned gracefully in to each other. When we parted lips, his lips continued over my eyes and cheeks. It was as if he wanted to feast on my face.

"Pierre," I pleaded weakly.

"No, Gabriel. You feel toward me exactly how I feel toward you. I know it; I've known it all these weeks during which I suffered being away from you. I thought I would try to stay away, but that was a foolish lie to tell myself. There was no hope of that. I could no more stop the sun from rising and falling than I could stop myself from seeing you, Gabriel."

"But, Pierre, how can we . . ."

"I've thought of everything," he said proudly. "And I've gotten it all accomplished before I came poling down this canal searching, hoping to see you along this bank. I must confess," he added, "I've been here before, waiting for you."

"You have?"

"Oui."

"But what have you thought of, planned? I don't understand," I said.

"Do you trust yourself, or me, for that matter, enough to get into my canoe?"

I looked at it suspiciously. "And then?"

"Let it be a surprise," he said. "Come along." He took my hand and helped me step into his canoe. Then he pushed off from the bank and turned the pirogue to begin poling away. Someone had taught him well. His strokes were long and efficient. In moments we were gliding through the water. "How am I doing? Will I make a Cajun fisherman yet?"

"You might," I said.

As we continued he described some of the work he had been doing since he had left the bayou, but how his mind always drifted back to me and to this natural paradise.

"And my cook loved your mother's herbs. She says your mother must be a great *traiteur.*"

"She is," I said. "Pierre, where are we going? I don't . . ." I paused when he turned the pirogue toward shore. There was a small dock nearly completely hidden in the overgrown water lilies and tall grass, and beyond it, what I knew to be the old Daisy shack, deserted ever since John Daisy had died of heart failure. He had been a fisherman and trapper. After he had died, his wife had moved into Houma to work and married a postman.

Pierre docked the canoe. "We're here," he said.

"Here? This is the old Daisy place," I said.

"Not anymore. I bought it a couple of weeks ago."

"What? Are you serious? You bought it?"

"Oui," he said. "Come see. I had it fixed up a bit. It's no New Orleans apartment, but it's cozy."

"But how did you do this without anyone knowing?"

"There are ways when you spend enough," he replied with a wink.

"But why?"

"Why? Just to be close to you whenever I want to be and when, I hope, you want me to be," he said. He took my hand. Feeling swept along, I could only follow him up the path to the shack. It was never anything when the Daisys lived in it, but it had fallen into some ruin after John Daisy's death. Pierre had had the floorboards repaired, the holes mended, the windows recovered, the tin roof restored, and the furniture replaced. He had a new rug in the sitting room.

"I brought that in from New Orleans myself," he said, nodding at the rug. "The shack has none of the modern conveniences, but I think that's what gives it all it's charm, don't you?" he said as I wandered through it. "The lamps have oil; there's something to eat and drink and the bed has new linens. What else could we ask for?" he said, and opened a cabinet in the kitchen to take out some glasses and then some wine from a cool chest he had filled with ice.

"I can't believe you did this," I said.

"I'm a man of action," he replied, laughing. He uncorked the wine and poured two glasses. "Let's make a toast," he said, handing me my glass. "To our dream house in our dreamworld. I hope I never wake up." He tapped my glass and brought his to his lips. After a moment I sipped my wine, too. "So? What do you think?"

"I think you're a madman," I said.

"Good. I'm tired of being Pierre Dumas, the sensible, brilliant, respected businessman. I want to feel young and alive again, and you make me feel that way, Gabriel. You wipe the cobwebs out of my brain and drive the shadows from my heart. You are all sunshine and cool, clear water.

"Didn't you think constantly of me these past weeks? Didn't you want me to return? Please, tell me the truth. I need to hear it."

I hesitated.

In the back of my mind I heard Mama's voice, I heard all the warnings. I saw myself heading toward a precipice, in danger of a great fall. All that was sensible and logical in me told me to leave, and as quickly as possible; but my feet were nailed to the floor by a love that rippled through my body as firmly as he claimed his did.

"I thought of nothing else," I admitted. "I, too, saw your face everywhere, heard your voice in every sound. Every day you didn't return was an empty day, no matter how much work I filled it with," I said. His face brightened.

"Gabriel . . . I love you," he said, and took me into his

227

arms. Then he scooped me up and carried me to the bedroom that would be our love nest.

After what Octavious Tate had done to me and what Virgil Atkins had said to me, I thought I would never taste love on my lips nor ever know what a soft, gentle caress of affection was like. I thought I would die resembling a wild rose, never seen, never smelled, never touched, a flower that would be kissed by the sun and the rain until it bloomed radiantly, but then would eventually wither and decompose, its petals floating sadly to the earth, its stem bending until the next rain pounded it into dust to be forgotten, to be treated as if it had never existed.

But in Pierre's arms, I felt myself blossoming, exploding with color and vibrancy. His kind and tender touch filled my heart with a warmth I never dreamed I'd feel. Nothing was rushed; nothing was grotesque. When we were naked beside each other, we were silent, speaking only with our eyes and our lips. His fingers made secret places on my body tingle, places I never imagined would ever feel as alive. I closed my eyes and clung to him when he moved over my breasts with his lips and touched me with the tip of his tongue. I felt as if I were falling, but as long as I held on to him tightly, I would be safe, forever.

He didn't rush to put his manliness inside me. It was as if he knew what I had experienced under the gritty, violent pawing of Octavious Tate, as if he knew I had to be brought back to a virgin state first and then, gently, affectionately, lovingly, taken on that ride young women dream about from the first day they realize what can happen between them and some loving man. It all happened now the way it was meant to happen. That horrible violation of me was erased with every tender caress, every word of love whispered.

When we coupled on the bed, we paused and gazed for a long moment into each other's eyes. It was then that I realized the act of love could be the ultimate confirmation of our deepest feelings for each other. We weren't taking from each other as much as we were giving to each other. I could hear Pierre's thoughts, hear his plea: "Come with me, soar with me, for these precious moments forget everything but us. We are the world to each other; we are the sun for each other: we are the stars."

It was wonderful to surrender myself completely and feel him submerge his identity completely into me. We were, as the poets say, one.

Afterward we lay beside each other, tingling, still touching each other with our lips as well as our fingers.

"This is our secret place," Pierre said. "No one must know. I will come to you as often, as many times, as I can for as long as I am able," he promised.

"But how, Pierre? You are married."

"My wife and I live separate lives right now. She is content being the queen of the block, one of New Orleans's royalty, a princess of the city. Her friends are not my friends. I do not enjoy the affairs she attends and the people with whom she surrounds herself. They are all . . . fops, dandies, artificial men and women who lie to each other and to themselves continually and then whisper behind each other's backs. But Daphne enjoys the games, enjoys being the center of things, being kowtowed to and catered to and treated like the blue blood she believes she is."

"But, Pierre, is it not sinful what we are doing?" I couldn't help thinking about Mama now and all her warnings. "Tell me that love makes this all right," I moaned, the tears burning beneath my eyelids.

"Shh." He put his finger on my lips and then kissed the tip of my nose and smiled. "Yes, darling Gabriel. Love does make this all right, especially a true love, for love like ours must be divinely inspired, blessed. It's too wonderful to be created by the devil and it's too pure. I love you without lust, but with affection; I love you without selfishness, but with only the hope to make you happy."

"But what if you're eventually discovered here? What if . . ."

"I would risk everything I have a hundred times," he pledged, "because what I have means nothing without you."

He kissed me and held me, and before we dressed to leave our secret place, we made love again. Afterward we returned to the pirogue and Pierre took me close to my shack home,

229

but far enough away to leave me off unnoticed. We kissed and held each other.

"I will return as soon as I can," he said. "I'll get word to you and you will find me there, waiting. Let every day become an hour, every hour become a minute, so I can see you sooner," he said, and kissed me again before pushing off. I watched him pole away, my apparition, my dream lover, until he was gone behind a bend.

It did feel more like a illusion than an actual event. I had to pinch myself to convince myself I was living this and not asleep on some rock conjuring the images. I walked on air, my heart full of contentment, but as I drew closer to the shack, I heard Mama and Daddy arguing about money. I paused by the window and listened.

She claimed he had gambled away what he had, and he swore it all went to expenses. He wanted her to give him what she had put aside, but she refused.

"I ain't helping you pay your new gambling debt, Jack. Gabriel and I worked hard for the little we've put away, and we ain't watching it get washed down some ditch, along with everything else you own."

"Ahh. You listen to me," Daddy said in a deep, threatening voice.

Suddenly Mama wailed and then I heard her cry for Saint Medad. She followed that with a string of gibberish only she understood, and a moment later, Daddy came rushing out of the house, his hair wild, his face flushed, his eyes bulging with fear. He practically leaped into his truck and drove off.

When I entered the house, Mama was collapsed in her rocker, her head down so that her chin touched her chest.

"Mama!" I cried, going quickly to her side and kneeling to hold her hand.

She lifted her head slowly. "I'm all right. I thought it was him returning," she said with a cold smile. Then her face saddened. "It's too bad I have to revert to mumbo-jumbo and superstition to keep him under control.

"I got our money buried all over this place, Gabriel, in places he ain't never going to find. It's better he don't know how much we have stored or he'll take it and leave us high and dry while he goes off on another bender. What he ain't got, he can't lose," she concluded.

"I'm sorry, Mama," I said. "I thought he was doing so much better."

"He was, but he's not constant; he'll never be dependable, I'm afraid. But," she said, rising, "we've got to make do with what we have now, don't we? I'll see to our dinner."

"Do you still love him, Mama?" I asked. I wondered how it would be possible, especially after being with Pierre and seeing how wonderful real love could be. Mama paused and thought a moment and then tweaked her lips into a tiny smile.

"Sometimes, when he's like he was, I feel the pitter-patter again. But," she said with a deep sigh, "it don't last."

It wasn't until that moment, until I had traveled on my own cloud of ecstasy and seen what love and true passion could be, that I fully understood Mama's burden and felt truly sorry for her. I wished I could tell her, but I knew if I uttered a single word that suggested anything, she would forbid me to leave the house and find a way to drive Pierre from my life quickly. Some secrets, I thought, were necessary, but I believed, I hoped, that maybe there would be a time when they wouldn't be.

Of course, I was still very young and had no idea how dark the future could be. Only Mama knew that; only she had the vision. For the moment I didn't want her to look into my future. I'd rather be like one of my swamp turtles and pull in my head until the storms passed. The question was, did I have as hard a shell with which to protect myself?

Daddy surprised us by not getting drunk and staying away as he usually did whenever he got into a row with Mama. He returned home that night, sober, and he was up early the next morning.

"I got me an important job today," he said when I came down to the kitchen. "Those rich people from New Orleans you were asking about the other day sent word they were returning for another hunting trip."

"Monsieur Dumas?" I said after a slight gasp.

"Oui. I'm buying a new pirogue because they're bringing a

231

few more with them," he told me. "Got me a loan yesterday. I have to pay a lot of interest because someone won't lend me the money without interest," he added, glaring at Mama. She pretended not to hear him complain. "Anyway, they're bringing me the canoe today," he said. "You can break it in for me. Gabriel. Take it out and put it through the paces, hear?"

"Yes, Daddy." I tried to contain my excitement. Would Pierre appear with his father? Would he be back that much sooner? How would I act? Would I reveal our secret love? Would Mama sense something even if I did nothing?

Late one morning toward the end of the week, three big cars appeared and the men from New Orleans stepped out. My heart skipped a beat. I had been waiting with a feverish insanity since I had awoken, but I wasn't disappointed. Pierre was among them.

Earlier we had had a downpour, but now the feather-brushed storm clouds were far off on the horizon and the sun had already dried the leaves and the grass. Daddy greeted Monsieur Dumas excitedly, and Monsieur Dumas introduced Daddy to the other hunters. As they spoke, Pierre remained in the background, glancing my way from time to time with a tiny smile on his lips. Because of the hour at which they arrived, it was decided Mama and I would feed the men first. They sat at our outside tables and we brought our shrimp étoufée, duck and oyster gumbo, Mama's homemade bread, and wine. It was an exquisite torture for me to serve Pierre without revealing my true feelings for him. I tried not to look at him because I felt the eyes of all the men on me.

"Your daughter is quite pretty, monsieur," Pierre's father remarked to Daddy. He grunted, looked at me as if just realizing I was there, and smiled. I felt a rush of color rise up my neck and into my face. I glanced quickly at Pierre and then looked down.

"She's going to be a great belle," Daddy said between gulps of food.

"Going to be? You would have to be blind not to see that she already is. How old are you, mademoiselle?" Pierre's father asked me.

"Nineteen, monsieur."

"Nineteen? Seems a pity to waste her talents here," one of the other rich men commented.

"She's not being wasted," Mama retorted sharply, and he lost his lusty smile quickly. Daddy scowled and Mama ordered me to bring something into the house.

Soon afterward, they prepared for their hunting trip in the swamps, all of them slipping into their hip-high boots. They checked their shotguns, with Daddy complimenting them on their fine equipment.

Pierre was going along this time, but before he got into the pirogue, he paused beside me, squeezed my hand surreptitiously, and whispered, "I'm going to remain behind at our secret place afterward. I've already arranged it."

"But your father . . ."

"Don't worry about him. Don't worry about anything. Can you come tonight?"

"Yes," I promised.

"Don't worry," he said, smiling as he started away, "I won't kill anything. I'm even a worse shot now that I've met you than I was before."

I laughed and turned to rush back to help Mama clean up. When I did, I saw her gazing at me from a window. Between the batten plank shutters, her face was as dark and as sad as one who just had seen the end of the world.

12

Following My Heart

Mama said nothing to me; her eyes did all the talking as she prepared our dinner and as we ate, flashing disappointment and sadness my way. Daddy didn't notice anything for a while. He was still beaming from the successful hunting trip and the good money he had made.

"To think I wasted all that time working for someone else," he lectured. "No one's ever going to take advantage of Jack Landry again and treat me like some swamp slave," he vowed. "No sir, I got respect. I think I might just invest in another building, a real boathouse, and eventually hire me an assistant," he continued, building steam as he rambled on. "I'll advertise my place in the papers, maybe even the New Orleans papers. We'll fix up this shack, put on new siding, do up the grounds, make it more presentable."

He paused and gazed at Mama. "What you so quiet about, Catherine? Ain't you happy about the money I gave you and how well we're doin'?"

"I'm happy, Jack," she said quickly. "I just don't want to hear any promises and pledges that ain't going to be kept," she warned.

"You see that, Gabriel? She says that after all I've done already. A Cajun man ain't got a chance with a Cajun woman. They're the stubbornest, most ornery females this side a hell. You give a Cajun woman an inch of rope and she'll stretch it into enough to hang you upside down from the nearest cypress and leave you dangling till the blood drips out of your hair." He ran his long fingers through his strands and then held out his palms. "Look here, it's happening to me already."

"Go on with you, Jack Landry," Mama said with a tight smile. "You look abused now, don't you?"

"I'm abused because I ain't appreciated enough," he complained.

Mama lifted her eyes to the ceiling as if to ask for divine guidance and then shook her head.

"Your mama's pretty though, Gabriel. That's why I grin and bear it," he said.

"Go on with you, Jack Landry."

"Pour me a little more of your good wine, Catherine," Daddy said with a different sort of look in his eyes. "It's time you and me did some celebratin'."

"I'll decide when it's time for that," Mama said, but she poured the wine and then flashed another sorry look my way. I finished eating and cleared the table.

"Let's us go for a little ride, Catherine Landry," Daddy suggested. "Like we usta," he added with a wink. It was the first time I could remember seeing Mama blush. She looked away quickly and went to fetch a light shawl.

"We won't be gone long," Mama told me.

"We'll see about that," Daddy said. "We might just stop to look at the moon over the dam at Samson's Landing."

"Hush up, Jack Landry, you fool," Mama snapped. Daddy laughed, put his arm around her waist, and hurried her out. She gazed back at me with a look of warning in her eyes, but Daddy rushed her into the truck before she could add a word. I heard them drive off, and the moment I was alone, my heart began to pound.

I completed cleaning up from dinner and then went quickly down to the dock to get into my canoe. The thumping in my chest was so hard and so fast, I almost couldn't pole and I was terrified I would lose my breath and fall out again. But I moved swiftly along the bank, and before long, saw the Daisys' old landing. There was just a sliver of moon tonight, and even that was blocked most of the time by thick layers of dark clouds rolling in from the Gulf. The cicadas were louder than ever, accompanied by a chorus of bullfrogs. A night heron landed on the dock before I arrived and strutted around for a moment before sailing off into the darkness.

From the dock I could see the tiny light of the butane lantern in the shack's rear window. It flickered like a candle. I hesitated, embraced myself and gazed into the darkness around and behind me. Everything felt forbidden; Mama had cast a blanket of taboo over the world with her dark gaze tonight. But inside the shack, the love of my life waited to feel my lips on his. His dazzling eyes danced on the inside of my lids whenever I closed them, and his voice was in the gentle breeze that lifted the strands of my hair and tickled the inside of my ears. I heard him calling, "Gabriel . . . Gabriel." I could practically feel his hand around mine, leading me, pulling me along, urging me to be at his side.

He didn't come out to greet me before I reached the shack, and when I opened the door slowly and stepped into the darkness, I didn't hear or see him. Maybe it wasn't Pierre; maybe someone else was in the shack.

"Pierre?" I called. There was no response; nothing but the drumming of my own heart against my chest. "Pierre?"

I walked in farther, reaching the steps and listening.

"Pierre?"

"Gabriel," I finally heard from the darkness above. "I'm up here, waiting for you."

My body trembled so. I had to hold on to the railing as I ascended. Slowly, wrapped in the darkness myself, I approached the doorway of the bedroom and gazed in at him, bathed in the dim light of the butane lantern. He was naked on our bed, his body gleaming.

"I shouldn't have come," I whispered, just loud enough for him to hear. "I should have resisted."

"You might as well try to hold your breath forever," he replied. "We can't refuse what our hearts desire. Gabriel, come to me," he said, holding out his arms.

Resembling someone under hypnosis, I walked slowly, my

legs feeling as if they glided on air to the bed. It was his idea that we not touch each other, not kiss, not caress, not even brush each other with our breaths for a while. He lay back as I undressed in the yellow glow of the small lantern. Then he shifted to the opposite side of the bed and I lay down, my head on the pillow, my eyes fixed on him. We gazed at each other, both our hearts pounding, the blood rushing through our bodies.

Every part of me longed to be touched. My lips tingled in anticipation. He smiled and brought his hand to within an inch of my breasts, moving over the air between us as if he were caressing me. I moaned, closed my eyes, and waited.

"It's exquisite, this torture," he said.

I squirmed, moaned again, and ran the tip of my tongue over my lips in anticipation of his kiss.

"Every inch between us is like a mile," he said. "Now you know how painful it is for me to return to New Orleans and what it is like for me to look out of my window toward the bayou and think of you."

I had come hoping to have the strength to refuse him, but now it was all I could do to keep from throwing myself at him.

"Gabriel," he finally said, and brought his lips closer and closer until we finally kissed. It was the most tingling, exciting kiss between us yet. I held him harder and tighter than he held me and then we touched and brought our bodies together. Our lovemaking was more frantic this time. It was as if we had driven each other mad by teasing each other with our desire. I didn't want it to end, and when it threatened to do so, I cried out and demanded more, digging my fingers into his shoulders and hips.

He laughed and we made love until both our bodies shone with sweat, our hearts ready to burst, our lungs unable to keep up with the demand for air. Gasping, but happier than ever, we lay back, our heads beside each other, his arm around my shoulders, and waited to catch enough breath to speak.

"Can you ever doubt my love for you?" he asked.

"No more than I can doubt my own for you."

"Good. Then let there be no more talk of resisting."

I curled up in the warm nook of his arm and listened as he described what it was like for him anticipating our rendezvous, planning it around his father's trip.

"We were so busy, I didn't know when we would be able to get back here, but my father was almost as anxious as I was."

"No one will miss you at home when they see you haven't returned with him?" I asked, meaning his wife.

"I'm on a business trip as far as anyone knows. It's not uncommon for me to do that, but I think my father has some suspicions."

"What will he do?" I asked, a bit frightened.

"Nothing. He isn't looking for any more unpleasantness. Despite the way he behaves with his friends, he is a very unhappy man these days. First, there is my brother Jean, as I told you, and second, there's . . ."

"What?" I asked when he hesitated.

"My wife's failure to be with child. He's been hoping for grandchildren. He's very disappointed."

"Is there no hope that your brother will someday recuperate?"

"No. The doctors believe the damage was permanent. He may improve enough to take care of his basic needs, but he'll never be the man he was," Pierre said, and sat up quickly. "I blame myself," he added.

I put my hand on his back. "Why? If you were caught in a storm . . ."

"I should have never gone out with him. If I hadn't, if I had listened to my own warnings and not let him taunt me into it, he would be fine today."

"But he was a good sailor, wasn't he? He should have known, too."

"Jean was always challenging me to be like him. I think that ego of his got the best of him. I should have restrained him. I'm older, wiser," he said.

"But you're a man, and every man has ego. I'm sure—"

"No," he said sharply. "It was my fault," he said firmly. "I've got to learn to live with that, but more importantly, I've got to find a way to bring my father some happiness before he dies. I try. I do the best I can with our businesses,

238

but it's never enough. My father is a very demanding person, you see.

"But," he said suddenly, turning back to me and smiling, "let's not talk about my family problems. Let's just talk about us.

"Let us make a pledge to one another. Let us pledge to care only about our own bliss and not think about the consequences of anything we do together as long as we do it out of love and for each other."

"It sounds like a very selfish pledge," I said.

"It's meant to be. I want to pluck happiness out of the jaws of sadness, drive the monster away and keep us protected forever and ever, shielded from the miseries, the jealousies, the evil, that seems to seep into everyone's life, even the richest and most respected people. No one will have the ecstasy we will have, Gabriel. I swear."

"You overwhelm me with your love for me," I said. "It scares me because I don't know if I can keep such a pledge, Pierre. I think my mother already knows about us."

"If she's truly a woman with vision, she will see how full your heart is and how good our love is and she will not want us to part."

"But you're married. We can't be lovers forever."

"We'll find a way, somehow," he said. "For now, let's not think about it. Let's not think about anything that takes from our love. Let's be deliberately blind and deaf to anything but ourselves. Can you do that?"

He didn't wait for my reply. He brought his lips to mine and then he kissed my chin and my breasts, laying his head in my lap. I stroked his hair and gazed down into his handsome face and pleading eyes and ordered the voices inside me that wanted to warn me to be silent.

Be still my heart, I thought, and listen only to my love's vow.

I lay back on the pillow. It started to pour, the drops tapping on the tin roof. He raised himself slowly and then brought himself to me so we could make love again to the rhythm of the rain.

It was still raining when I left the shack to pole my pirogue home. Pierre wanted to drive me, but I told him it was far from the first time I poled in the rain, even at night. He walked down to the dock with me and we kissed as we parted. He stood there, smiling, the drops trickling over his cheeks, soaking him, but him acting as if it were the brightest, driest day. I pushed off and waved and, after a moment, lost sight of him in the darkness. He said he was going to drive back to New Orleans tonight and he would let me know when he would be able to return to our love nest.

Mama and Daddy weren't home when I returned, which made it easier for me. I didn't like lying to Mama, but I had a story already prepared. I was long in bed and even asleep when they came home. I woke to the sounds of Daddy's laughter and Mama telling him to hush up. He knocked into a chair and Mama chastised him again. Then she helped him up the stairs and into bed. I heard her come to my doorway and sensed she was standing there awhile, but I pretended to be asleep.

Daddy slept late the next morning. When I went down to breakfast, Mama was up, sitting at the table, her hands cupped around a mug of steaming coffee. She gazed into the dark liquid as if it were a crystal ball.

"Morning, Mama," I said, and shifted my eyes quickly to avoid her penetrating gaze when she raised her head. It was as good as a confession. She waited for me to get some coffee and a biscuit before she spoke.

"You went out after your daddy and me left last night, didn't you, Gabriel?"

"Yes, Mama."

"Where did you go?"

"Just for a walk and then a short ride in the pirogue," I said. I put some jam on my biscuit.

"You met that man someplace, didn't you, Gabriel?" she asked directly. My heart stopped and then fluttered. "You can't lie to me, Gabriel. It's written in your face."

"Oui, Mama," I confessed. She was right: Keeping the truth from Mama was like trying to hold back a twister.

"Oh, honey," she moaned. "After what you've been through, you've suffered, to go and start with another married man."

"We love each other, Mama. It's different and it's not like anything I've ever felt before," I protested.

"How would you know?" she asked with a stern face. "You've never really had a boyfriend."

"It can't be this good with anyone else."

"Of course it can. You're just feeling your first real excitement, and with a very sophisticated, rich city man who probably has a half dozen young mistresses," she declared.

Such an idea had never occurred to me.

"No, Mama, he said . . ."

"He'd say anything to get you where he wants you, Gabriel." She leaned toward me so I couldn't look away from those all-knowing eyes. "And he would make any promise to get what he wants. If you believe him, it's because you want to, first, and second, because he's done it so many times before, he's good at it," she concluded.

I stared, thinking. Then I shook my head. "He can't be that way; he can't," I insisted, as much to myself as to her.

"Why not, Gabriel?"

"I feel him," I said, putting my hand over my heart, "deeply in here. My feelings have never betrayed me before," I insisted, building my own courage. "Since I was a little girl, I have known what is true and what is not. My animals . . ."

"Animals are so much simpler than people, Gabriel. They are not conniving and deceitful."

"Tell that to my spiders," I shot back. Mama's eyes softened for a moment with a little amusement, but then she grew worried again.

"All right, what of your spider who sets up such a seemingly harmless world around him, so innocent looking, the fly always steps into it and realizes it too late?

"A rich, sophisticated man like Monsieur Dumas has the power to weave a very inviting world around him. He will catch you in it, and when you realize it, it will be too late."

"Pierre is no more conniving than I am, Mama. You don't know him yet."

"And you do? Already?"

"Our feelings for each other have opened our hearts and

minds to each other. When you love each other deeply, truly, it takes only minutes to know everything there is to know. He has told me of his great unhappiness and I see how much he suffers, even though he is a wealthy man."

"And what of his wife, then?" she asked.

"They lead separate lives right now. She has been unable to give him a child and she is more involved with her society friends than with him," I explained.

"But where will all this take you, Gabriel?" she asked with despair.

"I don't know," I admitted.

"And for the moment, you don't care because you're blinded by your feelings and your excitement. Don't you think I know how desperate you are for a real love, how much you need someone who will love you truly, especially after your horrid experience? You're jumping on the first opportunity, only it's not an opportunity, Gabriel. It's like a false dawn. You're going to plummet into a deeper darkness."

She sat back firmly, her words lying heavy in the air between us.

"I want you to tell this man first chance you get that you won't ever see him again, hear? If you don't, I will, Gabriel, even if it means marching down that road all the way to New Orleans and knocking on his front door," she threatened.

"Oh Mama, please . . ."

"If I stood by and watched you drown, I'd be wrong, wouldn't I? Well, I ain't gonna stand by and watch this, neither," she vowed.

We heard the floorboards above us groan.

"It's best your daddy don't know nothing about this, Gabriel, hear?"

"Yes, Mama." I looked down.

"I'm sorry, honey, but I know what's best for you."

I shot an angry glance at her. Why did she always know what was best for me? She wasn't me. What did she think it was like having a *traiteur* for a mother, thinking all these years that my every thought, my every feeling, was as naked as a newly born doe before her eyes? Besides, I thought, when it came to love, Mama wasn't infallible. Look at the mistake she had made, the marriage she had. Defiant, I rose from the table and left the room.

"Gabriel!"

The front door slammed shut behind me as I jogged down the gallery steps and around back, heading toward the canal. I remained away from home most of the day, wandering through my paths, weaving along the water, sitting on a big rock and watching the birds and the fish. I spent most of the time arguing with myself.

The sensible side of me took Mama's side, of course, claiming she was only looking out for my happiness and trying to protect me from sadness and disappointment. That side of me warned against living for the moment. It ridiculed the pledge Pierre and I had made to each other. What sort of a pledge was it anyway, a pledge to ignore everything and anything but our own pleasure? Living for the moment was shortsighted. What would happen when that day of reckoning came?

The other side of me, the wild and free side that found its strength in Nature, that side of me which was never comfortable confined by clothes and houses and man-made rules, refused to listen. Look at the birds. They don't sit worrying about the winter; they enjoy the spring and the summer and feel the warm breeze around them when they glide through the air, free . . . happy.

And what of these people who have been sensible and who have married the so-called right person? What of these people who have never been naked under the sun and the stars, who have listened first to their minds and then their hearts? Trapped in their wise and reasonable decisions, they wither away wondering what it might have been like if they had followed their feelings instead of their thoughts.

But your mama followed her feelings instead of her thoughts, my sensible side retorted. That thought shut me up for a while. I sat there, brooding. My sensible side continued. She's only trying to give you the benefit of her wisdom, a wisdom unfortunately gained through pain and suffering. Can't you take her gift gracefully and stop being a stubborn, selfish little girl?

I swallowed back my tears and took a deep breath.

Still defiant, or tying to be, I turned my face to the wind and screamed.

"I love Pierre! I will always love him. I won't give him up. I won't!"

My words were swept away. They changed nothing. It didn't take very much effort to scream them; I could scream them again. What took great effort was to shut them up in my heart, to lock the door on that secret place within me where Pierre's face resided and his words resounded.

As I started walking back home, I wondered if every birth, whether it be the birth of a tadpole or the birth of a spider or the birth of a human being, was another beat in the heart of the universe. Maybe my birth was an irregular beat. I was simply out of sync with the rhythms of this world, and I would not ever find a place in it. I would never find happiness and a love that could be. I was destined to be an outcast. Maybe that was why I was so drawn to simple, natural things and felt safer in the swamp than I did in society.

Mama looked up from the clothes she was washing in the rain barrel when I appeared. She wasn't angry; she was very sad for me. She stopped working and waited as I drew closer.

"I'll tell him I won't see him anymore, Mama," I said.

"It's the best thing, Gabriel."

"The best thing shouldn't be so hard to do," I replied angrily, and went into the shack.

Almost a week went by before I heard from Pierre again. During that time I sat by the window in my room and looked out over the canals toward New Orleans and wondered what he was thinking, what he was doing. In my mind I wrote and rewrote my letter to him until I found the words, and then I sat at the kitchen table late one night after Daddy and Mama had gone to bed and put the words on paper.

Dear Pierre,

Some women think giving birth is the hardest and most painful experience of their lives. Afterward, of course, there is a wonderful reward. But I think the birth of these words on this paper is the hardest and most painful thing for me. There is no wonderful reward either.

I can't see you anymore. I love you; I won't lie and deny that, but our love, as beautiful as it seems, is a double-edged sword that will turn on us someday, perhaps sooner than we expect. We will hurt each other deeply, perhaps too deeply to recover, and maybe, just maybe, we will even grow to hate each other for what we have done to each other, or worse, hate ourselves for it.

I don't pretend to be a very wise person. Nor have I ever assumed I have inherited my mother's powers, but I don't think it takes a very wise person or a clairvoyant to see our future. We are like a stream, rushing, gleaming, sparkling, and full, that suddenly turns a corner and drops over a ledge to pound itself on the rocks below and then stagnate.

I can't let this happen to you or to me. Please try to understand. I want you to be happy. I hope your problems will end and you will have a good and fruitful life where you are, where you belong.

Sell this shack and go home, Pierre. Do it for both our sakes.

Gabriel

I folded the letter and put it in an envelope quickly. The next morning after breakfast, I went down to the dock, got into my canoe, and poled up to the Daisy dock. I hurried up to the shack and put the envelope in the center of the kitchen table where it would be prominent. Then I gazed around what was to have been our love nest for as long as we could have it. The tears streamed down my cheeks. I sighed, bit down on my lower lip, and ran out of the shack. I sobbed as I poled my way back, but when I reached our dock, I sucked back my tears, took a deep breath, and forced myself to stop thinking about what I had done.

I dove into the work Mama and I had to do, weaving, cooking, organizing, and I didn't permit myself to think about Pierre. Whenever his face came to mind, I started doing something else. Mama watched me all day through her wise eyes. She said nothing while I worked, but that evening, after dinner, she came out to see me on the gallery and just hugged me without speaking. We gazed into each other's faces.

Finally she said, "Don't think I don't feel your pain, honey. We're too close."

"I know, Mama."

"You're a good girl, a strong girl, stronger than me," she said, and smiled. I smiled back, but I didn't believe those words. If anything, I felt more fragile and thinner than ever.

Another day passed and then another and another. I began to believe that Pierre had come to the shack, found my letter, and returned to New Orleans. The longer time grew between us, the more I began to believe Mama might have been right about everything. I was saddened, but a little relieved.

And then, one night, just as I was about to go to sleep, I paused to gaze out of my window as I often did, and there in the moonlight, his form well outlined, was Pierre. He stood staring up at my window. I wanted to go down to him, to talk and tell him why I wrote the letter, but I didn't move. I watched him and waited. He stood there for nearly an hour, waiting, looking like a statue. My heart was bursting, but I stopped myself every time I went toward the doorway. And every time I returned to the window, I hoped he would be gone, but he wasn't.

Clouds came and blocked the moon. He disappeared in the shadows, but when the clouds parted, he was there again, waiting, watching, hoping.

I went to bed and pressed my face in the pillow, nearly smothering myself, squeezing, clinging to the sheets like someone who might drown if she let go. Finally, when I went to the window, he wasn't there. He had resembled my ghost once more, and once more, he had returned to that other world. I couldn't fall asleep. I lay there with my eyes open, wondering if he had returned to the shack to sleep or if he had taken my advice and gotten into his car to drive back to New Orleans.

All the next day I was tempted to pole up to the Daisy dock to look. I thought he might also pole down to see me, but he didn't come. I took my walks, did my work, watched the road every time I heard an automobile, but he didn't appear. It's over, I thought that night after dinner. I did it. The realization made me sick inside. I had to go to bed early. Daddy was off playing *bourre* and Mama finished cleaning up.

But just as I got into bed, I heard someone come to the front door. I listened hard. Was it Pierre? I heard the voices and realized it was Jed Loomis, a neighbor who lived about a half mile toward Houma. He had come by in his pickup truck to tell Mama that his mother was suffering something terrible from stomach cramps. She was in great pain. Everyone was very worried; his father wouldn't leave her bedside. They weren't sure whether it came from something she had eaten or if it was something worse.

Mama packed up her herbs and her holy water and then came up to tell me she was going.

"You want to come along, Gabriel?"

"No, Mama. Not unless you think you'll need me."

"No. There's nothing for you to do and it might take most of the night. I guess there's no sense in both of us staying up," she said. "If your daddy comes home early for some reason, you'll tell him where I've gone."

"Yes, Mama."

"You all right, honey?"

"Yes, Mama," I lied.

She paused a moment. "I gotta go," she said. "Poor woman's in pain."

"Okay, Mama."

She descended the stairs and was gone. I closed my eyes and tried to sleep, and for a little while I did fall into a deep repose, but suddenly my eyes popped open. My heart had started to drum as if it knew something I didn't. I lay there staring up into the darkness waiting for it to slow down. When it didn't, I sat up and then went to the window.

There he was, outlined in the moonlight, staring up at the house, waiting . . . Pierre. My ghost would not go away.

I threw on my dress and hurried down, closing the screen door softly behind me. He was waiting on our dock.

"Gabriel," he said as I approached. "I was afraid to come to your house to ask for you."

"I'm glad you didn't," I said, stopping a foot or so away from him.

"Why? Why did you write that letter?"

"I had to," I said as harshly as my lips would permit me to speak to him. He stepped toward me. "Mama knows," I added, and he froze for a moment. "She threatened to go to New Orleans and knock on your door if she had to," I added.

As the moon peeked over the shoulder of a passing cloud, the light caught his face and revealed a pained expression.

"What is it your mother thinks of me?" he asked softly. "What has she told you?"

"You are rich, Pierre. You can go anywhere, do anything, see anyone you want."

"Oui," he said. "That's true, Gabriel, but I didn't go anywhere else; I didn't do anything else, and I haven't seen anyone else but you. You were right in your letter. Our love, my love for you, is a double-edged sword, and when you said you couldn't see me again, I felt its sharpness in my heart. Do you know what it's been like being here, looking up at your window at night?"

"Pierre . . ."

"And during the day."

"During the day?"

"Yes. I've watched you from a distance, seen you walking, seen you working, talking to people, but I was afraid to approach you in daylight. Remember the exquisite torment of being beside each other and not touching? It wasn't exquisite this time; it was just torment.

"You think I have other lovers, don't you? You think because I am rich, I can go anywhere and have affair after affair and then one day pick up and leave, breaking someone's heart without caring?"

I was ashamed to say yes, but I had thought it. He nodded and turned away for a moment.

"Other men I know, wealthy, married men, fit that description. I would not deny it, but you are the first woman I have kissed passionately since I married Daphne. You must believe me."

"Didn't you love her?"

"I . . . thought so. She's a very beautiful woman and she comes from a family as distinguished as mine, although not as wealthy. Ours was more of an arranged marriage. We were thought to be the perfect couple, but things happen, things change. I'm a very lonely man these days, Gabriel, and despite what your mother might fear for you and even what you might think at this moment, I am not one to go wandering and philandering. I do not give myself liberally.

"But when my eyes feasted on you, when I first saw you, I felt something so deep and so sincere in my heart, I could not deny it; I will not deny it. I swear I'm not here to take advantage of you and then leave you in the lurch. I will never do anything to harm you or make you unhappy. Somehow, I want to be able to take care of you.

"I can't believe," he continued, raising his voice and his clenched hands in the air, "that this love is not meant to be. What a horrible trick Nature has played on us then. To bring me here, to permit me to see you and you to see me. To permit us to kiss and hold each other and pledge our feelings to each other, and then to rip us apart mercilessly like this . . . no. No!" he cried. "I won't permit it to happen. Tell me what I must do to be with you and I will do it."

"I can't ask you to do anything, Pierre. It's enough that you and I have been together while you are married, but I believed you when you said our love is so good and pure, it makes it all right. I wanted to believe you."

"Don't stop believing that, Gabriel. It's true. It's as true as the morning light and the evening stars." He stepped closer to me. "How can you deny that?"

"I don't deny it," I said softly.

"Good. Love me then, Gabriel; love me as purely as I love you and throw caution and unhappiness to the wind."

"Pierre," I said, whispering. He put his hands on my shoulders. I couldn't drive him away; I didn't have the

249

strength. God forgive me, I thought, but I love him more than I love what's logical or right or what's sensible. He kissed me and I kissed him back.

Instantly his arms were around me. He lifted me to him and held me.

"I thought I might kill myself," he whispered in my ear between kisses. "I thought I might throw myself into your swamp and let your snakes or alligators feast on my depressed body. It seemed a fit place to die."

"No, Pierre. Don't think of such a terrible thing."

"I won't as long as you will hold me and be with me and love me," he said. I promised I would and we kissed again. Then we stepped into his canoe. I lay back and watched him push off and pole us into the darkness.

The swamp seemed to come alive. It was as if all sound, all life, had been put on hold while we spoke, and now that we were quiet, Nature spoke. She spoke through the owl that hooted from the branch of the pecan tree onshore, the cicadas that raised their voices to drone their nightly symphony, the frogs that croaked at us every inch of the way, and the night heron that called from the darkness.

We returned to our love nest that night, and together, we burned my letter and watched the flames consume it.

"Let those dark thoughts evaporate with the smoke," Pierre said, and kissed me.

I lay back, too emotionally exhausted to resist or even to hesitate. Afterward, he brought me home before Mama returned from her *traiteur* mission. He told me he had to leave in the morning.

"I won't be able to return for nearly two weeks because I'm going on a business trip to Texas with my father."

"I will miss you and count the days until I see you again," I promised.

"I don't suppose I can come calling on you when I do return. Your mother wouldn't be too happy about that."

"No."

"I expect your father wouldn't be pleased either. But I can't just come by and stand waiting for you to see me, so here's what I'm going to do," he said, and took off the blue silk cravat he had around his neck. "When you find this tied to the northeast post on your dock, you will know I am here and waiting for you. Bring it with you when you come," he said. "Someday, somehow," he added with a sigh, "we might not have to be so secretive, but as for now . . ."

"As for now, let's not think about it," I told him. He smiled and kissed me good night. He waited as I ran up to the house and turned once to wave good-bye. He pushed off into the darkness as was gone, and I went inside.

As Mama had thought, she had to stay with Nicolette Loomis most of the night and was exhausted herself when she returned just before daybreak. Daddy didn't come home at all until the following afternoon. He made no excuses and Mama didn't ask him for any.

I said nothing to Mama about Pierre. If she knew anything by reading my face, she didn't reveal it.

Daddy had two hunting trips that week, and Mama and I were busy making food and selling our wares.

I went to town on an errand the following Saturday and spotted the Tates' automobile in front of the dry goods store. Neither Gladys or Octavious seemed to be around, so I wandered up the walk toward the car. When I peered into the rear, I saw the nanny and Paul. He smiled at me and I smiled back, but I moved away quickly when I thought Gladys Tate was returning. Even so, I had a long enough look at Paul to see how he had grown, how bright his eyes were and how beautiful he was.

Mama sensed a lightness in my gait and a contentment in my smile during those days. I could see it in the way she looked at me from time to time, but she didn't ask me anything, nor reveal she suspected anything. I was spending almost all my time working beside her or taking my walks in the swamp alone. I helped Daddy, too.

I hated being deceitful and secretive, but I told myself this was one of those times when it was better for everyone. I was afraid I was becoming a little like Daddy, who used to say lying and stealing were all right if they were meant to help someone you love or who needs it.

Mama, of course, accused him of just making up an excuse for his own evil ways.

"It will all come home to roost and haunt you in your old

age, Jack Landry," she predicted. "The ghosts of your sins will be your own company."

I was terrified, of course, that what she predicted for Daddy would fit my future, too; but every time I entertained a thought to try to end my love for Pierre again, his face, his words, his warm lips, returned to mind and drove those thoughts away, fluttering off like a flock of rice birds spooked by an alligator.

The weeks passed too slowly, and when the time came for him to be here, I looked eagerly for his blue silk cravat; but every day I looked, I found nothing. I was afraid he had tied it and it had come loose and been carried down the canal, so I even poled up to the Daisys' landing to check, but he wasn't there. Another week passed and I began to grow desperately worried. Had our love affair been discovered and his father forbidden him to see me again? Had Daphne found out and made great trouble between them? Perhaps something happened to him and he was sick or hurt, I thought. It was terrible having to live in ignorance and darkness when it came to him. After another day passed and there was no cravat, I entertained the thought of going to town to use a pay phone and call his residence in New Orleans; but the idea of hearing his wife's voice, or even a maid's or butler's, terrified me. I could get him in trouble, I thought. So I waited, growing sadder and more depressed with every passing hour, much less every passing day.

I tried to act cheerful whenever I was with Mama or whenever I thought she was watching me, but my face was like a glass pane to her. She finally asked me if I was feeling all right.

"I'm fine, Mama," I said. I thought quickly and added, "I saw little Paul in town the other day and he smiled at me."

"Oh," she said, thinking that was it. "Did the Tates . . ."

"No, I left before either saw me looking at the baby."

"That's good," Mama said. "We don't need any more turmoil in our lives," she added, raising her eyebrows. "No more, hear, Gabriel?"

"Yes, Mama."

I went on about my business. The next morning I found a lark had thatched a nest with goose down, but a family of field mice had made a home beneath it. The lark didn't seem to mind, and the wonder of Nature cheered me up for a while. Then, as I returned home from my walk, I gazed at our dock and saw the blue silk cravat waving in the breeze.

My love was back.

My heart was full again.

13

Secret Wife

In the days and weeks that followed, I lived for the sight of Pierre's blue silk cravat fluttering in the breeze. It was as if we had our own country, our own world, and the cravat was our flag, hoisted to announce our love. His arrivals were always unexpected, for he never knew exactly when he would be free to come. Sometimes we met in the afternoon, sometimes at night. He never stayed more than two days.

After a while there was no question that Mama knew, but she said nothing. A few times I caught a glimpse of her crossing herself while she looked at me. She wore that expression she always had when she believed something sad was inevitable or meant to be.

But these days Mama was distracted by and occupied more with Daddy than with me. Having some success and some money had gone to his head. Mama tried to get him to put something in the bank, but he never trusted banks or bankers. Daddy was suspicious and disdainful of anyone who made a living with his brain instead of his hands. To him it was just a more elaborate or sophisticated form of a scam that had its roots in the con games and tricks scoundrels employed to tempt hardworking people into investing their money in phony land deals or companies.

Mama told him if there was anyone who should know about that sort of evil, it was he, since the Landrys had a string of embezzlers, con men, and thieves throughout their family line. Those comments only started new arguments between them. The truth was, Daddy could be as stubborn as Mama, and what he claimed to be true about Cajun women was just as true about Cajun men.

With money in his pocket, a new truck, and the growing respect of other Cajun trappers and fishermen, Daddy became somewhat arrogant. He bought himself new boots and some new clothes, new knives and fishing poles, and paraded about the old haunts, buying some of his worst drinking buddies jugs of "Good Old Nongela" and rye whiskey, and going off with them to drink and gamble. His stash quickly shrunk and he started in again, day after day, demanding Mama share some of the money he had given her to hold for a rainy day.

"It's pouring now," he'd complain. "I need it."

"If it's raining, it's raining because you brought the storm clouds over yourself, Jack Landry. Stay home nights and think about ways to earn new money, not spend the money we have," she told him. She refused to give him a penny no matter how much he pleaded.

One night he came home drunk and started to pull the shack apart looking for hidden dollars. Mama was out treating Mrs. Bordeau for gout, and when she returned, she found me hovering in the shadows out front, frightened. She heard the racket coming from inside.

"What's going on, Gabriel?"

"Daddy's drunk again, Mama," I wailed. "He came charging into the house, demanding I tell him where you hid money. I told him I didn't know and he started pulling the pots and pans out, throwing them across the kitchen, and nearly hitting me with one. I ran out here to wait. I think he's pulling up floorboards now."

"This is coming to a quick end," she vowed, and charged toward the front door, her tiny body swelling up so that her shoulders rose almost even with her ears. She pulled open the screen door, reached into her basket, and came up with a statue of the Virgin Mary. She held it up in front of herself and walked in, chanting something in French. I heard the racket come to a stop. Mama shrieked something that sounded like voodoo and Daddy came out of the house, his face beet red, his eyes wild. He tripped on the gallery steps and fell. Mama appeared above him and shook a bottle of holy water at him. When the drops hit him, he howled as if he had been scalded. I had never seen anything like it before. He bellowed and crawled away, clawing the air to get to his feet.

"Don't you come back here, Jack Landry, unless you repent and are sober as a church deacon, hear?" she screamed after him. He practically flew down to the dock and into his canoe, poling off into the night as soon as he was able to push off. Mama sat herself on the gallery top step to catch her breath.

"He near wrecked our home," she moaned as I approached. "I swear," she said, her eyes full of tears and frustration, "the devil sent him to me as part of his battle against my good works. He's the curse I wear around my neck, and just because I listened first to the woman in me. You hear, Gabriel? You see what comes of paying more attention to this than this?" she said, pointing from her heart to her head.

"*Oui*, Mama," I said softly. I knew what she meant, but never in a thousand years would Pierre be anything like Daddy, I thought. His first concern was always my happiness. Whatever brought sadness to me brought sadness to him. There was a great difference. The woman in me hadn't blinded me to that truth. I looked down so Mama couldn't see my defiant eyes. I heard her sigh deeply.

"Nothing to do but fix up what he broke," she said.

"I'll help you, Mama."

I followed her in, shocked myself at the sight of smashed furniture, torn-out cabinets, ripped-up floorboards, and holes in the walls. We worked until we were both exhausted and had to go to sleep.

Nearly a week followed before Daddy returned looking meek and repentant. He had a small hunting party to take out, but he got into an argument with one of them before they began and the whole group marched off and drove away, leaving him cursing and spitting on the dock. It was more money lost, and because of his temper too. Mama bawled him out for that and he left in a huff, claiming his woman never took his side.

"If I had something decent to take, I'd take it!" she shouted after him. He muttered curses and drove away.

Things between them had never been worse. It saddened me deeply. I was very happy to see Pierre's cravat on the dock post the next day and couldn't wait to get myself up to the Daisy shack.

Now that we met more often at our love nest, Pierre brought food often and I would make us a romantic dinner. We had wine and bread he had brought from the fancy bakeries in New Orleans. We would eat by candlelight. We didn't have electricity, of course, but Pierre bought a wind-up phonograph and played records. We held each other closely and danced in the shadows and flickering light, his lips against my forehead, my ear against his chest, listening contentedly to the beating of his heart and knowing that it beat with love for me.

This time when I arrived, Pierre had gifts for me. He had bought me a fancy dress that had a billowing full skirt and he bought me a necklace with matching earrings. He had even bought me matching shoes. I put everything on and felt like I was going to a real ball.

"It's the latest fashion," he said. "A Dior. Daphne keeps up on those things," he added without thinking. I saw him press his lips together like the farmer who realized too late he had let the horse out of the barn.

"Does she have a dress like this too, then?" He stared at me. "Does she?"

"Yes," he admitted, "but despite her expensive hairdressers and makeup, she doesn't look more attractive than you."

"I doubt that," I said, the magic seeping out of my precious, special moment. "I never wore anything but a little lipstick. Mama says most of it is bad for your skin."

"And she's right."

"Why? Does Daphne have bad skin?" I snapped back quickly.

"She will," he said.

"The only perfume I've ever owned is the scents Mama concocts with her herbs and plants."

"And they're ten times better than what Daphne imports from France."

I shook my head. "I may look like a swamp rat, but I'm not that dumb."

"You don't look like a swamp rat. I'd match you against the most elegantly dressed debutante in New Orleans," he declared. "And you shouldn't dismiss your simple life out here. To me it looks like an idyllic world when I think of the turmoil, the phoniness, and the deceit I contend with day after day in the supposedly sophisticated city."

"Some idyllic world," I said, flopping on a chair. "My mother spends all her life helping people fight diseases and pains, bites and poisons, and then comes home to do battle with my drunken father."

"Why so sad, *chérie?*" Pierre asked, moving quickly to my side so he could take my hand. "This is not like you, especially when you talk about the bayou."

"It's Daddy again," I said, and described what he had done to our home and what had happened between him and Mama. "Money has made him worse, not better."

"I'm sorry. I wish there was a way to take you away and build you a castle someplace where you will always be safe and happy," he told me. He thought a moment. "Maybe I will."

"Don't be a dreamer, too, Pierre," I warned him. Thanks to Daddy, I knew too well what misery false promises could bring.

Pierre smiled. "My little old wise woman." He kissed me. "Come. Let's refuse to be sad. Remember our pledge? When we are here, we shut the rest of the world away and live only for ourselves." He put the music on again and held out his arms. "Come to me, Gabriel. Let these arms comfort and protect you forever and ever."

I softened. "Am I really as pretty as a rich and elegant New Orleans debutante?"

"They can't touch you. You are fresh and beautiful in ways they couldn't even begin to understand," he said.

My heart felt full again. He was right, I thought, we must

live up to our pledge and think only of ourselves and our own happiness. I rushed into his arms and we danced, had wine and coffee, and then made love as passionately as ever. It seemed we would never grow accustomed to each other, never stop discovering something new and exciting about each other.

I felt so complete, so full and satisfied, when I went home that night. Mama was already asleep, or at least in bed, and Daddy was nowhere in sight. I moved through the shack as quietly as I could, but the stairs creaked and the floor groaned. When I lay back on my pillow, I thought I heard the sound of Mama weeping. I listened hard and didn't hear it again, but even the thought of such a thing put a sword of ice through me. I felt terribly guilty for being so happy at a time when Mama was so terribly sad.

In the days that followed, Daddy returned to eking out a small living harvesting oysters and Spanish moss, which was used by furniture manufacturers for stuffing chairs and sofas. He trapped muskrats and did some fishing. He seemed angry all the time, and Mama and he said very little to each other. Pierre offered to give me some money for him, but I thought that would only make Mama angrier, and Daddy would only spend it on jugs of whiskey. There was nothing to do but plod on and hope for the best. Mama must have felt the same way. She seemed busier than ever with her *traiteur* missions.

One afternoon Pierre arrived earlier than usual and had a basket of food. He thought it would be nice to try a picnic. He asked me if I knew any place in the swamp that was interesting, quiet, secluded. Of course, I thought of my special place, my pond, but that was where Octavious Tate had raped me, and I hadn't been able to go there and swim or sun myself since.

"There is one place," I said, "but I don't think I can show it to you."

"Why not?" Pierre asked, and I explained. He listened, his face turning grim and dark.

"It makes it even worse if you permit what he did to destroy what you had," he said after I finished describing what had happened. "It wasn't Nature's fault, was it?"

259

"No."

"Then what we must do is win back your special place, win back its magic for you."

"I can't go back there, Pierre."

"With me, you can do anything," he said defiantly and firmly. "Take me as close as you can and I will do the rest," he declared.

My heart pounding, fearful and nervous, I did as he asked, bringing us right up to the overgrown cypress before stopping the canoe.

"Well?" Pierre asked, sitting up and gazing around. "Is this it?" He looked very disappointed.

"No." I smiled. "It's through there," I said, pointing to the cypress.

"You can go through there?" He stood up. "Let me have that," he said, taking the pole from my hands excitedly. It was my turn to sit and watch him work. He pressed us forward, the canoe penetrating the branches and leaves, which parted like a door, and then we were there.

The horror of what had happened to me began to rush back through the halls of my memory, charging forward, every image, every sound, as vivid as they would be had it all happened minutes ago. I grimaced, but Pierre didn't notice. He was drinking in the beauty of my pond.

"It is magnificent here," he said, gazing over the clear water. There was my pair of egrets, strutting over the big rock. I looked up at the top of the gnarled oak on the north side. The heron's nest was still there, but I didn't see her.

"Is that where you used to go to sun yourself?" Pierre asked, pointing to the rock.

"Oui," I said weakly. He pushed forward, tied the pirogue to the branch sticking up from the water, and stepped onto my rock.

"I, Pierre Dumas, do hereby exorcise any evil thoughts, memories, demons, creatures, and the like from this pond," he said, and waved his hands in the air. "There," he said, smiling down at me. "It's ours now."

I had to laugh. He did look handsome and strong standing there, waving his fist at my past horror. He pulled off his shirt and spread it over the rock. Then he sat on it and waited for me. Gradually, gazing about as if I half expected Octavious Tate to reappear, I stood and stepped onto the rock. For a while I just sat beside him gazing over the water, watching the bream feed, the nutrias scurry about the business of their daily lives. And then, as if it was meant to be a sign of renewal, my heron swooped in over the treetops, dipped toward the water to greet us, and then rose gracefully toward her nest.

"Beautiful," Pierre remarked. He turned to me. "Happy now?"

"Yes," I said cautiously. He smiled, kissed me, and then like an eager teenage boy, hurried to get our picnic spread on the rock. We did have one of our most beautiful days together. Although we kissed and stroked each other, laughed and even teased each other, we did not make love at the pond that day. Pierre was smart enough to go slowly. The look in his eyes promised we would next time, but for now, it was enough to conquer the old demons and reclaim my special place in the bayou.

I felt as if I had a glow about me when I returned home late that afternoon. I walked up from the dock, my eyes down, a small smile on my lips. As I drew closer to the house, I heard a strange voice and paused. The conversation was followed by some laughter and then the clink of bottles. Daddy was entertaining one of his friends, I thought, but I knew Mama never permitted him to do that at the house, so with great curiosity, I approached the front gallery. When I turned the corner, I saw Daddy sitting in Mama's rocker, and across from him sat Richard Paxton, Nicolas's father. The two looked my way sharply when I appeared.

"There she is!" Daddy exclaimed. "Lookin' as pretty as ever."

Monsieur Paxton nodded, his round face beaming as his lips twisted up into a smile. His son had his face, the same round eyes, the same rubber-band lips, always a pale red.

"Come on up here and say hello to Monsieur Paxton, honey. You know him. You've been in his store plenty of times. He's got the best and biggest store in Houma."

Monsieur Paxton nodded, his jowls shaking.

"*Bonjour*, monsieur," I said, and flashed a smile. I started for the door.

"Hold, up now, Gabriel. Monsieur Paxton has come to see me on behalf of his son. You know him well, too, don'tcha?"

"I know him," I said.

"You two graduated together, and Monsieur Paxton here tells me you're the only girl in these here parts he's taken a fancy to. Ain't that right, monsieur?"

"All he talks about is Gabriel Landry whenever we discuss marriage."

"Marriage?" I said, backing a few steps away.

"Sure. Why not?" Daddy asked. "Nicolas is going to inherit the store, right, Richard?" Daddy said, reaching across to slap Monsieur Paxton on the shoulder.

He laughed. "*Oui,* monsieur. He will that."

"See, honey? You can have a nice life, and Monsieur Paxton here says he will start you and Nicolas off with your own home, too. That's a good offer, ain't it?"

"No," I said quickly.

"No?"

Monsieur Paxton's smile evaporated. He looked nervously at Daddy.

"I can't marry Nicolas, Daddy. I don't love him."

"Love him? Hell, girl, you'll learn to love him. Those are the best marriages anyway."

"No, Daddy, please," I said.

"Lookie here," he cried as I moved quickly to the door. "I promised Monsieur Paxton you would—"

"No. *Never!*" I screamed, and ran inside. I heard Daddy mumble something and then follow. I was terrified. Mama wasn't home.

"How can you say no?" Daddy demanded. "What'cha wanna do, stay here the rest of yer life and play with the animals?"

"I don't want to spend the rest of my life with Nicolas Paxton, Daddy."

"Why not? You listen to me," he said, wagging his long right finger at me, "it's a father's duty to find a suitable husband for his daughter, and I did it. Now, you just march out there and tell Monsieur Paxton you will marry his son, hear?"

"No, Daddy. I won't," I said, shaking my head.

His face turned crimson. "Look how old you are already, and you know why you can't be so choosy," he said. "It's just luck no one else knows, too."

"I won't marry Nicolas, Daddy. I won't."

"Gabriel . . ." He took a step toward me.

"I'd rather die," I declared.

The screen door opened, but I couldn't see past Daddy. He hovered over me like a hawk.

"You put one finger on that girl, Jack Landry, and I'll curse you to hell," Mama declared.

Papa turned quickly and looked at her. "I was just trying to get her a good husband, woman."

"Tell that man to go home, Jack. And give him back whatever he gave you," she added.

"What? Why, he didn't . . ."

"Don't waste your breath on a new lie," Mama said.

Daddy gazed at her for a moment and then at me. He shook his head. "Two chicks from the same egg," he muttered, and went out.

Mama stood there looking at me.

"I'm sorry, Mama. I can't marry Nicolas Paxton."

"Then let's not talk any more about it," she declared, and went to put her things away.

Despite what Daddy had tried to do and how much he complained about my refusal to cooperate, the months that followed were the happiest of my life. Daddy finally stopped trying to get me to change my mind and went on about his business, which, more often than not, resulted in some new problem for Mama to solve.

But Pierre and I saw each other more than ever, and every time he appeared, he appeared bearing gifts. Our little love nest filled up with nice things, expensive things: pictures, throw rugs, more clothes for me, and silk robes and slippers for both of us. We ate there more often, poled to the pond, picnicked, made love in the sunlight and in the moonlight, played our music and danced, once until dawn.

Pierre spoke little about his life in New Orleans, occasionally mentioning something he had done with his business, but rarely talking about his wife or his father. I didn't ask questions, although they were always on the tip of my tongue. I knew that they would only bring sadness and pain to him, and we both guarded our pledge to each other religiously. The rule was, anything that would bring sorrow or unhappiness was forbidden from entering these four walls. This was a home for laughter and for love only. Anything else was to wait outside.

But Nature had taught me early in my life that everything has its season. Our romance grew and bloomed, flourished and ripened, with every passing moment, every kiss, every promise in our breaths. Happiness was a bird at full wing, gliding gracefully toward the warm sun.

I knew that clouds do come, that rain must fall, that shadows must darken, and that even though our love was good and pure and full, it wasn't strong enough to withstand the hard, cold truth that lay dormant at our doorstep, waiting like some patient snake, so still it was hard to distinguish from the surroundings, but ready and eager to strike at the first opportunity.

We weren't always careful when we made love. In the beginning our passion was so strong and overwhelming, we could no more hesitate to protect ourselves than we could hold back a hurricane. Afterward, when I had a chance to sit and think, I admitted to myself that it wasn't just carelessness or a devil-may-care attitude. I wanted Pierre's child. I wanted a part of him in me. I wanted to bond us some way forever and ever. Maybe he wanted the same thing.

Unfortunately, I knew the symptoms of pregnancy all too well. I didn't have to ask Mama what this or that meant. It came upon me one afternoon when I realized I was late, and all the other indications announced themselves with clarity and certainty.

Despite my feelings, I was frightened. I had no idea how I would tell Mama, but I thought I must tell Pierre first. He didn't return for nearly two weeks after I realized my condition, and when I saw the blue cravat, I felt a pang of trepidation along with a feeling of happiness.

Early that night when I poled to the Daisy landing and walked to the shack, my body was trembling. Was this the end of our love affair? Would he run from me once he learned what had happened? I couldn't prolong the answer and stop myself from drowning in that all too familiar pool of despair.

He was sitting at the kitchen table, waiting for my arrival. A bottle of wine was opened, more than half of it drunk already. He looked up with a smile.

But before I could blurt out what was happening, he greeted me with his own shocking news.

"Daphne," he said, "has found out about us."

"I didn't think she would even care," he said after having me sit at the table before telling me. He poured me a glass of wine and one for himself. He paced as he continued. "All this time I thought she enjoyed the freedom I was giving her, enjoyed her distractions, her charities and causes, her art gallery openings and dinners. She surrounded herself with so many people and lived for the society pages. Whenever I had to travel for business, she was unconcerned and disinterested. She never complained about our being apart.

"Apparently, her lack of interest in me and my affairs was just a smoke screen for her real intentions and actions."

"What do you mean?" I asked.

"She hired a private detective and had me followed and all this traced," he said, indicating our love nest. "Yesterday she came into my office, closed the door behind her, and revealed with glee all she had learned and knew."

"She knows my name?"

"The smallest details," he said, nodding. "She enjoyed rattling them off. Of course, she made threats. She would bring down my family name, destroy the Dumas reputation, but I know she would never do any such thing. She's terrified of putting a spot on her own reputation. The worst thing for Daphne is social embarrassment," he said confidently, but I couldn't keep the terror from jumping into my heart and bringing goose bumps over my arms.

"Maybe she will do something like that this time. You didn't expect her to have you investigated," I pointed out.

"No," he said, shaking his head. "It's all just a bluff. Right now she's playing the role of an abused wife."

"Oh, Pierre," I cried, and buried my face in my hands.

"It's all right." He laughed at what he thought was my reaction to only his news. "I just wanted you to know what was happening, but I don't intend for any of this to interfere in any way with our happiness. As far as Daphne goes—"

"You don't know the worst of it," I moaned, raising my bloodshot eyes to gaze into his proud, handsome face. "And at this time, too!"

"Worst? What could possibly . . ." He grimaced. "Something with your father again," he said. I shook my head. "Your mother?"

"No, Pierre. With me. I'm pregnant," I blurted. The words clapped like thunder in my own ears.

"Pregnant?"

"And there is no doubt," I added firmly. My tears rolled freely. With Daphne on the warpath, what would happen now?

"Pregnant," he said again, and sat, looking stunned for a moment. Then he smiled, a light springing into his soft green eyes. "How wonderful."

"Wonderful? Are you mad? How can this be wonderful?" I asked, my anxieties twisted into a tight knot.

"You're having my child; how could anything be more wonderful?" he replied. I shook my head in amazement. Sometimes, despite his urban sophistication, his formal education, his years and years in business and society, Pierre seemed more like a foolish little boy to me. Was this the power of love: to hypnotize and turn grown men into children again, children who lived in fantasy worlds?

"But you are married, Pierre. And you've just finished telling me how you were painfully reminded of that fact, *n'est-ce pas?*"

He stopped smiling. "That won't make any difference. Our child will have everything he or she needs," he vowed. "I'll build you your own house. I'll provide everything: clothes, money, private tutors, nannies. You name it and it's yours," he declared zealously.

266

"But, Pierre, if Daphne has had you followed and investigated, she will surely learn about all that quickly."

"What of it?" he snapped. "Daphne would never reveal such a thing. She would die of shame. Don't worry," he assured me with a cool, wry smile. "I know my wife."

"Mama will be furious with me," I wailed. How could he not realize the hardships and pain I would endure?

"I'll retire her and your father for life. I'm a wealthy man, Gabriel. Money will provide the answers to all and any problem. You'll see," he predicted. He thought a moment. "When are you going to tell your mother?"

"Tonight," I said. "I can't keep it a secret any longer."

He nodded. "All right. I was going to leave early in the morning, but I'll wait right here until you return to tell me what she has said and what she wants you to do. If you want, I'll go to see her."

"I'm afraid to tell her," I wailed. "After all her warnings, I let this happen."

"Because you wanted it to happen. I know I did," he confessed.

"You really did?"

"Yes. You don't know what it's been like for me thinking I might never have a child of my own. It's wonderful," he declared again, and jumped up to pour us glasses of wine for a toast. His exuberance overwhelmed me and made me question my own fears and doubts.

"We will have this private, secret life forever and ever," he promised. "Don't look so skeptical," he added, laughing. "It's almost a tradition for us Creoles, you know."

"What is?"

"Being married yet having the woman you really love as well. My father had a mistress and so did my grandfather. But," he said quickly, "you are more than a mistress. You are my true love. Don't worry. We'll take it a step at a time. First, we'll have our child. Then I will quietly build you a new home, a decent home for our child. You will have all the money you need so you will have only to raise our child. Sometimes," he continued, planning our dream life, "you will come to New Orleans and stay at the best hotels. We'll take trips to Europe, and when our child is old enough, we'll put him or her in the finest private school."

I stared at him. Could all this really be?

"Now," he said, kneeling at my feet and taking my hands into his, "how are you feeling? Do you want me to bring a doctor next time?"

"A doctor?" I laughed. "Mama is ten times better than any doctor. Don't forget she's delivered my baby before," I reminded him.

He closed his eyes. "That's not the same thing. This is a baby born out of love, a baby we want."

Although he didn't mean them to be, his words were like tiny arrows piercing my heart. I cried for little Paul and couldn't imagine any child more precious or beautiful than he was. I couldn't imagine loving a baby more.

"But if you feel confident, I feel confident," he said, and began to pace again as he thought aloud. "Of course, I'll try to visit you more often, and if there is the slightest problem or complication, I'll see to it immediately. The important thing is that you feel safe and happy. My father is going to be a bit of a problem, but I will tell him all of it now."

"You will?"

He nodded. "He'll understand," he said. "I don't think it will be all that much of a surprise to him. Well, that's not for you to concern yourself with anyway. Just dote on yourself, my *chérie*," he said. "Shall we eat?"

"Oui," I said, rising slowly. Already I felt twenty pounds heavier. Invisible burdens rested on my shoulders. Pierre embraced me to kiss me and reassure me. I smiled softly at him and prepared our meal. Afterward Pierre understood why I wasn't in the mood to make love. He held me and repeated his promises and elaborated on his plans. I left somewhat earlier than usual because I wanted to talk to Mama before she went to bed.

"Remember," Pierre said on the dock, "I'll be here if you need me."

"Yes. Good night."

"Good night, my secret wife," he whispered. He remained on the dock watching me glide over the water.

After I tied up the canoe, I walked to the house, and when

I turned the corner, I was surprised to find Mama still on the gallery, but asleep in her rocker. Daddy's truck was there, too, but he was nowhere in sight.

For a moment I just stood there staring at her in sweet repose. Mama didn't deserve me, she didn't deserve another burden, another thing to accelerate her aging. Daddy was enough of a weight around anyone's neck. I knew no one who was as caring and loving as Mama, no one who worried about the elderly, the handicapped, the sick and the weak, as much as Mama did. She was truly a saint to her people, and what amazed everyone was how so much compassion and so much wisdom and goodness could be packed into so small a woman.

Her eyelids flickered and then opened once, closed and opened again when she realized she was looking at me. She sat up in the rocker and scrubbed her cheeks with her palms for a moment.

"What time is it?"

"It's not late, Mama."

She took a deep breath and nodded at Daddy's truck.

"He's inside, sleeping on the living room floor. I had to sew up a gash in his head. He got into a fight in town and someone hit him with a crowbar. Least, that's what he tells me. He could have fallen over a railing, dead drunk, too, and smashed himself on something."

She looked at me again. "What is it, Gabriel? You've got something to say."

"*Oui*, Mama," I replied in a small voice. Her body tightened as if she were preparing to receive a blow herself. I guessed that's what it would be.

"I've been seeing Pierre for some time now."

"You ain't telling me anything I don't know, child. I might as well have spoken to the wind about that, no?"

I nodded. "I love him, Mama, and he loves me. It's not something we planned or something we can help. It happened and it is," I said, my head down.

"You're still not telling me anything I didn't know before, Gabriel," she said, rocking.

I swallowed back a throat lump and rallied all the courage I could muster.

"I'm pregnant, Mama."

She stopped rocking, but she didn't say anything. She gazed into the darkness across the road and then began to rock again.

"Pierre knows and he wants to take care of me and the baby. He wants to take care of all of us," I said quickly.

Mama didn't look at me. She kept rocking. "Of course, that's what he would say now. He would say anything."

"No, Mama, he means it. Pierre really does love me. He bought the Daisys' shack just to be near me and—"

"Buying a toothpick-legged shack in the swamp ain't much of an investment for a man like that, Gabriel. Taking care of a child from the day it's been born . . . that's an investment, not only of money, but of love and affection and concern. It doesn't come in an envelope every week either, hear?"

"I know that, Mama. But I want the baby more than anything. It's a baby that comes from love," I told her. I didn't even feel the tears that were streaming down my cheeks, but I felt them fall from my chin.

Mama sighed. "You're going to be some rich Creole man's mistress, have his child and live on his generosity for the rest of your life, Gabriel? That's what you want?"

"I want Pierre as much as I can have him, *oui,* Mama," I told her.

She closed her eyes and put her hand on her heart. "I'm tired," she said. "I think I'll go to bed."

"Mama, please . . ."

"What is it you want me to say, Gabriel? That I'm happy for you? That I'll help you any way I can? You know I will, but don't ask me to believe in promises like the ones you've been given." She stood and her face grew dark, serious, her eyes small.

"I don't know everything, honey. I don't know why the Legrands' five-year-old boy drowned last year; why Mrs. Kenner, who's only thirty-nine, had a heart attack and died on her rear gallery washing her children's clothes, and leaving Lyle with three young boys to raise; I don't know why hurricanes come and wipe out the fishermen and destroy natural, good things. I don't know why people are killing each other every day on the other side of the ocean.

"The world is full of mysteries and questions, and we struggle to understand our tiny part in it. I don't love anything more than I love you. I want your happiness more than I want anything else, but I can't pretend that what I know to be ugly and hard won't be.

"We'll do what we can and what has to be done. We always do and we always will as long as we have the strength and the breath, but we won't, or at least I won't, pretend to understand why what's happened, happened.

"Maybe," she said, looking into the darkness again, "maybe there's a reason for all this. Maybe it ain't all caprice, but we just don't have the power to understand. I guess we have to live with that faith if we're to live at all, no?"

She started to turn toward the door. My heart ached so, I thought my chest would burst open.

"Mama!"

"Don't apologize for anything, Gabriel. I don't love you any less than I did a minute ago."

I ran up the steps and threw my arms around her. She held me for a moment and kissed my hair, stroking it gently.

"You're a very special girl, very special," she whispered.

Suddenly the screen door was thrown open behind us and we parted.

Daddy stood there, his hair wild, his eyes so bright they looked filled with fireflies.

"I heard it all," he said. His lips twisted between his overgrown mustache and his beard to form a cold, hard smile. "So this is why you wouldn't marry Nicolas Paxton, huh?"

I started to shake my head, but he turned to Mama.

"Don't you worry, Catherine. Don't you worry 'bout nothin'. I'll fix 'im. I'll fix 'im good," he threatened, and pulled out his long, serrated fishing knife.

My legs turned into two sticks of freshly made butter. Mama screamed as I sunk to the gallery floor.

14

Up in Smoke

I woke on the sofa in the living room. Mama had a cold washcloth on my forehead and a glass of water ready for me. I groaned and sat up confused.

"What happened, Mama? Why am I on the sofa?"

"You fainted, honey. You'll be all right. Here, drink this," she said, bringing the glass to my lips. I took a few sips and she told me to follow that with a deep breath. As my senses returned, so did my memory.

"Daddy!" I cried, gazing frantically about the room.

"He's not here. I chased him away for frightening you," Mama said.

"Where's he gone?" I asked, a twilight gloom pervading my entire being as I recalled the things he had vowed.

"Off to blow some steam at one of his hangouts, I'm sure," she said with a smirk.

"I've got to warn Pierre about him," I said, standing. I wobbled for a moment and Mama steadied me.

"You can't go anywhere just yet, Gabriel. Just rest," Mama insisted. She forced me to sit and lie back on the sofa. "I'll mix up something to help give you strength. You're going to need extra nutrition, as you know," she added.

I swallowed hard, nodded, and closed my eyes. Mama went into the kitchen, but she was there only a moment before I heard her shout, "Oh, *mon Dieu!*"

I rose as quickly as I could and went to her.

"What's wrong, Mama?"

"There's a fire someplace," she announced, nodding toward the window.

Looking south over the tops of the cypress and willows, I saw where the sky was turning from pink to a darker red, and black smoke was billowing. A flock of rice birds was in a frenzy, madly circling. My heart stopped. It looked like the smoke was coming from the direction of the old Daisy shack. The blood that had been restored drained from my face again.

"Pierre!" I gasped, and turned to run out of the house.

"Gabriel! Gabriel, where are you going?"

I didn't wait to reply. Instead, I nearly tripped over the steps, but caught myself on the railing as I whipped around the corner and down the pathway to the dock.

"Gabriel! Come back!" Mama shouted behind me.

I broke into a run. As soon as I stepped into my pirogue, I gathered all the strength I could muster and pushed away from the dock. My chest felt as if I had swallowed a ball of pins, all sticking into my lungs, but I didn't pause even though the pole felt ten times as heavy. My shoulders ached with the strain. I grew dizzy again and feared falling over into the water. I could pass out and drown, I thought, but I took a deep breath and continued, determined. This was a very big fire! I had to see if Pierre was all right.

More of my strength returned as I gazed ahead and saw the sparks floating skyward on the shoulders of the smoke. Minutes later I could see the actual flames licking at the darkness. Their glow illuminated the water. Alligators, frogs, snakes, and even the fish retreated deeper into the swamp. By the time I reached the dock, the entire shack was engulfed, its walls crumbling, the roof collapsed. Despite the distance, I could feel the heat on my face.

"Pierre!" I called, hoping he was safe nearby. "Pierre, are you here? Pierre!" I heard nothing but the cracking of the

273

flames and the shrieking of birds. I remained in my canoe, searching the illuminated areas for signs of him. I called again and again, but to no avail.

Some of our neighbors and those who lived close enough to the Daisy shack to see the fire and smoke arrived to be sure the flames didn't spread. I heard their shouts. I docked my canoe and approached the fire, drawing as close as I could under the waves of heat that undulated from the conflagration. Way off to my right, I saw Jacques Thibodeau, Yvette's father, with two other men. I hurried toward them.

"Monsieur Thibodeau," I called, approaching.

"Hey, what'cha doin' here, Gabriel? It's dangerous. You get back, hear?"

"Was there anyone in the house?" I asked frantically.

"Not that I know," he replied, and looked at the others, who shook their heads. "Your pere's out there on the road. He'd be plenty upset if he knew you were back here so close to the fire, Gabriel, no?"

"Daddy's out front?" I asked. My hope that Mama had been right—that he had gone to a zydeco bar to blow off steam—was doused with the cold reality that what I feared the most had occurred.

"Oui. Now get yourself back home."

"Are there any strangers?" I inquired. "Anyone else nearby?"

"None I seen, but Guy here says the shack had been bought by some rich man from New Orleans. He ain't going to be too happy to hear about this, no?"

The three men shook their heads.

"Someone had to start that, for sure," Guy Larchmont said, nodding at the fire. "You seen anyone around here?" he asked me. "Some mischievous kids, maybe?"

I wagged my head, barely listening.

"Better get home before your pere sees you wandering about here," Monsieur Thibodeax warned. "He don't look to be in the best of moods as it is."

"Merci, monsieur," I said, and retreated from the fire, moving slowly back to the dock and my canoe. I watched the gallery cave in and the last piece of wall melt away. All of my precious gifts, my clothing, our wonderful love nest, went up in flames. The smoke carried our secret into the night. I felt as if I were at a funeral, watching Pierre's and my love cremated in sacrifice to some angry god.

I didn't pole home directly. Instead, I sat in the canoe, watching the fire burn itself out. More people arrived and drew closer as the flames weakened. Soon whole families appeared. A fire like this was special excitement in the bayou. The children were permitted to come along and sit in the automobiles or stand near them and watch the activity.

What had happened to Pierre? Surely he was there when Daddy arrived, I thought. He probably thought it was me returning. I felt numb all over, my stomach hollow. For a while I was dizzy again and wished I had listened to Mama. I rested, splashed water on my face, and finally stood up and poled myself back to our dock. Exhausted, I made my way to the shack, my legs trembling, my heart thumping. Mama was beside herself with worry.

"Where did you go, Gabriel? What's wrong with you charging out of here like that after you fainted?"

"Daddy burned the shack, Mama," I complained. "I know he did. He was there, watching with the other people. Pierre was supposed to be waiting for me. I don't know what happened to him," I wailed.

Mama embraced me. "There, there. I'm sure he's fine," she said. "Most likely he ran off and your father took his anger out on the shack. Come on inside. I want you to lie down and get some rest now, hear?"

I had no strength to resist, although I wanted to be awake and waiting when Daddy returned. He didn't come home until nearly morning, however. I learned from Mama the next morning that after the fire had burned itself out, he and some of his friends had gone to drink and talk about it. And when he came home, he was so drunk and tired, he collapsed in his bed.

He didn't rise until midafternoon. I sat on the gallery, rocking in Mama's chair, waiting to hear what had happened. Finally the screen door opened and Daddy appeared, his face pale, his eyes so bloodshot, I couldn't see the pupils. He scrubbed his hair, yawned and stretched.

"Where's your mama?"

"With Mrs. Sooter, treating her foot corns," I said. He nodded and started to go back inside. "Daddy. What happened last night? What did you do?"

"Do? I didn't do nothin'," he said quickly, turning his face to avoid my gaze.

"I know you did, Daddy. I know you set fire to the shack. Was Pierre there? What happened?" I demanded.

He turned back slowly and stared at me a moment. Then he shook his head with disgust.

"I wanted you to marry Nicolas Paxton, but you were too high and mighty for the likes of him. Instead, you go get yourself pregnant with some rich Creole who don't care a hoot what happens to you, your baby, or us who got to live here in shame," he replied.

"That's not true, Daddy. Pierre cares about me. What did you do? What happened to him?"

"Shoot," he said, shaking his head. "Cares." He spit over the side of the gallery. He paused and gazed in the direction of the Daisy shack. "He was there," he finally admitted.

"He was? What happened? Tell me!"

"I'll tell you. I ain't got nothing to hide. I asked him what he was planning to do to make up for what he had done, and he goes and runs off instead of facing me."

"He ran off?"

"Scurried away faster than a nutria. His shadow had trouble keepin' up with him," Daddy added. "So much for your rich lover man. Now what, huh? A daughter should live and work toward makin' her daddy proud of her. She should find ways to help him, too.

"Ahh," he said, waving at me, "your mother spoiled ya somethin' terrible, Gabriel, and I been too busy to do much about it. Now look at the mess you're in. I got to sit some and give it all a good think, no?"

He went into the house. I looked toward the road and thought about Pierre. I was happy that at least he had gotten away safely. I was sure he would contact me soon. A wave of relief passed over me and I permitted myself finally to close my eyes. I fell asleep quickly and didn't even wake when Mama returned and went into the house. Her and Daddy's shouting was what finally woke me. It was painful to listen to them. He was blaming her for what I had done and for what had happened.

"I'm the one who's no damn good. I'm the one who is a no-account, lazy so-and-so, and I don't provide; but where's her moral learning, huh? She goes and does this right under your nose, Catherine. You go and face your saints now, hear? You go and wave your wand and make this all go away.

"I won't be looked down on anymore," he emphasized. "You and your daughter ain't nothin' special. Just remember that and remember to stop cursing the Landrys, hear?"

Mama had no strength to reply. I heard her go into the kitchen and start dinner while Daddy continued to rant and rave to himself in the living room. When he came out, I pretended to be asleep and kept my eyes closed. I felt him standing there, staring at me, and then I heard him charge down the steps and go off in his truck, mumbling to himself.

I never felt so sick inside, so depressed and disgusted with myself. Poor Mama, I thought. She had to take the brunt of Daddy's rage. I went inside to apologize and found her sitting at the table, her palms pressed against her forehead.

"It's all my fault, Mama. I'm sorry," I said. For a moment she didn't move. Then she raised her head slowly, as if it weighed as much as a barrel of rainwater. She looked so tired and worn and she looked like she had been crying, too. It made my heart ache and tears burn the insides of my lids.

"What's done is done," she said. "Don't let your father's ranting bother you. He just looks for excuses to be the no-account man he is. He'll use this to justify getting drunk and wasting time and money, is all." She rose. "Let's eat."

"I'm not very hungry, Mama."

"Me neither, but we better put something good inside to help fight the bad outside," she declared, and gave me a tiny smile.

I went to her and we embraced. She stroked my hair and kissed my forehead.

"Pierre will be back to help, Mama. I know he will," I said to reassure myself as well as her.

"Oui," she said with a tired voice. "But until then, we better learn to help ourselves, no?"

Mama and I ate and then had some coffee on the gallery.

277

It was one of those nights when the air is so still, you think the world had stopped spinning. Nothing moved either, not a bird, not a rabbit, nothing. The stillness had a way of creeping inside you, too, making you feel hollow and full of echoes. Mama was just as quiet for most of the time, and then she suddenly put down her cup and turned to me.

"I guess this is as good a time as any to tell you the truth, Gabriel," she declared. "Goodness knows, I kept it locked up too long."

"The truth? The truth about what, Mama?"

"About me and your daddy. About you," she added.

Her bleak eyes told me it was a dark surprise. I held my breath and waited for her to continue. She had to swallow a few times before she did so.

"I often told you how handsome he was. He still can be when he cleans himself up and cares enough. Well," she said, "he courted me on and off for some time. He was unreliable then, too, but I didn't pay enough attention to that. My mother didn't want me to marry him, of course. She knew the Landrys, and warned me time after time, but . . . as I told you before, I let the woman in me have first say.

"The fact is," Mama said, turning to me again, "I got pregnant before I got married."

"You did?"

"*Oui.* We lied about our marriage date, pretended we got married by a judge months before we actually did. We had a church wedding just to satisfy the family. I didn't think your father was going to marry me when he found out I was pregnant, and I wasn't sure I was going to marry him, even then; but he surprised me by being happy about it and told me if I didn't marry him, he'd tell everyone in the world you were his child anyway.

"My mother was brokenhearted about it. She barely said a word after the actual wedding, but being married seemed to settle Jack Landry down for a while. He was productive and responsible, and then he just fell back into his old ways.

278

"But whenever I stop and have regrets, I think how lucky I am to have you, honey," she added, her face beaming.

"Oh, Mama," I wailed, "I just keep adding to your burden."

"Now, now . . . what I'm trying to tell you is I don't want you to apologize and feel bad about me. It says in the Bible that he without sin cast the first stone. I'm no one to cast stones, and your daddy, he couldn't cast a pebble at an ax murderer. Understand, honey?"

"*Oui*, Mama," I said.

"I mean it," she said firmly.

I smiled. Mama's confession gave me the strength to offer my own.

"Mama, I wanted Pierre's baby and I still do. Very much. I know it's wrong, especially because Pierre is married, but you know how terrible I feel about losing Paul."

"Yes," she said with a deep sigh. It amazed me how she could bear so much weight on those small shoulders. "We'll make do, somehow. We always manage. Great strength comes from great burdens, I suppose.

"But," she added, turning back to me with a very serious expression on her face, "we have to live here, and some of these people can be pretty mean and vicious when they want to, you know. I think it might be best to come up with some explanation down the road. I don't like lying to anyone, even to your father; but it may be necessary to stretch the truth a bit. We have so many other sins to be forgiven for, a little white lie don't seem like much to add, no?" she said with a smile.

"No, Mama. But I'm sure Pierre will help us," I added confidently.

Mama smiled. "We'll see," she said. She sat back, sighed deeply again, and then stood up. "I think I'll turn in. It seems like it's been a very long day."

"I'll be right behind you in a moment, Mama," I told her.

"Don't stay up late," she advised, and went inside.

I sat on the gallery and stared into the darkness of the road that ran by our shack and off to the main highway that would take anyone to New Orleans.

"He'll be back," I told the shadows that hovered around me. "And soon, too.

"And everything . . . will be all right."

Days passed into weeks and I heard nothing from Pierre. Every morning I would wake expecting something, a package, a letter, a messenger, and at night I would sit on the gallery after dinner and stare at the road in anticipation of something; but there was nothing but silence and darkness.

I knew Mama felt bad for me. If I looked her way and caught her gazing with pity, she would shift her eyes quickly and pretend to be interested in something else.

Daddy came and went, sometimes staying away for days. When he did come home, the first thing he would do was come to me to ask if Pierre had been back.

"He come around here, Gabriel? You tell, hear?"

"No, Daddy," I replied. He nodded, satisfied I wouldn't lie to him. I often caught him staring at me, though. He always looked like he was in deep thought. It made me nervous, but I didn't say anything about it to Mama or to him.

Weeks after the fire, I finally gathered the strength to return to the ruins of Pierre's and my love nest. It had been reduced to rubble, a pile of charred wood and metal. Wandering through the ashes, I saw the small remnants of one of my dresses and sifted through the soot to find some pearls. I gathered them quickly and cleaned them off. Then I put them in my pocket and brought them home to keep them close to me.

Even my nights alone, shut up in the Tates' attic room, weren't as lonely and as melancholy for me as the nights after the fire were. When I finally did go up to sleep, I would sit by the window and look out toward the canal, toward the places where I had seen Pierre waiting for me in the moonlight. I would hope and pray so much that my eyes would play tricks on me and I could swear he was there. Once, I even went out to see, and of course, found no one.

When I did fall asleep, I tossed and turned a great deal, fretting in and out of nightmares. In one I saw myself drowning and calling for Pierre to help. He was just standing in the pirogue, watching, and when he finally decided to pole in my direction to help me, someone called him back. I couldn't see who it was. I woke as my head sunk into the dark, tea-colored water of the canal. My heart was pounding, my face and neck were damp with sweat. After nightmares, I didn't fall back asleep until it was almost morning light, and when I heard Mama moving about, getting ready for the day, I groaned and got myself up to help.

"I want you to rest more, Gabriel," she told me, and studied me a moment. "You look like you're swellin' up faster this time." She pinched my arm gently and watched the color in my skin, nodding to herself. "Every time a woman gives birth, it's different. Makes sense it should be, the baby's different. You mind and take care, hear?"

I promised I would. These days I wasn't filled with too much energy and enthusiasm anyway. Even my walks were shorter, and I stopped my canoe trips through the canals. Occasionally I went along with Mama to town, but even that held no interest for me and I stopped. I spent hours at the loom or sitting on the gallery weaving palmetto baskets and hats. The mechanical work seemed to fit my empty thoughts. My fingers moved as if they had minds of their own, and I was always surprised to discover I had finished something.

Had Daddy really driven Pierre away forever? I wondered when my mind did work. What would become of our special love? Would it wilt and crumble like leaves?

The rumble of thunder and rugs of dark clouds that were laid over the sky fit my mood. When the rains came, they seemed to wash away my memories as well as plants and flowers. Hurricane winds tore off branches and blew over tables and chairs. The shack strained and groaned. I hovered under my blankets waiting for it to end, pressing my face to the pillow, wondering how so much gloom could have come so quickly to my world of light and hope.

And then one night after a particularly bad storm, after Mama and I had to clean up our gallery and the front of the shack, Daddy came barreling in with his truck, slamming the door and whistling as if he had won the biggest *bourre* pot of his life. Exhausted, Mama and I were sitting at the plank table in the kitchen, neither of us with much of an appetite. She looked up at him with disgust.

"Now you come home, Jack," Mama began. "After the storm, after we done all the work, man's work?"

"This house can blow itself down to hell, for all I care," he said. "It don't matter no more."

"Is that right?" Mama began, her eyes blazing despite the film of fatigue that had settled over them. "My house don't matter no more, you say?"

"Now, just hold on, Catherine," he said, raising his hands. "Sit yourself back in that chair, hear, and behave yourself. Otherwise," he said with a wide, silly grin, "I might just not tell you what I done and what's going to be."

"I'm probably better off not hearing it if it's something you've done," Mama mumbled.

"That so? See?" he said to me. "See how she's always smart-talking me all the time, putting me down, making me look bad to my friends and neighbors?"

Mama started to laugh. "Me? No one has to work at making you look bad, Jack. You do that the best."

Daddy's smile faded. He stared at her for a moment and then he took on the most self-satisfied leer I had seen on his face. He dug into his pants pocket and came up with a fistful of money, and planted it on the center of the table. As the bills unfolded, we saw they were fifties and hundreds. It was the first time I had ever seen a hundred-dollar bill.

"What's that?" Mama asked suspiciously.

"What's it look like, woman? That there's good old U.S. currency, and that pile there is for you to do with what you please, hear?"

Mama glanced at me before looking up at Daddy again.

"And where's it come from, a *bourre* pot filled with money folks can't afford to lose?"

"Nope. It comes from here," Daddy said, poking his right temple with his right forefinger. "It comes from being smart."

"Is that so? Well, this I gotta hear," Mama said, and sat back, her arms folded under her bosom.

Daddy went over to the cupboard, found himself some

cider, and poured himself a glass first. We watched him gulp it down, his Adam's apple bobbing. He wiped his lips with the back of his hand and glared at me.

"She may know the swamp and the animals better than most around these parts," he said, nodding at me, "but she don't know nothin' when it comes to men."

"Never mind Gabriel, Jack. We're talking about you now and what you done to get this money."

"Right. I think to myself, Jack Landry, why is it you've been the one left holding the hot potato here, huh? Why is it you got to be the one to figure out what else to do to feed another mouth, make a home, bear the brunt of insults, huh? Why is it those rich people can come in here and use us the way they want, use us like a . . . a towel and then throw us away, huh? Well, they can't, is what I say!" he exclaimed, pounding the sink top with his fist.

"Most men in these here parts don't know their right from their left when it comes to going someplace other than the bayou. Once you take them out of the swamp, they're confused, stupid fools. But I ain't no swamp rat, hear? I'm Jack Landry. My great-grandpere worked the riverboats, and my mere's great-grandpere was one of the best gamblers this side of the Mississippi," he boasted. "It's true, he was hanged, but that was a mistake."

"All right, Jack. I know how wonderful your ancestors were. Get on with it," Mama demanded.

"Yeah. You know. You know everything, don'tcha, Catherine Landry? Anyways, I upped and took myself to New Orleans."

"What?" I said with a gasp.

"That's right," he said, his eyes blazing.

"What were you doing in New Orleans, Jack?" Mama asked.

"I found out where those Dumas men live and I paid 'em a little visit. Turns out the old man is not really unhappy with what I come to tell him either," Daddy said, nodding.

Mama stared, astounded. She looked at me and then she leaned forward.

"What did you tell him, Jack?"

"I told him about Gabriel here and the condition his son

put her into," he said, standing proud. "That's what I told him, and I didn't spare no words, neither. I told him about the shack and the way he done seduced my little girl."

"He did not!" I cried.

"Hush a moment," Mama said, her eyes brighter, her face flushed. "Go on, Jack. What else did you tell him?"

"I told him I was about to bring Gabriel into New Orleans and take her to the newspaper people if I had to," he said, nodding and smiling. "I would let the whole city know what his fine, upstanding, well-to-do businessman son done to a poor, innocent girl in the bayou."

"Where was Pierre?" I asked, my heart pounding.

"Hiding himself someplace, I bet," Daddy said. "He didn't show his face the whole time I was there. They got a palace, not a house, Catherine. You can't even imagine the rich things in the house and the size of the rooms, and there's a tennis court and a swimming pool and—"

"I don't care about any of that, Jack. Just tell us what you told Monsieur Dumas."

"Well, I expected to get the money I needed to look after Gabriel here. You ain't gonna find yourself a good husband now, Gabriel," he said, turning to me and shaking his head. "A woman with a child and no marriage ain't got a chance and certainly ain't got the pickin's. Why, I couldn't even get you Nicolas Paxton now, and it's your own doin'."

"Never mind all that, Jack. You haven't told us anything we don't know."

"Right." He straightened up. "Well, Monsieur Dumas, he says his son already told him about what he had done. He knew the details, and what's more, he said his son's wife knew the details, so I couldn't threaten him none."

"His wife?" I gasped.

"That's right. That's what he says, and full of arrogance, too. I was about to protest and start ragin' at him when he puts up his hand, looks away for a moment, and then says he's willing . . . no, he wants to buy the child."

"No!" I cried.

"Not again, Jack?" Mama said. "You didn't go and make a bargain with the devil again?"

"This is different, Catherine," Daddy protested. "We got

no way to hide Gabriel's condition. We can't keep the community from knowing she's a fallen woman. I got to look after the future. These people are so rich, they make the Tates look like paupers. You see that pile of money there?" he said, pointing to the table. "Well, that's just payment for me to think on it. I'm going to get us enough to take care of us forever. We don't have to worry about Gabriel finding herself a good man, see? And you don't have to go running off at everyone's beck and call to tend to their insect bites and coughs."

Mama was silent a moment. The tears were streaming down my cheeks. Where was Pierre? How could he have permitted his father to make such an offer? Mama rose to her full height, which wasn't much, but with her eyes wide, she looked taller, and Daddy stepped back, shaking his head.

"You gotta admit I done good, Catherine. You gotta admit that."

"You done good? You done good? How, Jack? By running off to sell your daughter's child? You think children are just like a bag of oysters? It's part of her, which makes the child part of us, too. It's our flesh and blood."

"And it's our burden," Daddy said, his determination firmer than I had ever seen. He didn't flinch or retreat from Mama's anger as he usually did. "I know I done right." His courage mounted, his chest pumped. "I'm the man here, see? I make the decisions. You might be the best *traiteur* in these parts, Catherine, but you're still my wife and that's still my daughter, and what I decide is . . . is what will be when it comes to this family, hear?"

"Go to hell, Jack Landry," Mama said. Daddy's face turned so red, I thought the top of his head would explode. He looked at me. I was holding my breath, my eyes so wide, they hurt. It only added to his embarrassment. "Take your bargain back to the devil," Mama hissed.

Daddy didn't retreat.

Mama started toward him, and suddenly he swung his open right palm and caught her on the side of the face. The blow sent her flying against the table. I screamed. Daddy stood there, surprised at what he had done himself. He

285

started to stutter and stammer an apology as Mama shook the dizziness out of her head and stood up to him again. This time she pointed her finger at the door. When she spoke, it was barely above a whisper, her voice cold and throaty.

"Get out of my house," she said. "And never set foot in here again or I'll put the blackest curse on your head. I swear by my ancestors."

Daddy's mouth opened and closed. I felt so faint I thought I would collapse on the table myself. He looked at me a moment and then at Mama, but his eyes shifted from hers quickly. It was as if he were looking right into the heart of a blazing fire. He raised his hand as if to block a blow she might throw at him and retreated.

"You'll be sorry you talked to me like that, Catherine. I might just not return," he threatened.

"I'm telling you not to return, ever," she retorted. "Everything that's yours will be on that gallery in less than an hour. You come by and take it away, and with it, your dirty, filthy soul. Get out! *Get out!*" she shouted.

Daddy turned and pounded over the floorboards. He slammed the door behind him and marched over the gallery. I heard his footsteps on the stairs and then . . . a deadly, deep silence until I heard his truck engine start.

"I won't come back until you apologize!" he cried, and then the truck spun away.

Mama pivoted and rushed toward the stairway to go upstairs and do what she said she would: gather Daddy's things and put them on the gallery. I heard her rip through the dresser drawers and pull out the clothing from the closet. She heaved it down the stairs and then followed, pounding the stairs with such anger, I was afraid to get in the way. I spoke to her, but she acted as if I weren't even there. It took her only ten minutes to gather everything that belonged to Daddy. She cast it all out the door, just as she had vowed. It was the worst fight ever between them.

And all I could think was I was the cause of it all.

Daddy didn't return for his things that night. I kept waking up, thinking I heard him, but when I listened hard, there was only silence, no footsteps, nothing. Mama had gone to sleep early. She seemed to age years in minutes, and right before my eyes, too. I remained awake as long as I could, sitting by the front door, and then I went up to bed.

Mama was up earlier than ever the next morning. I suspected she had gone downstairs before the sun had risen. I had woken so many times during the night, my eyelids felt like they were made of slate. It took gobs of cool rainwater to snap them open. When I walked past Daddy's things scattered over the gallery, I felt my heart sink like lead in my chest. Mama wouldn't talk about it. She rattled on about the things she had to do all day and described some of the chores she wanted me to complete.

She moved in and out of the shack all day that day without as much as glancing at Daddy's things. I saw some of his socks had been cast over the railing, but I was afraid to touch anything. We had a few customers and Monsieur Tourdan brought his mother to get Mama to treat her warts. When anyone asked her about the clothing on the gallery, she looked at it as if she saw it for the first time herself and said, "That's Jack Landry's business, not mine."

The way she spoke about Daddy, it was as if he were some stranger, someone she barely knew. She avoided saying "husband." In her mind her husband was dead and gone, and this man, Jack Landry, a boarder, had to get his stuff away from here. No one said anything or asked anything. Everyone just nodded, understanding. Most people had often wondered how Mama had put up with Daddy all these years anyway, ascribing it to her healing powers.

It wasn't until dinner that I finally brought the topic up. "I just hate myself for causing all this, Mama," I told her.

She laughed. "You? Believe me, honey, the forces that caused Jack Landry to be the man he is come from the Garden of Eden. Don't you blame yourself for your father, Gabriel."

"Maybe Daddy was right," I said mournfully. "Maybe I'm wrong wanting to keep my baby. Maybe it is like hoisting a flag of sin in front of our house."

"If there is such a flag, your pere wrapped himself in it years ago."

I looked away and thought before turning back to her. "I

don't understand why Pierre hasn't returned to see me, Mama." My chin quivered.

"He got himself into a pot of gumbo, too, honey. I'm sure about now he'd like to be able to make it all disappear."

I shook my head, my hot tears streaking my cheeks. "But he loves me; he really does."

"Maybe so, but it's something he can't do. I'm sorry, Gabriel, but it looks like he's come to that realization. Don't expect him anymore. You're only adding to the pain you got, honey," she advised wisely. "Take a deep breath and turn the corner."

I nodded. It looked to me like she was right, just as she usually was.

Another day passed and Daddy didn't return for his things. But sometime during the night, he did. I heard his truck and I heard the truck door slam. I waited, expecting to hear the sound of the screen door, but all I heard were his footsteps on the gallery. After a few moments, he shouted.

"You'll all be sorry! Hear! I ain't coming begging to live in my own home, no! You'll beg me to come back. You'll see!"

His voice reverberated. It sent shivers through me. Mama didn't get up or say anything. I heard the truck door slam shut and then I heard him drive away.

The darkness seemed thicker, the silence deeper. I took a deep breath and waited.

My eyes were still open when the first rays of sunlight peeked through the moss-draped trees, but Daddy was gone. It had a sense of finality to it. Mama sensed it, too. There was a funereal air about our home. More than once that day, both of us gazed at where Daddy's clothes had been, but neither of us mentioned his coming and going. Mama finally picked up one of his socks he had missed. She crushed it in her hand and dropped it in the garbage.

Her eyes were frosted with tears when she looked at me this time.

"Mama?"

She shook her head. "I've really been a widow for a long time, Gabriel. It's just that now, I'm mourning."

I cried a lot that day. I cried for the daddy I never really had as much as the daddy who had left. I cried over the memories of the good times. I cried thinking about Mama's smile and the sound of her laughter. I cried for the sunshine and the warm breeze, the fiddle music and the steaming hot gumbos we once all shared. I remembered holding Daddy's hand when I was a little girl and looking up at him and thinking he was so big and so strong, nothing in the world could ever hurt me. I trusted his embrace when he carried me over the swamp and I had faith in everything he told me about the water and the animals.

He was a different man then. That which was good in him had its day, and maybe, because I was more like a boy than a little girl sometimes, he saw himself again and it made him feel good to reach back and be younger.

It's the death of a precious childhood faith when you become old enough to understand that the man you call Daddy isn't perfect after all. Then, desperate and afraid, you look elsewhere for your prince, for the magic.

He had come to me, just like in the Cajun fairy tale. One day he was there in the canoe, smiling, handsome, full of promises and hope, turning cloudy days to sunny ones and making every breeze warm and gentle. The world was once again filled with kisses and hugs, and once again I felt safe.

But now that was gone too.

Darkness came thundering over the swamp, rolling, seeping, thick and deep. We were drowning in it. I clawed out a little space for myself and curled up in bed, wondering what sort of a world awaited the child of love inside me. Being born was probably our greatest act of trust, our greatest faith. As we let go of the precious, safe world inside our mothers, we entered this one hopeful.

It's not really the mother who's expecting; it's the child, I thought.

I began to wish I could keep him or her forever inside me. That way there would be no disappointments.

I started to turn the corner, just as Mama had told me to do.

And I trembled.

And I was afraid.

And I had every reason to be.

15

Gone but Not
Forgotten

Time dripped by like molasses. Sometimes the sun looked like a wafer pasted on the sky, barely moving toward the horizon. Everything began to irritate me: the days without the slightest breeze, the overcast nights shutting away the stars and the moon, mosquitoes and dragonflies circling madly over the water or the tall grass, the screech of a night owl. Things that I had barely noticed before or even enjoyed were suddenly oppressive.

Mama was right about my swelling up faster than I had during my previous pregnancy. I saw the bloatedness in my face and felt it in my legs. I tried to eat less and Mama bawled me out for that.

"It's not food that's doing this to you, Gabriel. You can't diet like some lady worried about fashions. You need to keep up your strength," she warned.

But it wasn't just worry about my plumpness that stopped me from eating the way I should. These days I had little interest in anything that had interested me before, and that included food as well. Mama did her best. She made all my favorite things. Most of the time I ate more than I wanted to eat just to please her. She knew it and shook her head sadly as I moved mechanically at the table and around the shack.

I couldn't shake off this shawl of depression, no matter how I tried. With the feud between Mama and Daddy growing worse and worse every passing day, and with every day passing without my hearing a word from Pierre, the world turned gray, the flowers dull. Even when the stars were out, they lost their twinkle and resembled nothing more than flat white dots staining a shroud of sable. All the songs of birds became dirges. The swamps never looked as gloomy, the Spanish moss draped like curtains closing off the light. My precious canal world had turned into a maze of loneliness and melancholy.

I spent my days working beside Mama and listening to her stories about people she treated for this or for that. She rattled on and on, trying to fill the deep silences that fell between us. To cheer me up she would talk about things we would do in the future. She even began to describe how we would change the shack to accommodate the baby.

I attempted a little bit of reading every night, but my eyes would drift off the page and I would sit there for long intervals before realizing I was staring at nothing, my mind blank. It frightened me to see how I was dying in small ways. Mama had often told me about people she had known who had pined away when a close loved one had passed on. She said their absence created too great a hole in the hearts of the mourners, and eventually those hearts just stopped beating. I wondered if that would happen to me.

Occasionally either Mama or I would find something Daddy left for us on the front gallery. He was trapping and harvesting oysters for a living. We learned he had taken his things and gone to live in his daddy's old swamp shack. Usually he left some canned goods, sometimes some pralines. Mama didn't want to take them, and often left them there. I would bring them in before the bugs or field mice could get to them and I would put them away, but Mama would pretend she had never seen them or didn't know from whom they had come. She wouldn't discuss them either, or anything that had to do with Daddy for that matter. The moment I would mention his name, she would draw up her shoulders and sew her lips closed.

If she said anything about him, it was along the lines of "He's where he belongs, finally."

I couldn't help feeling sorry for him, no matter what he had done. One day when I was just strolling mindlessly along the canal, he came along in his pirogue. I heard him call me and then he poled to shore to show me the muskrats he had trapped, forgetting that I hated to see any of my precious swamp creatures caught and killed. As usual, there was the stink of whiskey on his breath.

"How's that woman you call Mama?" he asked, anticipating no hope of reconciliation.

"The same," I said.

"I just did what I thought was right and best," he claimed. "And I ain't ever going to apologize for it."

"I'm sorry, Daddy," I said.

"Yeah. Me too. Sorry about a lot of things," he muttered. "I'll come by later this week and leave something. She takes what I leave at least, don't she?"

"Not willingly, Daddy," I revealed.

He grunted. "Just the same, I'll come by," he added. As he poled away from the shore, he turned to me and said, "Those rich people ain't giving up on you, Gabriel. You don't close your ears and eyes like your mother, hear?"

I looked after him, surprised. What did he mean? What else would be said? Was Pierre included in his reference to those rich people?

Before I could ask, Daddy was pushing hard and moving away quickly, his long arms extended, the muscles in his shoulders and neck lifting and stretching with his effort. I watched him disappear around a bend. My heart hadn't thumped this way for a while. I thought about what he had said; in fact, I couldn't get it out of my mind, but it wasn't until nearly a week later that I heard any more about it, and how I heard was as surprising as what I heard.

It happened one night after dinner. Mama wanted me to accompany her to visit the Baldwins. Maddie Baldwin was pregnant with her fifth child, but she had been having complications, which included the most intense back pains she ever had. Her ankles were swollen something terrible too. Mama was afraid I was heading in the same direction.

But if there was anything I wanted to avoid these days, it was seeing another pregnant woman, especially one who was having problems. I told Mama I would rather stay home. She promised to return as soon as she could.

I sat on the gallery in her rocker after she left. I was just rocking gently, listening to the monotonous song of the cicadas and peepers, when suddenly a sleek, long white limousine appeared. It was so quiet and so unexpected, it looked as if it had popped magically out of the darkness. It came to a stop in front of our shack and the driver stepped out. He looked my way, spoke to someone in the rear, and then started toward me. I stopped rocking and waited, holding my breath.

He was a tall, caramel-skinned black man with strikingly green eyes, dressed in a chauffeur's uniform with a family crest on the breast pocket. He paused at the steps and removed his cap.

"Excuse me, mademoiselle. I am looking for Mademoiselle Gabriel Landry."

"That's me," I said.

He smiled. "I have been instructed to ask you if you would be so kind as to speak with Madame Dumas in her limousine," he said, and for a moment my tongue felt as if it had been glued to the roof of my mouth. I started to swallow and stopped to look at the limousine again.

"Who?" I finally asked.

"Madame Dumas," he said softly. "She wishes only a few minutes of your time, mademoiselle."

I didn't move; I didn't speak. He stepped back and gazed at the limousine and then he looked at me, his face full of anticipation, his smile frozen. I wasn't sure what to do. Madame Dumas? Pierre's mother was dead, so this had to be his wife. Why would his wife come here to see me? Was Pierre in the limousine as well?

"Is it just Madame Dumas?" I asked.

"*Oui,* mademoiselle." He raised his eyebrows.

Slowly I rose from the rocking chair.

"Why doesn't she come out of the automobile?" I asked, gazing at the sleek limousine.

"She prefers to speak with you confidentially, mademoiselle. I assure you, it's very comfortable in the limousine. There is something for you to drink, if you like," he added.

I was a little frightened of the idea, but I didn't want to appear afraid, nor did I want to appear ignorant. It wasn't just that I had never sat in a limousine. I couldn't imagine what would bring Pierre's wife here, and all sorts of dark thoughts passed through my mind.

"You'll be quite safe, mademoiselle," the driver said, interpreting my hesitation. "I assure you."

"I'm sure of that," I said as bravely as I could. "All right. I'll see her," I said, and started down the stairs.

The driver waited for me and escorted me to the automobile, the rear windows of which were tinted so that no one would be able to look inside and see the passengers. The driver reached for the door handle and opened the door, stepping back as he did so. I gazed into the dark interior and I saw her sitting on the far side.

"Entre, s'il vous plaît," she said. "I just want to talk to you," she snapped when I didn't move. I looked at the driver and then I stepped cautiously into the limousine. It had a large, plush black leather seat with a table before it on which there were glasses and a bottle of sparkling water. I was immediately struck by the heavy scent of jasmine. As soon as the driver closed the door, Madame Dumas leaned over and flipped a switch to light up the cabin.

For a long moment we contemplated each other. I could see she was a tall woman, perhaps as tall as six feet, with a regal demeanor. Her pale reddish blond hair lay softly over her sable shawl. She wore a dark blue ankle-length dress with a tight waist and a high collar. There were pearl buttons along the bodice and lace on the sleeves. So beautiful did she appear to me, with her big, light blue eyes and a mouth I couldn't have drawn more perfectly, that I wondered how any man could have risked losing her love, or would even contemplate turning from her, even for a short tryst. I thought I was in the presence of a movie star. Her radiant beauty and sophisticated demeanor made me feel so inferior, I felt sick inside.

Her lips cut a hard, cold smile in her rich peach complexion. She nodded as if to confirm a thought and then shook her head.

"You're just a child yourself," she said. "But that doesn't surprise me."

She pressed a button that lowered the window on her side and then she reached down to take a cigarette from her gold cigarette case. At the same time she pushed the lighter in and then plucked the pearl cigarette holder from the table. She didn't speak until she had lit her cigarette and blown some smoke out the open window. Then she turned back to me.

"Do you know who I am?"

"Yes," I said. "You're Pierre's wife."

"*Oui,* Pierre's wife. Whatever that means," she added dryly.

"Does Pierre know you've come here?" I asked.

"No, but don't worry. He will. I have no fear of telling him anything."

"What is it you want?" I asked sharply. I had my hand ready to grab the door handle so I could leap out if I wanted.

"I don't know what Pierre promised you or told you, but I assure you, none of it will come true." She took another puff of her cigarette and waited to see what I would say.

"I didn't ask for anything," I said.

"That's a pity and quite foolish. You have a right to ask for something. Your father has."

"I know. I didn't send him, nor did my mother," I told her.

She smiled coolly. "I have heard how you Cajuns can be stubborn and foolhardy. Perhaps it's a consequence of having to live in this godforsaken part of Louisiana," she commented.

"This is hardly the godforsaken part of Louisiana, madame. If God is anywhere, He is here. There is more beauty, more natural goodness, than there is in the city," I told her proudly.

"Oh? You've been to New Orleans?"

"No, but . . . I know," I said.

She smiled again.

"What is it you want from me?" I demanded. "Or did you come here just to gloat or threaten me? I didn't plan for what happened to happen, but it did."

"And you're not sorry, is that it?" she said, her eyes turning to glass.

"I don't know," I replied.

She softened, her eyebrows rising. "Oh?"

"I have brought a lot of pain to my family . . . to my mother," I said.

She stopped smoking and quickly crushed her cigarette in the ashtray. "I will come right to the point, Gabriel—if I may call you Gabriel?" I nodded. "I would like Pierre to have his child. It's something that his father wants very much, too. I suppose Pierre told you that we have been unable to have children. The failure to have a family has made my marriage something of a failure as well.

"My father-in-law told me of your father's demands and his willingness to permit you to give up the baby."

"And you would want this, too?" I asked, not hiding my surprise.

"I would like to see my father-in-law happy and . . . I'd like to have a child in the house. We could have adopted, of course, but he or she wouldn't have been a Dumas. You carry a Dumas and that means a great deal to my father-in-law.

"I have come here because your father has now informed my father-in-law that you refused to give up the baby, no matter how much money was offered. I hope to change your mind, but if you do, it will have to be immediately, for I am planning to take an extended holiday, during which time I will . . ."

"Pretend to be pregnant," I said. "I understand, only all too well."

"*Oui.* That is my plan. So you see, if this is to happen, there can't be any more delays. It will either happen or it won't now. Soon it will be obviously impossible for us, for me, to take the baby as my own."

"But no matter what you do, it won't be your baby, madame," I reminded her.

"It will be Pierre's child, and therefore, it will be mine.

We are married; we are as one, whether Pierre recognizes that fact or not. I have come to assure you I will accept the child as my own and I will raise him or her to be a Dumas. The child will have all the benefits, the education, the finest things, and will be with the father," Madame Dumas added pointedly.

I started to shake my head. "I can't give up my child. . . ."

"Why not? You think by holding on to the child, you will somehow hold on to Pierre?" she asked, her smile widening. "I assure you, Gabriel, Pierre is out of your life. He is a rich Creole gentleman. He's had flings before and I've over-looked them before, but this time . . . this time he's gone too far and he knows he has.

"Look at the alternative, Gabriel," she said, sitting back. She nodded toward the shack. "Your life will become more of a struggle. Your parents will have to work harder and harder. You will feel more and more guilty. It will affect the way you treat the child. *Oui,*" she said before I could protest, "it will. You won't even recognize it and maybe not even think it, but it will nevertheless.

"And if you should meet another man, someone who will want to marry you even with a child, you will be afraid that he will come to resent the child, that he will look at the child and think this is the child of another man, another man she loved, and not my child, and here I am working to support this child. Then there will be arguments and resentments.

"And if you don't ever find another man, what do you have to offer this child? What hope for the future? How will she or he attend school, for example? Will the other children in the bayou accept this fatherless child or will he or she always feel inferior? You know what happens then, Gabriel? The child begins to resent you for bringing her or him into such a circumstance.

"Are you prepared for all this? Why should you be?" she added before I could even think of a response. "Why should you have to worry and think about ways to avoid this hardship? I am the first to admit my husband abused you."

"No," I said. "He didn't do anything that I didn't want him to do."

"I see." She smirked and sat back again. "Then you are happy?"

"No."

She stared at me a moment. This woman with her expensive clothing, her well-manicured nails and styled coiffure, her makeup, jewels, and her urban sophistication, was so different from me, we could be speaking different languages, and yet our destinies had crossed and intertwined us in ways neither of us could ever imagine.

"You are a pretty girl," she said in a softer voice after a short pause. "A natural beauty and perhaps not as young as you appear." She leaned toward me, fixing those light blue eyes on me. "Whether we like it or not, pretty girls, beautiful women like us, are often victims simply because we are attractive. Yes, in some ways I am a victim, too. I know I look rich and successful to you, but like you, I find myself in circumstances I would like to change, but can't. Like you, I'm trapped. I'm in a different sort of cage, but nevertheless, I'm not free."

She looked away for a moment, and my heart, which had hardened against her from the moment I set eyes on her, softened a bit.

"I'd like to be a mother," she said, facing the window and gazing at the darkness across the way. "I'd like to be the mother of my husband's child."

She dabbed her eyes with an embroidered silk handkerchief and then gazed at me. "Will you do it?" she asked. "My father-in-law will give your father the money he wanted, too. It will help your family, your mother. . . ."

"I won't do it because of the money," I said. She nodded. "If I do it, I would do it for Pierre and because . . . because a lot of what you said is probably true."

"*Oui*. I am sorry. I wish I had given my husband more so he wouldn't have come here to spoil your life, too."

"He didn't," I said, and then felt foolish for saying it.

"Nevertheless, if I would have been able to give him his child, my marriage would have been more successful. It still can be," she said. "You and I can take hold of some happiness and turn something bad into something good, especially for the poor, unknowing child you carry inside you. *N'est-ce pas?*"

I thought for a moment and then I nodded.

She smiled warmly, beaming with tears in her eyes.

"*Merci,* mademoiselle. Oh, mademoiselle, *merci.*" She reached out with a hand full of rings to touch mine. I felt as if I were extending my arm from one world into another, from reality to illusion. She took hold, smiled, and then released my fingers.

"Would you like something cold to drink?" she offered, nodding at the bottle.

"No, thank you, Madame Dumas."

"You have given my father-in-law a new lease on life, Gabriel. I can't wait to return to New Orleans to tell him. He's mostly in a state of depression these days. Perhaps you know about my brother-in-law."

"*Oui.*"

"And my poor mother-in-law, who died shortly after the accident. So you see, rich people have no guarantee of happiness. Money can't buy everything."

"My daddy thinks it can," I said sadly. "And unfortunately, I'm only firming up that belief now."

"Yes, well, I'm sure he will realize the truth eventually. Thank you for listening to me," she added with a tone of finality. I recognized she wanted to leave. The moment my hand touched the door handle, the chauffeur opened it and stepped back. He held it open as I turned.

"*Au revoir,* Gabriel," Daphne Dumas said. She looked like a beautiful mannequin set in the corner of that long leather seat. "I don't expect we shall see each other again, but I promise to be a good mother."

I simply nodded and the chauffeur closed the door.

"Good evening, mademoiselle," he said, tipping his hat. He went around to get into the limousine. I stood there watching him drive it away, the white automobile moving like a ghost into the darkness. For a moment I wondered, had I really had this conversation, or had it all been a dream?

I returned to the gallery and sat in the rocker. I was still there when Mama returned from her *traiteur* mission. Orville Baldwin brought her home in his van. She was surprised to see me waiting up for her.

"I thought you would be asleep," she said as she approached the steps.

"I'm about ready for bed now, Mama."

"Me too," she said, stretching.

"How's Maddie?"

Mama shook her head. "I think she's going to have a hard delivery. I'm worried about the baby, too," she said in a dark voice. Despite the heat and humidity, her words put a chill in my bones. "I'll do what I can, of course," she said, and started for the screen door.

"Mama."

"Yes, Gabriel?"

"I've changed my mind about my baby. I've decided Pierre should have the child and should bring him or her up in New Orleans."

"What?" She stepped back. "Why?"

"It'll be best all around, Mama."

"Are you sure of this, Gabriel?" Her expression changed quickly as an angry thought rippled through her face. "Your daddy didn't come around here threatening or haranguing you now, did he?" she asked.

"No, Mama."

"Because if he did . . ."

"No, Mama. He didn't. I swear."

"Hmm," she said, still very suspicious. "And Pierre? Was he here?"

"No, Mama."

She thought a moment. "You've made up your mind on this?"

"Oui, Mama. I have," I said firmly.

She nodded. "Well . . . this has to be your own decision, Gabriel. If that's what you want." She opened the screen door. "Suddenly I feel twenty years older. That bed's looking better and better to me. You had better come up to sleep, too, honey."

I stood up. Mama's eyes washed over me quickly. "I know

you're hurting something bad, honey, and I'm hurting for you."

"I know, Mama," I said. I went to her and she held me for a moment, kissing my hair and my forehead. Then we went inside together, holding on to each other until we ascended the stairs and went to sleep.

Two days later Daddy appeared on the front gallery late in the morning. Mama was in the kitchen cooking, and I was folding some pillowcases and linen we had woven to sell. The moment the screen door squeaked, Mama turned. When she saw it was Daddy, she left the ingredients bubbling in her black cast-iron pot and came charging forward.

"Don't you set foot in this house, Jack Landry," she cried, holding the ladle up like a club.

He hesitated. "Now, just hold on, Catherine. I come by because I heard you and Gabriel have come to your senses."

"What?" Mama turned to look at me as I approached. She tightened her eyes into slits of suspicion and fixed them on Daddy. "Who told you that?"

"The Dumas," he said. "Why? Ain't it true?"

"What's true is you're still the scoundrel you was before. Nothing's changed as to that."

Daddy shook his head. "I swear, Cajun women can drive you mad. I just stopped by to discuss the arrangements," he protested. "Or did you think you'd sidestep me somehow? Did ya?" he asked, turning to me, now with his own suspicions clouding his eyes.

"No, Daddy."

"All right, then. Here's what's going to be. I'm asking for half the money now and half the money on delivery. I'll have some for you in a few days' time," he said, nodding.

"Don't you bring any of that blood money around here, Jack Landry," Mama said.

"What are you talking about? You act like you don't know nothing, and you're the ones who've gone and fixed it," he protested, his voice rising in pitch.

Mama bit down on her lower lip and stared at him. He got nervous and closed the screen door between them.

301

"All right. I'll come by another time and we'll talk about it again. But you're going to have to keep me up-to-date now, so I will know when exactly to tell them to be here, Catherine."

"Go back to the swamp, Jack, and sleep with your pack of snakes."

"You ain't cuttin' me outta this," he threatened, waving his long right forefinger at us. "You ain't. I'll be back," he muttered, and kept mumbling as he left the gallery. The moment he was gone, Mama turned on me.

"How did he find out? How did the Dumas family find out you changed your mind, Gabriel?"

"I'm sorry, Mama. I had hoped to take care of everything myself. I didn't want to cause you any more trouble."

"I had a inkling in my bones when I come home from Maddie Baldwin's the other night. Did you lie to me, Gabriel? Was Pierre here?"

"No, Mama." I paused and then added, "But his wife was."

"His wife?" She sat on the overstuffed chair, her face full of amazement.

"We talked a long time in her limousine and I saw she was sincere about becoming a mother. She made sense to me and opened my eyes to reality, Mama."

"His wife came pleading for you to give them the child?" she asked with disbelief.

"Yes, Mama."

She shook her head. "She wasn't embarrassed?"

"I suppose she was, Mama, but she's a very dignified and sophisticated lady. I saw how much the baby would be offered living with the Dumas family and how hard things would be for us here. Besides, that's a family that's suffered a lot of tragedy, Mama. Pierre's baby might just be the medicine to cure some of the sadness and give them hope."

"After what you've been through, I know how you wanted to keep your child, Gabriel."

"I got to do what's best for the baby, though, don't I, Mama?"

She was silent a moment and then she fixed her wise eyes on me. "What really made you change your mind about the

302

baby, Gabriel? I'm sure it wasn't just because they have all that money."

"No."

"Well?" Mama pursued.

"Madame Dumas said something that made me question why I wanted the baby so much, Mama. She said if I thought by keeping the baby, I was keeping a hold on Pierre, I was wrong."

Mama nodded.

"And then I thought, if I was doing that, I was being selfish and not thinking of the baby as much as I was thinking of myself. No bird, no nutria, not even an alligator, thinks of itself before it thinks of its babies."

Mama smiled. "I used to worry about your being out there in the swamp so much, but I see you got the best education from the best teacher," she said. She thought a moment. "That man will be back to be sure he gets his money. Keep him out of my sight.

"I know what I'll do," she said, and went to her cupboard to get a statue of the Virgin Mary. She took it outside and set it down in the middle of the top step. "The moment he sees that," she predicted, "he'll stop dead in his tracks."

Now that I had made my decision about the baby, a weight seemed to be lifted from my shoulders. However, my world still remained changed, and as time went by, I became even less and less energetic, dozing and sleeping longer and more frequently. My swelling continued. Mama had me taking different herbal drinks, but I still bloated and looked twice as big as I had during my first pregnancy at every step of the way. Mama was disappointed that none of this lessened during my second trimester when a pregnant woman usually felt better.

But Mama was heavily involved and distracted by Maddie Baldwin's delivery at the start of my own seventh month. Just as she had predicted, Maddie had a hard time of it, and after the baby was born, Mama said it was a very sickly infant. She didn't think he would last a week. Six days later, the baby died. It laid a heavy pall over everything we both did for days afterward. Mama always blamed herself, thinking there was something she could have done, something she could have added to the treatment and diet.

It seemed we were stuck on a merry-go-round of sadness these days, all the gloom somehow finding its way to our doorstep. It was like being in a storm that would never end. And then, a little more than two weeks later, a ray of sunshine broke through the clouds of despair.

I had finished eating a little lunch. There was the usual afternoon lull, but a wave of high clouds kept it from being too hot, and there was a cool breeze from the Gulf. So I decided to take a walk along the canal. I had stopped looking for it so long, I almost missed it when I turned the corner toward the path, but there on the dock post was Pierre's blue cravat. The surprise almost had me paralyzed. For a moment I thought I was seeing things; I was a victim of my own vivid, hungry imagination, but when I drew closer, I realized it was true.

I felt an aching in my heart, making it thud louder, making my blood race. As quickly as I could, I went to my canoe. My hands shook with excitement when I grasped the pole. My legs were trembling. I hadn't poled my pirogue for some time now and my palms had grown soft. The pole burned my skin because of my hurried efforts, but I could think of nothing else but Pierre. As the canoe moved toward the Daisys' dock, I turned and gazed ahead in anticipation, impatient with the few minutes it would take to bring me closer.

I didn't see him on the landing, but after I tied the canoe and stepped out, I saw him sitting on a wooden box right in the middle of the debris.

"Pierre!" I cried, and he turned. He stood slowly and looked my way. He was wearing a light blue suit, but he was also wearing his palmetto hat. He looked tanned and healthy and never more handsome. He started toward me and I quickened my pace, nearly stumbling over the overgrown weeds. In moments we were in each other's arms.

"Gabriel, my Gabriel," he said, and followed it with his lips over my forehead, my eyes, my cheeks, and then against my lips. "I'm sorry," he said as he held me to him, raining kisses. "I'm sorry."

"Where have you been, Pierre? Why didn't you come to me before this?" I asked, my eyes flooding with tears of happiness.

He let go of me and stepped back, his eyes down, his head lowered. "Because deep inside, I guess I am a coward, I am weak, I am selfish," he declared.

"No, Pierre . . ."

"Yes," he insisted. "There's no way to sugarcoat it. Your father appeared that day, wild, angry. I tried to say something, to explain and to make promises, but I saw he was not a man with whom words would work, so I ran from him. I stood by and watched him set fire to our love nest and I did nothing. When other people began to arrive, I fled to New Orleans, crawled back behind the safety of my walls and gates and left you here to bear the brunt of it all. You have every right to hate me, Gabriel."

"I could never hate you, Pierre."

"Haven't you suffered a great deal?"

"Only because I haven't seen or heard from you," I said, smiling.

He shook his head. "You're far too good for me. I'm sure you've borne insults, and your father . . ."

"He's out of our house. He lives in the swamp," I said. "He and Mama fought terribly."

Pierre widened his eyes.

"If it wasn't this, it would have been something else," I said sadly. "Mama and Daddy have been drifting apart for a long time."

"I see. I am sorry. Shortly after your father came here and I ran home," he continued, "I told my father everything and then he and Daphne discussed it."

"He and Daphne? Not you?"

"Not right away. Daphne has sort of stepped in to look after my father since my mother died. She's actually closer to him than I am these days, and especially now," he said with more sadness than bitterness.

"You know she came here to see me?"

"Oui. She enjoyed telling me about her conversation with you. I feel even more like a cad. Here I had gone and made all these promises to you about our baby, how I was going to take care of you and provide, and then she surprises me by going to see you and gets you to do this thing. But that's Daphne," he said. "She's a remarkable woman who finds it easy to take charge of everyone's life, not just her own."

"She wants to be the mother of your child very much," I said.

He smirked. "What Daphne wants, she usually gets, one way or another."

"I had the feeling she was doing this for your father as much as she was for herself and you," I told him.

He raised his eyes again and nodded. "Yes," he said. He turned away and gazed into the cypress trees. "I haven't been completely truthful with you, Gabriel," he said in a voice so weak and troubled, I couldn't help but tremble in expectation. "I let you think of me as a fine gentleman, a man of character and position, but the truth is, I don't deserve to stand in your presence, and I certainly don't deserve your love, or anyone's love for that matter."

"Pierre . . ."

"No," he said, pulling his head back to gaze up at the sky. "I want you to understand why I care so much about my father's happiness, even more, please forgive me, than I do yours and certainly my own."

He turned back to me.

"My brother's accident was no accident. Yes, we drank too much and we shouldn't have been out in that sort of weather, and yes, he should have known all this better than me, for he was the sailor.

"But he was everything in my father's eyes, even though he was younger. He was more of a man's man, you see, an athlete, charming, handsome. He could get more with his smile and twinkling eyes than I could with all my intelligence and knowledge.

"Even Daphne, who was my fiancée at the time, was more infatuated with him than she was with me. Ours was more of a marriage of convenience, the logical couple, but with him she was romantic, even radiant; with him . . . she was the lover," he said.

"And so, when we were out there on that lake and the opportunity came to do him harm, I did and immediately regretted it. But it was too late. The damage was done. Only I had struck a blow that reached even more deeply into my parents' hearts than Jean's. My mother suffered, had heart trouble, became an invalid, and died. My father went into deep depressions, and in fact, it was only Daphne who could bring him out of them.

"She was the one who suggested we come to the bayou to hunt. It was almost as if she knew I would find you. Of course, that's ridiculous, but still . . . Anyway, when she presented the idea to me in her usual businesslike manner, and when she told me how much my father wanted it, I couldn't stop her. I couldn't care more about my promises to you. I'm sorry. I've gotten you into a much deeper mess than you ever imagined.

"I deserve your disdain, not your love," he concluded.

"That will never be," I said.

"I won't be able to come back to see you again," he warned. "And certainly I won't be able to bring our child. It wouldn't be fair to Daphne."

"I know."

"I've never known anyone as generous and loving as you, Gabriel. I wish you could hate me. It would be easier to live with myself."

"Then you are doomed to suffer with yourself forever and ever," I told him.

He smiled. "Look at you," he said with a small laugh. "You're very pregnant," he added.

"Am I ugly now?"

"Far from it. I wish I could be there with you, holding your hand, comforting you."

"You will be," I said.

"I promise, I'll spoil our child something awful, just because whenever I look at him or her, I will see you," he vowed.

I nodded, my own tears burning under my eyelids.

"I'd better go," he said, his voice cracking.

We simply stared at each other.

"Promise you'll send word to me if you need anything, ever," he said.

"I promise."

He stepped toward me and we embraced. He kissed me and held me for a long moment.

And then he turned and walked away, into the dark path under the cypress, disappearing just as I imagined my ghost lover would. It seemed centuries ago when, on our way home from school, I had told Yvette and Evelyn about the myth.

But it wasn't a myth for me any longer.

For me, it had come true.

Epilogue

I don't remember poling home that day. One minute I was
saying good-bye to Pierre forever, and the next minute I was
sitting on Mama's rocker, staring out at the road, watching
the sun sink below the crest of the trees and the shadows
creep out of the woods and into my heart.

When Mama stepped out on the gallery, she was surprised
to find me sitting there.

"I've been looking for you, honey. Where have you
been?"

I smiled at her, but I didn't answer. She tilted her head for
a moment, studying my face, and then her eyes filled with
alarm.

"What's wrong, Gabriel?" she asked.

I shook my head. "Nothing, Mama," I said, and held my
smile.

Mama said I moved around the house like a ghost,
drifting from one place to the other after that. She said I was
so quiet, she thought I was walking on air. Suddenly she
would turn and find me beside her.

She told me I became a little girl again, confused about
time, easily hypnotized by something in Nature. She said I
would sit for hours and watch honeybees gather nectar or

watch birds flit from branch to branch. She swore that one day she looked out and saw me approach a blue heron. It didn't flee. She claimed I was inches from it and it had no fear. She said she had never seen anything like it.

I remembered none of this. Time drifted by as anonymously as the current in the canal. I stopped distinguishing one day from the next, and always had to be called to the dinner table. I wasn't very much help to Mama either, barely doing any of the work. If I started to do something in the kitchen, she would chase me away and tell me to rest.

It really was difficult for me to move around anyway; my stomach had gotten so big. I thought I would just explode. Mama examined me almost every day, sometimes twice, her face full of concern. Occasionally my underthings were spotted with blood and I began to have what Mama called false labor pains.

Daddy came by often during my last month. He would just wait outside, fuming. Finally, one day, while I was in the rocker, Mama stepped out to speak with him. She folded her arms under her breasts and kept her head up, her eyes cold, looking through him rather than at him.

"I'll let you know when to send for them," she said. "It's what Gabriel wants or I wouldn't do it. You're to keep them out of the shack, hear? I don't want them settin' foot on these steps, Jack. I'm warning you. I'll have the shotgun loaded and you know I won't hesitate. After the delivery, I'll bring the baby out myself."

"Sure," Daddy said, happy she was speaking to him, even though she was really speaking at him. "Whatever you say, Catherine. How much longer is it going to be?"

"Not much," she said.

"That's good. I got some money for you," he added.

"And I told you I don't want none of that money, Jack."

"Well, maybe Gabriel wants it," he said, nodding at me. Mama looked at me.

"I don't need any money, Daddy," I said with a smile. He looked at Mama, puzzled.

"Just go on, Jack. God have mercy on you," she told him.

He shuddered as if he had been hit with lightning and then put on his hat and stomped off. But he stopped by every day after that, sometimes twice. Mama would just come out and tell him, "Not today," and he would nod and leave.

"Too bad he couldn't have stayed so close to home before," she muttered sadly.

Almost a week later, I had a bad spell of bleeding and Mama kept me in bed all day. She didn't like the sort of pain I was having either. She fed me and washed me down and burned some banana leaves. She was praying all the time, and always trying to smile at me through a mask of worry.

"I'm all right, Mama," I told her. "I'll be just fine."

"Sure you will, honey." She squeezed my hand and read to me, and sometimes she put on the records and listened to music with me. She sat there and talked more about her childhood than ever. Her voice took on a rhythm and melody of its own, often serving as a lullaby.

At night I called to her in my dreams, and sometimes called for Pierre. I often saw him the way he was when we first met. If I stared out my window long enough, he was there in a pirogue, waving and smiling up at me, or just standing on the dock. His blue cravat was always waving in the breeze.

Sometimes Mama would come upon me and ask me why I was crying. I would have to touch my face to feel the tears.

"Am I crying, Mama?"

"Oh, honey, my precious little Gabriel," she would say, and kiss me.

Almost exactly two weeks after Mama had told Daddy I would give birth, I woke in the middle of the night with the most excruciating pain I ever had. My screams brought Mama hurrying to my side. She put on the butane light and gasped. My bed was soaked with my blood.

"Oh, Gabriel," she cried, and went to get hot towels. Daddy must have been sleeping under my window because moments later he was at the screen door. I heard him ask loudly what was going on.

"A baby's coming," Mama declared, and he was gone.

Soon after the bleeding started, my water broke. It was then and only then that Mama told me the most astounding news of all. She knelt at my side, took my hand into hers, and in a loud whisper said, "There'll be two babies, Gabriel."

"What? Two? Are you sure, Mama?"

"I've been sure for quite a while, honey, but I didn't want to say anything for fear that scoundrel would go and sell the other one just as quickly."

"Two?" My heart was pounding so hard, I had trouble breathing. Mama put a cool cloth on my forehead.

"You don't want me to give them both, do you, honey? It's a blessing. You'll have your child. Those rich folks won't have everything after all."

"You want a grandchild, Mama?"

"Oui," she said, smiling, but there was something else in her eyes, something she saw that I now saw, too. Maybe I did have some of the *traiteur* in me, I thought.

"I understand, Mama," I said.

Mama bit down on her lower lip and nodded, tears streaming down her face. Then she got to work.

My pains were so intense, I know I passed in and out of consciousness. It went on for hours and hours, right through the rest of the night. Morning came and still the first child had yet to be born. Mama was exhausted herself.

"They're fighting to stay out of this world," Mama said angrily. "We're wisest before we're born, it seems. Push, honey," Mama ordered. "Go on."

I reached back for whatever strength remained in my flesh and bones and pushed. It seemed to go on and on for hours, but it was only minutes later when I heard the cry of my first baby girl. The second baby girl followed soon thereafter, and Mama was so busy cleaning them off and wrapping them in blankets, she didn't have time to tend to me. I was too exhausted to speak and barely could keep my eyelids open. She put the second baby safely and comfortably in my arms and took the first into her own. She knew Daddy was waiting.

"I want to hurry," she said in a whisper, "so he don't hear the other one cry."

She didn't cry. It was as if she knew that she must keep still to remain with her mother and grandmere. I struggled to look at her tiny face and bring my lips to her cheek.

Minutes later, Mama was back upstairs. "It's done," she said. "God forgive us."

"It's all right, Mama. Pierre needs her, too."

"Your scoundrel of a father hightailed it with his money. It will be gone in days, I'm sure, gambled and drunk away."

"Look at her, Mama," I said. "She has ruby red hair."

"The other one did, too."

"I want to call her Ruby, Mama. All right?"

"Of course, dear." She smiled and then her smile faded when she gazed at the bed again.

"What is it, Mama?"

"The bleeding. Let me take the baby away for a while, honey, and tend to you."

The bleeding didn't stop. Mama said it happened when there was more than one baby, but I could see from the look on her face that this time was more serious than most of the others she had seen.

I tried to stay awake, but I kept falling in and out of sleep, drifting for longer and longer periods each time. In fact, I thought I was a little girl again, floating in my pirogue. Sometimes I would just lie back and let the current take me wherever it wanted to take me in the swamp. I would lie there with the sun on my face and try to imagine where I was. Then I would sit up and greet my surroundings with surprise and delight. Sometimes, because I was so still, an egret would land on the canoe and strut about bravely. And once, my blue heron did the same.

I heard Mama calling my name. She sounded farther and farther away, and I knew that was because I was drifting on in the canoe.

"Don't worry, Mama," I wanted to shout back to her. "I'm all right. I'm where I want to be, where I'll be safe forever."

Her voice grew so tiny.

Ahead of me the Spanish moss looked like the secret doorway again. My canoe passed under and through it and then I was in a small pond where all my birds waited to greet me. There were doe on the shore and nutria scurrying about happily. A lazy old turtle floated alongside the pirogue.

I felt myself sit up.

There, just ahead, his shoulders gleaming in the sunlight, was my mythical lover. As I drew closer, the features of his face became clearer and clearer until I recognized it was Pierre.

"I've been waiting for you," he said, stepping into the water. He took hold of the canoe.

"I came as soon as I could," I told him.

"It wasn't soon enough."

We both laughed. He held his hand toward me and I reached and reached and reached. . . . I just couldn't . . .

"Gabriel!" Mama was crying. "My Gabriel!"

I turned slowly and smiled at her. "It's all right, Mama. I'm fine now."

Slowly the world behind me began to shrink and darken, but when I turned back to my lover, there was only brightness and warmth.

I was home.

Truly.

I was home.

POCKET
BOOKS

The Rain Series
VIRGINIA ANDREWS®

RAIN

Book 1

Life isn't getting any easier for Rain Arnold. The ghettos
of Washington D.C. are a daily reminder that she must
struggle to hold on to her dreams. Unlike her tearaway
sister, she has battled against the odds to do well at
school and to be a good daughter. But Rain can't
suppress the feeling that she has never really belonged,
that she is a stranger in her own world.

Her instincts are confirmed when she overhears a
revelation from the past. A long-buried secret is about to
change her life beyond recognition. Suddenly everything
Rain has ever known is left behind, and Rain is sent to
live with the wealthy Hudson family. Just as she never
felt a part of the troubled world she was raised in, Rain is
also out of place in the luxury and privilege that now
surround her. Will Rain ever be able to fulfil her hopes
and ambitions – and find a place to call home?

0 6710 2964 9

£5.99

POCKET
BOOKS

This book and other **Virginia Andrews** titles are available from your book shop or can be ordered direct from the publisher.

		The Landry Family Series	
☐	0 7434 6832 5	**Ruby**	£6.99
☐	0 7434 6831 7	**Pearl In The Mist**	£6.99
☐	0 7434 6830 9	**All That Glitters**	£6.99
☐	0 7434 6828 7	**Hidden Jewel**	£6.99
☐	0 7434 6829 5	**Tarnished Gold**	£6.99
		The Cutler Family Series	
☐	0 7434 4026 9	**Dawn**	£6.99
☐	0 7434 4027 7	**Secrets of the Morning**	£6.99
☐	0 7434 4025 0	**Twighlight's Child**	£6.99
☐	0 7434 4023 4	**Midnight Whispers**	£6.99
☐	0 7434 4024 2	**Darkest Hour**	£6.99
		The Hudson Family Series	
☐	0 671 02964 9	**Rain**	£5.99
☐	0 7434 0914 0	**Lightning Strikes**	£6.99
☐	0 7434 0915 9	**Eye of the Storm**	£6.99
☐	0 7434 0916 7	**End of the Rainbow**	£6.99
		The Wildflowers Series	
☐	0 7434 4034 X	**Wildflowers**	£6.99
☐	0 7434 0444 0	**Into The Garden**	£6.99

Please send cheque or postal order for the value of the book, free postage and packing within the UK; OVERSEAS including Republic of Ireland £1 per book.

OR: Please debit this amount from my:

VISA/ACCESS/MASTERCARD ....

CARD NO .... EXPIRY DATE ....

AMOUNT £ ....

NAME ....

ADDRESS..

....

SIGNATURE ....